NIGHT

YOU'D BETTER STAY AWAKE

BY

IF YOU WANT TO STAY ALIVE

NIGHT

JACK JORDAN

CORVUS

Published in Great Britain in 2019 by Corvus, an imprint of Atlantic Books Ltd.

Copyright © Jack Jordan, 2019

The moral right of Jack Jordan to be identified as the author of this work has been asserted by him in accordance with the Copyright, Designs and Patents Act of 1988.

9 8 7 6 5 4 3 2 1

A CIP catalogue record for this book is available from the British Library.

Trade paperback ISBN: 978 1 78649 443 6
Paperback ISBN: 978 1 78649 442 9
E-book ISBN: 978 1 78649 444 3

Printed and bound by CPI Group (UK) Ltd, Croydon, CR0 4YY

Corvus
An imprint of Atlantic Books Ltd
Ormond House
26–27 Boswell Street
London
WC1N 3JZ

www.corvus-books.co.uk

For the Finns, the Jays, the Jacks

BEFORE

ONE

C

Rose lay in bed and counted the seconds passing on the clock. Twilight lit the curtains until the room had a sickly, sepia haze. Of all the hours she lay awake, it was the hour when night turned to dawn that she loathed the most. It reminded her that another night had passed, another day lay before her; for those sixty minutes, she was the loneliest woman in the world.

She loathed their bedroom. So many times she had lain there, watching the night morph into day as the sun blinked awake behind the curtains, reminding her of the empty hours she had spent waiting for it to arrive. She had counted every Artex swirl in the plaster on the ceiling, every petal and leaf on the floral wallpaper, every screw that knitted the bedroom furniture together.

Christian turned in his sleep, nudging her in the ribs with his elbow. She exhaled sharply as bone clipped bone and clamped her eyes shut.

It's not his fault.

She sighed, hot and stale in her nostrils, and blinked her eyes open again to take in his sleeping face, and imagined pinching his eyelashes between her fingertips and plucking them until he woke.

It wasn't his fault, she repeated to herself, but it didn't do any good. The better part of her shrank with every sleepless hour. After a restless night, she couldn't stop the hate infiltrating her mind as she thought of those she loved, had no control over her words as she spoke to them with unjustified rage. She often listened to herself snap at her children, or felt unprovoked tears rolling down her cheeks without any way to stop them. Ten years of insomnia should have been enough, she should have been used to it by now, but every sleepless night felt worse than the last.

She rubbed her face. The flesh of it felt like leftover meat, dry and rubbery. She worked out that she had been awake for over forty-eight hours. Another night of staring up at the ceiling as exhaustion vibrated beneath her skin. Usually she would be allowed a few hours of scattered sleep each night, but every so often she would be kept awake for days, her body and mind running on empty until exhaustion finally dragged her under, no matter the place or time of day. She hadn't fainted in public for a while; she had to be thankful for that.

Christian groaned from behind closed lips, his eyes moving beneath their lids as he dreamt. She watched his Adam's apple bob in his throat as he swallowed.

She used to think he was beautiful when he slept. His green eyes hidden, dark hair ruffled on the pillow, full lips framed with stubble. But as the number of sleepless nights grew, her admiration turned putrid with jealousy. Her chest burnt with it, rotting her from the inside. She swallowed it down and sighed.

It's not his fault.

But it didn't stop her from thinking of jabbing him in the ribs with her fingernail. It wasn't fair that she was awake, resenting every blink and breath, as the rest of the house slept.

She slipped out of bed and stumbled. Small white lights sparked in her vision. She leaned against the bedside table and waited for it to pass before slipping into her dressing gown and closing the door behind her.

4

The silence of the house taunted her; it was the sound she heard when the rest of the world slept, a piercing ring in her ears that started at ten each evening and screamed through until daybreak.

She crept along the hall, dodging the boards that squeaked, and slipped her head through the doorway to the girls' bedroom.

For identical twins, they couldn't be more different.

Lily was the wild one, her vibrant red hair like a bird's nest on the pillow, with her pale legs sprawled out and the duvet kicked half off the bed.

Violet was asleep on her back, her hair fanned out perfectly as though she hadn't moved an inch since closing her eyes. Her hands were clasped on top of the bedspread and her feet formed one neat mound beneath the sheets.

They were her world, but whenever she looked at them, she couldn't help but think about what she had lost. Her first sleepless night had been after she and Christian returned from the hospital with their newborn twins. She had cradled the girls in the crook of each arm, bobbing them up and down to soothe them back to sleep. Their cries had woken something in her, something that had been dormant her whole life until that first rattling scream. She hadn't just become a mother that day; she had become an insomniac. Motherhood came with a price: it had meant sacrificing her former self.

Rose crept down the stairs, her thirty-five-year-old body aching as though it belonged to a woman twice her age, and stood in the bright kitchen, squinting at the sun's rays reflecting off the marble countertop. She looked out the window at the new day.

The river bustled beneath the morning sun, winking with small bursts of light as the current drew the water under the bridge and through the rest of Rearwood. They had bought the house for the view, but now all she wanted to do was board up the windows and keep out the day.

She stood silently as the kettle boiled and caught her reflection in the glass of the microwave. The skin around her eyes looked bruised. The rest of her was cadaverously pale and thin on her bones. She had been called beautiful once. However, it turned out there was such a thing as beauty sleep; without it, she was a shell of who she used to be, the light in her eyes blown out.

She made a mug of tea and stepped out onto the porch. The cold morning tightened the pores on her face; the breeze was tainted with the scent of the water, a faint smell of salt from the Thames where the river originated. She sat on the rocking chair and swayed back and forth with her eyes on the river.

Smoking was the one thing she liked about being alone at night and in the dawn, allowing herself this small guilty pleasure, the one thing that was hers. In the day, she had to set a good example for the girls. But at night, she wasn't a wife or a mother; she was a woman marooned on her own deserted island, waiting for the sun to rise.

She took the pack and lighter from her dressing-gown pocket and lit a cigarette hungrily.

They would be awake soon. She longed to end the loneliness of the night, but dreaded having to slip into the facade: attentive mother, loving wife, a mask with a chiselled smile.

She closed her eyes against the wind and breathed in the fresh morning air, mixing with the cigarette smoke drifting up from between her fingers. Her heartbeat calmed as she listened to the quiet rush of the river in the distance, like water trickling in her ears.

'*MUM!*'

Rose jolted awake, knocking over the mug of tea by her feet.

The sun was higher in the sky and beaming down on the porch; her chest was a furious pink.

Lily peered down at her slumped in the chair, her young brow creased with disgust.

'You're smoking!'

Rose looked down at the cigarette burnt to the filter between her fingers, then up at her daughter. Tears filled her eyes and blurred her daughter's face, washing the frown away.

I had finally fallen asleep. Why won't you just let me sleep?

'Oh, this? I wasn't smoking, darling. I like the smell, that's all. Reminds me of my mum.'

Whenever Rose mentioned her family, she could see her daughters' wonder at the other life she'd had before them. They never had the chance to meet their grandmother. Calling her Grandma wouldn't have meant a thing.

Lily looked her up and down, at the tea running between the cracks in the patio tiles beneath their feet.

'Why are you crying?'

'I'm just tired, that's all.' She wiped away the tears and sat up. 'Where's your dad?'

Rose bent down and placed the mug upright again. She dropped the cigarette end inside.

'Gone. He told us not to wake you.'

Then why did you?

She looked out at the bridge, at the cars crossing like ants on a branch, and scanned them for his white four-by-four. She was thankful that he had left her to sleep, but felt a pang in her chest at not being able to say goodbye. Perhaps they still longed for each other after eleven years of marriage. Or maybe it was the guilt she had for resenting him, scowling at his sleeping face and envying every peaceful breath he took.

'Isn't it Sunday?'

'It's Monday.'

'Oh, yes. Bank holiday.'

Her memory dripped in and dried up; it never came in a steady flow. She vaguely remembered Christian telling her about a meeting he had to attend for his latest case for the court date at the end of the week, leaving her to look after the girls again. She could barely string a sentence together, put one foot in front of the other, and still he left her alone with them.

'It's our last game of the season today,' Lily said. 'Remember?'

'Huh? Oh, football. Yes, I remember.'

By the look in Lily's eyes, the lie was clear on her face. The facade was slipping.

'It's an away game,' Lily added.

'Yes, at the school in Longridge, right?'

'That was last month. It's at Fairmount.'

'Of course. What time is it now?'

Rose tucked her hair behind her ears and pulled at her nightdress where it had bunched around her waist. What must Lily think of her? Was she embarrassed? Ashamed? Scared?

Lily leaned in through the doorway to the kitchen and glanced at the clock on the wall. 'Seven forty-five.'

'What time is the game again?'

'Kick-off at nine.'

Maybe she could ask Heather to take them. The thought of sitting behind the wheel made her stomach lurch. But Heather had given her so many favours and never asked for anything in return. The mothers at the school had to be talking about her by now, absent from games, turning up with her coat inside out or dressed for summer in the rain, her words slurred as though she had been drinking. Is that what they thought it was? Was she known as the school drunk?

'Right, right. Best get cracking, then.'

Rose followed Lily into the kitchen where Violet was sitting at the island eating a bowl of cereal.

'Shall I clean up the tea, Mummy?' she asked with a mouthful of cereal, her line of sight on the puddle crawling across the tiles.

'No, darling, you eat. I'll clean it up later.' She leaned down and kissed the top of Violet's head. 'Have you eaten, Lily?'

Lily shook her head as she climbed up onto the stool beside her sister.

'What do you want?'

Lily looked at her sister's bowl. 'Shreddies.'

As the girls talked, Rose prepared breakfast, wondering how she was going to get through the day. Exhaustion burnt at the backs of her eyes and scratched her skin, as though insects were scurrying beneath. She felt sick with it, shook with it, but she had to be a mother. She had to stop letting them down.

She placed the cereal in front of Lily and turned back to clean up the pieces that had missed the bowl.

'I asked for Shreddies.'

'What?'

She eyed the bowl. Rice Krispies bobbed around in the milk.

'Can't you just have those?'

Lily glanced at her sister's breakfast again. 'But I wanted Shreddies.'

'Fine.' Rose dragged the bowl in front of her, her thumb submerged in the milk, splashing it on the granite top. 'I'll have it then.'

She looked back at Lily and watched the tears sheen over her daughter's eyes.

She could feel that her brow was fixed in a frown, her lips pressed into a hard line.

You're frightening her. You're a bad mother.

'Lily, I'm sorry. I'm not angry with you, I'm just tired. I'll get you some Shreddies.'

The girls were subdued by her swing in mood, which could change faster than they could blink. She smiled at them both, trying to prove she wasn't a monster, but neither of them would meet her eye.

She slipped into the larder and closed the door behind her to let the sob free, muffled behind her hand. Sometimes she wondered if it would be easier for all of them not to have her there. She whimpered into the palm of her hand until her lips felt hot and swollen. Tears filled the seal of her hand against her face.

After a brief moment, she took a deep breath to compose herself and wiped away the tears.

Pull yourself together. You'll be home before you know it. You can try to sleep again this afternoon.

She returned to the kitchen with the box of Shreddies and a forced smile straining her cheeks.

'There,' she said, after she had prepared the cereal and passed Lily the bowl.

She sat opposite them and took a mouthful of her own cereal, soggy now, like frog larvae on her tongue. She managed two mouthfuls before nausea crept up her throat.

The girls took it in turns to glance up at her, eyeing the red blotches on her face. The spoon shook in her hand, spilling cereal back into the bowl until all she got was a small slurp of milk.

Be good to them. They're the most important things in your life.

But deep down, in the small burrows of her mind, she knew she was lying. The most important thing in her life was something she could never have. The need for sleep wasn't from the heart, it was from the most archaic part of her brain that controlled her primal need for food, water, shelter and rest. She could lie to herself all she wanted, that her love for her children was the most important part of her, but beneath it the animal inside growled the truth.

You don't deserve to be a mother, she thought, before casting her mind back to the small sleep she'd had, just before Lily jolted her awake.

TWO

☾

Rose couldn't remember driving to the school. One minute they were pulling out of the driveway, the gravel crunching beneath the wheels, and the next they were pulling up in the car park.

Dozens of children and parents escaped SUVs and scrummed together in a hot crowd of bodies heading towards the playing field.

'Mum, there's a stain on my top!'

Rose whipped around and eyed Lily's football shirt.

'No one will notice. Here.' She licked her finger to work out the dried food with it, scratched it with her nail.

'But Violet's top is clean, why isn't mine?'

Tears were forming in her eyes. Her bottom lip began to quiver.

'Don't start, Lily.'

'It's not fair!'

Rose turned back and unfurled a hot sigh into her lap, clutching the steering wheel until her knuckles whitened. Lily whimpered behind her.

Maybe I can try to sleep here while they play, catch an hour or two. I'll be nicer then. I won't be such a terrible mother.

'I'm sorry. It'll be clean next time. I must have thought I put both in the wash.'

'You always forget about me,' Lily said, sniffling back tears.

'I'm sorry, Lily.'

You're screwing them up. All they'll remember of their childhood are your failures.

Violet sat quietly as she always did, her hands cupped neatly in her lap.

A fist banged against the window. Heather stood on the other side of the glass and burst out laughing when Rose jolted with the impact.

'Sorry, lovely. Didn't mean to scare you! Your face!' She laughed behind the glass, revealing a flash of white teeth. She had taut, ebony skin and long, dark hair that shimmered when the light hit it. Heather Forrest was the epitome of a rested woman; she was everything Rose wasn't.

Rose glanced at herself in the rear-view mirror. Her damp hair was scraped into a messy bun; she eyed the bruising around her eyes, and spotted a stray Rice Krispie hardened into the fabric of her T-shirt where she had tried to finish off the bowl before running out the door.

'Wipe your face, Lily,' she whispered as she scratched off the Rice Krispie and unbuckled her belt.

Rose stepped out of the car and forced a smile.

'Sorry, I was miles away.'

'Still not sleeping?'

'Is it that obvious?'

'You look fine,' Heather lied and stroked her arm. Rose's skin was so tender that Heather's touch felt as though it singed down to the bone. She forced herself to withstand it and steeled her muscles. 'You just look tired, that's all.'

'I'm fine.'

The girls got out of the car with their football boots tied at the laces and hung around their necks. Lily had wiped the tears away, but her lip still hung out and she had red blotches beneath her eyes. Violet gave Heather a timid smile, hiding the gap in her teeth behind her lips.

'What's up, girls?'

'Hi,' they said together.

'Violet's upset, I forgot to wash her top.'

'Lily,' said Lily. 'I'm upset, not Violet.'

'Yes, sorry.'

Sorry. Sorry. Sorry. Shut up, Rose, you sound pathetic.

'You look great, Lily love. The boys have run ahead, you might be able to catch them.'

The girls looked up at Rose, who nodded in approval. They scampered off for the field with their boots knocking against their chests.

'How are you really?' Heather asked, touching her again.

Tears welled in her eyes.

'Don't, Heather,' she said and covered her face. She turned her back on the parents pulling into the car park and faced the body of the car.

'Oh, lovey,' Heather said and placed a hand on her back.

'I'm sorry. I'm just so tired.'

'You shouldn't be driving this exhausted.'

'What else am I supposed to do?' she snapped.

Heather's expression fell.

'I'm sorry. It's just. . . the girls shouldn't be impacted by my failures. I wasn't going to drive, but I was so tired I forgot to call a taxi. We waited for it for twenty minutes, a cab I hadn't even booked.'

She laughed at herself, how pathetic she was.

'You're not a failure, Rose. Insomnia is an illness.'

'Well, I feel like I am. I'm always letting them down. I snap at

15

them all the time, forget things. They must hate me, think I don't love them, when I do, Heather, I really, really do.'

'I know you do, and they do too. Where's Christian?'

'Working,' she said.

'Aren't there any tablets you can take to help?'

'Don't you think I've tried that? I've been prescribed every drug out there. One made me a zombie, another made me vomit for three days straight. The others didn't even make a dent, I just remained awake, stumbling around like a drunk. I've tried everything, Heather.'

'Look, why don't you kip in the car during the game? I can watch the girls and then bring them back with me.'

'I can't ask you to do that. You're always helping me.'

'That's what friends are for, isn't it?'

She glanced at the passenger seat through the window and saw herself there, lying back against the reclined seat. She'd had so many opportunities to sleep last night, but it was now when she needed to stay awake that her body decided to shut down. She shook her head.

'I can't.' She walked round to the boot for her bag and arranged it on her shoulder, the camping chair poking out like a sail mast. 'I'm always letting them down. I need to be here for them.'

'If you're sure. . .'

'I am.' She shut the boot with a bang and locked the car.

The army of parents waited by the pitch, camping chairs arranged, tea poured into mugs from flasks, babies nestled against shoulders and breasts. A group of fathers stood close to the sidelines, huddled together like a third team waiting in the wings. All of the mothers looked pristine. Over thirty of them turned their heads at their arrival, some waving, some simply looking them up and down before turning their attention back to their children warming up on the pitch.

Rose looked down at the stained tracksuit she had pulled on, the flip-flops slapping against her heels, her naked nails bitten to the quick.

'Morning, ladies,' Heather said as she pitched up her chair with the same group they always sat with, six women who slept soundly.

Rose forced a smile in greeting and tried to ignore the women glancing her up and down.

Heather mingled, fitting in with the other mums effortlessly, unlike Rose, who stuck out like the runt of the litter, the pup with the lazy eye or undeveloped leg. She took out the camping chair, which snapped shut the moment she opened it up. She tried again. It snapped shut. The rage swelled in her, tuning out the natter and the whistle from the football coach ushering the children in, until all she could hear was the thump of her heart racing in her ears.

'Come on, you fucker!' she said, too loud.

She returned to the sound of gasps.

The mothers were staring at her, eyes wide and brows creased with disgust. The children on the pitch were a huddle of faces looking her way, gasps and giggles erupting in a sudden whoosh. Both of the twins burnt red and turned away.

'Let me help,' Heather said, crouching over her. Her sweet perfume filled Rose's nostrils.

Heather, you're perfect. Why can't I be like you? Like them?

'I'm sorry,' Rose whispered.

'Hey, it's probably the most excitement they've had all weekend.'

Heather patted the seat and ushered her down by her shoulders, as though she was guiding a stumbling drunk.

'Let's get you some tea,' she said. 'Adeline, can you spare some?'

'I only have eucalyptus infusion,' she said through pursed lips.

'Laura?'

17

'Green tea?'

Rose hated green tea. Laura knew that.

'It's okay,' Rose said. 'I have a flask of coffee.'

A second whistle blew and the game began as she rummaged around in the bag, filled with used wet wipes, empty chocolate wrappers, her one emergency cigarette crumpled beneath the mess, ground into brown dust and coating everything. She had forgotten the coffee. She could see it now, standing tall on the countertop, the metal flask twinkling in the sun as it poured through the window.

A tear fell into the bag.

Stop crying. You're an embarrassment.

She zipped the bag shut and dabbed her eyes with her sleeve. When she turned around, Heather was smiling, flask in hand.

'I never forget coffee.'

The other mothers were staring at her, her failures more alluring than the game.

'You're a star.'

'I know,' Heather said with a wink, pouring the black coffee into Rose's unwashed mug. Another thing she had forgotten to do.

The game began. Children in yellow shirts ran back and forth, mixing with the opposition dressed in green. The coffee was good, but the mug was as heavy as her eyelids, closing as though they were being stitched together and shutting out the light.

Her head dropped suddenly, and she woke with a gasp. All the mothers were staring at her. She glanced up at Heather from where she had slumped in the chair. Heather mouthed it was okay and gave her a reassuring wink.

Rose turned back to the game, looking for the twins amongst the masses of skin and hair.

Before she knew it, her head dropped again, so hard that

something clicked in her neck. A whimper escaped her lips as she woke.

'For God's sake,' Adeline hissed.

'Why don't you go and have a nap in the car?' Heather whispered, a hand on her arm with that painful touch again, as though she had slipped her fingers beneath the skin and was strumming Rose's nerves with her fingernails.

'I'm fine. Sorry. I just need more coffee.'

'Here.' Heather topped up her mug.

She breathed in the delicious scent and watched the steam curl up from the mug, but it wasn't long until her eyelids flickered and her head lowered as though someone was pulling her down by her hair.

'Mum?'

Rose woke up with a jolt. Cold coffee seeped into her tracksuit bottoms. It had felt like seconds since her last sip of hot coffee, and yet she knew time had passed from the sickness that clung to her. It was almost worse, sleeping so lightly.

Clouds had smothered the sky while she slept, throwing a grey tint on everything she set her eyes on. Mothers had wrapped themselves in cardigans and pashminas and were slowly packing away their things. Heather wasn't there.

Lily was peering down at her, her cheeks red with shame, mud flicked above her brow and streaked in her hair.

Rose looked down at the brown coffee seeping through her clothes.

'Shit.'

'Mum!'

'Rose, please watch your language,' Adeline said as she snapped her chair shut. 'You might raise your children differently to us at home, but here, you need to respect ours.'

Dispersing mothers glared back at her, muttering about her beneath their breaths.

'I'm sorry, I wasn't thinking,' she said and rubbed her eyes, unknowingly smearing her mascara into black clouds.

Adeline looked her up and down one last time and ushered her children towards the car park.

'How was the game?' she asked Lily. 'Did you win?'

'You would know if you'd been awake,' Lily said under her breath.

'We lost, Mummy,' Violet said from the other side of the chair. Rose hadn't even seen her. 'But it was fun.'

'You weren't benched,' Lily spat.

'Why were you benched? What happened?'

'Doesn't matter.'

Lily slumped off, kicking at the grass until green and brown clumps flew across the turf. Thunder grumbled in the distance.

'She'll be okay, Mummy. It was just a tackle.'

'I'm sorry I'm so crap, Vi,' Rose said, pulling her in for a hug.

'You're not crap.'

'I love you,' Rose said and kissed her daughter's forehead. Lily wouldn't let her give her affection; all she was allowed was a quick kiss on the forehead before she went to sleep, and that was only on a good day. It had taken some getting used to, feeling her daughter squirm to get out of her embrace and steel against her lips.

'I love you too,' Violet said. She licked her fingers and wiped the smudged mascara beneath Rose's eyes. 'You have panda eyes.'

'I must look a right state, huh? You're probably embarrassed of me.'

'No, I'm not,' she said, her voice tinged with the lie.

Thanks for trying, Vi.

'Come on, let's get you home.'

They headed off for the car to the first flash of lightning, and met Lily there, kicking at the gravel.

Rose waved at Heather who was grappling with her youngest to get him inside her car. Rose had wondered why Heather hadn't woken her; now she knew. Heather waved back, forming her hand to resemble a phone and putting it to her ear. Rose nodded and unlocked the car. She would call her once she had slept. She was only twenty minutes away from home. A short drive and she would finally be able to close her eyes; she just had to stay alert until then.

THREE

Rain pummelled against the windscreen. The brake lights from the car in front squirmed on the other side of the water. Rose glanced in the rear-view mirror at the back seats where Lily sulked with her arms crossed and a knitted brow, and Violet hummed along to the song on the radio, kicking the back of the passenger's seat to the beat.

The windows had steamed up and the heat from their bodies filled the car, weighing down her eyelids.

She shook her head roughly and clenched the wheel until her hands felt numb.

You'll be home soon. Ten minutes and you're home. The girls can crash in front of the TV while you sleep.

'What time is Daddy home?' Violet asked.

'I'm not sure,' she replied, grateful for the distraction. 'I'll ring him when we're back.'

The car fell quiet again. The song on the radio was slow and smooth, like a lullaby. Rose flicked between the stations, trying to find something with a beat to knock her awake.

'I liked that one!'

'Sorry, Lily, I need something livelier.'

Lily sighed heavily, tightening the knit of her arms. Violet drew hearts in the condensation on the window with the peel of a satsuma on her lap, the scent staining the air.

The car shuddered as it veered to the right, jutting over the cat's eyes in the middle of the road. An oncoming car honked its horn. She swerved back into the left-hand lane just in time.

'Shit,' she said and clenched the steering wheel until the leather squeaked beneath her palms. She eyed the car behind her in the rear-view mirror.

Just get over the bridge and you're home.

'Adeline said you shouldn't swear,' Lily said, after they had all caught their breaths.

Whose side are you on?

'Well, Adeline says a lot of things.'

They reached the bridge, its steel beams towering over them like ribs.

The river was dark and grey, reflecting the thick knit of clouds. Even through the metal of the car and the glass of the windows, she was sure she could smell it, the tang of the water ripping through Rearwood from the Thames.

Her eyelids flickered again. She shook her head, stared at the road until her eyes burnt, and lowered the window to feel the cold air against her face. Rain splattered against her cheek.

'It's getting on me!' Lily said behind her.

'Sorry.'

She closed the window and widened her eyes, not daring to blink, powerless as they cranked shut.

She woke to the girls' screaming and the sound of a horn blaring in her skull. She yanked the wheel to the left, missing the oncoming car by an inch, and collided with the side of the bridge.

Metal twisted. The headlights shattered. The car ricocheted off the bridge wall and spun across the road until the steering wheel turned wildly beneath her palms. The tyres screeched against the tarmac as the car veered head on into the side of the bridge again and thick, black smoke burst through the air vents. The airbag blasted out in a flash of white powder. Rose felt her nose crack, saw her own blood explode from her nostrils.

The side of the bridge split with the impact like parting lips, and spat them out until they were airborne, weightless for mere seconds before the car began to nosedive towards the river. Rose screamed and waited for the blow, her stomach forcing past her lungs and rising to her throat.

The windscreen cracked as the nose of the car hit the water, jolting them forwards. Her body wretched against the belt, cutting into her skin.

The river began to drag the car beneath the surface, creeping over the bonnet and edging up the glass, giving them a glimpse of the dark depths beneath.

'It's going to be okay,' she yelled, quietened by the whine of the sinking car. Glass cracked in the windscreen. Blood dripped from her nose and warmed her lips. 'I promise it'll be okay!'

The girls screamed as water poured through the air vents and filled the footwells until brown waves were chopping at Rose's feet. The radio was silenced with a quick spark and puff of smoke.

Rose fumbled with her seat belt, watching the dark water creep up the glass. Inside, it enveloped her feet and began to spit through the cracks in the windscreen in jet streams, creating new breaks, each larger than the last.

She unclipped the belt and snapped around, wincing from the pain in her neck, and reached for the closest child. Lily was red in the face, tears oozing from her eyes and snot from her nostrils. She had a bloody lip and a welt on her head. She put her hands out and clawed for Rose.

'We're going to be all right!' Rose shouted.

She unclipped the belt and dragged Lily forwards, untangling her small limbs to place her in the passenger seat. The water was so dark that she couldn't see the floor of the car. Lily screamed and dug her nails into Rose's arm until she bled.

'Lily, I need to get Violet!'

But Lily wouldn't listen; she clawed and screamed as the water crept over the edge of the seat and onto her legs. The glass in the windscreen continued to crack as the car sank and bubbles rose behind the glass. Jets of water sprayed at Rose's back, so cold that she flinched with the impact. The water seeped beneath her, numbing the flesh until it felt as though it was curdling the fat in her thighs.

'Come on, Vi,' she said as she leaned towards her and reached out for the belt clip. Violet was stunned, her wide eyes set on her mother's. Her skin was drained of blood and shimmered with tears. Her lips were red and wet. She stared down at the small tooth resting in the palm of her hand, felt the new gap in her mouth with her tongue and winced.

The water lapped around Rose's waist.

'Vi! Look at me!'

She looked up. Tears fell from both eyes.

'My tooth.'

Her voice was so delicate, so innocent, that Rose had to bite back the tears.

'I know, darling, but we have to go!'

She reached for her, fumbling with the seat belt as Lily's fingernails dug into the flesh on her back. She unclipped Violet's belt just as the car jolted, hitting the rocky bed of the river with a booming thud. Violet slammed into the back of the passenger seat just as Rose was pulled under water with the impact and dragged towards the break in the windscreen. Glass bit into the flesh on her back; her screams were nothing but bubbles of air. Water gushed around her body and forced her back into the car. She instinctively drew a breath and inhaled icy water into her lungs. She clawed wildly until she broke through the surface, hitting her head on the roof with a crack. Water spluttered from her lips and stung her eyes.

'Violet! Lily!'

She whipped her head around, but saw nothing but the chop of the water as it rose to the roof. The rear windscreen was dark with the water on the other side, waiting to be let in.

She couldn't see them. The water splashed against her chin as it rose. She took one last desperate breath, just as the water reached the roof.

She thrashed through the murky water and felt a small hand grip hers. She pulled the body to her and arms wrapped around her neck, just as the last of the windscreen shattered and the force dragged them from the car.

The current silenced their screams and ripped them this way and that, desperate to sever them. Rose held on to the small wrist so tightly that she felt bones snap beneath her grasp. The water was so cold that she couldn't move, couldn't think.

Suddenly she broke through the surface and gasped in air. Rain pummelled down from the sky and thunder clapped above her head.

The bridge was far away now, rising in and out of view from the choppy water, a gaping hole in the barrier where they had burst through. She spotted the bank and clawed towards it, listening to her daughter's cry close to her neck.

Which one have I saved?

Which one have I left behind?

The water stole the power from her legs, whipping them up and dragging her under. The river spat them back up and weeds tangled around her legs. She clawed her daughter upwards, her eyes curtained with sheets of water so she couldn't see which one. But her child wasn't crying any more. She was silent.

'No!' Rose screamed the word until she heard it echo amongst the trees on the side of the bank.

Rose kicked and kicked, clawed at the weeds with her one free hand, and dug her feet into the mud the second she felt it beneath her. The water broke around her in white sprays. She fought against the current until she breached the river and collapsed on the bank.

She lay there, shaking violently, the chill of the wind catching the water soaked into her hair and clothes. When her eyelids flickered, she forced herself up to a sitting position. She tried to stand but stumbled; it felt as though water had seeped in through her ears and filled her skull.

You can't give up.

She dragged her daughter's limp body further away from the river until they were both smeared with mud, and pressed shivering fingers to her neck.

Nothing.

She tried to blink away the water, but all she could see was the blurred silhouette of milky white skin, wet red hair, the yellow football top both of the girls had been wearing.

Rose pumped her daughter's chest, forced breaths through her lips that she couldn't afford to share.

She pumped and exhaled until water spluttered from the child's mouth, followed by a desperate heave for air.

Rose sat up, gasping in the ice-cold air and blinking furiously until her eyes cleared, and saw which daughter she had saved.

Lily was beneath her, shaking violently against the bank, her wild blue eyes locked on Rose's face. Her skin was so pale it was as though the river had drawn all of the blood from her body.

Violet.

Rose stumbled to her feet as the sob came, and rushed back towards the river. She felt the water climb up her calves and her thighs, until something caught her from behind. Hands were on her, wrapping around her waist and pinning down her arms, yanking her back towards the bank. A crash of thunder dulled the sound of her screams.

She kicked and thrashed. Flashing blue lights crept up from the town on the other side of the bank, their sirens carried with the wind.

The stranger ignored her screams, her threats, her desperate pleas. Every second she was held back was a second longer that Violet was without air. She turned to bite the stranger's hand, her lips curled back and teeth bared, and came face to face with the stranger, a man with jet-black hair, eyes wide with fear. A dog was barking further up the bank.

'You'll die!' he shouted, his warm breath blasting her face. 'You'll die if you go back in there!'

She couldn't do anything else but scream Violet's name. Tears blurred her eyes as lightning flashed on the surface of the river, the river that had stolen her little girl. The man clamped her against his body until she could feel the nervous rush of his heart. She screamed into his chest and her legs buckled.

I saved the wrong one, she thought. *I saved the wrong one.*

AFTER

◇◇◇◇◇◇◇◇◇◇

FOUR

Rose sat in her armchair before the window with her eyes set firmly on the bridge. Four years had passed, and yet she still heard their screams as crisp and slicing as the day of the crash, heard the whine of the car as it sank towards the river bed.

While Lily had transformed from a young girl into a teenager, the memory of Violet remained ageless. As Lily celebrated another year, Rose silently mourned three hundred and sixty-five more days without Violet. It was just Lily turning fourteen today. It was no longer *their* birthday.

Although Rose had seen Violet's body dragged up the bank by the divers after the search, she often dreamt she was still down there, her limbs drifting with the current and her hair fanned out in the water. In her dreams, she saved her. When she woke, she had to remember all over again.

The sun rose behind the trees on the opposite side of the bank, setting the sky ablaze. She glanced at the clock. It had just gone seven. She had managed a little over two hours' sleep in the chair, but still she felt drained, with the weight of exhaustion pressing against her forehead in a sharp pain, as though the tip of a knife was working its way down to the bone. She thought of Christian asleep in the guest bedroom above her study, and tried to remember the last time they had slept beside one another. He told her it was so he didn't disturb her with his snores, but she knew the truth – he couldn't stand the sight of her. She had killed his little girl.

The room smelt stale. Cigarette smoke lingered in the air, trapped in the room and pressing against the windows. Orange tar had begun to build on the glass and stain the ceiling above her chair. An ashtray filled to the brim with ash and filters rested on the windowsill. She spent most of her time by the window with the door shut behind her, her eyes on the bridge and her mind filled with memories. She couldn't bear to see the looks on their faces, feel the tension between them and her.

Lily left the room when Rose entered. Christian spoke bluntly with his back turned or his eyes averted. If one of them dared to meet her eye, she saw the hate dwelling within them, the kind of hate that was impossible to disguise. Christian hadn't touched her in so long that she couldn't remember what his hands felt like or recollect the taste of his lips. Sometimes she forgot the sound of his voice, only hearing it muffled from behind the study door as he cooked dinner for Lily and himself, while Rose ate alone.

Lily hid from her so well that Rose was often startled by the changes in her when they accidentally crossed paths: the length of her hair, the growth of her breasts, the womanliness of her face emerging as the puppy fat faded away. Life was passing her by, changing those within her own home, as she sat before the window cemented in the past.

Rose got up from the chair and turned her head left and right to stretch the muscles in her neck that had stiffened in her sleep. She was so accustomed to the room that she no longer saw the layers of canvases leaning against the walls with numerous paintings of Violet's face staring out at her, eyes following her as she moved. They wouldn't fetch any money like her old paintings used to, which had paid for the house that her husband now worked to keep. No one wanted a picture of someone else's dead daughter smiling out at them as they ate dinner, or the haunting scene of a child's white cadaver lying on a riverbank. She had depicted the same scenes over and over again, hoping to bleed them from her memory. So many times she had picked up her brush to paint something different, a landscape other than the view of the bridge from her window or the bustle of the river, but nothing came; all she could produce was her daughter's face and the dreaded day she lost her.

She opened the study door and listened for whispers of life upstairs. Silence. The rest of the house smelt fresh, with just the barely discernible scent of last night's meal. She tiptoed out of the study and into the kitchen, the tiles chilling the soles of her feet.

Apart from the occupants, not much else in the house had changed. The kitchen was the same as the day she had snapped at Lily for wanting a different cereal, the morning Violet ate her last meal. She peered towards the back door and remembered how the spilt tea had dried on the tiles, waiting for her when she arrived home from the hospital with one daughter instead of two.

She tried to remember the last time she'd made a meal. Exhaustion numbed the ache of hunger, brought a nausea that forbade her from eating. She would eat later, she told herself.

Christian cleared his throat behind her. She flinched at the sound and watched as he walked to the coffee machine, his eyes still hazed with sleep.

'Morning,' she said.

'Morning,' he replied.

She stood in silence as he moved around the kitchen to make a pot of coffee, never once meeting her eye.

'Is the birthday girl up?' she asked. If she'd noticed the forced cheeriness to her voice, he would have too.

'Since six,' he said gruffly. He moved slowly as the coffee brewed so that he wouldn't have to turn around and face her. She stared at his back and remembered how she used to claw at it as they made love.

'You can look at me, Christian. I won't turn you to stone.'

She watched his shoulders tense against her words. When he finally met her eye, she wished she hadn't said anything. There it was, the familiar hate staring her in the face.

He looked tired. The skin around his eyes was swollen from the early hour, and his hair was wild from sleep, but he was still as handsome as he had always been, even behind the dark stubble on his cheeks and neck, and the crow's feet beside his eyes.

'I'm staying away with work tonight,' he said as he turned back for the coffee pot and poured himself a mug. 'I'll come home for the birthday meal and then head out.'

'Again?'

'I've already ordered the takeaway for later.'

'I can cook her dinner.'

'You needn't,' he replied curtly. 'But don't forget the cake.'

He looked at her so coolly that she almost recoiled. She couldn't remember anything about a cake.

'From the bakery in town. I put the order in a month ago. Are you still all right to pick it up or should I do it in my lunch break?'

There was a distinct sharpness to the offer.

'Of course,' she said.

Which bakery? I could call both, check which place has an order under his name.

'I need to pack my overnight bag.'

Christian headed to the door.

'What's her name, Christian?'

He stopped in the doorway. She watched his back tense again, as if his muscles were shielding him from the risk of her touch.

She eyed his broad frame beneath the pyjamas, the bulk of his arms, the wide span of his shoulders, the way his back narrowed as it descended to his hips. She realised she would do anything to touch him again, if he would let her.

'Does it matter?' he said finally.

Each word hit her like a punch; instant nausea, burning in her throat, the blur of tears.

So it was true.

'It matters to me,' she replied croakily.

He hesitated, as though he was choosing the right words, but none came. He headed down the hallway and up the stairs.

If only she hadn't asked him to look at her. She could have lied to herself, held on to the hope that deep down he still loved her. But she had seen his hate, and knew that the love he'd once had was gone. Someone else had him now.

To outward appearances, they had stuck together after the death of their daughter. But within their home they were strangers, occupying different rooms, different beds, and avoiding each other's eyes.

He wasn't staying for her, she knew that much. He was either staying to protect his honour, to show the world they hadn't crumbled, or because he believed it was best for Lily, who couldn't stand to be in her company either.

Rose wiped the tear away and made her way back to the study, listening to the ring of the lifeless house before she closed the door behind her.

Rose stood before the mirror in her bedroom and dropped the towel. Her wet hair clung to the side of her neck and chest, while her pale skin revealed blue arteries in the soft creases of arms and groin. She eyed the shadows of her ribs protruding from beneath the skin, her visible collarbones and hips. Her body trembled with exhaustion.

She got dressed and brushed her hair, leaving it to dry on its own. As she fixed her necklace at the nape of her neck in the reflection of the mirror, she noticed how much older she looked, as though it had been a decade since her world fell apart and not four years. She moved the locket to the centre of her chest. Violet was enclosed inside, forever close to Rose's heart. She had worn the necklace the day she was sentenced in court. If she closed her eyes now, she could still smell the dull musk of the courtroom as she was committed to 200 hours of community service, fined heftily for damage to the bridge, checked into a sleep clinic for a month and banned from driving for life.

You have paid the ultimate price, the judge had told her that day. *You have lost your daughter by your own hand. That's a life sentence in itself.*

She shook the thought from her mind and tucked the locket beneath her T-shirt, out of sight. As she was about to leave the room, she saw a note on the dressing table.

I think it's time, don't you?

Her heart jolted. He had finally built up the courage to leave her. Yes, it would ease both of their pain, but it would also mean losing Lily, who would undoubtedly go with him. If she left, she would drift further and further away until they never saw each other again. After all, she knew how it worked. Rose had done it to her own father.

Then she spotted the business card beside the note and sighed. It was for the therapist he had been trying to push on her for years. The relief that they weren't leaving her was replaced with resentment, burning up her throat. There he was, bringing this up again.

It wasn't just any therapist, but Christian's own, who he recommended because he already knew their backstory. But it also meant that he had probably chosen sides before they'd even met; he had listened to Christian's criticisms of her.

But maybe this is his way of suggesting a fresh start, she thought. *Maybe if I see the therapist, he will try to forgive me.*

She stared at the card for a while, reading the doctor's name, *Dr William Hunter*, over in her head and eyeing the creases from wear, the yellowing of the white paper from all the years it had been inside Christian's wallet. She picked up the card and slipped it into her pocket.

Lily's gift sat on the side table. She had spent hours wrapping and rewrapping it, wanting every curl of ribbon and fold of paper to be perfect. But when she looked at the gift, her heart sank. Beneath the paper and decorations was a stainless-steel phone case engraved with the stencil of flowers, dotted with crystals. She had no idea if Lily would like it.

She headed down the stairs with the gift, stifling a yawn, and stopped in front of the open door to the living room.

A sea of wrapping paper littered the carpet: pastel pink, monochrome, silver shining in the sun as it beamed through the window. They had opened presents without her, presents Christian had chosen without even consulting her. She glanced towards the front door. Christian's car keys were gone.

Lily appeared in the doorway to the kitchen. Her red hair had grown down to the middle of her back, thick and ironed straight.

Her freckles had faded, revealing the youthful glow of her skin. She was as tall as Rose, but her posture was better. Lily stood upright with pride and youthful confidence; Rose seemed to shrink inwards, too exhausted to keep her spine straight.

'Happy birthday,' Rose said.

Lily stared down at the floor. Her school bag was over her shoulder. Her skirt was too short. Rose wouldn't dare tell her to change.

'I'm late,' Lily said.

'How are you?' Rose asked. 'School okay?'

'It's fine when I'm not late.'

Still she wouldn't look at her.

'Your hair has got so long. I always wanted hair that length, when I was your age.'

And then Lily looked up. Her glare was as cold as her father's. Rose flinched but refused to look away. She had to take every possible chance to talk to her, even if it meant standing in her path.

'I'll miss the bus.'

'I'm heading into town, maybe I could come with you.'

'No, thanks.'

'Another time then.'

Awkward silence filled the air. Her skin twitched with it. She watched the frustration rise through Lily's body.

'Here. . .' Rose said, and held out the present. 'Happy birthday.'

Lily gritted her teeth before heading towards her, each step forced, and took the present from her. Silence fell between them.

'I'm *late*.'

Rose stepped aside and watched her walk towards the door and snatch the handle; she was so desperate to get away.

'Do you need anything? You know, like tampons or—'

'Jesus,' Lily said, scrunching up her face. She opened the door and slammed it behind her.

Rose stood in the hall, listening to the tick of the clock on the wall, and blinked away the tears. It didn't matter how many years passed, the pain of being hated by those she loved would never ease. She hadn't just lost Violet on the day of the crash, but her whole family, as though they too had perished in the river.

Rose stared through the glass in the door and watched Lily walk down the drive. She crouched down by the bin bags ready for collection and shoved the gift inside before walking out of sight.

FIVE

Rose got off the bus in the centre of town and placed her hood over her head. It wasn't raining or particularly cold. This was just a way to protect herself from the town's stares. Rose Shaw would always be known as the woman who killed her daughter.

She headed aimlessly down the street. Twice a week she would go to town simply to listen to the sound of others' lives. She needed to be reminded that the world was still turning, remember the sound of babies crying, friends talking in cafés, the latest fashion in shop windows. In her study, time stood still.

She moved around people on the street with her eyes firmly on the ground, on the chewing gum trodden into the pavement and the odd cigarette end stamped flat. The fresh morning air clawed yawns from her lungs. Coffee. She would stop at the café and buy a cup.

She lit a cigarette in a cupped hand and turned left down another street towards the coffee shop she knew best. As she turned the corner, she knocked into a woman.

'I'm so sorry,' she said and looked up.

Heather stared back at her, her eyes widening.

'Rose,' she said.

Heather looked better than ever. Her skin was taut and without a blemish. Her body was toned in all the right places but still with womanly curves. She was immaculately dressed, from the cashmere coat to her high heels with red soles. She wore her hair short now, clipped close to her head.

'Heather,' she replied curtly.

People swerved around them. The day kept moving as they stood still, taking each other in.

'You look. . . good,' Heather said.

Rose looked down at herself: air-dried hair poking out from under her hood, baggy jeans that thickened the sight of her thighs.

Liar.

'Well, I won't keep you,' Rose said and headed down the street.

'Rose!'

She stopped and turned. Heather was making her way towards her, trying to find something to say to keep her from walking away again.

'What are you doing now? Shopping?'

'Coffee.'

'I should have guessed,' Heather said with a smile. 'Can. . . can I join you?'

'You don't need to do this,' Rose said finally.

'Do what?'

'You don't need to see me to clear your conscience.'

'I know,' Heather said. 'I want to, that's all.'

'What's changed in the last three years?'

Heather sighed, aware of the people on the street, weaving around them on the path.

'I owe you an apology.'

'So apologise.'

'I'm sorry, Rose. I just. . . I didn't know how to help you.'

'So the mums at the school had nothing to do with it? You weren't embarrassed of me?'

44

Heather looked away.

Rose threw the cigarette to the path and ground it beneath her sole. 'I needed you, Heather, and you cut me out, a year after my daughter died. I lost everyone – my daughters, my husband – and I needed you. I needed you and you turned your back.'

Rose walked away, but this time, Heather didn't stop her. She walked on, past the coffee shop, and another. She couldn't stop now, or the grief would hit her. She kept walking until her legs ached and her face flushed red with the cold. She was better off alone.

Rose sat at the table furthest from the window and sipped her coffee. The card for the therapist sat on the tabletop before her. She eyed it as she took another sip, reading the therapist's name over, and tried to straighten out the creases between her fingers.

If she didn't get help, she would remain in the vortex of grief, swirling around and reliving every memory. It wasn't the thought of talking to someone new, it was the judgement she feared. Would this man, this therapist, struggle to hide his disdain for her too?

She looked down at Dr Hunter's card.

The idea of opening up to a man was nerve-racking, but certainly better than meeting with a woman, who might be a mother and judge her even more fiercely. No, it was better to see a man, however uncomfortable the thought seemed.

She took her phone from her pocket and typed in the number on the card. The phone shook in her grasp. She looked around the coffee shop, eyed those closest to her, and pressed 'call'. She placed the phone to her ear and turned towards the wall to muffle her words.

'Dr William Hunter's office,' a woman said on the other end of the line.

'Hello, I. . . I would like to make an appointment.'

'Have you been with us before?'

'No.'

'Can I take your name?'

'Shaw. Rose Shaw.'

She listened to the tap of the keys on a keyboard and the distant murmur of reception-area music. She bit her fingernail.

'Mr Hunter has availability in two weeks' time. The morning of the second of November, at ten o'clock. Shall I book you in?'

That was too long to wait. There were too many nights for her to talk herself out of going.

'Isn't there anything sooner?'

'I can speak with Mr Hunter and get back to you, if you like. In the meantime, shall I pop you in for the second?'

'Yes, fine.'

'Is this the best number to reach you on?'

'Yes.'

'Thank you, Ms Shaw. We'll be in touch.'

She wanted to correct her, tell her she was Mrs Shaw, but it felt wrong. Perhaps it was best she wasn't listed as Mrs after all.

Rose placed the phone on the table and picked up the cup, finished her coffee in three gulps. The café buzzed with people. A grandmother was cutting up a cupcake for her grandson; a woman breastfed her baby as she talked with her friend; a man sat alone reading a book; but it was the woman around her age drinking hot chocolate with her college-aged daughter that she focused on. They smiled and laughed. The woman swiped whipped cream from the tip of her daughter's nose with her finger. It was agony.

She looked down at her phone and opened Instagram, scrolling through her timeline filled with photos from the only person she followed: Lily.

Rose's own profile was blank: no photos, no followers, and under a false name. The same for Facebook and Twitter – they were all created to keep up with Lily's life; it was her only way in. It worried her that Lily would let a profile so vague follow her, but she was grateful to have the opportunity to be a part of her life, even if she didn't know it. Rose swiped through the timeline, looking at photos of Lily with her friends, iced-coffee drinks with her name on them, a book she had read the week before. Rose read the comments left by Lily's friends, mostly girls, but some boys too. They wrote in another language, using emojis in place of words: flames to indicate she looked hot; girls calling Lily their 'wifey', both genders posting drooling faces or a face with hearts for eyes.

She worried about Lily. There was so much she had to learn, so many things she should know to avoid, and Rose couldn't help her with any of it; she wasn't even allowed to try. It wasn't Rose who Lily came to when she got her first period, it was Christian. Would he think to warn Lily not to send nude photos of herself the way so many teens did nowadays? Teach her to know her worth, and God forbid, tell her she had the right to say no?

Rose stopped scrolling when she stumbled across a photo of Lily and Christian together, in a place Rose didn't recognise. It was sunny, and sunglasses shaded their eyes, their smiles bright. But it wasn't the photo that made her heart jolt – instead it was the caption.

Can't wait for Daddy/Daughter night. #DaddysGirl

Jealousy coursed through her as she locked her phone with a shaking hand. Christian wasn't blameless – he had left her alone with them most of the time, including the day of the crash. Lily should hate him too.

'You look like you could let off some steam.'

Rose glanced up at the sound of the man's voice. He was tall and pale, with thinning red hair and a tired smile. His clothes looked old and worn.

He placed a card on the table with *Rearwood Rifle Range* printed across it.

She looked around the café to see if he had placed any other cards on the nearby tables. No one glanced their way.

'Do you approach everyone you meet in cafés like this?'

'Just the pretty ones.'

She scoffed.

'I didn't think people with impaired vision could have a gun licence, let alone a range.'

'Come on,' he said through a laugh.

'I don't like guns,' she said, choosing not to add that she thought men who did had something else to make up for.

'Well, if you change your mind –' he nodded towards the card and winked – 'name's Rob.'

As he turned away and headed for the counter, a short laugh cut from her lips. But the smirk stayed on her face. It felt good to be admired, even for a second. She stood to slip into her coat. The thought of therapy returned and wiped the smile from her face.

If she wanted to move on, she had to help herself. But the fear of letting someone in, a strange therapist she had never met, was too much to bear. She headed for the door with her head down, but not before sliding Rob's card off the table and slipping it into her pocket.

SIX

It was dusk by the time Rose made it to the graveyard. The church windows were emblazoned with the last of the sun's rays, and the grass between the dead was illuminated with rare flecks of gold. She walked up the gravel walkway and stopped before their graves.

Although the coroner had declared that her mother Lorraine had died of cancer, Rose knew that she had died of a broken heart. For years, Rose had watched the grief eat away at her until she was all but skin and bone, sitting in the same spot on the sofa until the cushions moulded to her shape and the ceiling was marked with a brown halo from the constant stream of cigarette smoke staining the plaster. Rose had resented her for allowing herself to be consumed by grief. As Rose entered adulthood, her mother was noticeably absent, even when they spoke or occupied the same room. Her eyes were vacant and her words were distant, as though she was running on autopilot as her core continued to fester in the past. It was only when Violet died that Rose understood her mother's grief, and mourned her all over again. Without even realising it, she had become her mother, the woman she had spent her whole adult life resenting.

Rose took a pair of scissors from her bag and trimmed the grass on her mother's grave, picking at emerging weeds. The gravestone was weathered with moss sprouting in the grooves of the words.

She took a mini screwdriver from her bag and worked out the moss until she could read the inscription clearly.

Here lies Lorraine Bartholomew,
a devoted mother and wife.

She surveyed the grave for any last blemishes, and finally forced herself to look at her brother's grave lying beside their mother's.

Jay had been too young to die. It physically hurt to think of him in the ground, like a migraine waking behind her eyes. His bones had never been given the chance to fully form. He never knew the sensation of a first kiss or a tender caress. He had never known what it was like to be loved by a partner, the unconditional bond that made sense of the mess of one's teenage years. At seventeen, he should have been happy, with the whole world before him.

Tears bit at her eyes as she remembered finding him, and looked around the graveyard to check she was alone. When the memory came, it was like an unstoppable wave, pushing into her and dragging her under. She closed her eyes and took a deep breath as the memory came flooding back.

She had passed the bathroom so many times that evening, banging on the door for him to hurry up and get out. All she had been thinking of was getting inside to prepare for her date with the guy from the local pub. She couldn't even remember his name now; the man's existence instantly became irrelevant, as did so many other aspects of her life. When two hours had passed without a word from him on the other side of the door, fear hit her suddenly. She took a coin from her purse and slipped it in the groove of the lock. She could still remember the quiver of her hand as she held the door handle and pressed down. Part of her knew what she was going to find. When the door drifted open, her whole life changed.

Jay was lying in the bath, the water red with blood. His skin was stark white, and appeared bruised in the grooves of his ribs where he had starved himself. A razor blade lay on the white tiled floor.

It had felt as though someone had taken over her body, moved her limbs for her, screamed without her consent. She snatched him up with such urgency that red water splashed over the rim of the bath and soaked into her jeans. She looked into her brother's eyes. She would never forget the emptiness of them, the serenity frozen onto his face. When she spotted the cut from his wrist to the crease of his elbow, her legs buckled. All she remembered after that was the sight of her brother's blood snaking between the floor tiles and the echo of her mother's screams.

When Rose came to, her gaze settled on the tombstone.

Jay Bartholomew 1982–1999

Twenty years, she thought. *I've been an only child longer than I was a sister.*

She swiped the tears away and took a deep breath. The cold air scorched her lungs. She tidied her brother's grave, picking at the dead leaves from the trees at the top of the hill.

'Rosie?'

She froze. Dead leaves crinkled in her fist.

'Don't,' she said and stood with her back to him.

'Rose, please.'

She turned and looked at her father with a piercing glare.

Tony had gotten so much older. His back had begun to curl. The skin on his cheeks drooped below his jaw. The few tufts of hair he had left were bone white. Sun spots littered his nose, with

51

broken capillaries on his cheeks. But his eyes, they were the same, filled with the same shame and pain.

'You shouldn't be here.'

'I come most days,' he said.

'Well, you shouldn't. They wouldn't want you here.'

Night was falling. The sky had lost its glow of the setting sun and the shadows in the yard were thickening. Silence grew between them. She bent down and packed away her tools.

'I see you here sometimes,' he said. 'But I know you don't want to see me. I usually wait until you're gone.'

She stood and slipped her bag over her shoulder. Blood rushed to her head and made her dizzy.

'But I had to see you,' he said finally. 'Even though you hate me.'

She moved past him, trying to ignore his familiar scent, the musky cologne he dabbed behind his ears and the bitter undertone of cigarette smoke clinging to his clothes. She noticed his hands were flecked with paint. He hadn't stopped painting either.

She turned back suddenly as hot rage crept up her throat.

'You don't get to do this,' she spat. 'You don't get to come to me after all these years and try to make amends. Where were you when my daughter died?'

'You. . . you didn't want to see me,' he said, baffled. 'You wouldn't come to the door when I called by.'

'Then you should have kicked the damn thing down. You should have tried harder.'

'But you've never forgiven me for. . . everything. How was I supposed to know what you wanted?'

She could see that her words were hurting him. His eyes began to sheen over, his bottom lip trembled and his words stuttered. She hated herself for it, but she had to hurt him, just as he had hurt her, Jay, and their mother.

'No, and I never will forgive you.' She stormed back to their graves and pointed to where Jay laid beneath the ground.

'He's down there because of you,' she said, watching tears build in his eyes. She moved her finger to her mother's grave. 'She's down there because of you too.'

'I'm so sorry,' he said. The tears finally broke. She had only seen her father cry three times before: as each of them was lowered into the ground, and when she swore never to speak to him again, just hours after her mother had been packed beneath the earth.

'It's too late for that. No apologies will bring them back.'

'Rosie. . .'

'Don't call me that!'

She stormed past him for the path and strode towards the exit, shaking with rage that only began to ease when she reached the gate of the graveyard. She looked back over her shoulder and could just see him through the lowlight, kneeling before their graves.

She could never forgive him. It was the only way she could withstand the hate from Christian and Lily; she understood their resentment well.

Rose walked through the graveyard gates and onto the street. The sun had almost set and had leached the last bit of warmth from the air. She dashed the tears away and felt how her cheeks had numbed with the chill.

The street was deathly quiet, with nothing but the sound of a siren calling from afar to break the silence. The air was so still, not even the trees made a sound. A fox froze mid-step by a parked car and dashed across the road as she drew near.

Rose walked on with her head down, thinking of Lily. She thought of ways to coax her out of her room to spend time with her, even considered bribing her with a shopping trip at the weekend or her favourite takeaway. But she knew that Lily would ask to go

53

shopping with her friends instead, and come down from her room to collect the food, only to sneak back up again without a word.

And then it hit her: Lily. Birthday. Cake.

'Shit!'

As if on cue, her phone began to vibrate in her pocket.

Christian's name flashed on the screen.

She immediately began to shake. However much she tried to love them, prove that she wasn't as awful as they thought, her exhaustion and poor memory were proving them right. She had forgotten Lily's birthday cake and hadn't turned up for dinner. She sighed and answered the call.

'Where the hell are you?' Christian asked.

'I'm so sorry, I lost track of time. I—'

'Did you at least get the cake?'

'I. . . I haven't slept properly in weeks. My memory, it's awful. I completely forgot. I'm so sorry.'

He sighed heavily into the receiver. She heard a door shut, perhaps to keep Lily from overhearing.

'So Lily won't have a birthday cake this year because you forgot about her?'

'I'm so sorry. Perhaps if I call now, I can—'

'I knew I shouldn't have left you with this.'

'Christian, I'm so sorry. I didn't mean to.'

'What were you doing that was so important?'

'I was at the graveyard. I completely lost track of time. I bumped into my father and—'

'Christ, Rose. You forgot about our living daughter because you were pining over the one we lost?'

'It wasn't like that.'

'I need to leave. Lily's staying over at a friend's. I'll pick up the cake tomorrow.'

'No, I'll do it. I promise I won't forget.'

'I don't think that's a good idea, do you?'

He sighed again.

'I have to go.'

'Christian. . .'

But he had already ended the call.

She closed her eyes and clenched her hands into fists to feel something, anything other than the guilt burning through her.

No wonder they hate you, she thought as she headed down the street with her eyes on the ground.

Rose reached the centre of town in forty minutes, and followed the cobbled streets until she reached North Lane that would lead her out of the town centre and towards home.

She hadn't seen a single person during her walk, and had become so accustomed to the silence that the growing patter of footsteps made her stop and turn.

Only a few of the street lamps worked down the lane, and those that did flickered pitifully like strobes.

Behind her, a man ran beneath one of the beams.

The hood of his coat was up, throwing a shadow onto his face. He was tall and broad, dressed head to toe in black or colours deepened by the night. In a split second, he was in the dark with her again.

He's a jogger. There's no need to be afraid.

But even as she thought the words, her chest tightened, making it difficult to breathe.

She turned and continued to walk through the darkness, suddenly aware of every sound. She heard the buzz of a security box outside the shoe shop to her left, the ruffle of her coat, the sound of her trouser legs grazing at her thighs. The man's laboured breaths grew louder, closer, until she froze to the spot with her pulse pounding in her ears. There was enough space for him to run around her. It would only be a moment before she was alone again.

The force of him threw her to the ground. She had no time to put out her hands, and hit the ground with a thud. The side of her face slammed against the cobbles and instant pain ricocheted through her jaw. She heard the man land with a groan.

As he stumbled to his feet, Rose scurried on her hands and knees to the doorway of the nearest shop and rested her back against it, panting in the shadows. Her pulse hammered all over her body: her temples, her neck, her heart seizing in her chest. She tried to find him in the dark.

He wasn't looking for her, but back the way he'd come. She could see his chest heaving, clouds of breath dispelling in the air. He crouched down and swept the ground with his hands, searching for something, his breaths growing more desperate with each second, before he got to his feet and burst into a sprint. His silhouette disappeared into the night and the sound of his footsteps slowly died until she was alone again.

Her hands shook before her in fists she didn't remember raising. Her heart was beating so hard that she felt her pulse beating against the door.

Had she been mugged? It had all happened so quickly.

She had dropped her bag. She could taste blood on her tongue. Her head was spinning.

Her phone wasn't in her pocket.

The locket was gone from around her neck.

She snatched at the skin on her chest for the chain and crawled, her hands running over the cobbles, in case it had fallen from her on impact. Her shaking hands touched moss, grime, something sharp. Her bag wasn't far from where she'd fallen and she slipped the strap over her shoulder to search for her phone on the ground. At last, she grazed the cool screen of the mobile with her thumb. She breathed a sigh of relief and used the screen as a light to search for her locket and any other belongings that might have fallen from her bag. It was just metal, a photo she could have printed again, but tears coated her eyes.

Please, don't let it be lost. I can't lose her again.

She hovered the light over the dark ground, the beam shaking in her grasp, and caught a glint of gold. She snatched up the locket and pressed it to her lips. The chain was broken, but easily replaced. She slipped it into her pocket and stopped. There was something else on the ground.

The light hung over a black notebook, wrapped with an elastic string keeping the covers together.

It had to belong to the man.

She snatched it up and stumbled to her feet.

'Hey!'

The word echoed down the lane, and fizzled out into silence again.

He was gone.

SEVEN

Rose arrived home and rested her back against the door. She was safe – she was home.

The man clearly hadn't meant to run into her, but having someone almost twice her size knock her to the ground had drummed fear into every muscle and bone. Her legs shook beneath her from running the whole way home. Something in her gut told her to lock the door, and quickly.

Calm down, she told herself as she swiped a lock of hair from the side of her face, slick with sweat. *It was dark. He didn't see you, that's all. You're safe.*

The house was silent. Every evening would be like this when Christian and Lily inevitably left: just her and the quiet. She listened to it ringing through the rooms; the sound would drive her mad within a week.

She turned on the hall light and caught her reflection in the mirror. Her cheekbone was starting to bruise, following up the curve of her eye socket and shadowing the dip in her cheek, making her look gaunt. One side of her jaw had swelled. She pressed her fingertips against the graze beneath her eye and winced. Almost an hour had passed, and her hands were still shaking.

She headed down the hall to the kitchen and put the notebook on the countertop. The pages were waved and yellow with age, and the cover had stray scratches from a pen. She wouldn't look in it. Whatever was inside was private. She would take it to the police station tomorrow so they could get it back to the rightful owner, if they even did that sort of thing.

She slipped out of her winter layers and made a mug of tea. The house had an empty chill to it, so much so that she considered wrapping her scarf around her neck again. When she made her way up the hall, she whacked up the heating and opened the door to the living room.

This room used to be her favourite place, but now it looked as though it belonged in an entirely different house. Over the years, the sofas had been moved and decorated with different cushions and throws. Even the scent of the air had changed. A calendar she hadn't seen before hung on the wall where the family portrait she'd painted once used to be. Now, it rested against the wall in the furthest corner of the room, their faces against the wallpaper. Rose wondered if it was her or Violet they were trying to avoid.

She walked towards the calendar on the wall and checked the dates highlighted in different colours: yellow, pink, green. Her throat thickened. They had movie nights together each week, marked with whose turn it was to choose the film. Christian noted when he would be away, giving Lily time to make plans so she wasn't left alone with her.

She marched back into the kitchen and threw her tea in the sink. Tonight, she was going to have a drink. Tonight she wouldn't give a damn that alcohol was a stimulant insomniacs should avoid. Her family hated her – the least she deserved was a glass of wine. She took a bottle of red from the rack and the biggest glass from the cabinet. She carried them into the living room and set up her own spot on the sofa. The room wasn't just theirs, but hers too.

She turned on the TV and flicked through the channels. Every colour on the screen seemed to glare out at her, flashing in her eyes until her head ached. She needed to sleep; her heart was beating irregularly. Running home had made it worse. She was more awake than ever.

She picked up the wine and the empty glass. It was a bottle with a cork, not a screw lid. She swore under her breath and returned to the kitchen, rifling around in the drawer for the corkscrew. When she turned back for the door, her eyes fell on the notebook.

Maybe she could read the first page. After all, the man hadn't even checked she was okay. She snatched it from the countertop before she changed her mind.

Back in the living room, she settled on the sofa with the notebook in her lap and stared down at the black cover. Was it filled with personal entries, or business plans, to-do lists? Were the pages written on at all? The owner's details could be in the front. She should look, for his sake.

She poured herself a glass of wine, removed the elastic string, and opened the front cover. Nothing was written on the inside flap. She turned the page and saw neat, cursive handwriting scrolled along the lines.

My name is Finn Matthews and if you're reading this, I'm dead.

Rose slammed the journal shut.

Of all the things that could have been written in it, she hadn't expected that. It was a joke, or a work of fiction; it wouldn't be real. She took a generous gulp of wine and opened the journal again.

I wish I could tell you my killer's name, but he has fooled me – he has fooled us all. The only thing left for me to do is look back over the past few months and document the events that occurred, to try and explain how it all began, in the hope that, should anything happen to me, the truth will be revealed.

He will kill me, that I'm sure of. He has hunted me for months, invading my home, my mind, and I have no power to stop him. He is everywhere, lurking, nameless. The police don't believe me. I have no friends here, no family. I'm alone, waiting for him to end this. And there's only one way this will end. I know that now.

From the outside, I look insane.

I'm starting to feel it on the inside, too.

This is not a joke. This is not a game.

Please, if nothing else – believe me.

Rose closed the journal again, speechless.

Silence filled her ears. When she noticed she was holding her breath, a bout of nervous laughter slipped from her lips. It was just a story, and there she was with shaking hands, sweat breaking on her forehead.

But if it were true, she was holding a potential crime in her hands. The man had been running from something, perhaps someone. Had it been Finn? Had he been escaping from the man who was set on taking his life?

She looked up and eyed the night pressing against the window. Someone could be out there, watching her from within the darkness, and she wouldn't have a clue.

It's not real, she told herself. *It's just a story.*

Her skin immediately felt hot. She stood quickly and closed the curtains before returning to the sofa.

She had to find out what happened next.

EIGHT

☾

Rose was numb in the back of the police car with the scent of the river stained into her skin. She sat with her bare feet in the well behind the police officer's seat. The river had taken her shoes. Lily clung to her, blue-lipped and catatonic, with her arm in a sling where her wrist had broken in Rose's grasp. Water had soaked into the upholstery of the seats and sent fresh shivers up their spines.

It had been hours. The storm had passed but the clouds remained, casting a shadow upon the bridge, lit only by the blue lights of the ambulances and the police cars blocking either end of the bridge. Cars were backed up for miles. Passengers got out to enquire, only to lurk at the barrier.

Rose refused to go to the hospital; she wouldn't leave Violet in the water; she had always been afraid of the dark. Paramedics had checked them over, and returned every ten minutes to flash lights in their eyes, check their blood pressure, their temperatures, adjusted the foil blankets wrapped around their torsos that rustled with every breath. Lily wouldn't leave Rose, and Rose wouldn't leave Violet. They sat in limbo, waiting for the divers to pull her from the depths.

The crane was stationed at the edge of the bridge with workmen ushering the pincer towards the water. She wished she could hear what they were saying, understand their occasional glances towards the car, peering through the back window and looking away when she met their eyes.

DS William Montgomery sat silently behind the wheel, occasionally eyeing them in the mirror. He'd challenged her when she refused to leave the bridge, but then Lily had screamed when they tried to prise them apart. The only thing he could do was usher them into the back of his car.

'Do you feel ready to talk about it?' he asked suddenly.

Rose's head snapped towards the mirror.

She wanted to, but the words wouldn't come. She parted her lips, only to close them again.

'We've spoken to the drivers who witnessed the crash. But we need to hear from you, to get to the bottom of this.'

It was my fault.

His colleague, DI Eva Rey, who had introduced herself as the lead investigator of the crash, stood at the barrier of the bridge, watching the divers sink into the depths of the river, tethered to the bank so they weren't whisked away. She stood tall and still, her deep ebony skin flecked with rain.

'I don't know if I should talk about it yet. . .' Rose said finally. Her voice sounded as though it had been shredded with a blade. She had screamed for so long that she could taste blood when she swallowed.

'Without a lawyer?' he asked.

She nodded her head.

'And . . . I should talk to my husband first.'

I have to tell him that I lost her.

She looked down at Lily, clinging to her tightly. Her other side was empty, where Violet should have been.

'He's on his way.'

They fell silent again, listening to each whine from the crane as it moved.

Her clothes and skin were torn from the rocks of the river bed. But she couldn't feel the pain; it was as though the water had devoured the very part of her that helped her to feel, to taste anything other than its salt. All she could do was stare before the break in the barrier.

DI Rey glanced at the car and locked eyes with Montgomery in the front seat. She nodded solemnly.

'Stay here,' he said and got out of the car.

Rose watched him stride over to Rey. They looked down at the water.

'Lily, stay here,' she whispered and reached for the door.

'No!'

Lily immediately began to sob again and clawed at her with her one free hand. Red marks trailed down Rose's arm.

'I want to come with you!'

'I need to go to her. I need to go to Violet. I'll be right back. You'll be safe here.'

She pulled away and silenced Lily's screams with the slam of the car door, squinting from the blow of the wind as it whipped locks of hair against her face. She walked along the bridge, almost as though she was floating.

She reached the break in the barrier just as her car rose into sight, water gushing from the smashed windows, the grille, the exhaust pipe. The roof had caved in. A set of wheels dangled from one axle, and the paintwork had large, jagged scratches raked into the side. The driver's door creaked open, snapped from its hinges and fell from sight, followed by a gush of dark brown water.

And then she saw it in the corner of her eye, the little white body being guided across the surface of the water towards the bank.

The divers were dressed head to toe in black with tanks on their backs and masks on their faces. Rose thought about how terrifying it must have been for Violet, seeing them approach through the turbid water like beasts, clawing in through the windows.

She walked along the bridge in a haze, ignoring the hammer of Lily's fists against the window of the police car, and walked slowly behind the officers so as not to catch their eyes.

At the end of the bridge, police tape flapped in the wind. A crowd of faces stood behind it, watching her every step.

She weaved through the ambulances, ignoring the glances from the paramedics, their desperate calls for the police officers further along the bridge. She walked around the numbered markers on the ground, highlighting each tyre mark, broken glass reflecting the clouds, a drop of blood that could have been from any one of them.

A uniformed officer approached her from the barricade at the bridge with her hands by her sides, open and ready to grab her.

'You can't be here, miss. . .'

Rose burst into a sprint and ran around the officer for the edge of the bridge, just missing the snatch of her hand. She ran for the slanted path that led to the bank, the sound of thudding footsteps collecting behind her and strangers calling her name. All she could think about was Violet.

She ran down the slope without slowing, cutting her feet on jutting rocks, stumbling and slipping in the mud until she landed on the bank on all fours.

'I'm coming, Violet!' she yelled.

She ran fast, mud squelching between her toes, with her eyes locked on the shadowy figures carrying her daughter in from the water.

As she reached them, a hand snatched her from behind, but she pulled away and stumbled into one of the divers. She slipped against his slimy wetsuit and fell to her hands and knees.

Violet was beneath her.

Her lips were purple with stagnant blood. Everything vibrant about her had gone: her freckles had faded away; her auburn hair had lost its glow; her skin was the colour of putrid milk.

Rose screamed until her ears rang. She threw herself over Violet's body, her head pressed to her small, motionless chest. She held her tight, longing for the faint beat of her heart against her cheek.

'I'm so sorry,' Rose whispered.

She looked at her face and tucked a lock of wet hair behind her ear. She snatched her up and rocked her gently.

'I love you,' she said between sobs, breathing in the scent of the water, and not the scent her daughter used to have; sweet and milky. 'I love you.'

'Rose.'

When she heard the stranger's voice she jumped, and slowly opened her eyes.

They had formed a circle around her. The divers had taken off their masks. The uniformed officer who had chased her down the bank was still panting. DI Rey stared down at the ground the moment Rose caught her eye, but DS Montgomery looked on, his eyes searing into hers. Figures in green arrived behind them.

'It's time to let go, Rose,' he said. 'We need to let the paramedics do their job.'

She breathed back a sob and looked down at Violet's ghostly white face nestled against her chest.

'I'll never stop loving you,' she whispered, pressing a kiss on her lips. Two tears landed on Violet's cheek. 'Never.'

Hands began to untangle her limbs from around Violet's body, clamping down as she fought.

'NO! Don't take her away! Please let me stay!'

The officers tugged at her arms and waist as the paramedics swooped down over Violet like vultures ready to feast. She watched until the sight of them blurred with tears and the woodland beside the bank echoed her screams.

NINE

R ose woke with a desperate gasp.

She could still smell the water, taste it on her lips. She licked it from her bottom lip and looked down. It wasn't Violet in her arms, but a cushion clamped to her torso.

She longed for sleep, but when it came, the past was waiting for her. She craved rest, but dreaded it in equal measure.

Sunlight sliced through a crack in the curtains. She had fallen asleep on the sofa. Her clothes had twisted in her sleep, stuck to her skin with sweat. She closed her eyes and breathed deeply to calm her heart.

Despite her nightmare, she felt almost rested for the first time in weeks. She sat quickly and reached for her phone to check the time.

'It's almost nine,' he said.

Rose flinched and looked towards the doorway.

Christian had to have been home for some time. His face was freshly shaved, and he wore a different suit from the day before, the tan-coloured one that clung to his body in all the right places.

'I slept for seven hours,' she said. 'I didn't wake once.'

For a brief second, he looked elated for her.

'That's good,' he said. His smile fell. 'What happened to your eye?'

She saw him take an instinctive step towards her.

Immediately, she remembered.

The man, the journal, the crime.

The skin on her cheek pulsed with her heart. She felt the hot flesh with her fingers.

'It's nothing, I. . .'

She was going to lie to him, but didn't know why. She looked down at the journal lying on the carpet beside the sofa.

'I wasn't paying attention. Hit my cheek on the corner of the chest of drawers as I unplugged the hairdryer.'

'Put some ice on it,' he said.

She nodded.

When the silence grew between them, as it always did, they looked away from each other, thinking what to say next to fill the void.

'You haven't been in here for a while,' he said.

She couldn't tell if he was pleased to see her there, or whether her presence was an invasion. It had been hers too, once. She wondered if he had forgotten that.

'No, I haven't,' she said.

'Did Lily come home before going to school?'

'I wouldn't know. Do you know the friend Lily stayed with last night?'

'She's a new friend from school. They've grown quite close. Nice girl.'

'I see.'

Where had she been, when Christian met Lily's friend?

Silence swelled between them again. They listened to the tick of the clock from the hall.

'I'm at home this weekend,' he said suddenly.

'I know, I saw it on the calendar. Your turn to choose the film, right?'

He blushed and looked away.

'You can join us on Saturday. . . if you want.'

She couldn't hide her elation. She had waited so long for an olive branch like this, but the more she thought about it, the more she heard the force with which it was shared, and her elation withered.

'I can't imagine Lily would be happy with that.'

'No, I don't suppose she would.'

The silence returned, the kind of silence that made it difficult to breathe, silence that felt like unwanted hands closing around her throat.

'She's out tonight,' he said. 'Over at Samantha's again.'

'Right.'

The two of them had been so close before her insomnia emerged. They never ran out of things to say or got sick of each other's company. Sometimes they talked for hours, and only stopped when they saw the sun start to rise behind the curtains. They would often finish those nights by making love, starting in bed but ending up on the floor, their limbs entwined, her head on his chest listening to the beat of his heart. And once Violet was gone, they practically became strangers. She could never have imagined them ending up like this.

'Just so you know,' she said. 'I hate this. I really, really hate this.'

'I do too,' he said, before glancing at his watch. He couldn't wait to get away from her. Just like Lily. 'Look, I've got to run, I'm late.'

'Right,' she said.

'I'll, er. . . see you later.'

He headed for the front door.

'Christian.'

He turned back.

'If you hate this too, then maybe you'll help. I may never get you back – that's not up to me – but please, help me with Lily.'

She thought of where he had been the night before, who the mystery woman was. Her stomach clenched like a fist at the thought of them together, their bodies linked the way theirs used to be.

He held her gaze for a while, nodded briefly.

'See you later,' he said again and turned away. She listened to the front door shut behind him.

They couldn't keep living like this, but she couldn't bear to let them go either. In four years Lily would be off to university, and things would have to change, if they hadn't already. Living with them was hell, but the thought of living without them, left alone with her grief, was unbearable.

It would just be the two of them tonight. She remembered the happiness in his eyes when she'd told him how she'd slept. However hard he tried to hide it, he still loved her, but in a new, guarded way. She couldn't remember the last time they'd been home alone together for an evening. Her chest gave the slightest of flutters. Maybe he did hate this as much as she did. Maybe this was her opportunity to make it right.

But there was something she had to do before then.

The journal.

She had read it from cover to cover before she slept, devouring every flick of the stranger's pen. She saw how his neat handwriting got messier as his fear grew; the pen had practically broken the paper in the last few passages.

She had read it like a novel until she reached the last page, and realised that the victim and the abuser weren't fictitious characters, but living, breathing people – or at least they had been. What happened to Finn Matthews wasn't a turn in a plot, it was the destruction of an innocent man's life. Had she found the journal too late? Was he already dead?

A new fear shook through her.

Who was the man she'd bumped into? Was it the victim? Or the man who hunted him?

She stood up from the sofa and headed for the hallway with her eyes on the stairs. She couldn't do much, but she had to do something – she had to go to the police.

FINN'S JOURNAL

8th January 2018

The day my life changed for ever was supposed to be the best day of my life. It was my first day as assistant editor for the local Evening Herald, *a position I'd been working towards for years. But the best day of my life would soon turn out to be the worst, only I didn't know it then. If only I had. I might never have met him. I might have stood a chance.*

I had been in town merely a week, and despite the awkwardness of settling in and meeting my colleagues, I was in my element. After three years at university and nine years in the business, I was finally another position up the ranks and that much closer to getting into the hot seat as editor-in-chief. But the whole experience was dirtied by the fact that I'd had to come home to achieve it.

Rearwood wasn't technically home – that was twenty-five miles north – but the two towns were eerily similar, evoking memories I'd fought for years to forget. The people of Rearwood were just like those of North Heath: closed-minded, hidden from the world and content with their lot. However much I had tried to escape home by moving to London, life had dug in its claws and dragged me back.

I left the office at midday on a coffee run to avoid the endless small talk that was slowly curdling my brain and felt totally overwhelming after a week of being alone in the silence of my new flat, unpacking and making it a home.

I crossed the street and stepped inside the café. I knew immediately that I was in a unique establishment: teapots with knitted cosies, odd tables and chairs, the café's history framed on the walls with photos of the owners arranged in a family tree; the business had been passed down to each generation, a strange discovery after living in London for so many years where a Pret A Manger sat on every street corner.

'There's a face I've never seen before,' said the woman behind the counter. She was large for her height, with brown hair, red blotches on her face, sweat on her lip.

I smiled nervously.

'Hazelnut latte, please.'

Her smile vanished.

'Not even a hello?'

I blushed. 'I'm sorry, I didn't mean to be rude. I. . .'

'Where're you from?'

I looked at the queue of people behind me. They all looked back at me like the woman. The café was silent.

'London,' I replied.

Everyone in the queue nodded, as though that small, two-syllable word explained everything.

'I see,' she said, her spine straightening. 'Well, here, we say hello to one another.'

'I'm sorry, I didn't mean to offend. . .'

'Two-eighty.'

I handed over the change and waited for my coffee, my cheeks still burning as people continued to stare.

'Here,' the woman said as she placed the takeaway coffee

cup in front of me. 'We don't do any of that fancy syrup stuff. There's your latte.'

I thanked her and left with my head down. In my desperation to escape their glares, I rushed out onto the street in a blind hurry, and straight into him. The cup burst open and threw scalding coffee over us both.

'I'm so sorry, I. . .'

The man stood before me his white shirt soaked. His face was bright red with either fury or pain or both. He had dark hair, wide shoulders and cold, bottomless eyes.

I loathe confrontation, especially with men; it reminds me of all the abuse I received in my youth, taunts that have never truly left me. I stood before him shaking, waiting for a homophobic slur or punch to the mouth. I couldn't even feel the coffee burning my skin, just the heat of his eyes looking me up and down as he decided what to do with me.

But then our eyes met and the rage suddenly vanished.

'I was running late for work and I. . .'

'It's all right, you didn't do it on purpose.'

'I'm so sorry.'

I was a mess. Sweating, twitching with nerves.

He smiled. 'You can make it up to me by buying me my coffee,' he said with a smile.

I looked into the café.

'I don't think they'll want me back in there. I didn't make a very good first impression.' I rummaged around in my pocket for my wallet. 'I'll give you the money for it.'

I picked at the change with a shaking hand.

'I don't want your money,' he said. 'I was after your company.'

I stopped and looked up at him. No one had ever been this forward before. My immediate thought was that he was joking, that this was some sort of game. Were his friends sitting in the café by the window, laughing with him. . . at me?

'We could go to the café down the street, they're much nicer.'

I glanced at my watch. Coffee had splattered on the glass face.

'I really should be heading back to work.'

'Where do you work?'

'There,' I said, indicating the building behind him.

'Oh, the paper.'

'Yeah. I'm so sorry again. . .'

I crossed the road, thinking of how I was going to explain my soaked shirt and burnt-red skin to a roomful of new people. There was a clothes shop a few doors down that I'd passed on my way to work. I decided I would buy a new shirt and hope no one noticed.

His voice broke through my thoughts.

'Can I have your number, then?'

I turned. He had followed me across the street.

'Pardon?'

'Your number. You said you didn't make a good first impression, so you must be new here. Weird way to make friends, throwing coffee on people, but it's a start.'

I laughed nervously.

He took his phone from his pocket and handed it to me. I tapped my mobile number in, saved it under my name, and passed it back.

'Bye.'

'Bye, Finn.'

I walked up the street towards the clothing store, bewildered and sweating, finally feeling the burns on my skin, with no idea that I had just met the man who was going to kill me.

TEN

R ose paced outside the police station puffing on a cigarette, her hair darting to the north with the wind.

She was going to sound mad. But however it sounded, she had the journal filled with crimes in her possession. She could tuck it in a drawer or throw it in the bin, but if she did that, she would never know what had become of the man who had written it, the man who was convinced he was going to be murdered.

The whole thing could be a joke, or the first draft of a novel, maybe even some sort of perverted fantasy. But if she didn't find out, she would never know for sure. She remembered the last sentence the man had written on the first page, before he began to document his own living hell.

Please, if nothing else – believe me.

She dropped the cigarette to the pavement, ground it beneath her shoe, and stepped inside the police station.

The reception was empty but for a police officer sitting behind a glass partition shielding the desk. Chairs lined the left wall, screwed to the floor. She approached the reception desk and stood before the glass. The policewoman reluctantly looked up from the computer screen: she looked young but tired around the eyes.

'Good morning,' she said with a false smile. 'Can I help you?'

'Morning,' Rose said, and took a breath. 'This is going to sound odd, but I've found a journal with tales of abuse written inside.'

The officer frowned and looked her up and down.

She thinks I'm crazy.

'Confessing what?'

'Stalking, breaking and entering, a range of assaults, quite a lot of things. But the most disturbing part. . .'

The officer waited.

'The author of the journal was convinced he was going to be murdered.'

Rose spotted a flicker of interest in the other woman's eyes.

'Do you have it with you? May I see?'

Rose took the journal from her bag. The officer stood from the desk and walked towards a door in the glass partition. Rose followed her, her heels clipping against the lino floor. The officer opened a hatch in the door and took the journal.

'Where did you find it?' she asked as she returned to the desk and opened the cover. Rose followed her on the other side of the glass.

'Last night I bumped into a man, or rather, he bumped into me. He was running – away from something, I think. He dropped it and left it behind.'

She watched the woman scan the page before turning it over to assess the next.

'I probably shouldn't have read it,' Rose said, filling the silence. 'But I looked inside for his details in the hopes of returning it, and well, the content caught my attention.'

'Does the journal contain any names?'

'Yes, but. . .'

'And you've read it all?'

'I have.'

She stood in silence while the young woman read a passage, turned another page to eye the other side. She closed the journal and looked up. 'I'll pass this on to one of our detectives and see what they say. I've. . . I've never come across anything like this before.'

Rose suddenly realised that she didn't want to part with the journal, but what had she expected? She watched the policewoman slip the journal into a bag and place it inside her desk drawer.

'Could you get in touch and let me know of the outcome?'

'Yes, the detective will be in touch. Should this go any further, we'd need a statement on how you came across it.'

Rose hadn't done anything wrong, but the idea of being questioned by a detective made her chest tighten. She had always been that way when it came to authority figures, but since the day she'd lost Violet, she'd seen the police as a threat. She couldn't be questioned again.

The policewoman slipped a form beneath the glass barrier. 'Fill out this contact form with your details, please, and we'll be in touch.'

As Rose filled it out, she noticed her hand was shaking.

You've done nothing wrong, she thought. *You're doing a good thing.*

She slipped the form back beneath the partition.

'Thank you –' the officer looked down at the form – 'Mrs Shaw. We'll be in touch.'

Rose headed for the door.

'Mrs Shaw. . .'

She turned and swallowed. Perhaps the officer had recognised her name: Rose Shaw, the woman who drove her daughters off a bridge. The policewoman was eyeing her expectantly.

'Yes?'

'The pen.'

Rose looked down at her hand. She was still holding the biro she had used to fill out the form. She laughed nervously and returned it beneath the partition with hot cheeks.

As she left the building and braved the cold again, she lit a cigarette and headed up the hill towards the town centre. She took her usual route around the lanes, but it felt different from before. Something was missing.

That morning, the journal had given her a purpose. Now, her life had no importance once again; she was simply the woman who drove her daughter to her death.

Rose stopped outside the library. The emptiness hadn't left her. All she could focus on was the man from the journal.

She had to put a face to his name. Without it, the people, the crimes, they didn't seem real. But it could take weeks to hear back from the police to confirm the contents of the journal, if they got in touch at all.

She looked up at the library, and felt a nostalgic twang in her chest. Insomnia hadn't just taken her child, it had sapped every ounce of pleasure from her life. It was only now as she had a clear head from a full night's sleep that she remembered what life had been like before.

Before insomnia and motherhood, she had been a ferocious reader. But the disease had whittled down her attention span to mere seconds. She would read a sentence and lose her place, skip lines without realising, forget what she had read the day before. It had stolen memories of her children, her desire for her husband, the enjoyment of food that had become nothing but tasteless fuel, like ash on her tongue.

Jay had loved reading too. Whenever she had read a book after he died, she wondered whether he might have enjoyed it. But death had claimed him and left her without answers, just like the man in the journal, his fate left hanging on the last page.

Finn Matthews had been the assistant editor for the local newspaper. If it were true, she might be able to find him in the library archives. She would be able to put a face to his name.

She stepped inside the library. The smell of books hit her instantly, paper that had been touched by hundreds of hands, year after year. She went to the reception desk and smiled down at the woman behind the counter, who tidied away a half-eaten muffin and wiped crumbs from around her mouth. She looked up through thick-lensed glasses that magnified her eyes.

'Good morning,' she said.

'Hi. I'm hoping to look through some old newspapers. Do you keep a record here?'

'You can access the newspaper archives from the computers upstairs.'

'And that will have copies of the local paper?'

'Sure does.'

The librarian made it sound easy, but Rose had no idea where to start. The woman noticed her reluctance.

'Here –' she wrote down a web address on a slip of paper and handed it over – 'use this. It'll have what you're looking for.'

'Brilliant, thank you.'

The woman looked at her face for a beat too long, as though she was putting her face to a name. Rose turned away, her cheeks already beginning to burn. She knew what was coming.

'It's Rose, isn't it?'

She stopped in her tracks.

'I'm sorry about what happened with your daughter,' the woman said to her back. 'Terrible thing, that.'

Rose couldn't face her; she couldn't stand the pity in people's eyes, nor the silent blame that always festered beneath.

'Thanks,' she said finally, and headed up the stairs, fighting the urge to take them two at a time.

The library was deathly quiet, with the exception of the odd rustle of a page or a stranger clearing their throat. She headed towards one of the computers and hung her coat on the back of the chair, then sat down and rested her hands on the keyboard.

After following the instructions taped to the desk to log on to the computer, she brought up the website the receptionist had written down for her and typed in the name of the local paper.

The date of events in the diary began in January 2018, the month he had started work at the local newspaper; almost two years ago. She pulled up the newspaper issues that month and flicked through page after page, looking for articles on new staff appointments, read the names of the authors by the articles, but upturned nothing. She checked each issue a second time, until her eyes burnt from the strain and she began to yawn. It had been a long time since she had given herself any mental stimulation; she forgot how tiring it could be. As the minutes passed, she began to wonder if it really was just a fantasy jotted down on paper.

As she opened the last issue of the month to read through once more before giving up, she spotted him.

Whether it was magazines or newspapers, she had a habit of skipping over the editor's note at the front of each issue; the habit had been so ingrained in her that she had completely overlooked him.

It had to be him. The man in the photograph by the editor's letter fitted his description perfectly: blonde hair, a white smile, even green eyes when she neared the screen and squinted. She thought back to the man in the street. Had it been him? But it had been too dark to spot the colour of his hair or eyes. She read the write-up and spotted his name.

Finn had been appointed as the new assistant editor of the local paper, after working as a digital content editor for another newspaper in London. But that wasn't what interested her.

The man from the journal wasn't a figment of someone's imagination. He had been a living, breathing person. But what had happened to him?

What had become of Finn Matthews?

ELEVEN

Rose returned home with an energy she hadn't had in years.

She had bought a slab of steak from the butcher's shop on her way home, Christian's favourite, and a flan for herself, with flowers for the table and the best red wine she could find. She was going to show him that she still loved him. He usually returned home just before seven. She had time to prepare dinner and get ready before he walked through the door.

She peeled potatoes and rolled them in garlic and rosemary, oiled a frying pan for the steak, and foiled a baking tray for the grilled vegetables, all the while thinking of him that morning and the flicker of affection she had caught in his eyes. It had been years since he had looked at her like that. She wouldn't let the opportunity pass.

She put the flan, potatoes and vegetables in the oven and headed upstairs, stripping the sheets from her bed and replacing them with a fresh set. She showered, blowdried her hair, applied make-up for the first time in months, and fished out the lingerie that had been pushed to the back of her underwear drawer.

It had been years since she had dressed herself to be desired, and in that time, her reflection had changed. She stood before the mirror in the black lingerie and eyed the way her skin had slackened in places, the shadows between her ribs and the sharpness of her collarbones, but it was still the body he knew, the same skin he had kissed every inch of.

She slipped into her favourite black dress and ran her hands over the fabric. The fit was looser than it used to be at her chest, and tighter around her hips, but the cut of it helped to give her more of a proportioned shape, rather than the uneven body which grief had left her with.

She returned downstairs and fired up the hob for the steak, turned the potatoes to brown on the other side. She lit candles for the table and arranged the flowers, poured herself a glass of wine for courage, and left the bottle to breathe.

When the clock struck seven, she arranged the food on the plates, placed them in the oven to keep warm, and waited.

And waited.

By quarter past seven, she had finished her glass of wine and poured another. Her foot tapped against the floor as she watched the seconds move around the face of the clock, each second feeding her doubt. He was coming, he was just held up at work, or stuck in traffic. He had said he would see her later. She took the plates from the oven and placed them on the table, hoping to tempt fate. He would be back any second. He would.

When it reached seven thirty, the make-up she had applied felt stale on her skin, and her teeth furry from the wine. She checked her phone in case he had texted her about a hold-up. She had no messages.

The dinner was cold, and the bottle of wine was half-empty. She unlocked her phone and typed out a message.

Are you still coming home tonight?

She had finished the rest of her second glass by the time her phone pinged. She opened his message with a racing heart.

> Sorry if I wasn't clear earlier. I'm away
> tonight, home Saturday and Sunday.

Her heart dropped.

Of course he wouldn't stay at home with Lily away. Rose had known him for half of her life, and heard him use the phrase *See you later* to mean *See you soon* countless of times before. She wanted to believe that deep down she had known all along he wouldn't come home with her there, but she had truly believed he wanted to make it work.

Tears built in her eyes and blurred the flicker of the candle. She wiped them away as they cascaded down her cheeks. The meals sat uneaten on the table. Candle wax had melted down the silver holders. She tried to steel herself against the tears, clenching her teeth and tensing the muscles across her chest, but the tears refused to be buried. Of course he wouldn't want this. She looked down at herself, at the dress she had pulled out from the back of the wardrobe, the lingerie hidden beneath.

You're a fool. He would never want you. Not after what you did.

She stood and pulled at the dress, snagging the zip when it caught, ripping the fabric from her with a desperate cry. She wanted to shred it, burn it, forget she had ever tried.

She stumbled to the utility room and took a clean pair of pyjamas from the ironing basket, ripping the lingerie from her body. She couldn't bear the touch of silk on her skin. But even when she was dressed in her pyjamas, the humiliation refused to budge. She shoved the lingerie and dress deep into the bin. She wouldn't be able to look at them again without remembering the embarrassment of it all. She leaned over the table and blew out the candle, smoke curling up towards the ceiling, took her wine glass and the bottle and shut herself away in the study.

If only she could sleep to forget. But she knew that insomnia would keep her awake for hours, leaving her to fester in her own shame.

TWELVE

☾

Somehow she kept walking, one step after another, up the slope and onto the bridge. Her feet were frozen and cut on the soles. DS Montgomery guided her with an arm around her waist to keep her from buckling. She could still feel the tickle of Violet's hair against her face, the icy chill of her daughter's chest against her cheek.

They both stopped at the sound of her name.

Rose blinked away the tears. Christian stared back at her with bloodshot eyes. His hands were clenched into fists by his sides, his knuckles white to the bone.

'What have you done, Rose?' he asked hoarsely. His voice quivered as a sob clawed up his throat. 'What have you done?'

She watched a tear slip down his cheek, listened to agonised sounds that she had never heard him make.

'WHAT HAVE YOU DONE?'

She jolted as the sound echoed down the bridge. Montgomery stood quietly by her side; the onlookers at the barricade continued to stare, their eyes burning into her back like flames.

Not here, she thought. Please not here.

He wanted to know what she had done, but she couldn't bring herself to say the words, or believe them herself. Only that morning she had kissed Violet on the head, hugged her tight. Now she was on the bank, as cold as the river bustling beneath them. Every second she stood without speaking, his rage seemed to rise closer to the surface, dilating the veins in his neck, turning his face and neck crimson.

'She's. . . she's dead, Christian. Violet's dead.' Then she broke down, gasping for precious air. Montgomery clamped on to her when her legs threatened to buckle.

The words seemed to hit him physically, sucking the life from his eyes, every ounce of strength from his limbs. He collapsed to his knees and covered his face with his hands.

She instinctively went to comfort him, but Montgomery kept her at his side.

'Don't,' he whispered.

She stood helplessly and watched her husband, taking in every sob, every quiver of his body. She was watching his heart break.

Christian screamed into his palms. His face went bright red, anger scalding his skin. He lowered his hands and bellowed deep from his gut, until spit flew from his mouth and strung between his teeth. She watched helplessly as he beat the tarmac with his fists, thrashing the ground until the skin on his knuckles broke and bled. She could imagine he was thinking of her beneath him, her bones snapping with each blow.

He stared at his quivering hands, at the blood dripping from them and onto the tarmac, and finally met her eyes.

She knew he loathed her. He wished it had been her dead on the bank, rather than their child.

He stood and turned without a word, and marched towards the police car. Rose pushed away from Montgomery and followed the drops of blood in his wake.

He opened the rear door and bent inside, returning into

view with Lily clinging around his neck.

'Stay away from us,' he said as she approached.

'Christian, please. . .' she sobbed, snot and tears glistening on her face. She reached out and touched him.

'STAY AWAY!'

She backed into Montgomery, who had followed close behind. It was all too much. She was light-headed and shaking all over. She reached out for him again.

'Please don't leave me. Please don't take Lily away too!'

Montgomery held her back gently. She was too weak to fight him.

Christian walked further along the bridge, with Lily watching her over his shoulder, her blue eyes wide with fear, taking in the sight of the break in the bridge, the mess of car metal and glass littered on the road.

'No!' Rose shouted. 'Please!'

She snatched herself away and raced behind him. Glass bit into her feet and the wind cooled her tears. She couldn't lose them too. She grabbed the back of his shirt in both fists.

'Please don't leave me!'

He turned swiftly and pushed her away. She fell to the ground with a thud; the air was forced from her lungs.

'You stay away from my daughter,' he spat, pointing a finger at her face. Blood ran along it, etching around his fingernail. 'I never want to lay eyes on you again.'

She took in his reddened face, the venom in his eyes, and knew that in that moment, he could have killed her without regret.

He turned and walked on, holding Lily tighter.

'No. . .' She tried to stand but stumbled, fell back to the tarmac. 'NO!'

Mist crawled across the bridge, drinking in the view of them until they were nothing but shadows.

She hadn't just lost Violet. She had lost them all.

THIRTEEN

C

Rose woke from the memory to a sudden sound.

She had fallen asleep at dawn with the sun rising against her face. It was higher in the sky now, but the birds still sang. Her tongue and teeth felt furry from the wine, and she remembered why she had hit the bottle. Her gut twisted with the memory. She longed to return to sleep.

She remembered the happiness she had felt as she bought the steak from the butcher's, the stupid smile she had worn all the way home; the hope that had flared in her gut as she cooked for him and set the table, arranged and rearranged the flowers so they could see each other over the petals and leaves.

What a fool she had been. All he had done was show her some kindness, and she had taken it to mean so much more.

I'm pathetic, she thought.

She looked out the window and caught her reflection in the pane. Her make-up had smudged beneath her eyes; her lips were stained crimson from finishing the bottle of wine, drinking herself into a brief coma. Suddenly it hit her.

The door. She had woken to the sound of the front door closing.

The table was still set for two.

She darted from her chair and stumbled out of the study, her limbs still slow from the wine.

Christian was standing before the table, looking down at the food that had congealed on the plates, the stray splotches of red wine on the tablecloth. One of the flowers had drooped in the vase.

Her throat and cheeks burnt. She quickly began clearing the table.

'Rose, I—'

'Don't, please.'

She placed her plate over his and chucked the cutlery amongst the food. Her grip on the plates moistened with the slop as she headed for the sink.

'I'm sorry. I had no idea.'

Tears built. She blinked furiously.

'Christian, please. It was stupid. Forget it.'

'Let me help. . .'

'No. I'm fine.'

She turned quickly so he couldn't take them, and cutlery fell from the top plate and clattered to the floor. The plates followed, slipping from her hands and smashing against the tiles.

'*Jesus!*' The word rang through the house.

She looked down at the mess, her hands shaking by her sides, and turned towards the kitchen window above the sink to hide her tears.

'If I'd known. . .' he said.

She couldn't trust herself to speak. If she did, she was sure a sob would rip up her throat. She dropped her head and closed her eyes.

A brief silence swelled in the room. Christian moved behind her back. He swept up the broken china, took sheets of paper from the kitchen roll to wipe up the slop. She couldn't hold herself together. He had to leave, or she would only humiliate herself further.

'Christian, please,' she begged, tightening her grip on the rim of the sink. 'I need you to leave me alone.'

'Okay,' he said.

She would rather he laughed at her, left the room the moment he saw what she had planned for them, but instead he pitied her with a soft, remorseful tone, moved gently around the room so as not to break her.

He opened the bin and paused. She turned to see him looking down at the dress and lingerie she had thrown away the night before. His cheeks reddened and his jaw clenched. He emptied the dustpan into the bin and left the room.

Staring out the window, she let the tears fall and dry on her face. While she had been preparing the meal, he had been getting ready to see another woman.

Her phone rang from the study and broke her from her thoughts. She tried to wipe the tears from her face, but they had dried on her skin in salty trails.

She sat down in her chair before the study window and answered the call.

'Hello?'

'Hello, is this Mrs Shaw?' a man asked. She recognised his voice from somewhere.

'Yes.'

'This is Detective Inspector Montgomery.'

Air caught in her lungs.

Montgomery.

She was too stunned to speak. She breathed down the line as the memories hurtled back. He had witnessed the worst day of her life, seen first-hand what she had done.

'I was calling about the journal you found. Are you available to come to the station this afternoon?'

How could she face him? Look him in the eye when he had seen her daughter dead on the bank, all because of her?

'Or I can come to you,' he said, filling the silence.

'No!' she replied, too quickly. She couldn't have him in the house. If Christian saw him, it might reignite his hate and make everything worse. 'I'll come to the station. What time?'

'Is midday too early?'

'Midday is fine.'

'Great.'

They both lingered on the line, listening to each other's breaths. He had to be thinking of the past too.

'See you then,' she said, and hung up.

She looked out of the window. Her eyes travelled to the river. She thought of Montgomery dragging her from Violet, the look he had given her as she rocked the limp little body in her arms.

She couldn't meet him like this, not when she felt so vulnerable.

She sighed into her lap and snatched up her bag in search of cigarettes. But there was something else inside that caught her attention. She took the man's card from her purse, and remembered meeting him in the café, his cheeky, sideways grin. *Rearwood Rifle Range*. It was exactly what she needed. She took up her phone again and dialled the number.

'Rearwood Rifle Range,' Rob said as he answered the call.

'I need to let off some steam,' she said.

He chuckled into the receiver. It felt good to make a man laugh again.

'What time can you get here?'

FINN'S JOURNAL

11th January 2018

I saw him again that Thursday. I thought it had been a coincidence, something that came with living in a small town. I had no idea then that he had been following me, noting my every move, waiting for the perfect opportunity to infiltrate my life again.

I had almost survived my first week at the paper, and my new colleagues had pressured me into going for a drink with them to celebrate nearing the end of my first week, and although all I wanted to do was go home and read a book, I agreed. It had been so easy to shrink into myself in London, a city where it was near impossible not to be lost amongst the crowds. But I had to make an effort; I had spent far too many years alone already.

They took me to a series of pubs, each one dingier than the last, but as the night went on, I cared less – my colleagues refused to let me pay for my drinks, and by ten p.m. my thoughts and worries were swimming in gin.

We were in the Fox and Pheasant when I spotted him, or should I say, when he spotted me.

'No coffee on you this time?' he asked as he approached with a smile, his hands raised in mock surrender. 'I'm safe?'

'Well, I've drunk my body weight in gin, so I wouldn't be too sure.'

'You never did get me that coffee,' he said. 'How about a beer?'

'Of course,' I said quickly, slightly slurred.

He expertly whisked me away from the comfort of my colleagues towards the bar, spoke to me in an endless stream. I leaned on the bar to order his drink, my shirt sleeves soaking up a puddle of beer from a previous punter.

'So, you're new in town?' he asked, when his drink arrived. He took a sip, licking foam from his top lip.

'Yeah, only been here a couple of weeks. I grew up not too far from here though.'

'Where was that?'

'North Heath.'

'Finn!' Lindsay said, bursting between us.

Lindsay wrote the back pages – obituaries, ads, the small stuff – and was convinced that I would become her 'gay best friend', as if my attraction to men made me a far more remarkable, exciting pal to have. Harmless, but intense.

'We're having shots and then moving on.'

'If I have another tequila I'll throw up,' I said. 'I'm going to grab some chips and head home.'

'No!' she whined, dragging out the word. 'It's your night, you have to stay!'

'Honestly, if I stay, I'll vomit,' and on cue, the hiccups came.

'I'll walk you home,' he said.

'Who's he?' Lindsay asked, stumbling on the spot.

'Michael,' he said, holding out his hand. 'Finn and I met earlier this week.' Lindsay didn't even look at him. 'Stay, Finn, it'll be fun.'

'He said he wants to go home,' he said, sternly. His tone almost sobered me up. Almost.

Lindsay looked at him then, her brow creasing.

'You go and have fun,' I interjected. 'I've had a great night, thank you. I'll see you in the morning.'

I said goodbye to her and the rest of the group, with Michael behind me, waiting. I didn't want him to walk me home, but I didn't want Lindsay to cause a scene either. She was staring at him, thinking of the right words to say. I got out of there as quickly as I could.

The cold night was fresh in my lungs, and cooled the sweat on my brow from the hot room. I'd almost forgotten about him until I felt his breath on the back of my neck as he stepped out into the cold.

'So, which way?'

'Oh, erm. . . this way.'

I have never been good at saying no. After years of being told I was abnormal, a freak, even mentally ill for loving the same sex, some way along the line the need for people's approval, the hunger to be accepted, became ingrained into my psyche.

'That Lindsay's a live wire,' he said.

'Yeah, she's a fun one,' I said with a forced laugh. Surely he could sense my unease, the way I stepped back from him when he got too close, looked away when he tried to meet my eye.

'You're shivering. Here.' He slipped out of his jacket.

'No, honestly, I'm fine. You keep it.'

'Don't be silly, you're freezing.'

He draped it over my shoulders. I felt his body heat radiating from the fabric. He was trying to be romantic, but instead of being comforting, his warmth made me cringe. Mistaking it for the cold he pulled me in, rubbing my arm roughly to bring the heat of my blood to the surface.

'Thanks,' I said and slowly put distance between us again.

For years, I had watched straight couples walk hand in hand in the street, kiss whenever the mood took them, and felt sick with jealousy at their freedom, to express themselves in public without fearing for their safety; now I had a man trying to be affectionate in the same way, but it felt wrong, coming from him. Rushed.

We walked in silence, turning from one road to another. The sounds from the bar had gone, drunken shouts and laughter replaced with the scuffle of our feet and the whistle of the wind.

'Were you alone in the pub tonight?' I asked. Even then, drunk out of my mind, I was beginning to doubt him. I should have listened to my gut, thrown his jacket to the ground and run.

'My friend cancelled last minute. I was about to leave and then I spotted you. Had to get that drink, didn't I?'

He laughed, so I laughed too.

He spent the rest of the journey telling me about himself, and I believed him; but now I know the truth, that everything he told me that night was a lie. When we reached the top of my road, I stopped.

'This is me.'

'I'll walk you to your door.'

'No, honestly, you've already gone out of your way. I'll be fine.'

'I insist,' he said. 'It might not be London, but we have our fair share of nutters too.'

I've often wondered if he thought of himself when he said that, whether it was some sick joke, or if he truly believed that he was exempt, that his actions were justified and not those of a madman.

I gave in, as I always did. I let him walk me straight to my door, a decision I would spent many sleepless nights wishing I hadn't made.

'Thanks,' I said as I stopped outside, and turned to say goodbye. His hands were on me in an instant, clamping me down before him. His lips were on mine before I even had a chance to take a breath. His kiss was so hard it hurt. His stubble scratched my face; his hands pressed against my body until I could feel the ache of his grip against my spine. I pushed his chest and stepped back, wiping my mouth with the back of my hand.

Even then, I knew I shouldn't anger him. There were so many signs, but I had batted them away, longing to ignore them, to believe I was safe.

'Night.'

I shot up the steps towards the communal front door and rushed to find the keys. Dropping them in my haste, I heard him breathe a laugh behind me. He was still there, lurking. I found the key, turned it in the lock so hard it could have snapped, and closed the door without looking back.

Now he knew where I worked and where I lived. He knew my name and had my phone number. All I knew of him then was the false life he had created for me, and that he didn't take no for an answer.

I let myself inside my flat. The door swung wide before I'd even turned the key, the slight pressure of my hand enough to open it. I swore under my breath as I stepped inside and shut it behind me. I locked it, my hand pressing it firmly into the frame. My landlord had promised to fix the faulty lock before I moved in – it was one of my conditions before signing the lease. I vowed to call him the next day and demand he have it replaced.

I liked my flat, before he took it from me. The ceilings were high, with floor-to-ceiling windows looking out to the street. The main space was one large room, with the living area at one end and a small dining table separating it from the newly refurbished kitchen at the other. Off it was a small corridor leading to the bathroom and my bedroom.

I undressed lazily, leaving my shirt crumpled on the back of the sofa and my jeans in a pile on the floor, and stumbled to the kitchen to get a glass of water.

I got into bed with a relieved sigh, and groaned when I realised I hadn't lowered the blinds. I staggered out and held the blind cord, freezing as I caught sight of something on the other side of the street. A shadowy figure.

Through my drunken haze, I didn't even think it could be him, watching me from outside as I stood before the window in just my underwear. I didn't think much of it at all, until later when everything began to fall into place. I lowered the blinds and returned to bed.

The countdown to my death had begun.

FOURTEEN

The taxi pulled up outside the gun range an hour later, but Rose's need for release had died on the journey. All she wanted to do now was ask the driver to turn around and take her home again.

'This is the right place, yeah?' he asked.

She couldn't see his lips, but she could tell he was smirking by his eyes, as if driving her all the way out there had been a joke and he was waiting for her to deliver the punchline.

'I said the gun range, didn't I?' she replied and thrust the fare towards him.

She stepped out of the car and walked towards the entrance without looking back, but when she tried to open the door, she found it locked. She refused to look round, and imagined the driver laughing as he turned and drove back down the gravel drive.

Just as she began to worry that Rob wouldn't turn up, that it really was all some kind of joke, she saw movement inside through the glass in the door, and sighed quietly as he appeared on the other side. He unlocked the door with a grin on his face.

'Hey,' he said.

'Hi.'

'Come in.'

'No one else around?' she asked as she stepped inside.

'We don't usually open at midday in the week, but we make the odd exception.'

Fear ached behind her ribs. It had begun to form on the journey over as she thought of meeting with a man she didn't know, a man passionate about deadly weapons, but now they were alone together, she realised what a stupid decision she had made. He locked the doors and her mouth dried.

'Can't have anyone waltzing in and leaving with a gun,' he joked.

'Am I allowed to do this? Just turn up and shoot a bunch of guns?'

'With me here you can,' he said, putting his hands in his pockets as if to make him seem smaller, less intimidating.

She relaxed a little.

'I was giving out flyers for an open day next month to rope in some more members, but I gave you my card instead.' He winked again, but it wasn't crude, more playful.

She relaxed some more.

He was better-looking than she remembered. He had a kind smile; white teeth and a full bottom lip, carved cheeks and jawline covered in stubble. His eyes were both green and blue, ocean-like. She eyed the broadness of his shoulders and chest and laughed out loud suddenly.

'I have no idea what I'm doing here.'

'Don't overthink it,' he said, smiling back. 'Let's just have some fun. I'll show you around.'

The entrance hall was like an old American lodge with rifles on the walls and a buck's head over the reception desk. She met its glassy eyes and looked away.

'We do clay-pigeon shooting –' he nodded towards the window at the sprawling lawn – 'but I've always preferred the inside range.'

He headed to the desk. 'Would you mind signing up for our newsletter? We have targets to hit each month and we're falling behind.'

'Sure.'

She signed her name, jotted down her email and home address.

'This way,' he said, leading her through a doorway as he opened another on to a narrow staircase.

'I've laid out some guns I thought we might try.'

She followed behind him, barely listening as he spoke. Her heart was hammering in her chest. She had never liked guns, and yet here she was, moments away from pulling a trigger. She was locked in a room with a total stranger and no one knew she was there. It was madness.

They stepped out into a large room, separated by booths that faced a large open space where bullet holes littered the walls and paper shooting targets hung, waiting to be torn to shreds.

'Why did you approach me?' she asked suddenly. 'In the café.'

'Am I not coming on to you hard enough?' he said and laughed.

Tell him you're married.

His eyes turned serious.

'You looked. . . lost. I know how tough life can get sometimes. You looked like you needed to take control. I get that feeling here.' He clapped his hands and rubbed them together. 'Right, let's get started.'

He led her over to a booth where a row of guns waited for them, growing in size and presumably power. He talked her through them, picking up a shotgun that looked small in his hands but large in hers. He showed her how to load and reload, check the safety, demonstrating how to hold them and where to look. She watched and nodded in a blur, only taking half of it in. She didn't belong here, surrounded by dangerous weapons. Her hands shook as she

107

took the safety equipment from him, placing the noise-cancelling ear protectors on her head and the plastic glasses over her eyes. He helped her slip into a vest to ease the recoil of the gun. And suddenly it felt very real. She was about to shoot a gun.

'Ready to get started?'

'You go first,' she said. Even her voice was shaking.

'All right.' He lifted the shotgun, talking her through as he went, and took the first shot. She jolted with the sound and instinctively covered her ears and clamped her eyes shut. When she opened her eyes again, she saw him lower the gun and smile towards the target. A gaping hole where the head should be.

Her whole body was jittering. Adrenaline pulsed through her.

'Ready?'

She was on the verge of tears but didn't know why. She laughed nervously and nodded.

'Right, so. . .' He placed the gun in her hands and arranged them in the correct places, telling her where to put her thumb and not to hold the trigger until she was ready to shoot. He moved the butt of the gun to the right position on her body, and stood behind her, instructing her where to look, to raise the end of the gun to meet just above the desired spot. She felt safe there with him behind her, with his hands over hers.

'Ready?' he asked.

She nodded and placed a shaking finger on the trigger.

'Don't overthink it,' he said.

She pulled the trigger and her whole body jolted with the power of the gun, the butt of it thrusting into her like a punch to her shoulder. Adrenaline exploded in her chest. Even with the protective gear, she could hear the ring of the shot.

She had hit the target in the neck.

'Great,' he said.

Tears rolled down her cheeks and a manic laugh burst from her lips. He laughed with her, which only made her laugh harder. This was the most foolish, exhilarating thing she had ever done. She had the sudden urge to kiss him, to keep hold of the rush she was experiencing.

'How was that?' he asked through a grin.

'Again,' she said breathlessly. 'Let's do that again.'

FIFTEEN

R ose stood before the police station and stared at her reflection in the glass doors. Her hair whipped up with the wind, shining like copper as it hit the light. The positioning of the sun cast shadows in the pockets of her eyes, and with her pale skin, it was like staring at a bare skull.

The exhilaration she had felt at the range had been replaced with exhaustion, which clung to her again and pulled at each limb. It was as though the full night's sleep she'd had before had been a dream. She scoffed at the irony. *I could only have dreamt it if I had been asleep.* She had been a different woman at the gun range: she wasn't the woman who had killed her daughter, the mother hated by her only living child and resented by her husband. She was a woman with a gun, and a desired one at that. But the moment she'd left in the taxi, reality had seeped in again. Anxiety had given her the willpower to step out of the cab and walk the short distance to the station, but now it had her by the throat. Her past was waiting for her inside.

She had almost turned back twice, but somehow her legs had kept going, each step heavier than the last. But she couldn't put the thought to the back of her mind now: after all these years, she was going to see Detective Sergeant Montgomery in the flesh again.

Detective Inspector Montgomery, she reminded herself. He was an inspector now.

Everyone had moved on except for her – the policeman from the bridge, her daughter all grown up, Heather now a friend of the past, her husband living a separate life – but by the sound of the detective's voice on the phone, Montgomery remembered the day on the bridge as vividly as she did.

This isn't about you or Violet, she told her reflection, trying to meet her eyes through the shadows. *This is about Finn. Do it for him.*

But deep inside her chest, burning like a flame, she knew this wasn't just about Finn. However much she tried to bury the similarities, she couldn't escape the fact that she was seeking justice for Jay too.

It had been years since she had lost him, but no amount of time passing could lessen her longing to know the one question that haunted her every time she closed her eyes: why? He left no suicide note, no concrete reason for them to cling on to. Something particular had to have happened to him to push him to the brink, but he never spoke of his ordeals or his pain, not to her at least. He locked it up inside until it devoured him, until the only way to release it was to let it flow with his blood.

She paced before the doors, the familiar wave of guilt tightening the muscles across her chest, as the question she had asked herself for years began to whisper inside her head.

Did you know?

She knew that he got a hard time from their father and people at school, but life had been so busy that she had missed all of the signs. She hadn't known the scale of the abuse he had experienced until the day of his wake when his best friend, Emma, cornered her, her breath reeking of cheap Chardonnay.

You don't get it. Jay couldn't walk down the street without someone calling him a faggot, pushing him or laughing at him unprovoked. They were strangers, Rose; they weren't people he knew. They saw him, singled him out, and continued on with their day. Imagine that happening every ten steps, because it did. Imagine being told that you're worthless, over and over again, until eventually you believe it yourself, and the words aren't just being thrown at you on the streets, but from a voice inside your own head. He had bullies at college, but the people of this town are just as much to blame. Every single person in this shithole put a nail in his coffin.

Rose could still remember the quiet resentment Emma exuded for her and her family, for not doing something before it was too late.

She hadn't known enough, not until that day. That's what Rose told herself.

Had she questioned him about his abuse, perhaps she could have intervened, or got the names of his frequent tormentors and had them punished in some way. If she had cared more, hadn't been so self-absorbed. But she couldn't punish everyone in town. The people who led him to his grave were still out there, breathing the air Jay deserved to breathe.

She couldn't get justice for her brother.

But she could get it for Finn.

She took a step forward. The doors slid open, stealing away her reflection.

A man was sitting at the reception desk this time, talking into the phone with his eyes briefly meeting hers before looking back to the computer screen. The doors closed behind her.

She walked up to the desk and rested her hands on the countertop. They were already shaking. She buried them inside her pockets as the officer ended the call and gave her a tired smile.

'How can I help?'

He was a handsome man, with dark hair and olive-coloured skin, but she could tell he had already been working a while by the tired slump of his shoulders. Dark circles framed his eyes, but they were nothing on hers.

'I have a meeting with Detective Serg—' She shook her head, cleared her throat. '*Inspector* Montgomery.'

'Can I have your name?'

'Rose Shaw.'

She caught a flicker of recognition in his eyes. There it was, the familiar peak in a person's interest before it came to them, the reason why her name was familiar. When he realised, he blushed and looked away, pressing the phone to his ear.

'One moment, please.'

Rose sighed quietly and turned away, shame burning her cheeks. It had been four years, and people still reacted when they heard her name. She wondered how many more years it would take until her name was forgotten, or whether it would for ever be ingrained in people's minds. She hoped the memories of what she did would fade as the years passed. But deep down, she knew: the town would never let her forget.

Left to her thoughts, the anxiety slowly built again, drying her mouth until her tongue felt cracked and furry.

This isn't about you, she repeated, clenching her hands into fists to bring the life back into them. *This isn't about you.*

A door clicked open behind her.

She hadn't seen Montgomery for four years, but as she turned and took in the sight of him, it could easily have been a decade. His short hair had started to grey, his skin had weathered, but his eyes were still the distinct, piercing blue she remembered.

He looked at her with equal fascination, witnessing how grief had aged her, stolen the life from her eyes.

He gave her a close-lipped smile and walked towards her, shifting his weight onto one leg, which made him seem so much older than forty. She wondered what caused it.

'Rose,' he said. 'Long time.'

'Yes,' she said. It was all she could muster. The sight of him brought a flood of memories until she was drowning in them.

'This way,' he said, and limped towards the door.

She followed behind him, her heart quickening, and jolted at the sound of the door closing loudly behind her. She tried to keep her eyes on the floor, listening only to the sound of Montgomery's uneven steps, but as she got further into the building, she slowly recognised her surroundings. The floor, the walls, even the smell in the air, they were just the same as they had been the day she came to the station to tell the police how she'd killed her daughter.

Montgomery opened a door to one of the interview rooms and held it for her. She walked through and sat down at the desk, and realised it was the very same chair she had sat in all those years ago. When she noticed, her whole body turned cold. She placed her bag on the floor against the table leg and gripped the sides of the chair until the plastic dug into her palms.

The journal was on top of the desk in a clear bag.

Montgomery sat on the opposite side of the table and settled into his seat with a sigh. When he looked at her, it took all of her strength not to turn away. She was faced with the past every day, but today, she had to look it in the eye.

'How are you?' he asked.

'Fine,' she lied. 'Great.'

She had already committed to the lie that morning, layering her face in make-up to conceal her exhaustion, to hide the pain permanently etched into her face. But she couldn't hide her bloodshot eyes or the gauntness of her cheeks; she knew she wasn't fooling anyone, especially herself.

'I'm glad.'

'How're you?' she asked.

'Things are good. My wife and I took over my late father's farm a few years back.'

She knew of it; there was only one for miles, resting on the outskirts of town. The thought of such a set-up seemed foreign now, when everything was apparently prepared in factories. But that was Rearwood, holding the past in a chokehold.

'My wife sells eggs from the hens and tends to the vegetable garden. We don't have any other livestock – too much hassle. I do what I can when I'm not here.'

He paused, as if he was deciding whether to mention the past. She could almost see the memories in his eyes, the words forming in his mouth as his lips parted.

Please, she thought. *Please don't.*

'How's Lily?' he asked finally.

'Fine,' she lied.

'Good. And Christian?'

Stop it. Just stop.

'What happened to your leg?' she blurted out.

His eyes widened a fraction.

'I'm sorry, that was really rude of me. . . I—'

He raised his hand.

'It's fine. Let's just say some criminals hold a grudge.'

She tried to keep the curiosity from her face, but he spotted her eyes wandering to his hip, just in view from the edge of the table.

'A man I arrested some years back, he stabbed me in the thigh the day of his release. Nerve damage. Never did catch him again.'

'I'm really sorry.'

'Don't be. I have it easier now, no more running around and making arrests. I have a desk with a nice view and a stack of cold cases to solve.'

He laughed nervously and clasped his hands together on top of the table. His elbow grazed the clear bag with the journal inside.

'Is that what this is? A cold case?'

They both looked at the journal. He took it in his hands; the bag crackled in his grip.

'In short, yes.'

All of Finn's pain and torment left in the dark. She wondered how his family felt, whether his mother's grief was similar to hers. But it couldn't be – Finn's mother didn't kill her child.

She cleared her throat.

'In the journal, Finn said he reported the abuse.'

He looked from the journal to her, as if deciding what to tell her.

'We followed protocol, but we didn't have enough evidence to convict, not by a long shot.'

'But now that you have the journal, maybe you can—'

'Everything he wrote in the journal was documented in the case file. You've read it front to back?'

She nodded.

'Then you'll know that there wasn't enough information for us to act on. No witnesses, no concrete CCTV footage to convict. We only had Mr Matthews's word and untraceable leads, and even then, he didn't have enough information on the man for us to act. This happened almost two years ago, and we haven't had any further reports of harassment from Mr Matthews.'

Rose looked at the cover of the journal and thought of how many times Finn had held it, if tears had marked the pages. How could all of his pain and terror not be enough? Why hadn't they hunted for the man until justice was served?

'What became of him? Do you know?'

'When we reviewed the case, we discovered he had left his job and moved. His phone was cut off, meaning he likely changed his contact details as a deterrent.'

'But how do you know that his abuser didn't follow him?'

'Rose, if Finn wants to move on, we have to let him.'

'But he didn't leave a forwarding address, at least? A new phone number?'

Montgomery sighed and ran a hand over his cropped hair. His wedding ring glinted in the glare of the overhead lights. She wondered if he was in a happy marriage; she'd forgotten what that was like.

'When people are stalked, their whole lives are turned upside down. The simplest tasks like picking up the phone or walking down the street become seemingly impossible. It isn't abnormal for people to take themselves off the map – move away and start again with a clean slate.'

'But what if something happened to him?'

'We can't know that for sure. We can't search for a man who doesn't want to be found, especially with no evidence that foul play was involved.'

'But doesn't that worry you? That something might have happened to him?'

'With the information we have, I don't believe he came to any harm. He voluntarily moved out of his flat. To me, that's a clear indication that he *chose* to leave, that he wanted to be untraceable.'

'But in the last journal entry, Finn was convinced that his stalker was going to come for him before he had the chance to leave Rearwood. His future didn't sound secure at all.'

'He was clearly in a very delicate mental state. Stalking can make a person extremely paranoid.'

'Couldn't you trace his health records? His GP from Rearwood might be able to confirm if he signed on to a new practice.'

'Not everyone signs up to surgeries in their catchment, and people who experience this kind of ordeal tend to remove any chance of them being found.'

'So you can't do anything? We just have to assume he's okay?'

'There is no evidence to suggest he isn't.'

'He was convinced he was going to be murdered. It's right there, on the very first page.'

'Paranoia and stalking do tend to go hand in hand.'

'But now you're saying he's vanished. Can you honestly say that his stalker didn't go through with his threats? Are you one hundred per cent sure that Finn Matthews is alive?'

He thought for a while, genuinely weighing up her question.

'I know it's hard to accept, Rose, but we can't always get the answers we want, not in this line of work. I'm sorry. Without a reason, we can't chase a man who doesn't want to be found.'

Her eyes fell on the journal. She thought of Finn's words inside, destined to be forgotten. She couldn't let Rearwood forget Finn the way they had forgotten Jay.

'I hear you and Christian were able to make it work,' he said from the other side of the table. 'I'm glad.'

Just when she had felt in control, the past was back, kicking her legs from under her. Immediately she remembered the day on the bridge, the hate in Christian's eyes, the way Montgomery's firm grip kept her from buckling. He had witnessed it all – from the body of her daughter to the breakdown of her marriage, all in a single day.

'I. . . I'd like to go, please.'

She stood too quickly. Blood left her head in a rush; white spots pricked her vision. She leaned on the table for balance.

'Are you okay?'

'I'm fine,' she replied, blinking the spots away.

'I'll lead you out.'

He stood up with a laborious breath and made his way to the door, each step stiffer than the last.

I'm not the only one haunted by the past, she thought as she watched Montgomery try to mask his pain, but she could see from the paling of his complexion that his injury was causing him agony.

Life marks us all.

She took one last glance at the journal on the table. Finn's past was destined to be locked away in a dark room. But worst of all: he was destined to be forgotten.

She stepped out of the room with her eyes on the floor, thinking of Finn, of the man whose heart had been poured into the journal only for it to be ignored – and slammed into a man's chest.

'I'm so sorry,' she said, a wisp of dislodged hair moving with her breaths.

The man towered over her, his breath warming her face. She stepped back and took in the broadness of his chest and shoulders, thick arms from weightlifting. His hair was thinning, revealing the milky skin on his scalp, but there was a glint in his eyes that told her he was younger than she was.

'I. . . I wasn't looking where I was going, I'm sorry.'

She couldn't stop looking at his eyes; there was something dark about them, a festering rage dwelling within the pupils.

'This is Rose Shaw,' Montgomery said behind her. 'Rose, this is Detective Seb Clark.'

His lips turned up in a smirk. At the mention of her name, he knew what she had done too.

She didn't like him one bit.

'Monty,' he said, talking over her head. 'Need a word with you.'

'No problem. I'll just escort Mrs Shaw out and then I'll meet you in your office.'

The man nodded and looked at her one last time, the smirk reappearing briefly before he turned away and walked down the narrow corridor, his broad shoulders making the tight space appear that much smaller. Rose spotted a woman lurking at the end of the passage, but she shot out of sight when their eyes met.

'This way,' Montgomery said behind her, placing his hand in the small of her back. Just the way he had on the bridge. She blinked the memory away.

Montgomery led her the way they had come, until they were back in the reception area and stood before the doors. Outside, trees thrashed with the wind and covered the path with their leaves.

'Rose,' he said. 'If. . . if you ever need someone to talk to, I'm here. All right?'

He took a card from his pocket and held it out to her.

Pity. She saw it in every face, every expression. The moment she lost Violet she had ceased to be a woman and had become a walking trauma to be gawked at. Just seeing it in a person's eyes gave her the urge to claw them out with her fingernails.

She took the card with a swift nod and turned for the doors, stepping out with the heat of his eyes on her back.

The clouds in the sky had turned everything in sight a melancholy grey: the buildings, the roads and paths. She headed up the hill, trying to bury the loss she felt. She thought of the journal on top of the table and shook her head to rid it of the thought.

I don't even know him. The journal was never mine to keep. Forget him, Rose. Just forget it all.

'Mrs Shaw!'

She turned and saw a woman running towards her, dressed in a grey suit with a bag hanging over her shoulder. Her cheeks were a warm pink. It was the woman from the corridor. Dark brown hair lashed across her face with the wind. She couldn't have been older than thirty-five.

'Yes?'

'You came to us about the Finn Matthews case, didn't you?'

Rose nodded.

'Look, I shouldn't do this, but if you're going to look into it, there's more you should know.'

The woman briefly looked behind her before turning to her again, her voice a notch lower.

'I have an ex-colleague who you could speak to, who could fill you in on some of the things that go on within the force, things that might have jeopardised the case.'

Rose stood before her, taking in every freckle and line, every heavy breath.

'Why. . . why are you telling me this?'

'Because I can't do anything about it and I'm sick of it.'

'But what can I do?'

'Here.'

Rose took the scrap of paper from the woman's hand. A name and number had been scribbled onto it. She shoved it inside her pocket.

'Tell him Anna told you to give him a call. And please, don't tell anyone else I did this.'

The woman held her eyes until she was sure she could trust her.

'Why are you?' Rose asked. 'If you can't do anything about it, how can I—'

'You don't have to do anything, but something tells me you will. Here.' She took her bag from her shoulder and removed the journal. She must have sneaked inside the interview room and taken it before Montgomery returned. Anna pressed the journal into Rose's hands and turned back before she could speak again.

Rose watched the woman run down the hill again until she was back in the station, not using the main entrance, but a door further along the side of the building. Even with the distance between them, the woman hesitated in the doorway, and their eyes met before she stepped inside the station and closed the door behind her.

Things that go on within the force, things that might have jeopardised the case.

Rose had gone to the police to help find out what had happened to Finn Matthews. She hadn't even considered they might also be to blame.

She looked down at the journal in her hands. It was back in her possession; now she had to figure out what the hell she was going to do with it.

JOHNNY

29th November 2005

Johnny sat at the dining table in his usual place. He would call it his spot if his father didn't constantly remind him that he was living under his roof on borrowed time, and that everything in the house was his and his alone. His sister Harriet sat opposite him, with their parents at each end of the table. They ate in silence but for the occasional scrape of metal against china and the chew of tough beef, all with their eyes set on their plates. None of them could look at the bruise darkening around Johnny's eye. Occasionally Harriet would glance at him, consider the way his eyelids had swollen with the punch. When he looked across the table, her gaze dropped to her plate again, her cheeks redder than before.

They had followed him home after their shift at the factory where half the boys in his year had ended up after school. They had taunted him the whole way until words weren't enough and the first fist hit the back of his skull. He'd fallen to the ground with his ears ringing, did nothing as he was turned over with rough hands and punched again by a different man. They were all men now, but it felt like none of them had aged a day. It was the same three boys from school who had made it their mission to ensure that each day was worse than the last, the same boys who made him wish he had never been born. He thought that the fear would subside after a while; he would get used to their taunts, their fists jabbing in his ribs as he walked down the school corridor, the kicks littering his body from his head to his ankles after the last bell rang, the summers when they shoved grass cuttings down his throat after the groundskeeper had mown the fields. But each word and touch was as fresh as the first. As they assaulted him, he wondered what it would be like to die, and if it would hurt like everyone said, or if it would be painless and the idea of pain was a lie people told to keep others from taking matters into their own hands.

His father dropped his cutlery with a clatter and everyone looked up from their plates. They watched him rub his face, the slack, ageing skin moving with his hands. Johnny glanced at his mother as she eyed his father sharply, warning him not to start, but he wouldn't look at her. She knew what was coming. They all did.

'You need to stop making it so easy for them, John,' his father said finally. He said it with anger or frustration, Johnny couldn't tell which. Maybe it was hate.

'Andrew,' his mother said sharply.

'No. He needs to hear it.' He looked back at Johnny. 'The way you walk, the way you talk, you're basically. . . well, it's like you're. . .'

Asking for it, Johnny thought.

'Andrew, that's enough!'

'If you didn't act like such a. . .' He stopped, shook his head. 'If you just acted like a normal bloke, they'd leave you alone.'

Normal.

'Andrew!'

'Damn it, Lin, he needs to hear this!'

'Fuck you.'

Silence fell upon the table. All eyes shot towards Johnny, shocked at the words that had left his lips. But none of them were as shocked as him. He touched his lips where the words had fled.

'What did you say to me?'

Johnny stood up. Andrew snatched his wrist and tightened his grip.

'Say it again.'

'Andrew, please. . .'

He looked into Johnny's eyes, his grip tightening and tightening as the anger flooded his face.

'Don't you dare speak to me like that, not when you're under my roof.'

Johnny tore his wrist from his father's grasp and headed out of the room. He snatched a coat from the hook, not knowing or caring if it was his.

'If you leave this house, don't come back!'

He listened to his father's words ring down the hall and the quiet sobs from his mother. He opened the door and slammed it shut behind him.

The rain pummelled down, following the slant of the street in streams beside the kerbs. He shrugged into the coat and raised the hood, his throat burning with unshed tears. He wouldn't cry over them. He was done crying.

He headed down the road and turned right down the next, walking without a destination in mind. He had nowhere to go, no one to turn to. He didn't have grandparents. He didn't have any friends in town; the only few he'd had were off at university. They had left school with good grades. They hadn't been scared stupid at their desks, watching the clock ticking down to the end of the day when the beatings began. They'd escaped the town and left him there.

He walked through the rain, breathing quick, visible breaths into the night, remembering every word his father had said.

It's like you're asking for it.
If you were a normal bloke.
Asking for it.
Normal.

He walked until his legs ached, wandering for miles without really seeing. When he stopped, he looked up from the path and saw the bridge that led out of town. It was then, as he stared at the only route of escape, that the tears fell.

He would never be able to leave. He had no savings, no car, nothing to offer the world. The people who he had once called friends had changed so much in their short time away at university that he didn't recognise them any more; they had all grown up, while he remained in the past. His father didn't want him, and his old friends wouldn't either. He would work in the factory until the day he died, just like his father.

He wished them dead. He wished the entire town dead.

'Hey.'

He jolted with the sound and stumbled back.

A car had pulled up beside him. A man with dark hair sat behind the wheel, looking up at him from inside the car.

'You all right? It's pouring down.'

Johnny almost looked behind him to check the man was talking to him. He was attractive with a kind, straight smile. He couldn't remember the last time someone smiled at him.

'Do you need a lift somewhere?'

Johnny looked at the road out of town, and then back the way he'd come. He couldn't go back, but he couldn't go forwards. He was stuck there with nowhere to go. More tears came.

'Where are you headed?'

'I . . . I don't know.'

'Get in, you're shaking. You need to call someone to pick you up?'

He tried to think of someone to call, anyone at all. The rain stalked down his face, hung on the ends of his eyelashes.

'I don't have anyone,' he said absently.

The man looked him up and down, something flashing in his eyes. Johnny was used to pity.

'Get in,' the man said. He leaned over and opened the passenger door.

He was kind, the only kind man in the entire town. His face was familiar, although Johnny couldn't pin it down, but he had eyes that made him easy to trust, a smile that made Johnny feel like crying again.

'Come on, the seat's getting wet,' he said.

Johnny got inside. He slammed the door shut, quietening the rain until the downpour was just a patter against the roof and glass.

The man smiled beside him and locked the doors.

SIXTEEN

☾

Rose reached the top of the drive, trembling all over with a blue tint to her fingers. Her clothes clung to her body and dripped from every hem.

The bus journey home had almost lulled her to sleep. She had steeled her muscles against the juddering of the engine, but the soothing motion was like being rocked to sleep. If she had slept then, she would have woken at the last stop and had to wait for another bus or walk back; or she would have dozed for ten minutes before jolting awake again, only to spend the rest of the night awake. When she had the opportunity to sleep, it evaded her, but when she couldn't, it attempted to drag her under; an endless battle she was too exhausted to fight.

She looked up at the house, darkness lurking behind every window.

Surely Samantha's parents would get sick of having Lily to stay so often; perhaps her mum would start asking questions. She imagined the mothers talking about her the way they used to.

Is everything all right at home? Lily has been staying over an awful lot.

Oh, you didn't know? Rose fell asleep at the wheel with her children inside; only her and Lily survived. Lily can't stand the sight of her now.

Maybe she wasn't at Samantha's. Perhaps it was a lie, and she had no way of knowing. It was as though she wasn't a mother at all.

Rose walked up the gravel driveway with her teeth chattering in her ears and the journal clamped firmly under her arm. She reached to her shoulder for her bag.

It wasn't there.

She swore under her breath and rubbed her face. Her phone, purse and house keys were inside. She imagined her bag unattended at the bus stop; strewn out across the road, the valuables gone and the rest scattered by the wind. Perhaps she had left it under the seat on the bus; she might still get it back. If she had left it at the police station, they would have called.

But how can they call if they have your phone, you idiot?

She looked up at the house, hopeful for a sign of life behind the glass, and moved further along the drive. Night was falling, and the chill in the air was getting sharper. She cupped her hands around her face and peered through the living-room window until her breath steamed up the glass. Darkness.

All she wanted to do was change out of her wet clothes and collapse into bed, but if Lily and Christian were staying out, there was no way she was getting inside.

She opened the side gate to the garden and lapped the house, hoping to find an open window, maybe a light on in Lily's room. Every window was fastened, reflecting the evening sky. She eyed the brick they used to prop the door open in the summer, and for a brief second, considered breaking a pane of glass in the back door to get inside. She walked back around to the front of the house.

Without her purse, she couldn't check into a hotel. If her annual bus pass hadn't been in her pocket, she might have realised sooner. There were no phone boxes she could walk to, no neighbours she could rely on. She couldn't bear to give them anything else to gossip about. She tried to think of someone, anyone, who she could turn to. She had no one.

No one, she thought, except her father.

A week ago, she wouldn't even have thought of him, but seeing him at the graveyard had brought him to the surface again.

She couldn't go to him; every time she thought of him she remembered all the pain he had caused. It would be a betrayal to Jay and their mother. But her only alternative would be to sleep on the doorstep and hope someone returned, or stow away in the shed until dawn.

She had to face her father.

She had to go home.

Rose stopped outside the family home, a barrage of memories hitting her like a fist. She remembered Jay's first blundering steps across the living-room carpet, heatwaves spent in the garden, her mum tending to the flower beds. She remembered the Christmas mornings when it was the four of them, and then three, until it was just two left, spending the day apart.

Even in the dark, Rose could see that the house had lost the essence that had made it home. Thick layers of dirt coated the windows and the gutter was packed with rotting leaves. The grass had been left to grow untamed, and litter blown from the wind had caught in the reeds. Knee-high weeds swayed from their roots between the grooves in the path. It seemed the house had died with them.

The hallway light was on. She couldn't decide whether she was relieved or disappointed. Perhaps it would have been better to spend the night on the doorstep, waiting for Christian or Lily to come home.

Before she had the chance to change her mind, she walked up to the door and rang the bell. The paint on the front door was peeling off, revealing the bare wood beneath, which was rotting from years of rain. A dog barked inside the house next door.

As she waited for him to appear in the frosted glass, her stomach turned over, spitting bile up her throat.

This was a mistake. She still had time to turn back.

Just as she began to turn on her heel, a figure hobbled into view, edging down the hallway towards the door.

No turning back now.

A key turned in a lock and a chain moved across the other side of the door. She held her breath as the door opened.

Tony looked even older than he had at their graves. White stubble littered his cheeks and neck. He wore an off-white shirt covered in food stains, and old, yellow sweat soiled the fabric beneath his arms. Worn slippers poked out from beneath ill-fitting tracksuit bottoms.

His eyes widened and looked her up and down. She couldn't believe she was there either.

They stood in silence and stared at each other over the threshold.

'I. . . I lost my bag. Christian and Lily are out, and I'm locked out of the house for the night.'

He jolted back to life.

'Oh, right,' he stammered, moving aside for her to pass. 'Come in.'

'This doesn't mean anything.'

She peered down the hallway. Cardboard boxes were stacked up against the walls, leaving only a narrow path into the house. Dust coated everything in sight: the clock on the wall that had frozen at four minutes past midnight, on top of the boxes like a thin coat of fur, lining the picture frames on the walls; she noticed the photos had been taken out.

He followed her gaze as she took in the state of the house and blushed.

'I haven't had a visitor in a while.'

She took a tentative step inside and pressed herself against a box as her father shut the door. He squeezed past her and led her down the narrow corridor.

'This way,' he said, as if she hadn't lived there for two decades of her life.

It was as though he couldn't see the mess. She wondered how long he had lived like this, if whatever was in the boxes was hers, or her brother's or mother's, the past hidden away, each box taped shut to keep the memories at bay.

She followed him down the hall, squeezing past the banister, and stepped into the kitchen.

Her jaw dropped.

Crockery and pans towered from the sink, coated in old food and mould. Food containers were strewn on the floor and countertops, where stains had been left to harden into a thick crust, so baked on that she couldn't even remember what colour it was beneath. The floor was littered with wrappers and dropped cutlery left to stick to the lino. Flies buzzed languidly around the single light bulb.

'I can't believe—'

A mouse shot out of an old cereal box by her foot and scurried along the skirting board beneath the kitchen units. She screamed and jumped back, pressing herself against the door frame. The black bag beside her tipped over; maggots wriggled underneath.

'What the hell?'

'It's only a mouse, Rosie!'

'A mouse in your bloody kitchen, Dad!'

'I'm sorry. I would have tidied up if I'd known—'

'This doesn't need tidying, it needs *fumigating*!'

She stayed against the door frame, her chest racing, and eyed the floor for any more emerging creatures. Just being near the filth made her skin itch.

When she looked at her father, his eyes were on the maggots twisting and turning on the floor.

'I didn't know about those. . .' he said glumly.

'What the hell is going on?'

He stuttered as he struggled to find the words, his eyes darting around the mess.

'When. . . when you live alone, you let things slip. It's only me who sees it.'

'You could get ill. This is dangerous.'

She stepped further into the room and cringed at the sight of a blackened banana peel stuck to the work surface and left to rot. Dead ants framed the sink; live ones slinked in from the broken seal around the window. Mouse droppings were scattered everywhere she looked.

She couldn't stay here; even the air felt dirty in her lungs.

'I'll tidy up the living room,' he said nervously, as if reading her mind. 'It's not so bad in there. I could make a pot of tea, or something.'

She couldn't stay here. It was a hovel, a cesspit of filth and disease. She would catch something within the hour.

'Yes, tea in the living room,' he decided quickly, and made for the door. He turned, his eyes pleading for her to follow. She noticed a yellow tinge to the whites of his eyes and wondered if he still drank.

She had nothing to feel guilty about – he had broken three

hearts – and yet, standing amongst the mess, she felt it burning in her chest. She was all her father had left, and she'd cut him out.

He stared at her, his eyes sheening over. She sighed inwardly and followed him out of the kitchen.

The living room was just as dire. An array of junk was hidden beneath blankets of dust: old TVs set aside instead of thrown away, mould growing on the pages of books jutting from the mess. Takeaway containers littered the floor with food trodden into the odd flash of carpet. There was a rotten stench in the air; perhaps forgotten food or worse, the body of a rodent hidden amongst the mess.

Tony busied himself picking at the rubbish, collecting takeaway containers in his arms to clear a path.

'How long have you been living like this?'

He didn't reply, and she knew it was a stupid question to ask. They both knew the answer. He had been living this way since she cut him out after the death of her mother.

'You make yourself comfortable,' he said, somehow breathless, and passed her with his arms full of mess.

She stood on the spot, taking in the room she had been in thousands of times yet no longer recognised. All these years she had been focused on her own pain, her own guilt; she hadn't thought of her father's for a minute.

She heard the patter of plastic containers joining the mess in the kitchen as he chucked them aside, the clap of his hands as he dusted them off.

'Do you still have sugar with your tea?' he asked from the doorway.

She couldn't bear to sit amongst the mess, surrounded by his misery and her neglect. Her head was pounding from breathing in the dust and filth.

'I . . . I think I just need to sleep.'

'We could chat for a little while, maybe. It's been a long time.'

'Yes, and there's a reason why.'

'Then we should talk about it.'

Fury rose through her like heat. He had the audacity to try and weasel into her life now, after all this time? She clenched her hands at her sides, begging herself not to give in to the anger. The words came out all on their own. She spun to face him.

'Okay, what would you like to talk about? About how you bullied your own son, and raised him to believe he wasn't a real man or a real son because of who he was?'

He looked away.

'Stop it, Rose.'

'Oh, I know. How about we talk about how you used to pretend he didn't exist, that he hadn't shut himself away in his room as depression ate away at his mind until he had no other choice but to kill himself!'

'Rosie, please.'

He began to shake, but she couldn't stop. He needed to know about all the pain he had caused. Tears stung at her eyes. She wouldn't let him forget.

'Or how you were embarrassed of him, and made excuses not to bring him to the country club when all your other misogynistic golfing buddies brought their families along. You wouldn't be seen with him anywhere, would you?'

'Rose. . .'

'He was the nicest, kindest person I have ever met and you treated him like he was vermin!'

Hot tears slipped down her face. She gasped for breath as the sobs came, but she couldn't fill her lungs quick enough, each breath shuddering.

'All he ever wanted was for you to love him, and you shut him out. He needed you. He needed you and you pushed him away, and then he—'

'Enough!' he bellowed. He shook on the spot with tears spilling down his cheeks, the skin on his jaw rippled from gritted teeth.

They stood amongst the mess, breathing heavily and sniffing back tears. She watched his strong resolve break: his jaw relaxed, his shoulders lowered, his face returned to a normal pink.

'Look around you,' he said. 'You don't think I regret my actions every living day? That I don't miss my son? All these years I've. . . punished myself like this. I hate myself for it.'

Not as much as I do.

She shouldn't be here, dragging up the past when it would do no good. It wouldn't bring them back.

'I should go,' she said, wiping the tears from her cheeks. 'This was a mistake.'

'No,' he said. 'You'll stay in your room.' He made his way around the mess for the stairs. 'Bottles of water in the fridge. Turn the light off on your way up.'

The stairs creaked under his weight, a sad whine, as though the house was as miserable as he was. A door closed above her, and silence fell upon the house, the house she had grown up in but didn't know at all.

She should never have come. Old wounds had been ripped open, memories clawed up from the depths. She could no longer push the thought of her father from her mind, not now that she knew the life he was living.

She forced her way through the mess and took to the stairs. The landing was small with four doors off it, leading to the family bathroom and the three bedrooms in the house. All the doors were closed. Light glowed from beneath her father's, and when she stopped at the top of the stairs, she could hear the sound of muffled sobs.

The dent in the bottom-right corner of her door was still there, years after she had kicked it open during her first teenage tantrum and slammed it shut behind her. She turned the handle, listening to its familiar creak, and turned on the light.

Her bedroom was spotless.

SEVENTEEN

Rose had been dreaming of Violet again. All night she had been back on the bridge, locked inside her past as the event replayed in an endless loop. Each time, she tried to save her in a different way: unclasping the seat belt seconds sooner, grabbing on to her wrist and refusing to let go, pinning her and Lily to her body just before the windscreen broke away. But however hard she tried, she always lost her. The seat belt jammed, or the current ripped them apart. Holding the two of them was too difficult, and Violet was always the one to slip away. On nights like this, when she lost her again and again, she woke with the guilt of wishing it were Violet in her arms rather than Lily, and told herself that she would have thought the same thing had Violet survived and Lily perished. But there was always a small lack of conviction to the claim, cementing her guilt.

She had only managed three hours of broken sleep, waking each time from the dream only to return to it when she closed her eyes again.

She sat up and rested her back against the wall, and it was only then that she remembered: she was in her childhood bedroom.

It hadn't changed at all since her teenage years: pastel-blue walls, carpet stained with make-up and a long brown burn from the curling iron she had used to death. The cheap perfume she used to wear lingered faintly in the air. Photos plastered all over the walls of her with friends she hadn't seen in years and no longer knew. She wondered what had become of them, and if they ever thought of her, if they'd heard of what she did. Amongst the old faces, she spotted a photo of her and Jay. She looked at her long, auburn hair, the protective arm draped over his shoulders. Jay had blonde hair like their mother, and green eyes like their father. His smile was beautiful yet timid, forced for the camera, his pain evident in his eyes. Even then, he was struggling. How could she not have known?

A muffled clatter sounded from downstairs. Her father was up; perhaps he hadn't slept at all. He had always had trouble sleeping, and over the years she wondered if she had inherited her insomnia from him somehow. She wanted to believe they were nothing alike, but when she looked at their lives, at their equal misery, she couldn't escape the similarities.

She couldn't stay here another minute, but to leave, she had to go downstairs and face him in the light of day. Could she go back to her life without him, knowing that he was self-destructing like this? That she was partly to blame?

She had to get out of there, before she got in any deeper.

She stole out of bed and opened the curtains, squinting at the daylight. Her clothes were crumpled on the floor next to the journal, still in its plastic bag.

She hadn't decided what she was going to do. The police weren't intending to do anything. She pulled the scrap of paper from her trouser pocket and read the name and number – it hadn't been a dream.

Even if she did meet with the ex-cop and find out about errors within the investigation, what could she do about it? She had just wanted to do the right thing, but now, the whole responsibility had been dropped on her back.

She picked her clothes up from the floor and got dressed, purposely ignoring her reflection in the mirror. She had looked into that glass so many times, imagining a future so different to the one she'd been dealt. So many hopes and ambitions. So blissfully naive.

Once dressed, she looked around her room one last time, and impulsively took the photo of her and Jay from the wall and slipped it within the cover of the journal to keep it safe.

She pulled the door open as quietly she could and flinched as it screeched on its hinges, trying to remember which boards creaked, and descended the stairs.

Tony was picking at the rubbish in the kitchen and shoving it into bags. The back door was open, letting in a cold, moist breeze. She stopped briefly and watched him take some bags out the back.

He was trying. She could help him. She could be a better daughter and work through their problems with him.

She opened the front door and closed it quietly behind her.

$$\smile$$

'Where the hell were you?' Christian said from the doorway.

Rose stopped abruptly at the doorstep, shivering from the chill.

'I lost my bag. I couldn't get in. You and Lily were out.'

'You should have got in touch somehow,' he said, standing aside. 'I've been worried sick.'

'How could I get in touch if I didn't have a phone? I don't even know where you spend all your time.'

She stepped inside and shut the door behind her.

Christian sighed. 'Do you remember where you left it? The bag?'

'No. Probably on the bus.'

She stood before him as the silence settled, rain dripping from the hem of her coat and onto the doormat beneath her feet. Even with his infidelity, the coldness of his tone and the chill in his eyes, she longed to reach out and touch him, feel the beat of his heart and the warmth of his chest.

'You're late for work,' she said, desperate to say anything to break the silence.

'Yes, I was. . . I wanted to know when you came home. I'll head into the office now.'

You wanted me home, and now I'm here, you can't wait to leave.

'Right.'

She watched as he slipped into his coat and picked up his briefcase, ready and waiting by the door. She smelt his aftershave with his movements, and longed to bury her face in his neck.

He stood awkwardly before the door, waiting for her to pass.

'Bye,' she said and walked along the hall, refusing to look back. She heard the door close as she reached her study and shut herself in.

The room stank of stale cigarette smoke, each breath like a fresh hit of nicotine. She dropped her coat to the floor, kicked off her shoes and sank into the chair, which had morphed to her shape and lost its firmness; she could almost feel the wooden frame of it beneath the padding. But she would never get rid of it; she had lost too much already.

She picked up her iPad and checked Lily's social media, each timeline filled with nothing but her. There was a series of photos of her and her friends in the school toilets that morning, one girl applying gloss in her reflection, Lily and another girl pouting in the mirror for the camera. Perhaps one of the girls was Samantha. She scrolled and scrolled, looking at the funny videos Lily had shared, the comments she had left on other people's posts, until a single status stopped her in her tracks.

What sort of mum stays out all night without telling anyone? #DirtyStopOut #IHateMyMum

Tears scratched at her eyes. She took a deep breath and clicked on her profile to check who she was friends with, who would know that her daughter hated her. She typed in names of people she used to know, and found that Lily was friends with all of the mums Rose had seen each week at the football games, each afternoon at the school gates. Heather's name screamed out from the screen.

Rose locked the iPad and placed it beside the chair and out of sight. How could she do that? Humiliate her in front of everyone she knew?

On the other side of the window, the morning fog almost smothered the metal spine of the bridge. Rose wondered if Lily would ever forgive her, or if she would ever be able to forgive herself.

She pulled out the crumpled piece of paper from her pocket and stared at the phone number, reading the name scribbled above: Shane Hughes. There had to be something she could do. She had to distract herself from the pain, lose herself in something that would dull the agony of having a daughter who hated her, a husband who couldn't bear to be in the same room. She left the study with the piece of paper in hand and picked up the home phone.

He picked up the call after three rings.

'Hello?'

'Hi, is this Shane Hughes?'

'Speaking.'

What should she say? What had the policewoman said to her? She had been so tired, the words had failed to sink in. She couldn't even remember the woman's name.

'Hello?' he said again.

'My name is Rose Shaw. . . Your ex-colleague told me to call you, about what happened to you when you worked for the police in Rearwood. I'm looking into a missing person, and –' the name came to her suddenly – 'Anna told me you could give me some information about the police force, perhaps a reason why the case wasn't looked into appropriately.'

He was quiet for a long time, breathing down the line. He was thinking, most likely considering ending the call. Just as she was about to speak again, apologise for wasting his time, he spoke.

'Can you meet me tonight?'

'Where?'

'High Gate Park. By the gates.'

'Won't the park be locked?'

'Not a problem for us. Eight p.m.?'

'Yes. I'll meet you then.'

A beat sat between them, both stumped at what to say, strangers pulled together with an ominous cause at the heart.

The second he ended the call, her stomach dropped. What the hell was she getting herself into?

EIGHTEEN

C

Rose arrived outside High Gate Park and lingered before the locked iron gates, pulling up the collar of her coat to protect herself from the night breeze. Her pulse was beating in each of her fingertips where she had bitten her nails to the quick on the journey; dry blood framed the nail on her thumb.

She had agreed to meet a stranger at the dead of night, in a secluded location, with no idea what he looked like, and without telling anyone where she was going. If anything happened to her, no one would know what she had done with her last hours.

A police officer gave me the contact, she told herself. *Nothing will happen to me.*

But then she remembered how quickly the events had turned when she bumped into the man with the journal.

The night was dark and silent, with the moon hidden behind a thick knit of clouds. The only sounds were those of the occasional icy breeze whistling through the iron details of the gate, and the reluctant sway of the trees within the park.

She had no phone, no way of calling for help except for her own scream; and High Gate Park was vast. If the man attacked her deep within the grounds, she had very little chance of being heard. This was reckless and irresponsible – she was asking for trouble – but she had to know. Someone had to do something. Another truth flickered like a persistent flame, one she was too ashamed to admit, even to herself: she had to have something to do with her lonesome nights. She had to have a reason to keep going.

Her head shot up at the crack of a twig. Slowly, footsteps began to echo from the other side of the gate, growing louder as they approached. She peered through the gate and into the darkness and took an instinctive step back.

A silhouette breached the shadows: toweringly tall, the beam of a torch at his feet. The man appeared before the gate, his hand with the torch resting on the handle. The beam shot upwards, revealing his face.

He was an attractive man, she guessed in his early thirties, with pale skin lit yellow from the glow of the torch, and dark hair lost amongst the shadows. He didn't look dangerous; he looked as weary as she was.

'Rose Shaw?'

The torchlight whipped to her face. Blotches burst in her vision, blinding her. She squinted and covered her eyes.

'Yes,' she stammered. 'Shane Hughes?'

'Yes.'

The light fell to the ground beneath his feet, revealing black boots with mud dried on the tips. She heard the jangle of keys and the scrape of metal against metal as he turned the key in the lock. The gate screeched on its hinges.

The light from the torch had been emblazoned in her eyes, and followed her everywhere she looked. They stood on either side of the threshold, each waiting for the other to be the first to speak.

'I haven't got long,' he said.

She nodded and walked towards him, scraping her shoulder against the gate as she passed. He smelt of cigarette smoke and something sweet. She listened as he locked the gate behind her.

'You're locking it?'

'Can't have anyone sneaking in,' he said over his shoulder.

'How did you get a key to this place?'

'I'm the groundskeeper,' he said and placed the keys back in his pocket. 'I live in the cottage down by the lake. After leaving the force, I wanted a quieter life. Shall we?'

He walked ahead, and she followed obediently, listening to his heavy footsteps crunching on the stone path. They walked in silence, following the track as it curved around the hills of the park. They were two complete strangers, thrown together and thrust into the dead of night. By the sound of his fast breaths, she knew he was as nervous as her, but it didn't ease her anxiety. She didn't know what to do with her hands, and awkwardly held them together in front of her, then behind her, before finally burying them in her pockets.

'What do you want to know?' he asked finally. 'Or more importantly, why?'

Rose realised she had no idea what she wanted from him – she knew nothing about him or his past, or how he might be able to help; all she knew was that the policewoman had given her his number. She stole a look at his profile, admired the straightness of his nose, the unconscious pucker of his lips, and took a deep breath.

'I found a journal. The man it belonged to, Finn Matthews, wrote of being stalked, and how the police failed to help him. I took the journal to the police, but nothing was done, and they couldn't tell me what happened to him. It was then that your ex-colleague spoke to me, and told me to get in contact with you.'

He was silent for a beat, but she could almost hear him thinking, his mind ticking over. She spoke again.

'Finn feared the police weren't taking him seriously because he was attracted to men. . . and so do I.'

Shane didn't speak for several minutes. They walked along the path as it curved down a hill, and it was then that the moon appeared through a break in the clouds, releasing a sheen of light on the surface of the grass and the tops of the trees swaying in the breeze. In the distance, the lake reflected the night sky, with clouds drifting across the rippling surface, and perched above it on the hill was a small cottage with a thatched roof, and one lit window on the ground floor. She wondered if Shane had a partner inside, waiting for him to return home, or whether he lived there alone, behind all the locked gates and the endless silence of the park.

'You're right to be worried,' he said finally. 'The force in Rearwood is a team of close-knit locals, made up mostly of *traditional*-minded heterosexual men with old-fashioned values. From the outside, each cog seems to turn like any other force, but inside, it's a hierarchy built on toxic masculinity and prejudice. Homophobia has been institutionalised in the force, and not just in Rearwood. It's everywhere.'

Of all the things she had imagined him telling her, she hadn't even considered that.

'Did you hear about the four gay men murdered by Stephen Port in London back in 2014?' he asked.

'No, I didn't,' she said.

'I'm not surprised. The police failed to share news of the killings, so the press didn't catch wind until it came out about how poorly the case had been handled. Not because of lack of staff or funds, but because the men were gay.'

Rose didn't want to believe that people were still penalised and ostracised for their attraction to the same sex; she thought that as a society they had come such a long way, become a place where men like her brother could have thrived, or at least had the right to live peacefully.

'Despite numerous connections between the murders, each blindingly obvious clue was overlooked, leaving Stephen Port to kill again and again. Port was messy, leaving numerous mistakes in his path, but he continued to get away with each murder because the police failed to act in numerous ways. They didn't appeal for public information until the last body had been discovered; the public weren't even aware that there was a serial killer targeting a minority group, and gay men in London had no idea that their lives were in danger. The police failed to make the obvious connection between the two bodies that were found in the same location just three weeks apart. Evidence was left untested for DNA, and we're talking crucial items found by the bodies, the sheets they were wrapped in, a forged suicide note written by the killer that not only wasn't analysed by a text specialist, but wasn't even tested for fingerprints. The worst part is, they had the killer's DNA on file after a previous arrest. Had they actually done their jobs, the number of victims would have been three, not four. They had the chance to catch Port and turned their backs at every opportunity. It wasn't only Stephen Port who killed those men – those who worked on the case killed them too.'

'I. . . I had no idea that sort of thing went on, in London of all places. I can't believe. . .'

'It's not just London, Rose. It's a nationwide problem. In fact, it happens all over the world.'

'And here,' she added.

'Yes,' he replied. 'Rearwood too.'

'What do they do, in Rearwood?'

'Victims are unsupported, abuse and assaults swept under the rug. Even if someone in a cell wasn't gay, you'd be sure to hear them being regarded as a queer. And if they were, they were treated differently: more force, less support, their rights waived depending who was on shift. I couldn't watch victims of crimes be turned away any more. After a while, I noticed that hate crimes stopped being reported. That wasn't because the number of hate crimes had decreased, it was because victims stopped reporting them; they knew they wouldn't be helped.'

'Is that why you left the force?'

'I didn't have a choice. Once my colleagues knew I was attracted to men, they made it their personal mission to weed me out, as if they wanted to make the force *pure* again. But it's anything but – it's rotten to the core.'

'You shouldn't have to, but couldn't you have moved stations, continued your career?'

'And have the reason why I was transferred printed in black and white? The news would spread through the new force like a forest fire. I couldn't go through that all over again.'

'But there are women on the force, surely they aren't as bad as the men? Couldn't they help?'

'Women in the police force are only a notch or two above us. If they spoke up, their careers would be in as much danger as ours, and there are still women who think of us as unnatural just as the majority of the men do.'

Even in the dark, she could sense his pain; he seemed so lost, as though he had fallen apart and been stitched back together in scars.

'I'm so sorry.'

She thought of her brother, and how he hadn't gone to her for help. Did he truly believe he had no one to turn to? Was she as bad as them?

'So this Finn Matthews, you think he's missing?'

'The police make it out like he moved away on his own accord. But towards the end of the journal, he seems terrified, depleted, sick with nerves. His fate doesn't sound planned or safe at all. He was convinced his stalker was coming for him. I can't stop asking questions until I know he's alive and well.'

She thought of the man in the dark street, colliding into her and looking back the way he'd come, as though he had something to fear.

Maybe Finn's still in Rearwood.

'That's why Anna must have given you my number,' he said. 'To warn you of what you're up against. Whatever you're trying to do for this man, you won't have help from the police; if anything, you'll have to work against them. If there was any neglect of duty on their part, they'll want it buried.'

'Maybe I could go higher up. Speak to someone who manages every force in the county?'

He exhaled in a short laugh.

'Them too?' she asked.

'Yes, them too.'

She had been so focused on his words that she hadn't realised that they had looped around the park and were approaching the iron gates again, the black metal glinting in the moonlight.

'Why are you doing this?' he asked. 'I understand wanting to right a wrong, but this is a tough challenge you're about to face.'

'My brother,' she said. 'He committed suicide when he was seventeen. He was constantly berated and abused for who he was, and he couldn't take it any more. I couldn't save Jay, but I can try and get Finn the justice he deserves.'

The torchlight flickered at their feet. The night was cold, but she could barely feel it from the heat of the rage burning through her.

'I hope he gets it,' he said.

As he retrieved the keys from his pocket and unlocked the gate, Rose was reluctant to leave him. The thought of him locking himself inside the park and returning to the cottage alone made her throat ache.

He opened the gate again to the same squeal of rusted metal. Without thinking, she hugged him. His body tensed against hers, but eventually he took a breath and relaxed into her. One hand rested on her back for a beat, before returning to his side.

'Can I come again?' she asked as she pulled away.

'If you have any other questions, give me a call.'

The torch flickered again and slowly died, leaving them to the darkness. The gate shut with a clang, which echoed around them, and the key twisted in the lock, firming the seal between them.

He headed back towards the park. Just as she turned to walk home again, she heard gravel crunch beneath his boots.

'Rose,' he called.

She turned back.

'Good luck.'

She watched as he walked out of sight, his silhouette lost to the shadows of the night.

FINN'S JOURNAL

12th January 2018

I woke the next morning, the memory of him yet to surface, and looked around my bedroom. Even with a hangover beating at my temples, I smiled. It wasn't London, but it was progress; after a few years as assistant editor at the local Evening Herald, I would be back in the bustle of the city with the same title but almost twice the salary. I was on the right track to becoming the editor of a London paper before the age of forty.

I was so naive.

I rolled over and took my phone from the bedside table; it was a text alert that had woken me, just fifteen minutes before my alarm was set to sound. I blinked my eyes awake and looked at the screen.

I really enjoyed seeing you last night.

Immediately I felt the scratch of his stubble around my lips, the lingering scent of his aftershave and sweat. I remembered his calm yet authoritative tone, nudging me into doing what he wanted with each word.

I had to let him down easy, before it went any further.

Although it was a small town, it was big enough for me to avoid him; I needn't see him again.

I had no idea that I didn't have a choice.

I planned to respond after my first cup of coffee, but before I could, my phone pinged again.

You have the softest lips I've ever
kissed. I can still taste them.

I read the text and forced a laugh to hide my fear, even from myself. Even then I seemed to sense that giving him what he wanted would feed a fire that I had no way of putting out.

I left my phone on the bed and showered and dressed for work, the thought of him fleeing to the back of my mind as I went over my to-do list for the day. I had meetings until late afternoon. A good thing about my new colleagues: they kept the coffee flowing. By my third meeting, my hangover would be gone.

I walked to work tenser than usual. I wasn't able to take in the sights and sounds of my new home, or force a smile at each passer-by as I tried to shake off everything I had learned in London to fit in. I couldn't, because my phone vibrated in my pocket every ten steps.

It would be emails dropping into my inbox; someone must have got to the office early to tackle theirs before a day away from their desk. He wouldn't be as desperate as to text again and again without a single response.

I arrived outside the office and checked my phone.

He had texted ten times.

My heart quickened. The phone shook lightly in my hand.

I wrote out a quick text; I couldn't have my phone going off every five seconds. I had a reputation to build.

I'm at work. Talk later.

I left the office at the end of the day feeling sick with exhaustion. Too much coffee had my hands jittering at my sides. Staff writers had been sending articles for approval all afternoon, and I had spent over an hour on the phone to a freelance journalist chasing payment for an article that had been printed months before. Not to mention all of the meetings, each one providing a problem for me to solve.

I turned on my phone as I headed up the street and slipped it back in my pocket as it booted awake. Each breath I took unfurled in a visible cloud.

I stopped in my tracks.

My phone was going berserk, alerts almost overlapping each other, the vibrations stinging against my thigh.

I immediately thought of everything that could have occurred. A death, or an accident. I was miles away from London, with only my phone to keep me connected to my past life. Something terrible had happened and I had been none the wiser.

I removed my phone and scrolled.

Thirty-nine missed calls.

So many texts there were too many to count.

All of them from him.

I had completely forgotten. The day had been so hectic, I hadn't given him a second thought.

I tried to open my inbox but my phone froze, overwhelmed.

Anxiously, I looked up and down the dark street. Shop shutters were lowering over the windows; the odd person milled around further down the street, only distinguishable when they passed under a street lamp.

I looked back down at my phone and tapped his name, bringing up the thread of unread messages.

What are you doing tonight?
Fancy grabbing a drink?

We could go to the pub again,
or try somewhere new.

Hard to get, huh? Dinner then. On me.

Hope work's okay.

You there?

What could be so important that you
can't take a second to reply?

I scrolled further, my heart beating harder and faster as his frustration grew, as his words got nastier, filthier, threatening. The phone began to shake in my hand. I couldn't move from where I stood.

Pick up the fucking phone, you cock-tease.

You do this to all the guys? String them along
and then drop them like a sack of shit?

Fuck you.

You're not even that hot, you just think
you are. You're not special. You're nothing.
You ugly fuck.

I hope you fucking die.

'Excuse me.'

I jolted so hard that I dropped my phone to the tarmac.

An elderly couple were behind me. A man pushing his companion in a wheelchair. Both were wrapped up warm in winter layers and waiting to pass.

'Sorry.'

I snatched up my phone and walked ahead, too embarrassed to look back. The screen had cracked, the light behind brightening each break until they looked like veins in a sun-lit leaf. But even through the cracks, I could see his last message.

The world would be a better place without
scum like you.

I walked home with my head down, my heart pulsing in my throat. I couldn't stop myself from flinching at the slightest sound, peering down every road and path. My mouth dried until my tongue stuck against the sides of my teeth. Even though I was freezing, sweat began to form on my brow and beneath my clothes.

By the time I reached my front door, I was shaking all over. I dropped my keys in my rush to get inside, and snatched them up again, shooting a glance over my shoulder in case he was there, remembering the sight of him at the foot of the stone steps the night before, his eyes looking me up and down.

I locked the door behind me the second I got into the flat, but it wasn't enough. The lock was unreliable, and I wouldn't rest until I was certain that he couldn't get in.

When I look back, it's almost like I knew what was coming.

I shoved the back of a chair beneath the door handle and rushed to each of the windows, eyeing the darkness of the street before dropping the blinds.

I stood in the middle of the flat, panting, and snatched my phone out of my pocket.

A new message. From him.

I'm sorry.

I dropped the phone to the sofa as though his text had bled into the hardwiring of the phone, made it dirty.

He was deranged, he had to be. No one sent messages like that to someone they barely knew.

I thought of the man who had walked me home – overly keen, but not terrifying. Then I imagined that same man typing out the words in my phone. It was like they were two different people.

I sat on the sofa and picked up the mobile. This was going to end now.

He had to understand that I wanted nothing to do with him. I had to tell him no.

First, I texted my landlord and told him to fix the lock as soon as possible, reminding him of his promise before I signed the lease, scolding myself for not asking for it in writing, before opening a new message to send to Michael.

I was at work, I always turn
my phone off at work. . .

Why was I making excuses? I deleted the message and started again, writing numerous versions until fury and fear were quaking through me, giving me enough courage to tell him what I wanted, clear as day.

I'm not interested in you, and after
your messages, I never will be. Contact
me again and I'll go to the police.

I sent the text and dropped the phone to the sofa. It was done.

NINETEEN

R ose's welcome at the police station had been different this
time. The man at the front desk, albeit a new face to her,
seemed to know exactly who she was before she even uttered her
name.

'The detectives will be with you shortly,' he said, and signalled
for her to take one of the seats in the waiting area. She sat in the
chair closest to the door.

The measly hour's sleep had caught up with her. Her eyes
stung, every muscle ached, her heart beat sporadically, unable to
fall into a steady rhythm. She hadn't eaten breakfast or lunch –
even the thought of food made her feel sick – but as she sat waiting
for the detectives to arrive, she could hear her stomach whining
beneath her coat.

Detectives, the man had said. She wasn't just meeting with
Montgomery, but someone else too. She thought of the woman
who had chased her down, searching her mind for the name that
refused to stick, and hoped that perhaps the woman had spoken
to Montgomery herself; maybe they were going to do something
about it. Anna, that was her name.

But when the door opened, the tired smile she gave Montgomery
quickly fell as she eyed the man following behind him: Detective
Seb Clark.

'Rose,' Montgomery said, forcing a tired smile of his own. 'You wished to speak with us about Finn Matthews.'

The muscles in his face seemed tight, as though pain had set his expression into a permanent grimace.

Detective Clark was watching her closely, his lips set in a straight line, his eyes even darker than before.

'Yes, I do.'

'Come this way,' he said.

Rose stood and followed Montgomery, passing Clark as he held back to follow behind her, as though she was a prisoner who needed escorting through the building towards one of the cells.

Because of Montgomery's limp, it took them longer to walk down the corridor and deeper into the building, but Clark continued at a fast pace, the tips of his shoes occasionally kicking her heels. He was so close she could smell his breath with every impatient sigh, a vile cocktail of coffee and cigarette smoke.

I won't be intimidated by you, she told him internally, but on the outside, her body was squirming to get away from him.

The doors to the usual interview rooms crept into view. She braced herself for what was to come, further questions she felt unequipped to answer, but Montgomery didn't slow down, and they passed the doors without even a glance. Her pulse quickened, pounding at her neck and wrists. It was then that she realised she was truly out of her depth.

All she had to go on was a journal, written by a man who might or might not have gone missing. She wasn't a police officer or a detective; she didn't know the man, or anything that might give them information on his whereabouts, and yet she had thrust herself into the situation. She clenched her hands into fists by her sides – she had to remember why she was doing this, and how far the corruption went within the force. She was doing this for Finn. For Jay.

They walked deeper into the station, past officers who had to press against the wall to let them pass, suited men and women sitting at desks, too engrossed to look up from their screens.

They piled into a lift, Rose in the middle with a man on either side, listening to their even breaths and trying to calm her own. Her pulse sounded so loud in her ears that she wondered if they could hear it too.

The doors opened, and the air from the corridor, although stale, felt fresh to her after a minute of unbearable silence and recycled air. Montgomery led them to the right and towards a door. The plaque read:

Chief Constable Timothy Mann

Her mouth dried.

Montgomery gave her a timid smile and knocked on the door, only opening it when a gruff voice on the other side invited them in.

The room was of a good size, but the bareness of the office gave it an empty ring, with shelves barely filled and a desk so clean she could see the reflection of the window and clouds drifting across the surface.

Montgomery led them inside and ushered her towards the desk. Clark hung back, shutting the door behind them and taking a lone seat by the door.

The Chief Constable sat behind the desk. He stood and gave his hand.

'Rose, pleased to meet you.'

She shook it wordlessly. Her hand was damp with sweat; his was bone dry.

'Take a seat,' he said, settling back in his chair.

Rose sat and Montgomery took the seat beside her, releasing a small but noticeable grunt as he sat.

Just like the walk to the office, she had one man before her and another man behind, both the chief's and Clark's eyes on her as though they were burning through her skin to meet.

'Now,' he said, his hands clasping together on top of the desk. 'I understand you have some concerns about a Mr Finn Matthews.'

'Yes, I do,' she replied, sounding stronger than she felt.

'I've read over the information you gave when you handed us the journal allegedly written by Mr Matthews, and have spoken to Detective Montgomery, and unfortunately there isn't much we can do at this stage. No one has declared him missing, except for yourself, but you don't actually know this man, do you?'

'No, I don't.'

'I see.'

'But in the journal, he writes about fearing for his life. He believes the man who harassed him was going to murder him.'

'Having spoken to the officers who dealt with this case, I can't say he mentioned a fear of being murdered.'

'Perhaps he had lost faith in you by then.'

The words came out, quickly and unforgivingly, and she immediately regretted them. The air in the room changed. She sensed Montgomery tense up by her side, heard Clark scoff behind her. A room full of men, and her slap bang in the middle of them.

'Mrs Shaw,' he began. 'Mr Matthews let up the lease on his apartment and left town. Everyone in this room has the right to do the same, if they so choose, without being hunted down by the police, who are needed to work on urgent cases.'

'But no one in this room has been stalked. The circumstances are entirely different. Finn thought he was going to die.'

'And what would you like us to do?' Clark asked behind her.

'Fund a wild-goose chase for a man that fancied a change of scenery?'

'But can you be sure of that?' she asked, refusing to meet his eye. 'Or is that just an assumption so you don't even have to try?'

'No one has reported him missing.'

'Would you have listened if they had? I spoke to an ex-officer who used to be on the force here, and he told me about the lack of support for minority victims, and the prejudice that men attracted to the same sex received from your team.'

'And who was that?'

'Shane Hughes.'

She would stand her ground, keep her eyes on the man in charge, even if she could feel her knees jittering against each other, her throat beating with her heart.

And it was then that she saw the meeting for what it was: on the surface, it seemed like they were simply letting her down easy, but fear seemed to simmer beneath. They didn't want her digging up the past. They weren't going to help her. This was an intervention. At the mention of Shane, she sensed a barrier had come up between them and her.

'Mrs Shaw, I'm afraid we won't be going any further with this. We can't spend money on an investigation unless strong evidence permits it. There are too many crimes, too many victims, that need our attention.'

'Had I not been called in to your office, I would have agreed with you. But here I am, sitting with the chief of police, who seems set on trying to steer me away from looking into this any further.'

'No, I'm trying to protect police resources, and frankly, I can't have you wasting any more of my detectives' time.'

'But it was relevant enough to waste yours?'

'This isn't up for debate, Mrs Shaw. This will not be pursued.'

'Not by you, perhaps,' she said, and stood.

Each of them rose reluctantly, their confident air now far weaker than when she had first walked into the room.

'Please show Mrs Shaw out,' the chief said. 'Montgomery, a word.'

Montgomery nodded and sat back down, as Clark stood and opened the door for her to pass.

'Mrs Shaw,' Chief Constable Mann said.

She stopped in the doorway. 'Yes?'

'After your previous visit to the station, the journal in question went missing from our interview room. You wouldn't happen to know anything about that, would you?'

Sweat instantly broke on her back.

'No. Why, do you think I took it?' She looked to Montgomery. 'Did you see the journal in my possession when you escorted me from the building?'

'No,' he replied.

'Then I guess you can cross me off your list.'

Chief Constable Mann continued to stare. He didn't believe her.

'Are you going to search me?'

He looked her up and down, as if considering it.

'No, Mrs Shaw.'

'Right,' she said, and headed down the hall.

Clark shut the door behind her and led her wordlessly down the corridor, tapping his foot as they waited for the lift. When the doors opened, she was the first to step inside. The sooner she was away from him the better. The doors closed and the lift rumbled into motion.

'Why are you mixing yourself up in this?' he asked suddenly. 'Don't you have a job? Friends? Everyone already knows about the family situation. . .'

She ignored him, staring ahead. She could almost hear his thoughts ticking over, thinking of ways to get her to break.

'I knew your brother,' he said beside her.

She shot him a look. He looked ahead, at their reflections in the steel doors, chewing gum with that sly, slanted smile.

He was playing with her.

'We were in the same year at school. It was a shame what happened to him.'

Clark had seemed to master the art of barely muttering a word, but saying just enough to evoke pure hatred. Just hearing him mention her brother made her want to rip out his tongue.

'If he were around, he'd probably tell you. . .'

The doors opened on the ground floor. A woman in a skirt suit stepped aside for them to pass. Rose watched him wink at the woman and instantly felt sick. She headed down the corridor, refusing to be led. She didn't want to hear what else he had to say, what other punches he would throw just by parting his lips, but his stride was wider than hers, and soon he was back by her side.

'If he were around, he'd tell you I'm not the best person to get on the wrong side of.'

She stopped in place, just before the door to the reception.

'Is that a threat?'

'Not a threat, a friendly warning.'

He smiled, but without a single speck of sincerity. His stare spoke volumes.

'Maybe you should get a hobby,' he said, opening the door. 'Or a job. Use your time more productively rather than running around after someone who doesn't want to be found.'

The waiting area was empty except for one man. He was around her age, but looked better for it. Dark-haired and meticulously groomed, not a hair or stitch out of place. He looked her up and down.

She reached the main doors and stopped.

'That's right,' she said loudly enough for the man to hear. 'I have all the time in the world. I have nothing better to do than to get to the bottom of this, and you can rest assured that I won't stop until I get the answers Finn deserves.'

Clark's eyes changed, like two suns eclipsing, darkening.

'Good luck,' he said, another ominous threat, and turned towards the man. 'Come on up, doc.'

The man in the waiting room stood and followed Seb further into the station, glancing at her over his shoulder.

Rose stepped outside, her legs like jelly, hands shaking.

There was no room for doubt now.

The police wanted the case buried.

It was up to her to dig for the truth.

JAMIE

(

Jamie walked with his head down and his heart hammering in his throat.

He was being followed.

Jamie couldn't see the man, but he could feel him, his glare scratching at his skin like small nicks from a blade.

He shouldn't have walked through the woods. The safer route was through the streets, but it would have taken longer, and he just wanted to get home and shut the door behind him, hear the satisfying click of the lock sliding into place. He hadn't thought of how vulnerable he would be out here, with no one to hear him call for help if he needed it.

Sweat poured down his body, giving his lips a salty taste when he licked them. It seemed like he was checking his phone every ten seconds, waiting for the signal to pick up again so he could call a friend. If anything happened to him, they would hear it down the other end of the line. He could tell them where he was and they could get the police to come.

He looked behind him, saw no one.

He was being paranoid. There was no one there; all he could see were trees with green moss on the trunks, autumnal leaves coating the ground. The only person he had seen was the dog walker heading in the opposite direction a mile or so ago. But his gut was churning like it had all those times he had seen the man watching him from afar, the man he was sure had sent him the text messages.

I know what you are.

The first message had turned his blood cold. Not who. *What.* The man knew the secret he had kept from everyone, the secret Jamie hadn't even admitted to himself until he read the message.

As he headed out of the woodland and into the open field, he thought of all the times he had gone to tell his friends what was happening, but if he did that, he would have to tell them who he really was, or as the man put it, *what* he was.

The urge to run burnt in his legs. He turned to eye the woodland and saw nothing but trees. There was no reason to run, but as he turned back, he broke into a sprint. His backpack slammed into the middle of his back with every stride, and sweat slanted down the sides of his face in warm streaks. His mother would be waiting for him with the same look she had given him ever since the messages started, knowing something was wrong but not wanting to pry.

He ran across the field and through the next, until he was back in the knit of trees. He stopped and leaned against the nearest trunk, panting for air. His lungs stung from the freshness of it, the chill that had numbed his throat. He closed his eyes and listened to the race of his heart, waiting for it to slow.

A hand covered his mouth and his eyes shot open.

A man stared back at him, so close he could smell his breath. 'Shh. . .'

It was him. The man he had seen so many times. He was so

close the tips of their noses were touching. He blinked calmly, but his eyes were wide, darting left and right before settling back on Jamie's face.

Jamie instantly went rigid with fear, his body hardening against the tree trunk, recoiling from the press of the man's body. His eyes were so wide they felt close to bulging from their sockets. He murmured beneath the man's palm, grimaced when he tasted the sweat on it.

'I just want to talk,' the man whispered. 'If I take my hand away, will you let me talk?'

Jamie nodded. A tear fell from his eye and traced the seal of the hand against his face.

The man lowered his hand slowly, as if he was getting ready to clamp back down, and watched Jamie's face without blinking. When he was sure he would comply, he sighed and stepped back.

And then Jamie released a deep, terrified scream.

The sound echoed through the woods, slicing between the trees until birds flocked from the treetops.

There was a split second when the scream stopped and they stared at each other with shock painted on both of their faces, as though time suddenly stood still, before Jamie bolted into a run and screamed again for help.

He sprinted across the uneven ground, covered in leaves that hid dips in the earth, roots of the trees, fallen branches that broke and squeaked beneath his soles. His foot dropped into a hole in the earth and the ankle twisted, throwing him to the woodland floor, but he scrambled back up and ran through the pain, stray leaves that had stuck to his clothes falling off him in his wake. He ran until he could taste blood at the back of his throat, and the cold air stung his eyes and made them stream.

And then everything stopped.

One second he was running, and the next he was on the ground, staring out at the woodland from the side with a hot pain spreading through the back of his head. His right ear was ringing, piercing down to the ear drum. Boots appeared in his line of vision. A thick branch fell to the ground, blood and hair matted on the end.

My blood.

My hair.

The man knelt down and wedged his arms beneath him.

Jamie tried to scream as he was lifted in the man's arms, but all that escaped was a broken murmur. Rain began to cut through the trees and patted on his face. He closed his eyes against the drops and let the darkness take him.

TWENTY

Rose looked up at the newspaper building from where she stood on the street and squinted as sunlight sliced through the clouds. Exhaustion buzzed in every exhale, and her eyes were dry and sore, but her fury from the meeting at the station was still eating away at her. If they wouldn't look into Finn's disappearance, she would.

She had walked past this building so many times before, but this was the first time she really took it in, eyeing the dark bricks, the single-paned windows with chipped paint. The paper's logo was emblazoned above the main entrance, weathered from numerous seasons of scalding heatwaves and thrashing rainfalls.

Finn had spent so many hours of his life behind those walls, and all he had got in return was grief. She thought of him standing where she stood, seeing the building through his eyes, and wondered which painful memory would come back to him first.

She looked across the street at the café, eyeing the path where Finn first met his stalker. It could have been anyone, but fate had chosen him. She had known Rearwood all her life, walked into every shop, driven down every road, but seeing it through Finn's eyes, she couldn't ignore the darkness that lurked within the town she thought she knew through and through.

She steeled herself and stepped inside the building, the doors parting as she neared. The lobby was small, and the struggle of the printed newspaper business was evident from the scuffed floor to the walls desperately in need of fresh paint.

A woman sat behind the reception desk, talking quietly into the phone. It was only when Rose got closer that she heard the rushed end of a personal conversation on the company's time.

'How can I help?' the woman asked with a forced smile.

'I would like to see the editor.'

'Do you have an appointment?'

'No, but—'

'I'm afraid you'll need an appointment,' the woman said quickly.

Rose wondered how many people requested meetings like this and how many times the receptionist had said the same sentence. It sounded as though the words were imprinted into her brain.

'The person in charge will be interested in what I have to say.'

'Well, when you have an appointment, I'm sure she will be happy to hear it. But until then, I'm afraid I can't let you up.'

She. When Finn worked there as assistant editor, the editor of the newspaper had been a man. She immediately felt thrown, but forced herself on.

'If you could give her a call and tell her that I would like to speak to her regarding the disappearance of Finn Matthews, I'm sure she will want to see me.'

The woman's confidence slipped from her face. Her lips parted.

'Are you a reporter?' she asked suddenly.

'No, merely a concerned member of the public.'

The woman hesitated, her eyes glancing to the left.

'Is there a problem here?' a man asked behind her back.

Rose turned and saw a security guard, his thumbs hooked inside the loops on his belt.

Shit.

'No problem,' Rose said quickly and turned back to the receptionist, her eyes flicking to her name badge. 'Maggie was about to call upstairs to confirm my appointment before I went over to *North Heath Press* instead.' She turned back to the guard. 'It would be better for the *Evening Herald* if I shared my information here – it's to do with the disappearance of an ex-employee after all, and the gross misconduct from the paper at that – but I'll leave it up to Maggie to decide.'

Both Rose and the guard turned to the receptionist. Her face had grown pale.

'One moment, please,' she said, and picked up the phone.

Rose smiled at the guard. He looked her up and down before turning back to his station by the door.

Rose faced the desk again to hear the end of the call.

'Yes, Finn Matthews.' Maggie looked up at her. 'What's your name?'

'Rose Shaw.'

'Rose Shaw,' she repeated into the phone. 'Okay.'

Maggie placed the phone in the cradle.

'Take the lift to the fourth floor. She will be waiting for you.'

'Thank you.'

Even through her sleepless haze and the pull of her aching joints, she couldn't help but smirk at her triumph. After so many years of keeping her eyes to the ground, it felt good to hold her head high.

She stepped into the lift and took out her phone the moment the doors closed to search her browser for the name of the new editor of the newspaper. She hadn't anticipated this, but she could spin it back to Finn. Her phone buffered, the connection faltered from the lift, and failed to give her the name before the doors opened on the fourth floor.

A woman was waiting for her in a dark brown suit, pulled in at the waist, padded at the shoulders, neat lines pressed into the front of her trousers all the way down to the tips of her heels pointing out from beneath the hem. Her hair was dyed dark brown, almost black, and starting to show grey at the roots. When she smiled, Rose thought she wore too much make-up as she watched it cake between the lines around her eyes and mouth.

'Rose Shaw,' the woman said confidently, holding out her hand. 'Miranda Lawrence, editor of the *Herald*.'

'Pleased to meet you,' Rose said.

'My office is this way – we can chat there.'

Miranda led her confidently through the open-plan office with a quick stride. Rose had felt confident before, but Miranda seemed to ooze with it, each movement sharply executed, as though each breath and word had an important purpose, and anything that didn't was a waste of her time.

'Here,' she said, opening the door to a small office and holding it open for Rose to pass. 'Can I get you a drink? Tea? Coffee?'

'Coffee, please,' Rose said as she took a seat before the desk.

'Lindsay, coffee,' she called out into the office, and closed the door.

Lindsay. The colleague from the bar.

Miranda made her way round the desk and sat quickly, every second precious, and clasped her hands together on top of the desk.

'How can I help?'

Rose had never trusted journalists. There was something cold-blooded about them, a ruthlessness they had to have to bag the best story, a trait she couldn't trust. Whatever Rose gave, she knew this woman would counter with a question of her own. But however she planned to spin this, Rose would leave with the upper hand.

'Finn Matthews is missing.'

'I'm sorry to hear that,' she said quickly, her voice void of any sign of genuine concern. 'I never met him, but I heard good things about his work.'

'Did you also hear of the abuse he received during his time in Rearwood?'

'I am aware he may have experienced some difficulties.'

The door to the office opened quickly, pressing into the wall with a bang. Miranda jolted behind the desk and closed her eyes briefly, the bones of her jaw clenching beneath the skin.

A young woman entered with a tray and placed it on the desk. Two cups, a pot of coffee, sugar and milk. Sugar granules fell from the bowl in her shaky grip.

'Thank you, Lindsay,' Miranda said between tight lips.

Rose eyed the woman properly for the first time. Ashy blonde hair flat-ironed to within an inch of its life, heavy eye make-up and bold red lips, with a skirt suit too tight for her frame and ballet pumps on her feet.

She nodded quickly and headed out of the room, closing the door with a quiet click.

'I was hoping you could tell me if you knew where Finn was,' Rose said, as she watched Miranda pour the coffee, shaking her head when she offered sugar and milk. 'Perhaps he asked for a reference for another employer? Had his P45 sent to a new address?'

'We don't have that information, I'm afraid,' the editor replied, stirring sugar into her cup before taking a sip. 'And even if we did, I wouldn't be at liberty to share that sort of private information with you.'

'Right,' Rose said, jumping to plan B. 'Then I would like to put this in the next issue of the *Evening Herald*.'

She took the folder from her bag and pulled out the sheets of paper. It had taken less than an hour to mock up in the library, and a kind woman at the computer next to hers had read over the paperwork to check for spelling mistakes, in case her tired brain had missed any. The woman's eyebrow had risen in an arch as she read the headline, but she was too polite to ask.

Miranda took them with a steady hand and read for a moment. 'I'm sure we could slip this into the ad pages somewhere. . .'

'No,' Rose said sternly. 'The back page. All of it.'

'Mrs Shaw, we can't just pull planned ads from an issue and replace it with. . . something like this.'

'We both know you can. And wouldn't you be putting the company first? Yes, backing from advertisers must be helpful, but I'm sure support from the town, your entire demographic, is more important. I'll be doing a lot of talking about this, about Finn. It's up to you whether I tell the town about the lack of support you at the paper had for him. I have a good way with words too, Miranda.'

The woman eyed her coolly from the other side of the desk, but one corner of her mouth twitched with a threatening smirk. She was impressed.

'You can have the ad space if you pay double. I won't upset a devoted advertiser if it's going to put us at a loss.'

'Fine.'

'Don't you care how much it is?'

'Do you prefer cash or card?'

She smirked again, both corners curling with it this time, and pressed a code into the phone on her desk. 'Rick, bring me the necessary paperwork for taking ad space at the back of the paper.' She hung up swiftly, giving little time for the person on the other end of the line to reply.

Miranda leaned back in her chair and looked Rose up and down, the smirk never leaving her face.

'Have you ever thought about selling your story?'

It was as if the woman had taken Rose's confidence, ripped it off like a second skin, and pissed all over it. Her past meant that anyone who knew of it could snatch back control within a second. Her most dreaded memory was public, a weapon everyone in the town knew to use. She crossed her arms.

'No.'

'It could help close that chapter in your life. It's been what — four years?'

'I'm not selling my story.'

'It would help pay for the ad too. You could have all the ads you wanted.'

'I have the money.'

'It could help your cause. If people see you in a good light, as a mother controlled by her insomnia, rather than someone irresponsible and reckless, you might have more people willing to help you with this.'

Rose snorted. 'Please don't try to act like you have some sort of moral integrity. You'd spin the story in a second.'

A man entered the office with a pile of papers, as flustered as Lindsay had been. Miranda had clearly made an impression on the office, but she didn't scare Rose. She had stared death in the face; Miranda Lawrence was nothing.

'Think about it,' she said, before her smirk dropped and she eyed the man standing beside the desk. The paperwork shook in his hands. She signalled for him to put it in front of Rose with a sharp tilt of her head.

'Sign where it's crossed,' she told Rose. 'And fill in your payment details towards the back. Your ad will run in the paper next week.'

'Next week?' Rick asked. 'But Miranda, that space is—'

'I didn't realise I needed to consult you on this, Rick.'

'You don't,' he said. 'Sorry.'

Rose took the pen he gave her and signed by the crosses, flipping past pages of text she was too exhausted to read. It wouldn't do her 'strong woman' persona any good if she fell asleep face first on the desk. She signed the last page and placed the pen on the desktop.

'Pleasure to have met you, Rose,' Miranda said and shook her hand. 'And think about what I said.' She clicked her fingers. 'Rick, show Mrs Shaw to the lobby, and then process the forms.'

He nodded quickly as he snatched up the paperwork and rushed for the door, holding it open for her. Rose walked through, excitement buzzing in her gut. She had done it. The first real step in finding answers. All she had to do now was wait.

Rick led her back the way they had come, past the desks piled high with paperwork, the distant bleep of a phone the only persistent sound in the room. Lindsay stood from her desk, smoothing down her skirt and slinging her bag over her shoulder before heading across the office, through a door for the ladies' room.

Rose stopped before the lift.

'Can I use the toilet before I go?'

Rick checked his watch nervously, glancing back at Miranda's office.

'I won't be long,' she said.

'Okay, there's one just off the reception. I'll show you.'

'I . . . I'd prefer if I could go now.' She waited a beat. 'Ladies' problems.'

'Right, of course,' he stammered. 'You can use this one.'

He ushered her towards the door.

'Thanks.'

The room was small, with just two cubicles and a lone sink beneath a smeared mirror. The light bulb flickered briefly above her head. The floor appeared clean, but stuck to the soles of her shoes as she stepped closer to the mirror.

One of the bathroom stalls was shut. Lindsay moved around inside, pulling at the toilet paper dispenser.

Rose stood before the mirror and almost flinched at the sight of the woman staring back at her. The dark shadows around her eyes made it look as though the sockets had sunk inwards. Her hair was ruffled and the first signs of grease shimmered at the roots. Insomnia had a way of sucking the life from a person, paling the lips, dulling eyes, thinning the skin. It had been years since she'd recognised herself in the mirror.

The toilet flushed behind her. She fussed with her appearance in the mirror to look busy, and watched as Lindsay left the cubicle, zipping her pencil skirt up behind her back.

'Sorry to ask,' Rose said. 'But do you have a tampon?'

'Yeah, sure.'

Lindsay took a tampon from her small bag; clearly her time of the month if she was traipsing back and forth to the bathroom with it.

'Thanks. Lindsay, right?'

'Yeah, sorry about. . . her. Was Miranda nice to you?'

'She was fine. Although Miranda doesn't seem like the easiest person to work for.'

'That's putting it kindly,' she said as she lathered her hands in soap.

'You knew Finn, right?'

Lindsay stopped instantly at the sound of his name, bubbles coating her hands as water continued to run into the bowl.

'He disappeared,' Rose continued. 'I'm worried about him. He said he was having some trouble with a man, which started the night you all went for drinks. Do you remember? A man from the bar walked him home.'

'He was a twat,' Lindsay said, washing the soap from her hands.

'How old did he look?'

'I don't know. Forties maybe?'

Lindsay was young, in her twenties. She would think anyone over thirty-five was in their forties. Rose didn't want to know how old Lindsay thought she was.

'What did he look like?'

'Black hair,' she said, remembering, and snorted. 'Probably a dye job. He seemed like the vain type. All right body from what I could see of it. Plain old face you'd forget in a minute.'

'Were there any distinguishing features you can remember?'

She thought back for a moment, chewing lightly on her bottom lip.

'Now I remember why I didn't like him,' she said. 'He was wearing a wedding ring.'

'What a pig,' Rose said, goading her.

'You're telling me. My dad was a cheat, completely broke my mum. Can't stand guys like that now. Makes me feel sick even looking at them. I mean, he even wore it when he was out on the pull. Crazy, right?'

'Right. Crazy. What did it look like, the ring?'

'Just a simple gold band.'

'Had you ever seen him before?'

'No, nor since.'

She dried her hands with paper towels, taking her time, as if delaying her return to the office.

'Would you recognise him again, if you saw him?'

'Maybe, but like I said, I haven't.' She headed for the door, but

184

hesitated. 'It's funny, isn't it? You can live in a town all your life and still stumble across people you've never met.'

Rose smiled and thanked her again for the tampon she didn't need, and watched Lindsay leave.

Rose wasn't worried about suspecting people she hadn't met in Rearwood before. She was worried about the people she already knew.

C

Rose turned off the path at the head of the drive and noticed there were lights on in the house. They were actually home, for once. It had to be both of them; neither of them liked to face her alone.

She stopped outside for a moment, silently preparing herself for the tension she would be welcomed with. It was almost possible to watch them shutting her out just by looking in their eyes and watching as they cooled. Trying to chip away at the barriers they put between them and her every day was exhausting.

When she headed up the steps for the front door, she stopped, her hand clapping against her lips.

Her bag was lying in front of the door, burnt to a crisp. The top step was charred from extinguished flames. Her phone was on the step beneath, away from where the flames had been, perched against it so the screen reflected her face in the glass. She snatched it up and saw an unsent text message.

If you play with fire, you're going to get burnt.

The front door burst open. She stumbled back, the phone clenched in her grasp. Christian stood in the doorway, chest flared.

'What the hell is this?'

Anger radiated from him. She looked down at the bag, just as the breeze wafted the scent of burning fabric between them. It was eye-watering. She met his eyes again. He had found the mess and gone inside so she would find it like he had when she returned home.

'I lost it,' she said, looking from her bag to him. 'I thought I'd lost it. But obviously someone took it.'

'But why? Why would anyone do that?'

Christian would never understand why she was doing this. If he knew, she would have to face the pity in his eyes. For once she wanted something that was just hers. Lily had her friends, Christian had his mistress; all she had was the hunger for justice for a man she had never met.

'I don't know.'

'What do you mean you don't know? The message said you were playing with fire.'

'You looked through my—'

'Rose, what have you done?'

'I haven't done anything!'

He scoffed and turned away, striding down the hall. She pocketed her phone and stepped over the bag, closing the door behind her.

Music was booming from upstairs, so loud she could almost hear Lily's bedroom door shuddering in its frame.

Rose strode down the hallway and found Christian in the kitchen, pouring himself a whisky.

'Where were you today?' he asked.

'Where were you last night?' she retorted.

'Don't be so childish, for Christ's sake.'

'So you get to do whatever you want, see whoever you want, with no regard for me? And yet I'm expected to answer to you?'

He finished off his drink in one. It was clear it hadn't been his first drink of the evening; the whites of his eyes were red, his pupils glassy.

'Whatever you were doing pissed someone off. They know where we live. Don't you care about Lily's safety? She was the one to find it, by the way. She came home from school to your shit melted to the doorstep.'

'If you were here more often, maybe she wouldn't have been alone.'

'I think you're forgetting I have to work to pay for the roof over our heads.'

'The house I bought, Christian, don't you forget that.'

'Yes, and a house I have to work day and night to keep.'

'Why?'

'Why what?'

'Why do it? Why stay? You clearly don't love me. So why are you still here?'

'You want me to go?'

'You should want to go. You said you were as sick of this as I was, so why put up with it? You've met someone else, you see her more than you see me, see *us,* and yet you keep coming back.'

She had asked the question, but she couldn't bring herself to stay for the answer. She snatched the bottle of whisky from the top of the island and headed for her study.

'And if you don't know the answer to that, I suggest you start thinking about it. We can't live like this for ever. *I* can't live like this for ever.'

She slammed the door behind her and retreated to her chair, just as the first tear fell. She had done it, uttered the question she had longed to ask for years, knowing full well that once it had been spoken aloud, she would never be able to take it back. She had practically given him an ultimatum: work to fix their mess or leave. Deep down, she knew which option made more sense.

Worst of all, he had been right. Following this path could mean putting Lily in danger. Whoever did this wanted her to stop. She thought of her brother, and how no one had helped him. Finn had no one looking out for him either, no one who cared, no one except for her. And pitifully, Finn was all she had. There was something comforting in knowing that he was lonely too; just knowing that someone else had felt so isolated made the silence a little easier to bear.

She checked her phone and looked through the unread messages. All of them were from Rob.

I had a great time with you today. Give me a call if you want another round.

Fancy grabbing a drink tonight?

As friends, I mean, if that's what you'd prefer.

Have I done something wrong?

The light caught her wedding ring, flashing in her lap. She buried the phone in her pocket and closed her eyes.

FINN'S JOURNAL

23rd January 2018

It was more than a week until I saw him again.

I had completely forgotten about him. My new role had demanded all of my attention: working all hours, skipping meals, falling straight into bed the moment I arrived home, only to wake up and do it all over again. Working as hard as I did gave me no time to ponder on how alone I was; the minute I stopped working, reality trickled in: I had no one, nothing except for my work. I would jump in again, keeping the cycle in motion, distracting myself to keep reality at bay. So when I hadn't received a response to my text message, I thought it was over, dealt with.

It was a Friday, and I was hours away from completing my second week on the job. The first edition of the paper that was partially under my helm was about to go to press, and I walked to work with a new rigour, even with puffy eyes and the fizz of exhaustion inside my skull. I didn't stay up all night worrying that my landlord still hadn't fixed the lock on my door, or that I had yet to make any concrete friends inside the office; my ambition was enough to put a smile on my face; soon I would be holding a copy of the newspaper in my hands.

When I saw him, my smile fell.

He blended into the morning rush well; to anyone else on the street, he was just your typical man nearing middle age, waiting for a bus or a friend. It was astonishing how normal he looked. Dark hair swept back with gel, a black suit that made his shoulders look even broader, an off-white shirt without a tie at the collar. He was scrolling through his phone with a cigarette burning between his fingers. He was waiting outside my office.

I watched him from across the road as he fidgeted restlessly, gave the occasional glance down the street, first left, then right. He was looking for someone.

He was looking for me.

I checked my watch: five to nine. If I stalled any longer I would be late for the morning briefing. But the sight of him froze me to the spot, as though his hands were on me, pinning me there.

I knew I had to move before he spotted me. If his presence alone could scare me into submission, I couldn't risk meeting his eye.

I crossed the street with my head down, my heart fit to burst. The street was heaving with people, a sea of coffee cups and frustrated tuts. I knitted my way through the crowd for the doors and dared to look in his direction.

He was staring right at me.

I will never forget the look on his face. In just a glance, I could see the madness in his eyes; a specific, unhinged glint that sent a shock of nerves through me.

I rushed inside the lobby and allowed myself to breathe. My legs were shaking and my head felt light. The security guard by the door gave me a concerned glance. I forced a smile and made my way to the lift.

Maybe it was a coincidence that he was outside my office. I had no idea what he did for a living; perhaps he worked in the same building. After all, I had met him outside the coffee shop across the street. Maybe he wasn't there for me at all.

But, however many times I told myself that it was just a coincidence, I was unable to forget that look of glee in his eyes when our gazes met.

I ordered in for lunch that day, and didn't leave the office until long after dark, telling myself I was there to catch up on work and not because I didn't want to leave the safety of the building. I found myself constantly eyeing the window as the sky darkened, making the walk home all the more terrifying, but I couldn't find the strength to rise from my seat and slip into my coat. By the time the clock struck seven, I forced myself away from my desk and collected my things, ignoring the light tremble of my hands.

I stepped outside the office and immediately looked to where he had stood that morning. He wasn't there.

That was the first time I wondered if I was going mad, if it was really me who was unhinged, terrified of a man who had only tried to woo me and taken the rejection to heart. I wasn't used to being desired; I had never thought myself worthy of it, too shy to meet a man's eye, constantly misconstruing their advances as politeness or a gag to humiliate me. Maybe my fear of being wanted had gone so far as to make me fear a man I didn't even know.

I walked along the street and raised the collar of my coat. Night had fallen, firmly in winter's grasp, making it so easy to mistake a shadow for a dark silhouette or the echo of my footsteps for a second pair of feet. Even though I was the only person walking along the street that night, I could feel the presence of someone else, as though eyes were blazing into my back. No matter how many times I looked around and found myself alone, I couldn't shake the feeling. Every fibre in my body knew something was wrong.

I got home, flustered and sweating, and fought my key into the lock on the front door of the building. I shut the door firmly behind me and pressed my back against it, listening to the rush of my heart. This was madness – I had been alone the whole way; the only thing I had to fear was my imagination. I was a grown man, not a child, and yet somehow, meeting him had made me afraid of the dark again, made me doubt my own sanity.

I sighed and peeled myself away from the door. It was all in my head. I'd worked too long; drunk too much coffee. I took my post from the pigeonhole on the wall in the hallway and let myself inside my flat.

The apartment still didn't feel like home; it had an empty chill to it, housing simple furniture and beige walls without a single clue of who lived there; it could have belonged to anyone. I think I wanted that on a subconscious level: I wouldn't be here for long. Rearwood was just a pit stop.

I went to the windows and closed the blinds before even turning on the light, conscious of not wanting to be seen from the outside. I left the post on the coffee table and sank onto the sofa, resting my head to close my eyes.

I had to give myself time to settle, that was all. I was overwhelmed by so much change: new job, new town, new flat. I was bound to be on high alert, taking everything as a threat. It was in my nature to worry.

My phone vibrated in my pocket. I opened my eyes and blinked furiously, my contact lenses sticking to them like glue. I checked my phone.

Like your post?

Him.

My eyes shot to the envelopes on the coffee table. Three envelopes, two white, one brown.

He sent the text the minute I got home, which meant he had to have been following me. I hadn't been imagining it.

I picked up the envelopes, my hands already shaking. The first would be a bill; it had a sticker on it, indicating the reroute to my new address. The second envelope was the same, with my bank's logo in the bottom right-hand corner. The brown envelope just had my name, written by hand.

I turned the envelope over and peeled back the lip, tearing it open with the swipe of my thumb. Slowly, I slipped my fingers inside and withdrew the small piece of paper – a newspaper cutting with part of an article and the page number in the corner. I turned it over.

It was the photo of me that the paper had printed to mark my employment. Jagged crosses blacked out my eyes, and a penis had been drawn beside my mouth, with drops of ejaculate doodled onto my face, as though it was running off my chin.

I dropped the cutting to the floor and stared ahead, feeling his presence behind the curtains, as though he was out there, somehow able to see in. I swiped a chair from beneath the table and pressed it beneath the handle on the front door.

My phone vibrated on the coffee table, far longer than before. I edged towards it.

He was calling.

I watched the phone shiver across the surface of the table, seemingly louder and harsher with each ring. Even when I shut myself in, lowered the blinds, barricaded the door, he still found a way to get to me.

I took a deep breath and snatched up the phone.

'What do you want?' I barked, trying to sound as brave as I could, but the fear was evident in my voice; it had me by the throat, squeezing the words out of me.

I listened to him breathing down the line. Goosebumps bristled up my arms, as though each breath was unfurled on my skin.

'You,' he whispered.

The call ended.

TWENTY-ONE

Rose sat in her chair before the window and fought back tears. It wasn't the sight of the bridge, but sheer frustration at yet another sleepless night. Her whole body ached as though exhaustion was slowly rotting her from the inside out.

On the other side of the window, the day was overcast, making the river water grey, and the trees colourless skeletons. She refused to look at the bridge – it would only provoke more tears. Once she started, it was almost impossible to stop.

She rose from her seat and headed out of the study, her throat parched and longing for a tall glass of water. She stepped out just in time to see Lily as she reached the bottom of the stairs. She was already in her uniform, with her hair straightened and swept across her shoulders. Her skirt was hiked too high, the waistband folded over and hidden with a belt, to reveal more of her legs, the pale skin hidden by thick black tights. She headed for the door.

'Lily, wait.'

Rose strode up the hallway, striding into a jog as Lily opened the door and kicked the burnt bag out of her way. Ash flittered with the wind.

'Have you eaten breakfast?' she called after her. 'Do you have money for lunch?'

Lily kept walking and disappeared around the corner.

Rose sighed and went inside for cleaning supplies: a bucket with hot soapy water and a sponge, broom and bin bags.

She swept away ash and bagged up the debris before pouring some of the water down the steps, watching the soot turn the suds black. She knelt down and began to scrub, until the sponge blackened in her hand and ash was bedded beneath her fingernails.

She had known Violet inside and out. Violet had shared everything with her, told her every thought, secret or worry. But Lily always preferred Christian, even before the crash. As a child, she would never tell Rose anything, or come to her without being prompted. Rose had had to tease the smallest truth or thought from her. But now, she didn't even get the chance to do that. Her own child was a stranger.

Stop thinking about what you cannot change.

She remembered Rob's messages and the day at the range. He had been kind, funny, flirtatious, and it terrified her. Christian might be able to move on while they were still married, but she couldn't. Tethers held her life together; pursuing whatever was between her and Rob could destroy it beyond repair.

As she scrubbed, she thought of who would have gained from making the mess. She had lost her bag the day she attended the police station. If the police had anything to hide, could they have left this as a warning? It seemed Detective Seb Clark was capable of something like this, just by the look in his eyes, the smirk he had given at the mere mention of her name. But if he did, then why?

Maybe Shane regretted speaking with her, and had decided he wanted the past to be left alone. But he hadn't had access to her bag, not like Detective Clark. Perhaps she had just left it on the bus. Or maybe the bag had been returned after all, and Lily wanted to get her back in some small way.

But that doesn't explain the message, she thought, as she chucked the remainder of the water across the steps to wash away the bubbles.

If you play with fire, you're going to get burnt.

There was only one way to make sure. She had to speak to someone who knew the police well.

She left the bin bag on the path just beside the drive and headed back into the house to scrub her hands clean before messaging Shane and asking to meet again.

They could threaten her all they wanted; she had lost so much, had been hurt so many times, she had nothing left to lose.

If they wanted her to stop, they would have to do much better than that.

TWENTY-TWO

Night had fallen by the time Rose reached High Gate Park. The chill in the air had seeped through her clothes and skin. Even though her teeth chattered and her body was numb, the empty chill was familiar. Exhaustion did that to a person, it sucked the heat from their bodies, hollowed them out; drifting, empty vessels, asleep on their feet.

She checked her phone for the time, her tired eyes watering at the brightness, and waited for Shane by the gate.

When she'd spoken to him that afternoon, he'd sounded more open to talking than the first time, but as the minutes passed and the silence stretched, a voice crept from the back of her mind: *He isn't coming. He's changed his mind.*

Gusts of wind curled through the iron gates in a high-pitched whistle, pulling them against their hinges, the sound like grinding teeth. The rustle of leaves silenced as the wind fell. Flowers had closed their petals. As she stood alone in the dark, a familiar breed of loneliness crept in.

Ten minutes passed. Twenty. Twenty-five. She checked the text messages again. Perhaps she had turned up on the wrong night. It wouldn't be the first time. But it was right there on the screen: he had confirmed tonight, nine on the dot.

Something had to have changed his mind.

She pressed herself against the gate and peered down the pathway, numbing her cheek against the cold metal. The iron gave way beneath her hands. The gate creaked open. She stood before it, watched it sway with the wind.

If Shane no longer wanted to see her, had decided to leave his past behind, who was she to bring it all up again? She had to respect his wishes. But she also had to find out the truth about Finn Matthews.

She stepped inside and shut the gate behind her.

At thirty-nine years old she was still afraid of the dark. Shadows crept from beneath the trees, darkened the lawns until everywhere she looked was a sea of black. It wasn't the darkness itself that scared her, but what might be lurking within. She picked up the pace with her head down, the wind whipping locks of hair against her face.

Reaching the end of the path she headed down the hill, pulling her coat to her torso as the wind swept across the open field, the grass moving with it in waves, and stopped before the cottage.

The front door was ajar.

A beam of light shone through the break in the doorway. She edged forward to peer inside.

A telephone table had been knocked over. The phone was lying away from its cradle to the endless sound of the dialling tone. The mirror on the wall had been smashed, reflecting the rest of the house in each shard like the view from a fly's eye.

A clock ticked from a distant room. The wind howled behind her, picking at her hair. She pushed the door open.

Dark drops of blood stained the carpet. Muddy footsteps had been ground into the fabric. The wallpaper had been slashed with a knife to form a word.

She tried to swallow, but her mouth had dried. When she went to call out, the word caught. She cleared her throat and tried again.

'Hello?'

She stepped inside, trying to avoid the blood, red streaks smeared into the carpet and packed down with dirt from a stranger's boots. She returned the phone to its cradle to cut the sound.

The mess on the floor led through an open doorway off the hall.

Her senses exploded with the slightest sound. Her legs jellified. Nerves stung through her.

She pushed the door wider. The light from the hall sliced through the dark room.

A table had been overturned. Pictures had been slashed and thrown to the floor, their frames broken into splinters. Glasses had been smashed and cushions gutted, their feathers trodden brown with earth and kicked about the room. She eyed the blood and mud at her feet, following the path as though someone had been dragged.

A man lay before the fireplace, naked and quivering.

'Shane?'

She couldn't tell. His eyelids had sealed shut. His lips were cut and bloody, his cheek and jaw had swollen as though he had been stung. His ribs were already bruised, maroon clouds swelling in his skin. She looked around the room, but failed to spot his clothes. Amongst the mess was a blanket, twisted up beneath the sofa that had been thrown onto its back. She tugged it free and rushed to him, covering his naked flesh.

'Shane?'

He jolted with the sound, like a man waking from a dream in which he was falling, waiting to hit the ground, and instinctively protected his face with his hands. Marks had been left on his wrists where someone had held him down. The fingers on his right hand were twisted, surely broken.

'It's Rose,' she said. She wanted to comfort him, stroke his cheek or take his hand, but she couldn't find a single part of him untouched.

A tear leaked from one swollen eye.

'I'll call an ambulance. I'll ask for the police and—'

'Don't.'

'But Shane, you're—'

'Don't call the police,' he said and tried to sit up. The tear fell silently to the floor.

'But whoever did this needs to be punished. You can't let them. . .'

He hunched over, a hand on his ribs, and looked at her properly for the first time. She could just see his eyes through the swollen slits he now had for lids.

'You can't call the police. Who do you think did this?'

'Rose, stop, you don't need to do that.'

She couldn't think what else to do. She had tried to sort out the mess and treat his wounds. The first thing she did was drag him up onto the sofa and wipe each cut and graze with salt water, comb the dried blood from his hair. When he began to drift, she upturned what furniture she could and piled the unsalvageable items out on the lawn. Still, it didn't feel like enough. She wanted to make the room look as though it had never been touched, as though the mayhem had never occurred.

'I don't know what else to do,' she said, stopping for the first time. Sweat coated her brow. She ripped off her winter layers and left them in a heap.

'You shouldn't have come,' he said.

She stared at his broken body. His bruises were darkening by the minute and his eyes had almost sealed shut. When he spoke, he sounded as though he was talking around dislodged teeth. Every time she looked at him, fresh tears sprang to her eyes.

'This is all my fault, isn't it? I did this. I mentioned you by name. This is my fault.'

'No,' he said. 'The responsibility lies with them.'

'I forgot to bind your fingers,' she said suddenly.

'Leave it.'

'No, I'll do it. Do you have plasters? Tape?'

'Medical drawer beneath the kitchen sink.'

She made her way to the kitchen, passing the mud and blood trodden into the carpet, and returned with the box, opening it with shaking fingers.

'Why would they do this?' she asked.

'Because I know what they've done. If you're digging into this, they could be found out. Whatever you're up to has got people talking.'

'What exactly have they done?' she asked. 'What have they got to hide?'

She taped one purple finger to another. When he sighed, a bubble of blood formed from the crack in his lip. He licked it away.

'While I was on the force, they made my life hell. At the station they hid parts of my uniform to get me pulled up, stuck me with the jobs nobody else wanted, excluded me from meetings, claiming they'd forgotten to add me to the list. But that was nothing compared to what they did outside the station.'

He was silent for a moment. Rose stayed kneeling before him, too scared to move in case any slight movement might be enough to change his mind. She had to know.

'I was a year into the job, and I was put on the late shift for patrol. Seb Clark's partner had an emergency and had to cancel his shift, so I was stuck with him, just the two of us driving around in the same car in silence, the only sound being the occasional natter of the radio and Seb's impatient sighs. When the clock on the dashboard flashed midnight and our shift came to an end, he asked me if I wanted to have some fun. I didn't know what he meant, but he was a man I knew I should try to please, to make my own life easier, so I nodded. He radioed his boys to meet him at the park. They radioed back that they were already there.

'"The party's started," an officer said.'

'This park?'

He nodded.

'We got there in about fifteen minutes, and as we walked through the park, he started asking me questions about my personal life, asking if I had a girlfriend, but I knew he knew – it was all a game to him. I hadn't told anyone I was attracted to men...' He caught the look in her eye. 'Not because I was ashamed, but because I had to protect myself. They treated me like shit with just the possibility of me being different to them – confirming it would have been a death sentence.

'He led me down by the lake, where the public toilets are. That's when I heard them, the officers laughing.

'We turned the corner and I saw them. Two men, stripped naked and lying on their fronts, the officers' torches lighting up their pale backs. They were soaking wet. I thought they had been in the lake at first, held under for a joke, but then I smelt the piss. The officers had urinated on them.

'The man on the left was older. Grey hair. White skin. The one on the right was younger, early twenties maybe, so thin I could see his ribs.

'Officers Watts, Leech and Benson were surrounding the men in a circle and they cheered when they saw Seb and me turn the corner.

'"Found them in the gents," Officer Watts said. "This one on his knees."

'He kicked the man on the right. He didn't make a sound, merely flinched with the impact, exhaled a chestful of breath.

'"You know them, Shane?" Watts asked, laughing when I shook my head. "Well, you'll know them after tonight."

'"You want to be one of the lads, don't you?" Seb asked me, and nudged my shoulder before stepping over one of the men and taking a can of beer from Leech. They all had a wild glint in their eyes, like animals surrounding their prey. I watched Seb chug down the beer, dribbling down his chin. He crushed the can in his hand and launched it at the nearest man's head.

'"So what're we doing with them tonight?" Benson asked.

'Seb began to circle the men, his eyes shimmering with ideas, each darker than the last.

'"If Shane wants to be one of us, I think it should be him who teaches these scum a lesson. Don't you agree?"

'Everyone agreed. Everyone but me.

'"I could write them up," I said. "Public indecency."

'They laughed so hard that tears glistened in their eyes and their faces turned bright red.

'"Fuck, he's such a pussy," Watts said, wiping his eye. "*Write 'em up.*"

'"String 'em up, maybe," Leech said. He was mumbling around a cigarette before lighting it in a cupped hand.

'"Gimme one of those," Seb said. Leech passed him the cigarette and lit another.

'Seb took one drag, knelt to the ground, and picked up the smaller man's head by his hair. He blew the smoke in his face.

'"What should we do with you, huh?"

'"Please. . ." the man said. He didn't have a chance to finish what he planned to say. The moment he opened his mouth, Seb shoved the lit cigarette inside and pounced on the man's back, clamped his hand over his mouth. The man writhed around, screaming behind Seb's hand as the officers laughed and cheered. The older man beside him sobbed into the dirt.

'"No!" I yelled. I couldn't stop myself.

'Seb looked up at me. His lips turned up with a smirk.

'"You're in charge," he said, and released him. He stood and dusted off his hands as his victim spat out the cigarette, followed by a blood-curdling cry. His tongue was black with ash.

'"So if you don't want that, what would you like to do?"

'"Let them go," I said.

'Seb approached me, spun me around by my shoulders, and led me away a few steps. He came in close – so close I could taste the beer on his breath.

'"If you don't do this, they'll do it to you. You want to protect yourself, right?"

'"You wouldn't," I said, but I knew he would. They all would.

'"There's only one way to find out."

'He went to return to them.

'"Wait. What would you have me do?"

'He turned back with a smile.

'"Beat some sense into them, that's all. They'll heal up in time, but they'll know not to come back here again."

'I couldn't do it. I froze on the spot, felt my bladder longing for release. I shook so hard I could feel my cap rattling against the sides of my head.'

Rose watched silently as Shane faltered mid-story, cleared his throat. She couldn't bear to hear of such cruel, senseless violence, but she had to know. She had to know everything.

'Seb's smile fell,' Shane continued. 'He snatched me by the collar and dragged me back to the men, pushed me to my knees.

'"Do it!" he barked. Just the shock of his voice made me piss myself. I started to cry.

'"Fucking pussy," Watts spat.

'"We can sort him out too, then we almost have one each," Leech said.

'"You hear that, Hughes?" Seb asked, leaning down until I felt his words against the side of my face. '"If you don't do this, you'll join them."

'"I can't!"

'"Lads, show Shane what will happen to him if he doesn't."

'Seb dragged me to my feet as the officers rained down on the men. Kicks, punches, spit. I cried until I couldn't see them any more, just hear their cries, the officers' taunts, the sound of thumping fists, bones breaking.

'I would have said and done anything to make it stop.

'"All right! All right!"

'The officers backed away, sharing satisfied smiles, clouds of laughter escaping their lips. Seb pushed me to my knees, above the men.

'The younger of the two was already swelling beyond recognition. The older man coughed up a tooth. Blood was trickling silently from his nose and mouth.

'I looked into the younger man's eyes, and saw the sheer terror of having their secrets exposed and punished for them. Perhaps they had been too scared to live openly, so hid away in the dark, coming together for brief encounters to feed their longing. I couldn't do that sort of thing, but I understood why. People who did that were afraid of being treated just like this.

'"I'm so sorry," I whispered. I watched a tear run down the man's cheek, the slight nod of his head, telling me it was okay.'

Rose couldn't hold it in any more. The sob burst out from her chest. She hid her face until her palms were hot and wet.

'I had to do it,' Shane said, crying too. 'I had to, for them and for me. If I didn't, they might have killed them. I tried. . . I tried to go as light as possible, but when I didn't hit or kick hard enough, a fist would crack against the back of my head.'

'Stop,' Rose begged. 'Please.'

All Rose could think about was Jay, lying naked on his front and being beaten into the earth. Did that happen to him? Had the same officers given him his cuts and bruises, the marks she shouldn't have let her father ignore?

'They goaded me afterwards,' he said glumly. 'Slapped my back and my arse in some sort of sick celebration, fell around laughing when they saw I'd pissed myself. Benson laid a rough kiss on my lips as some sort of sick joke.

'Then Seb led me back to the car, leaving the other officers behind. I never heard what happened to them. I'm not a religious man, but I still pray that they lived. I pray every night.

'When we got back inside the car, Seb turned to me.

'"You know what'll happen if you tell anyone about this, don't you?" he said.

'I couldn't speak. I couldn't even breathe. All I could do was cry silently, breathe in the smell of my own piss and the blood of the men.

'"What happened back there? That's nothing compared to

what'll happen to you if you open your mouth. Understand?"

'I pissed myself again, right there in the car. He nodded and drove us away. We never spoke about it again.

'I stuck it out another six months, so they wouldn't come after me in fear that I would talk. I had panic attacks before every single shift. That was three years ago and I can still smell the blood, feel them beneath my fists. I took this job so I could be closer to them somehow, and protect other men from being treated that way. I lie awake at night, waking at the slightest sound, as if I'm waiting for it to happen again, giving me the chance to do more – protect them more. Fight back.'

'And the officers did this to you? Tonight?'

He nodded.

'Do you think they could have done something to Finn too?'

'I don't know.'

She hated Seb, and these other men she had never met, couldn't even place faces to.

'They won't get away with this, Shane.'

'They already have.'

'No.' She took his hand, watched him flinch with the pain. 'I promise you, they won't get away with this.'

'How are you going to stop them? What could you possibly do?'

'I don't know, but. . . I have to do something.'

'Well, you can't do it alone.'

'But I can't drag anyone else into this. Look what happened to you.'

'Don't you care what happens to *you*?' he asked.

'I don't have anything to lose.'

He took a deep breath.

'I'll speak to Anna, maybe she can help from the inside. Where's my phone?'

'Here,' she said, getting it from the mantle. She had found it by the fireplace, its screen cracked.

He stared at the damage briefly and tapped out a message with his one good hand.

She looked up at the clock on the wall. It was two in the morning. She had been there for hours.

'I'll stay here tonight, so you're not alone.'

'Don't you have a family waiting for you?'

She thought back to how Christian had reacted to her staying the night at her father's house, the post Lily had left on social media.

'It's complicated.'

'Go home,' he said. 'Your life is about to become more complicated than ever. No point making it bad at home too.'

'I'm not sure it can get any worse. And you can't be on your own – what if they come back?'

'They won't,' he said. 'They've made their point. And I won't be here much longer.'

'You're leaving?'

'I've stayed long enough. Almost like I've been punishing myself for what I did to those men. But I can't stay now.'

She took his hand again, rubbed his knuckles with her thumb.

'I'm so sorry,' she said.

'I'm sorry too.'

She got up to leave, but stood in the middle of the room. Her world was different now. After tonight, there was no going back. The moment she stepped out of the cottage, she had a job to do. She had to make them pay.

She leaned down and kissed him on the forehead.

'Goodnight, Shane.'

'Goodnight.'

She left the room and opened the front door, staring out at the park where it had happened. She would never look at it the same way again.

She wasn't just doing it for Finn and Jay any more. She was doing it for all of them.

'Rose,' he called.

She rushed back inside and stood at the threshold of the room.

'Anna's texted back. She's on the night shift.'

'Tell her to meet me at the station. I can be there in thirty minutes if I walk fast. Text me her number.'

She left the cottage and powered up the hill. The night wasn't over yet.

TWENTY-THREE

Her feet were covered in blisters, her toes moist where they'd popped. She had walked miles. She could have caught the night bus or called a taxi, but she wouldn't. Tonight she loathed people for what they were capable of, what they did to each other. She had to be alone.

The police station looked different at night, more menacing, or maybe that was because she knew the truth about the establishment now. The reception was lit but the rest of the windows were blacked out. It was supposed to be a sight that calmed one's senses, make those in the town feel safe in times of terror. But now all she could see was the pain the force had caused, the hate that fuelled their hearts. She would never see an officer in uniform again without remembering Shane's busted lip, cracking as he spoke, or the tears that slipped from between his swollen eyes.

Anna had texted back almost immediately, and planned for them to meet in the alley behind the station. *No one will see us there,* she'd said.

Rose walked around the side of the building and turned down the alley. A single street lamp flickered above her head. She kept on walking until she was in the dark again, lost in the shadows with the overflowing bins, the scurry of a rat or a mouse gnawing through the darkness. A figure emerged from the shadows, her face like that of a skull where the shadows collected in the sockets of her eyes. Anna.

'I can't help you,' she said immediately.

Rose stopped in her tracks.

'It's too dangerous,' Anna continued. 'You don't know what it's like in there. You've got everyone on high alert. If I were caught helping you. . .'

Rose couldn't believe it, the cowardice shivering off the woman. Her eyes were wide like a doe's, shifting from Rose to the mouth of the alley.

'I don't know what it's like? I've just come from Shane's home. Detective Clark sent his officers there. They nearly beat him to death. I've spent the night cleaning his wounds.'

Even in the dark, Rose saw the woman's complexion pale. She looked awful. Her suit was creased. Her hair was a mess. The night made the angles of her face look sharper, inhuman.

'*Officers* attacked him?'

'You sound surprised.'

'Why wouldn't I?'

'Don't you know what goes on in there?'

'I don't *want* to know,' she said. 'I just want to do my job. I have rent to pay. A kid to feed. I can't screw this up.'

'You're a coward.'

Rose went to leave the way she had come, rage swelling in her chest, but a thought made her turn back.

'It's all right for you, isn't it, to look the other way when it doesn't affect you? You say you don't want to know, but it's your *job* to know. You're supposed to protect the people of this town. You're supposed to care.'

A car rushed past. They both turned to see the cop car's red and blue lights pass in a flash.

'You got me into this. You chased me down, dragged Shane's name into it, and now you're turning your back on him. On us. You're just as bad as them.'

Rose turned away, biting her lip to keep her from saying any more.

'Wait.'

Rose stopped.

'The guy you were talking about, from the journal. I looked into it, and there was a report of similar abuse on the system, from about three years ago. I don't know if it's the same guy who harassed Finn, but it's worth a shot. His name is Adam Morant. I remembered his name from years ago. You'll find him in the Lakes.'

'The Lakes,' Rose said. 'As in the mental-health facility?'

'Yes.' Anna stepped closer, her shoes scuffing against stones. 'I asked around. It sounds like he's still there.'

'I'd never get in.'

'I can set it up. But then I'm done.'

She wouldn't thank her – one good deed wasn't enough to make up for turning her back. Rose headed up the alleyway, but stopped with a thought.

'It's funny, isn't it? You pretend not to care, but you still remember that man's name.'

She left Anna there in the dark.

FINN'S JOURNAL

15th February 2018

The police have always instilled fear in me. Whenever I drive past a cop car, my hands tense on the wheel. If I see one in the street, my whole body becomes rigid; I try to prove my innocence in the way I walk, even though I've done nothing wrong. I have never been good around authority figures. It's in my nature to go along with what I'm asked to do. A pushover, my father used to call me. A wet blanket, a pussy who needed to man up. He tried to make a man of me, but all he did was deepen the fear.

So when I was ushered into the interview room inside the police station, I couldn't stop myself from shaking; every muscle in my body was tense. A uniformed officer sat me down, offered me tea, and left. I waited alone, watching the door for a detective to enter the room, to tell me everything was going to be all right.

It wasn't like the films I'd seen; there was no two-way mirror, just a camera blinking in the corner. There was a simple desk, scuffed and scratched with stray swipes of ink, three plastic chairs, and a clock on the wall loudly ticking off the minutes. There was nothing to distract me from the beat of my heart, quickening with every thought, spiking with every new fear. What if they didn't believe me? What if I didn't have enough to give them?

When the door clicked opened, I flinched in my seat. A different uniformed officer entered the room, the first officer trailing behind him with a polystyrene cup of tea in hand. No detective – just uniforms. Both sat on the other side of the desk. I thanked the one who placed the cup before me. The new man, with a black beard trimmed close to his face and small, dark eyes, spoke first.

'Mr Matthews, I'm Sergeant Martin Lycett, and this is my colleague, Officer Mark Byrne. I understand you've been having some trouble with a man called Michael King.'

'Yes. I've brought everything with me. Printouts of the text messages, the call log, and the post he sent to my address.'

I splayed them out on the table in a nervous jumble, edging them towards their side. A sheet slipped to the floor. I reached down to pick it up, but Officer Byrne found it first and added it to the pile. I watched him bang the bottoms of the pages onto the table until they were neatly stacked, and begin to read, his eyes skirting across the words.

'Could you tell us how it all transpired?' Lycett asked.

'Yes. . . well, I'm new in town. I've only been here a few weeks. I bumped into him on my first day at the new job, outside the coffee shop on Queen's Street. I work for the local paper.'

Lycett nodded for me to continue. My throat seemed to swell, as though it refused to let me speak the words of my ordeal. If I said them aloud, it was really happening.

'I was in a rush and bumped into him, spilt coffee down his shirt. As I went to leave, he asked for my number.'

It was small, but impossible not to notice. I was sure the sergeant flinched.

'And is that normal?' he asked. 'For men to ask for your number brazenly like that on the street?'

'Well, I. . . I suppose it's the same as a man asking for a woman's number. I thought no differently about it, in that respect.'

My attention swayed towards Officer Byrne as he took the newspaper clipping from the envelope and fought to hide a smirk.

He thought it was funny.

'And you gave him your number?'

'I. . . well, I was in a rush. I needed to get back to the office, and I felt bad for spilling coffee on him.'

When I said it out loud, it sounded as though I had made it easy for my stalker to get the wrong idea. But I hadn't, I was simply too polite for my own good, said yes when I really wished to say no. But by the look of them, I knew they wouldn't have understood.

'Then what happened?' Lycett asked.

'Later that week, I went for drinks with my new work colleagues, and. . .'

Lycett turned to Byrne.

'Is there a gay bar in town?'

'How would I know?' he replied defensively.

'No, we didn't go to a gay bar. We went to the pub on Linchfield Road. The Fox and Pheasant?'

'Oh, right.'

'He was there, and spoke to me. I'm sure he was alone. I can't remember all of it – I'd had quite a bit to drink – but he ended up walking me home.'

I noticed Lycett arch his eyebrow.

'I didn't want him to, but he made it difficult to say no.'

'I'm surprised,' he said. 'A tall, strapping guy like yourself, I'm sure you could get someone to leave you alone if you wanted to.'

I didn't know how to react. Had they never met a man being stalked before? Or male victims of domestic violence? It was like I was sitting in front of my father.

Man up, you pussy. Be a man.

'Well, we got to my home and he. . .'

I stopped suddenly. If they had struggled with everything I had told and shown them so far, I couldn't help but worry about how they would react when I told them that he kissed me. I laced my fingers together in my lap and clenched as hard as I could. I had to be strong.

'He what?' Lycett asked.

'He kissed me.'

'Right,' he replied, looking away.

Byrne cleared his throat.

'I pulled away and let myself inside. I thought that was the end of it. But the next day I woke up to the messages –' I nodded to the paperwork in Officer Byrne's hands. 'I replied that evening, after all of the calls and messages I'd received that day, and made it clear that I didn't want to pursue a relationship of any kind with him. Then a week later, I spotted him outside my office. I received the newspaper cutting later that evening.'

My eyes flashed to Byrne, the man who thought the disturbing image, my fear, the defiling of my face, were funny.

'He had texted me, asking if I'd liked my post. Then he called me. I asked him what he wanted and he said. . . me. He wants me.'

Lycett nodded. Byrne placed the paperwork down and looked my way.

I had come to the police because I'd thought they would help. I thought they would understand my experiences, and put actions into place to make it stop. But as I sat before them, I felt the need to make them believe me, to talk and talk until the reality of my situation sank in. It wasn't funny – I was terrified.

'I'm being stalked,' I said aloud.

'We will have a word with Mr King and issue a warning. There are some ways around this. From now on you need to ignore all attempts at communication from him: calls, texts, face to face. Keep a diary and record the time and place of every attempt at contact or any sightings of him, noting car registrations if this applies. If you feel it's necessary, there are safety measures you can take. Obviously, make sure your home is secure. You can carry a panic alarm device on your person.'

He turned to his colleague.

'I think we have one. Go and get it, would you?'

Byrne left the room, leaving the door ajar.

'If you receive any further mail from him, please deliver it straight to us, and avoid leaving fingerprints.'

'And this will make him stop? He'll leave me alone?'

'We'll talk to him.'

An awkward silence grew between us as we waited for Officer Byrne to return. I had not even considered that my attraction to men, or my gender, might be an issue. I'd thought they would help, not because of particular factors, but because I was a victim of a crime. But as I sat opposite the police officer, I felt like a joke.

Byrne returned with a small device. He showed me how to use it, and I nodded, my cheeks burning as the lesson went on. They made me feel cowardly. By the glint in Byrne's eye, I could tell he found the whole thing amusing, as if only women had been given the alarms until me. I took it from him and buried it in my pocket.

'We'll be in touch,' Lycett said.

I nodded and rose from my seat, eyeing the paperwork I had brought with me. I had prepared it all with the idea that the police were going to fix everything, that they were going to be on my side, but as I was escorted out of the building, I wondered how long they would spend reading it.

I left feeling defeated, but forced myself to believe in them. It was their job to help me; they couldn't let me down.

I had no idea then how wrong I was.

TWENTY-FOUR

I t was four in the morning by the time Rose got home. She had
crept through the door with her keys in a tight fist to keep them
from jangling, and premeditated each step so the floorboards
wouldn't creek. For the first time, she was disappointed by the
sight of Christian's car in the driveway. She didn't want to have
to justify why she had been out all night. She practically shared
the house with strangers who went in and out as they pleased, but
when it came to her, they held the right to know where she was,
judge her for breaking from the norm.

She sat in her chair and tried to doze, only to give up at dawn,
and read through the journal from front to back, to remind her
of why she was doing this. Jay. Finn. Shane. The two men in the
park. There were so many victims out there, waiting for justice,
and no one but her gave a damn.

It wasn't long before she heard them wake above her head: the
creak of floorboards, the rumble of the hot water in the tank. She
kept to her study as Christian and Lily moved about the kitchen
and raced up and down the stairs, even though her bladder was fit
to burst. Just like Shane's had the night of the attack. She thought
of Detective Clark straddling the young man's back as he rolled
around beneath him, the ember from the cigarette scorching his
gums, ash coating his tongue and teeth.

She had known there was something dangerous about him the moment she met him; it was something in his eyes, a permanent fury flickering like a flame. She wondered if Montgomery knew of the monster that lurked within the man.

When the front door shut and the house rang empty, she stood from her chair and winced. Her feet were raw; blisters had popped between her toes. She hobbled to the door and stepped out into the kitchen, relishing the chill of the tiles beneath her feet.

'Where were you last night?'

'Jesus!' She clapped her hand against her chest.

Christian was sitting at the breakfast bar, his hands clasped on the counter. He was dressed in one of his navy suits, tailored so perfectly to his body that she wondered how he managed to move without thread pulling from the seams. His briefcase was waiting in the hallway beside the front door, the buckle of it gleaming in the morning light. She checked the clock on the wall; if he didn't leave now, he would be late for work. But he continued to sit, waiting for her to answer.

'Do you really think you have the right to ask me that?' She took a glass from the cupboard and went to the sink. 'I never know where you are.'

'I'm worried about you,' he said. 'I heard you come in last night. It was gone four.'

'Don't you stay out all night when it pleases you?'

'You don't have to tell me where you go, just. . .' He slicked back his hair. She noticed how tired he looked around the eyes, the new streaks of grey hair at his temples. He sighed heavily. 'You don't have to tell me anything.'

He got up and headed for the door.

'How's Lily?' The question burst from her. She craved her the way she craved sleep. But seeing her was almost worse. At least from a distance, Rose could pretend her own daughter didn't hate her.

'She's fine,' he said without stopping and snatched up his briefcase from beside the door. He took his keys from the sideboard and shut the door firmly behind him.

She sighed and sat at the breakfast bar where he had been, feeling the warmth of his body on the seat, the closest she had come to touching him for months. She couldn't understand him. Everything he did told her that he couldn't stand the sight of her, a quiet loathing that simmered with every look and word, and yet he had waited for her to emerge from the study to ask where she'd been. A part of her hoped it meant he still cared, that somewhere deep inside, he still had her in his heart. But he seemed to think he had more of a right to know details about her than she did him. Suddenly, she didn't feel like the woman he might love, but property he wanted to keep in his sight.

Her phone vibrated in her pocket.

A text from Anna.

Meeting with Adam Morant at 5pm.

Blunt. Cool. Rose hoped that Anna's conscience kept her awake as insomnia did her. If Anna wouldn't help her, she was aiding Detective Clark, whether she meant to or not. Her silence gave the men their power. All it would take to regain control was a collection of strong voices that refused to be silenced.

But if Anna wouldn't help her, she would do it alone.

ADAM

☾

2nd May 2016

Adam drove along in silence, watching the mirrors for signs of someone tailing him. The road was dark but for the red glare of his rear lights.

But he could feel someone watching him, had done for months.

He was forgetting things at work. Missing appointments. Ignoring calls and texts from friends because each time he heard the phone he thought of him and the panic rose, clamping down on his windpipe.

He turned off the road and down the country lane that cut past the woods to the north of town. He would be home in twenty minutes if he put his foot down.

The road narrowed where the woodland encroached the tarmac. Twigs snapped and popped beneath the wheels. He looked in the rear-view mirror and saw nothing but the shadows of the woods behind him. He tightened his hold on the wheel.

The lights on the dashboard flickered. He put his foot down. The headlights seemed dimmer than before. The car began to slow. He put his foot down again, but the car continued its slow decline.

He just saw the fuel dial on empty before the dashboard went dark and the headlights vanished. The car rolled to a stop in the middle of the lane, swallowed by darkness.

'No, no, no, no, no!'

He turned the key in the ignition. Nothing. Not even a splutter of life from the engine. He tried again, and again, and again, the panic rising until tears scratched at the whites of his eyes.

There was no way the car had run out of fuel. He had filled up the petrol tank on his way to work. He felt the passenger seat in the dark for his bag, whipped out his wallet and phone and used the light on the screen to inspect his receipts. There it was, proof that he wasn't going mad. He had spent £40 on petrol at 8.49 that morning.

It was him. It had to be. Could he have drained the tank? The car park didn't have CCTV. He could have planned this, knowing he would take the shortcut home because he had been following him for months.

It's a trap.

He froze the moment he saw them: two balls of light in the rear-view mirror, growing in size as they neared and lit up the inside of the car.

A car was heading up the lane.

Adam instinctively locked the doors and clenched his eyes shut.

He heard it pull up behind him, its brakes whistling as it stopped.

He had nowhere to hide. He shook in his seat, silent tears slipping down his cheeks.

A door opened and shut.

Footsteps crept up to the driver's side, crunching on nature's debris.

A knock on the window.

Adam opened his eyes, knowing who would be on the other side of the glass. 'Open the door, Adam,' he said.

Adam shook his head roughly. Tears plummeted to his jaw.

He knocked louder. Harder.

'Adam, open the door.'

'Leave me alone!'

He tried the door handle. Adam jolted and held the door and finally looked at him on the other side.

Even in the dark, Adam could see that his face was set with rage: tense jaw, creased brow, eyes that pierced through the glass and into his.

'Please. . . please, just leave me alone.'

He pulled harder on the handle, so hard Adam was sure it would snap clean off.

'Please!'

He covered his face and sobbed into his hands until his palms were wet with tears, warmed by his frantic breaths.

I'm going to die. He's going to kill me here and no one will ever know.

He stayed there, hidden behind his hands, until he finally found the courage to lower them again and look out.

He was gone.

Adam whipped around, looking through each of the windows, both of the windscreens. The other car's door was open on the driver's side. He could hear the distant sound of an alert beeping into the night, but otherwise there was nothing around him but trees, shadows that bled into the darkness.

The window smashed beside him. Glass ricocheted against his face, littered his hair, and hands were on him and dragging him out of the car before he even had the chance to scream. He punched and kicked blind, the struggle echoing between the trees. Glass sliced his back from his shoulders to his waist as he was yanked out of the window and thrown to the ground.

Adam looked up, his desperate breaths expelling in clouds.

He was standing above him, panting too.

A metal tool lay on the ground. Adam lunged for it and swung it with all his might.

The man's kneecap cracked on impact and he fell to his side with a cry, snatching Adam by the shirt before he could make a run for it.

A fist landed in Adam's mouth, again on his cheek. His vision spun. Blood coated his teeth. Hands were pinning him down.

He rose the tool again and swung it through the dark until it met with something hard, the thud of metal against bone. The man fell beside him, spitting something dark onto the road.

Adam scrambled to his feet and ran for the trees, his shirt stuck to his back with blood, flittering where the glass had shredded the fabric. He ran into the shadows, the man's words echoing behind him.

I will find you, Adam. I will find you.

TWENTY-FIVE

The Lakes looked worse than she remembered. The years had been cruel, leaving streaks of mould on the brown bricks, tiles lying askew on the roof.

Every room stretched across one storey so as not to give the patients a platform off which to jump.

She didn't know much about Adam Morant, only what Anna had told her. There was nothing about him online; whatever his story was, it was hidden and hidden well. But if he could tell her anything about Finn's stalker, it was worth pursuing.

She stepped inside and approached the reception desk where a woman sat alone, her lips turned downwards.

'Hi, my name is Rose Shaw. I have a meeting with Adam Morant.'

The woman looked up.

'So you're the mystery guest.'

Rose looked down at the name badge on her pale purple tunic: *Linda*. She forced a smile.

'You with the police?' Linda asked.

'No.'

'He in trouble?'

'No, no. I just want to speak with him.'

'Good luck with that,' she said. 'Hasn't spoken to anyone in a long time. Surprised the police didn't tell you that.'

Would Anna send her to a dead end? She had thought Anna was merely being a coward. She hadn't considered that she was working against her too.

'Nevertheless, I'd like to see him.'

'Wait here,' Linda said. 'I'll buzz his key worker.'

Rose signed in to the visitors' book and walked away from the desk, setting her eyes on the car park through the glass doors, the grey sky reflecting in the windscreens. She could feel the heat of the receptionist's gaze on her back. Perhaps she had recognised her name.

A door buzzed behind her and a young man stepped into the room. He had brown hair shaved closely to his head. His face was unremarkable until he smiled. The teeth weren't straight or gleaming white, but there was a kindness in the way he set his lips.

'Rose?'

'Yes, hi.'

She stepped forward and extended her hand. He shook it softly.

'I'm Adam's key worker, Seth. I'll take you to him.'

'Thanks.'

He held the door for her and waited until she had crossed the threshold before shutting it behind her. They were confined in a small hall between the door to the reception and another leading deeper into the facility. There was barely room for the two of them. The air quickly heated with their breath.

'This is a semi-secure facility,' he said. He tapped a card against an electronic box on the wall. 'A lot of stopping and starting, I'm afraid.'

The door opened, leading to a long, wide corridor with multiple rooms off either side. Seth led her at a relaxed pace, the only sound being the click of their heels on the lino floor. The way he spoke and moved made her think he was a stoner; words drifted from his mouth, his limbs moved glacially. She noticed a hole in the wall, the kind made by the tip of a shoe.

'Are you with the police?' he asked.

'No,' she said.

'We wouldn't usually allow visitors in like this. You must have some pretty high-up friends.'

I wouldn't call her a friend.

She gave him a closed smile.

'Adam is a good guy,' he said, tapping his card to a door on the left, waiting for the buzz before opening it. 'He's been through a lot. He's mostly quiet, keeps to himself.'

They continued through the building, passing through door after door.

'How was he found? Has he ever spoken about what happened?' she asked.

'Adam? No. He hasn't said a word.' He hesitated, as though unsure what he should and shouldn't tell her. 'You're working with the police, right?'

'Kind of,' she lied.

'He was found wandering in the woods, delirious with the cold. They found his car deeper in the woods. Something happened to him out there, but he won't speak of it. When he relapses, he talks of a man hunting him. His relapses are always spawned by "him coming back".'

There was a ring in the air. She had expected many things from her visit, but at no point had she expected silence.

'There aren't many people around.'

'We've got a motivational speaker in the hall tonight, someone who has been through the mental-health treatment experience. It's good to give patients a light at the end of the tunnel.'

He slowed before a set of double doors. 'This is Adam's wing. There's a communal area where you can both sit.'

He opened the doors with a key card and walked into an open-plan living space: a large sitting area with three big sofas and a television, armchairs covered in plastic by the windows that overlooked a small rose garden. A kitchenette hid partially behind a wall on the right. Rose noticed there were no pictures, no rugs or colour, nothing to give the space a personal touch, just a room of furniture echoing their footsteps.

'Wait here,' he said. 'I'll get Adam.'

She watched him head through another set of doors and took one of the armchairs beside the window. The sun was setting, burning the sky. The roses were closing with the coming night. She wondered why the chairs were covered in plastic.

'Rose,' Seth said, returning a few moments later. 'This is Adam.'

She didn't know what she had expected, but it wasn't the man who stood before her. He had the frame of an undernourished teen, far too little fat for a man so tall. He stood with a slight hunch, as if to make himself smaller, curling in on himself, and his skin wasn't pale, but stark grey. His eyes, although a warm emerald, had an emptiness to them. She wondered how much of the man he used to be was still behind those eyes.

'Hello, Adam,' she said softly. 'My name's Rose.'

Seth led him to the armchair opposite hers. He sat down with almost no sound, just the soft ruffle of his clothes against the plastic.

'Do you fancy a cup of tea?' Seth asked him.

Adam didn't say anything, simply set his gaze on the roses.

'I'll make us all some,' he said, and looked at Rose. 'Or we have coffee?'

'Tea is fine. White, no sugar. Thanks.'

'I'll just be a minute,' Seth said, and patted Adam on the shoulder. There was no response.

Seth crossed the room to the kitchenette, unlocking cupboards to retrieve mugs; even the kettle was shut away.

'Adam, I'm a friend of a man called Finn. A woman called Anna from the police station suggested I meet you, as you and Finn have similar stories. Would you mind if I asked you a couple of questions?'

His attention never left the window. The blazoned sky reflected in his eyes.

'Finn is missing,' she said. She looked back towards Seth. He was standing checking his phone as the kettle boiled. 'He has been missing for a while. I'm trying to find him.'

She waited for a flicker of a response in his eyes. Nothing.

'He seemed to be having trouble with a man. A man who treated Finn the way. . . the way your attacker treated you.'

A muscle twitched beside his mouth.

'I. . . I don't know what happened to you. You don't have to tell me anything you don't want to. But I'm trying to find out if the man who hurt Finn might have been the same man who hurt you.'

His eyes darted to hers. His mouth fell slack.

'Is there a possibility that the man who—'

'No. . .' he said. His voice was soft but broken. She wondered how long it had been since he last spoke. 'No. . .'

'No what, Adam? It's not the same man?'

His eyes shifted left to right, shimmering with emerging tears. He murmured so quietly that she couldn't make out the words. His whole body trembled. His lips opened and shut as he tried to speak, strings of saliva connecting his lips.

'I'm sorry, Adam. I didn't want to upset you, I just—'

She heard incessant drips of water, and instinctively looked for rain on the other side of the window. The glass was dry. She looked down. Urine was dripping from his seat. A dark patch was soaked into his crotch. Now she knew why the chairs were covered in plastic.

'Adam, I'm so sorry, I didn't mean to frighten you. I only want to know if it's the same man. If it is, I promise I will find him. I promise—'

'He's back,' Adam whispered. Tears fell, one after the other. Spit bubbled on his lips. He held himself tightly, pressing his fingernails into his arms until the skin turned white. 'He's back!'

'Hey, hey, hey,' Seth said, placing the plastic mugs down on a nearby table before he approached. 'What's up, mate?'

Adam turned and clawed at Seth, pulling his clothes.

'Don't let him get to me. Please. . . please, don't let him get to me!'

'Hey, you're safe here, you know that. Come on, mate.'

Rose flinched as he made the first hit. Adam launched his fist into his own face. Once. Twice. She heard his knuckles clash against his cheekbone, the crack of his own nose. Seth snatched his wrists.

'No, mate, don't do that.'

'He's going to get me!' Adam looked wildly around the room, a small trickle of blood running from his nostril.

'No one's going to—'

'He said he would. He said he'd find me!'

He yanked one wrist free and clawed his face, just enough nail growth to leave jagged scratches in the skin.

'Press the buzzer,' Seth said to her. 'On the wall!'

Rose leapt up and rushed to the button. An alarm sounded over her head.

Adam thrashed in the chair. The tighter Seth held on, the more Adam fought.

'Get off me!' he spat. 'Get off me!' He bared his teeth, attempting to bite himself free, just as the doors burst open. Three people in purple tunics headed towards them, forming a circle around the chair.

'Let's get you to your room, Adam.'

He kicked. He screamed. He spat. The carers jumped on him, holding him so that he couldn't fight back. Adam had gone red in the face, blood slowly leaking from the claw marks in his cheek. His eyes were bulging from their sockets.

Rose pressed herself against the wall and watched them escort him from the room, his feet barely touching the ground. But even when the door closed, she could hear the haunting echo of his screams.

He's going to get me. Please don't let him get me.

TWENTY-SIX

Something fell from Rose's lap with a clatter. She looked around in a daze. Empty seats, windows fogged up with breath. Strip lighting flickered above her head. It had been light when she got on the bus, but now the sky was dark with the night, thick blackness pressing against the windows. The journal was lying open on the floor where it had fallen from her lap.

Ever since getting the journal back from Anna, she had been reluctant to part with it, and carried it around with her like a necessity: phone, keys, wallet, journal. She picked it up and tried to press a bent page flat before stuffing it back into her bag. She looked around. The only people on the bus were the driver and a youth sitting at the back with his hooded head pressed against the window.

She pulled her phone from her bag and checked the time. It was gone ten. She must have been on the bus for hours, travelling round and round the town. So many people could have seen her, slack-jawed against the window. Lily had the right to be ashamed. But at least she had finally slept.

She sat up in her seat and righted her clothes where they had twisted around her and got up from her seat, stumbling from pole to pole towards the driver. She stared out of the windscreen but didn't recognise the road.

'Where are we?' she asked croakily.

'Coming up to the last stop,' he said, his eyes on the road.

'Shit.'

'Didn't want to wake you,' the driver said. 'The shelters get so full now, sometimes this is the only place for you guys to sleep.'

She looked down at herself: the loose hooded sweatshirt, old, faded jeans. Her hair was a mess from her sleep.

'I'm. . . I'm not homeless.'

The driver cleared his throat and pressed his foot a little harder on the accelerator.

She would have been offended, if she didn't fit the look.

She swayed with the motion of the vehicle and thought back to where she had been. Adam Morant. The carers had practically dragged her out of the Lakes. She hadn't meant to push Adam over the edge – she'd simply wanted to find out more about Finn's stalker. If she could, maybe he would lead her to Finn. All she knew now was that the man responsible for Finn's harassment had ruined not just one life, but two.

'Last stop!' the driver shouted, jolting her back to the present.

The bus pulled up on the side of the road with a whine. The doors opened, letting the cold night drift in.

She peered out from the doorway and looked up and down the street. Shops were closed for the night, their steel shutters shimmering under the full moon. There was no one else, nothing but the howl of the wind.

Rose got off the bus and headed down the street, stumbling every few steps. She blinked furiously to wake herself up, breathed in the night. The bus rumbled up the street until the night fell quiet again.

Footsteps echoed behind her. The youth from the back of the bus must be walking the same way.

She instinctively searched her bag for her keys. If she ever found herself out late at night, she slipped one between her fingers like a weapon to make her feel safe. Behind her, the footsteps grew faster. She picked up the pace, her search growing more frantic. A hand landed on her shoulder, hard like a slap.

She turned just in time to see the hooded figure inches from her face and pushed against his chest, missing the kerb. She fell and her head smacked against the tarmac with a crack. Bright sparks of light burst and spun in her vision.

The hooded figure stood over her, panting visible breaths.

It wasn't a hooded youth.

It was the man who had dropped the journal, she was sure of it.

He lunged towards her and searched her body, grabbing at her pockets, her bag that had been caught beneath her in the fall.

He was after the journal.

'Get off me!'

She tried to get away, clawing at his clothes and kicking out her legs. The man pressed his whole bodyweight on top of her, forcing every bit of air from her lungs. When she tried to call for help, the word escaped only as a hoarse whisper.

He pulled her bag from beneath her and the contents burst out across the path, rolled into the gutter. Her keys caught the light of the street lamp. She snatched them, slipped the nearest one between her fingers and launched it into the man's ribs. Spittle landed on her face as he cried out with the impact. He coughed with the second blow and gasped for air, stealing upwards as he struggled for breath.

This was her chance. She slipped one leg from beneath him and launched it into his crotch, pushing herself from under him with the force. He buckled over, holding his ribs with one hand, his crotch in the other, and stumbled to his feet just as she did.

She held her bag to her chest and staggered. Her head was still spinning; she could taste blood in her mouth. They eyed each other through the darkness, breathing in clouds.

'Did you kill him?' she asked.

She tried to see his face behind the shadows of his hood. The bridge of his nose pierced the darkness, but nothing more. He was Caucasian, that she could see.

'Finn Matthews. . .' she said breathlessly. 'Did you kill him?'

The man hesitated for a moment. He lowered his hands, his fingers twitching by his sides, as if preparing to lunge at her again. She clenched her keys in her fist in case he suddenly struck.

'Answer me!'

He stumbled back and ran up the road, limping from the attack, until it was just her in the street, clutching her keys and panting for breath. Only when she was alone did she let the fear rise to the surface. Her fury simmered and tears filled her eyes. She could still feel his weight pressing down on her chest.

Finn's stalker knew who she was.

And he knew how to find her.

☽

Rose reached the driveway just before midnight with her bag still clamped to her chest. The straps had broken in the struggle. She knew that if she looked at the skin on her chest, it would be bruised from where his arm had pinned her down. The back of her head was throbbing with her pulse.

The keys had remained in her fist the entire way home. She was too shaken to get a cab, to face questions from a curious stranger eyeing her quivering body in the rear-view mirror. She had to be alone with her thoughts. She had to let the reality sink in: she had wanted to find the stalker, but in the end, he had found her.

A car she didn't recognise sat in the drive behind Christian's. She stopped in her tracks. Would he invite his mistress to the house? Had she really let things go this far?

Before becoming a mother, she had been so strong, so confident. She had flown all over the world exhibiting her art. She had walked into every room with her head held high. Now she was weak, trampled down by grief and guilt. Somewhere along the line, insomnia had stolen her inner fight, and she had let others chip away at her until she no longer recognised the woman in the mirror, glaring back at her with bloodshot eyes.

She slipped the key in the lock, turning it loudly so those inside could hear, in case they needed to pull their clothes back on, yet slowly enough to brace herself. Bile collected in her throat, which burnt with threatening tears.

She shut the door behind her. The kitchen door was open, lit dimly from the lights underneath the wall cupboards. Silence rang from the room. She listened for life upstairs as she passed, wondering if she would be able to hear the squeak of bed springs from the ground floor. She clasped her stomach with a shaking hand and stepped into the kitchen.

Christian and Heather were sitting at the island unit, watching her in the doorway.

Heather's lips were ajar, eyes wide. She moved on the stool so her knees weren't so close to Christian's.

The shock of seeing her there in her home with her husband was like a swift punch to Rose's gut. Christian didn't look embarrassed or ashamed, and she hated him for it. All she saw was the familiar pity in his eyes. She bit the inside of her lip to fight the urge to cry.

'Are you okay?' he asked.

'I'm fine,' she said, her chest tight. The words barely escaped her lips.

'Hi, Rose,' Heather said.

Rose shot her a look. Heather looked down at her lap.

She had to get out of there before she was sick. Just seeing them together made her stomach twist, her throat close up.

'I'll leave you to it,' she said, and headed for her study.

'Rose, wait,' Christian said, but she couldn't. The tears had already started to fall. She shut the study door behind her and clapped her hand over her mouth as the pain erupted, then slid down the back of the door, sobbing into her hand.

Christian and Heather. Her husband and her best friend. Not only had she lost her daughters, the love of her life, her best friend, but now she was made to watch as they continued to exist, to love, without her.

She lay down on the floor with her knees pressed against her chest and let the tears soak into the carpet.

TWENTY-SEVEN

Rose paced outside the gun range, limping slightly from the night before. But she had no room to think of the man in the street, the way his hands had searched her up and down.

The two people she trusted the most had betrayed her in the worst possible way. She had lost them both a long time ago, but seeing them together had been like the final, fatal severing. She hadn't just lost her husband, but her best friend too. Even though she had woken that morning with grazes and a smarting hip, it was the betrayal that hurt the most. She wondered what else happened in her absence, as she slipped her wedding ring off her finger and into her pocket.

'I didn't think I'd hear from you again,' Rob said through a smile as he opened the door.

'Sorry, I have a lot going on. It's not you, it's—'

'Me?' he said through a grin.

She couldn't help but smile back.

'Except it's not a lie.'

'I believe you. Come on in.'

She rubbed her arms to rid herself of the cold clinging on to her from the outside.

'You fancy a coffee or anything?'

'Please.'

'This way.'

He led her past the door down to the basement and into a kitchenette. She stood in the doorway, watching him move.

'You're here a lot,' she said. 'Do you live here or something? Sleep amongst all your guns?'

'Something like that,' he said as he poured coffee from the pot. 'Milk, sugar?'

She shook her head and looked at the floor.

'Sorry, I've never been good at jokes.'

He handed her a mug and gave her a kind smile.

'I'm finalising my divorce. The rent was up on the flat I'd moved into when my ex and I separated. Thought I'd save some money and crash here until the house is split between us.'

'How long were you married for?'

'Nine years. Two kids. You?'

This was it: the moment the flirting stopped, and any opportunity of going further was crushed.

'It's complicated.'

'I saw your wedding ring last time.'

She could almost feel it burning a hole through her jeans.

'He's seeing someone else,' she blurted out. 'My best friend, in fact. Something happened four years ago, and we've been effectively separated ever since, but under the same roof. We're married on paper. In reality we're. . .' She thought of the way he avoided her, the contempt she saw every time they met each other's gaze. 'Strangers.'

'I'm sorry about your best friend,' he said.

'Thanks.'

'Want to blow holes in shit, and pretend they're our exes?'

She laughed, a real laugh with a smile that made her cheeks ache.

'Yes. Let's blow holes in shit.'

He led the way down to the basement and dressed her in the safety gear before himself. She watched his hands move, wondering what they would feel like on her body: warm, strong, tender.

Stop.

He picked a gun for her and one for himself, going through the motions with her until it had sunk in enough for her to pull the trigger. She had her own booth this time, directly beside his. When he raised his gun, she did the same. He winked at her before turning his sights on the target.

'Fuck you, Erika!' he bellowed, and pulled the trigger. The paper-head ripped open in strips.

'What's your husband's name?' he asked breathlessly.

'Christian,' she said.

'Fuck you, Christian!'

He pulled the trigger again, blasting the target through the heart.

She jolted with each of the blows, adrenaline exploding behind her ribs.

'Your turn.'

She focused on her target, breathed a laugh.

This is crazy.

This is weird.

This is fun.

'Fuck you, Christian!'

She pulled the trigger, jolting back with the force. She missed the target by an inch.

'FUCK YOU, CHRISTIAN!'

She shot again. This time, she ripped his head clean off.

When she saw it she laughed, the exhilarating hysteria clouding her mind again.

'What's your best friend's name?' he asked, prompting her.

'Fuck you, Heather!'

Bang.

Reloaded.

Bang.

Bang.

Her whole body was vibrating. The rush was like a drug. She didn't want more: she needed it, craved it.

'Nice,' he said.

She looked at him and took in his body, his smile, and moved without thinking. She put down her gun and marched to him, throwing her arms around his neck, pressing her lips against his, tender at first, until their hunger grew and each caress became a desperate grab.

In the basement, she wasn't the mother who'd killed her child, but the woman who was desired, who could do anything she wanted. For the first time in four years, she left her grief at the door.

(

Rose lay with her head on Rob's chest, listening to the sound of his heart, and closed her eyes. He had fallen asleep with his arms around her, and it was the safest she had felt in years. She didn't want the life that was waiting for her outside the lodge; she wanted to stay here in his arms, where the past couldn't reach her.

A heavy knocking sounded from the front door, slicing through the silence. She jolted. Rob stirred beneath her.

'Someone's at the door,' she whispered.

'Shit, what time is it?'

'I don't know.'

He looked at her through a sleepy smile. She kissed his lips without thinking, as if they had been hers to kiss for ever.

The knocking persisted.

'Christ, I'd better answer it.'

They got up and dressed, laughing as they hobbled and lost their footing. Something strange was happening in her chest. It was warm, light. 'You can stay here,' he said. 'If it's regulars, I only have to let them in – they do the rest.'

'I should go,' she said, taming her hair with her fingers.

He came to her and kissed her again, holding her body against his. She breathed in his scent: aftershave, sweat, the lingering scent of sex.

It had been four years since she had been touched, and each time he put his hands on her, she wanted to keep them there, hold them down with her own.

'Are you going to pick up the phone next time I call?' he said.

'Yes,' she said.

'If it's going too fast, tell me, and we'll slow it right down. Just tell me what you want, and I'll do it.'

Her heart ached.

Shit.

'The door,' she said, when he tried to pull her back.

He kissed her one last time, tender but quick, and led the way to the door.

A group of men were waiting outside, jeered when they saw him approach. When she recognised one of the faces, she stopped dead.

Detective Seb Clark.

She scanned the other faces.

They were all policemen.

When he opened the door, she watched them hug him the way men often did: hardly touching, slapping each other on the back, more like an assault than a greeting. Just seeing Rob with them made her recoil.

When Seb saw her, he smirked.

As the other men greeted Rob, Rose and Seb stared silently at each other across the room.

'Good to see you're getting some, Rob,' Seb said, and clapped him on the back. 'Although I'm sad to see your standards have slipped since you split with Erika.'

Rose strode for the door, slamming her shoulder against him to clear the way, and shot out onto the drive.

'Rose!' Rob called after her.

She picked up the pace, but he was faster.

'I'm so sorry, I don't know why he would say something like that.'

'I need to go, I'm sorry.'

'Rose, I–'

Seb called his name. Rose picked up speed and turned right onto the road.

Just because Rob is friends with them doesn't mean he's one of them. It doesn't make him a monster by association.

But already she was thinking of him differently, walking faster to put further distance between them.

She knew what it had been now, that warm, light feeling in her chest: happiness. It had been so long that she had forgotten how it felt, and as the icy cold sadness crept in again, she remembered it, mourned it.

She walked through the dark, and thoughts of the night before crept in.

The man from the bus had wanted the journal, and had been willing to hurt her to get it. He knew who she was and seemingly found her with ease. Did he know where she lived? If he did, she wasn't just putting herself in danger, but her family too. In a single moment, the idea of unearthing the truth of what happened to Finn Matthews seemed too daunting, too much of a feat for just one person. Shane was leaving. Anna refused to help. The police were working against her, and the man responsible was closing in. Every person she went to for help had turned their backs.

Her mobile vibrated in her pocket.

She had been with Rob all day and hadn't even thought to check it.

Missed calls.

Text messages.

Emails.

Social media notifications.

The newspaper ad had been published.

Her heart beat faster. She scrolled through the list of unsaved numbers, opened message after message.

Finn is not the only one.

My son went missing.

The police wouldn't help us.

Rose lowered the phone, stopped on the dark lane.

Finn wasn't the only one.

The phone vibrated again. It was a call from an unsaved number.

'Hello?' Her voice was strained. Fear had clamped down on her neck.

'Hello, I, erm. . . I found your ad in the paper, about the missing man.'

Pain reverberated from the woman's voice. It was so distinguishable, as though grief lined the vocal cords, hardened the skin of her throat.

'My son,' she said. 'He was murdered eight years ago, and the police can't tell me why.'

Rose took a breath to speak.

'But there's more,' the woman said. 'There are more of us. Families who have lost our loved ones without explanation. We want to meet you.'

The words caught in her throat. She bit down on her lip. This was too much.

'Please,' the woman said. 'We've had so many years without answers. It's given us hope to know that someone out there cares, that we're not alone –' she took a rattling breath on the other side of the phone – 'and that our loved ones aren't alone in this either, that there are more waiting to be found, stories that need to be heard. Please.'

Rose stared out into the dark. Her whole world had changed the moment the car burst through the barrier, and only now, looking into Finn's disappearance, did she feel alive again. Christian had moved on. Lily had grown up. Rose might not be able to paint for a living any more, or sleep through the night, but she could do this. It gave her heart a reason to keep beating. Doing something good eased the guilt of doing the unimaginable. If the missing men were connected, the families could have information to help solve Finn's disappearance, and in the hunt for justice, she might be able to help them get answers too.

She took a deep breath, closed her eyes. Once she said the words, there would be no going back. When her eyes opened, her decision was sealed.

'Where would you like to meet?'

FINN'S JOURNAL

18th February 2018

Three days had passed since giving my official statement at the police station, and for the first time in weeks, I woke with a sense of peace. My chest was no longer lumbered with the weight of fear; I breathed deeply and clearly. My first thought wasn't of him.

When I rolled over and checked my phone, it wasn't to check if there were any messages from him, or a reel of missed phone calls and voicemail messages clogging the inbox to the brim, but simply to check the time.

But without fear came the realisation of another feeling: loneliness. I had been in Rearwood for almost a month, and spent the majority of my time in the office, even the weekends, so as not to sit inside my apartment waiting for Monday. I could join a book club, or sign up to an app to meet people in the area, maybe even get a cat, but each time I considered attempting to branch out, I would push the thought away. It was safer not to let people in.

I got out of bed and drew back the curtains.

It was him.

He was standing on the other side of the street, leaning against a lamp post. It wasn't like before, when he attempted to fit into the crowd by checking his phone, diverting his attention up and down the street. This time, his eyes were set firmly on the window, and I was sure, looking directly into mine.

I clambered over the bed and snatched my phone from the bedside table. The pressure was back on my chest. I dialled 999 and followed the steps, refusing to take my eyes off him in case he left.

It wasn't a coincidence. Not like before, when he could have been waiting for someone, or about to head into the office. He was standing directly outside my house.

He was there for me.

'999. What is your emergency?'

'My stalker is standing outside my house. I reported him to the police just a few days ago. They said they were going to talk to him, they said—'

'Okay, try to slow down. I'm here to help. Are you alone?'

'Yes.'

'And is your home secure?'

I strode across the apartment and propped a chair beneath the door handle.

'Yes, it's secure.'

'Okay, I'm going to need some details from you, and then we will send someone to take a look.'

I gave her all the details she needed, all the while peeping through the blinds in the living room, watching as he eyed every window, smoked a cigarette to the filter and immediately lit another, his attention never wavering from the front of the building.

'How long will you be?' I asked.

'Officers will be with you as soon as possible.'

It took the police car two hours to arrive.

I spent the time standing at the window, refusing to take my eyes off him, watching his eyes flit from window to window, crossing one leg, then switching it to the other. I called my landlord to chase the repair of my door, phoned the office and told them I would be running late. But after two hours of standing by the window, I needed to use the toilet, couldn't hold it any longer. When I rushed back to the window, he was gone. Just when the police car pulled into view.

As the officers got out of the car and walked up the stone steps towards the door, I realised I wasn't prepared for them at all: I was still in my underwear, my teeth unclean, my hair a wild mess, but I didn't give a damn. I could barely think of anything else but my fury. I wrapped myself in my dressing gown and rushed back towards the front door.

I removed the chair from beneath the handle and strode down to the main front door of the building, swung it open before they even had a chance to press the buzzer.

'Where the hell were you?'

It wasn't the officers that I had met at the station, but two new faces. They removed their hats, almost in sync. One was a woman with warm, ebony skin and almond-shaped eyes. The other was a man, with pale skin and freckles, and hair dampened by sweat. The woman spoke first.

'Mr Matthews? I'm PS Angela Croft, and this is my colleague, PC Alan Spelling.'

'We didn't see the man you described, Mr Matthews,' PC Spelling said.

'Of course you didn't! You're two hours late. He left before you arrived.'

'Can we come inside? We'll need to take a statement.'

'Will you document that you were two hours late?'

'We're sorry for the delay,' Croft said. Her colleague seemed aloof, almost as though I was taking up his time. 'But we'd like to make a statement to document what's happened here today.'

I headed back towards the flat and held the door open for them, waiting for them to file in before shutting it behind them.

They stood awkwardly in the living room, perhaps waiting for an invitation to sit down or to have a cup of tea. I would offer them neither. I crossed my arms across my chest, and PS Croft cleared her throat.

'First things first,' she said. 'I've spoken to the officers who took your initial statement, and I can confirm they have spoken with Michael King.'

'Well, clearly it didn't work. He was stood outside my house for hours.'

She continued, undeterred by my tone. 'When questioned, Michael King not only denied harassing you, but stated he had never even met you.'

'That's. . . that's bull.'

'Do you have any witnesses who will be able to confirm your story?' Spelling asked.

'It's not a story, it's fact. Michael King is harassing me.'

'Do you have any witnesses?' she repeated.

'And you won't believe me if I don't?'

'It would make it easier for us to prove he's lying.'

Or me, I thought. I focused on the memory of each time I had encountered him, and whether anyone could possibly prove it had occurred. But I was new in town, I didn't have any family or friends to tell. I was on my own. Perhaps that's why he pursued me, because I was alone with no one to turn to.

'There could be CCTV footage,' I said finally. 'Outside the café, or perhaps the route to my house, or outside my office building.'

'We can look into it,' she said, and wrote something down on a small pad.

Spelling took the statement while Croft asked the questions. As I answered, I watched the clock tick off all the seconds I was away from my desk. I still needed to shower and dress, walk to work quickly if I wanted to get there by noon. I should have asked to work from home that morning, but I couldn't have taken my eyes off him for a second.

By the time the questioning ended, my anger had dropped to a simmer, but I still couldn't bring myself to act with kindness towards either of the officers.

My stalker had pretended not to know me, and without proof, without further harassment confirmed by a witness or CCTV, the police would believe him.

TWENTY-EIGHT

Finn smiled up at her from the back of the newspaper and followed her eyes as she adjusted the pages in her grasp. It was the same photo she had discovered in the library, but blown up ten times the size. So many people in the town would be looking into his eyes, admiring his smile, reading the headline that would be impossible to miss. She read the ad over, her heart beating quickly in her chest.

WHAT HAPPENED TO FINN?
Finn Matthews disappeared on 19th April 2018. The police have done nothing because he is attracted to men. If you have seen him, or have any information about his where-abouts, or know anything that might help, please come forward. You can do so anonymously. Help us find Finn.

The ad was hard to miss. The words practically screamed off the page. Finn had eyes that caught one's attention, a smile that demanded a second look. Not only would people in the town learn of his disappearance, but she was sure the person responsible would be looking at it too.

Rose shoved the paper back in her bag and paced on the street corner, lighting her third cigarette in a row.

She stared her own guilt in the face every single day, but to encounter that of others, of the families of the victims, would be something else entirely. She was out of her depth. Somehow, she had stumbled into something that was far too big for one person to deal with alone. But there was no one who she could turn to for help. No one, she thought, except her father.

Letting him back into her life after everything he had done felt like a betrayal to Jay and their mother. But she had thought on it all night, and knew she would have to enlist his help. Not for herself, but for Finn. For all of them.

She took her last drag on the cigarette and dropped it down the drain. The street was peaceful. Detached homes lined each side of the road with mature, manicured gardens, cars sparkling clean in the driveways. She walked up the street and stopped outside house number twenty-two.

This was the home of Lucy Nightingale, the mother of a murdered man. Before the call, Rose had wanted to believe there was a chance that Finn was alive, that he was hiding away somewhere, too frightened to show his face in case he was found. But the moment she heard the word 'murder', she couldn't help but consider the worst: she wasn't searching for Finn's whereabouts, she was trying to find a dead man.

Multiple cars were parked in the drive, different models, ages and price tags; different lives brought together by the same pain.

The house looked neat – too neat. Every shrub had been symmetrically clipped, the grass was so short that it was barely an inch from the mud. There wasn't a single weed or blemish. Rose imagined Lucy there, day after day, snipping and pruning and mowing to keep herself from stopping, from allowing thoughts of her son to trickle in. Even though she had never met the woman, just seeing her home made her feel akin to her.

She took a deep breath and walked to the door, knocked twice. She hid her shaking hand in her pocket and looked down at herself. After being mistaken for a homeless woman, she was set on making a good impression: a silk blouse, dark blue jeans that hugged her legs, heels she hadn't worn in years. The make-up on her face felt too thick, as though she had aged herself by ten years. She was considering wiping off the lipstick when a figure emerged in the hall, swimming behind the frosted glass in the front door. When the door opened, a sweet, floral scent filled her nostrils.

'Rose?' the woman said.

She was tall and slim, almost too slim. Her chestnut-brown hair was long but thin, and her face was pretty, though there was a hollowness to her eyes.

'Yes. Lucy?'

She nodded and stepped aside. 'Please, come in.'

Rose stepped inside. The carpet was a spotless cream, almost white. She immediately slipped out of her shoes.

'Thank you for coming to see us,' Lucy said. It was only then, when Rose heard the shake in her voice, that she realised Lucy was as nervous as she was. 'This way.'

Rose followed her down the hall, eyeing the family portraits on the wall, how they went from a family of four to a family of three. A tall, handsome man vanished from the photos. He had warm brown hair and his mother's eyes. He was tall, towering over the rest of the family, with a smile that would have made Rose weak in the knees when she was his age.

'My son,' Lucy said with a pained smile. 'Phillip.'

'Handsome man,' Rose said.

'Yes, he was.'

Lucy gave her another forced smile and stepped through a doorway off the hall. Rose followed and stopped on the threshold.

A roomful of people stared back at her. Three men and five women with sullen faces and bags beneath their eyes, lips downturned even when they attempted to smile.

The room was a good size, but seemed small with all of the visitors crammed inside. Two armchairs were placed beside the brick chimneybreast; a sofa in the bay window, another against the wall, each space taken by a grieving soul.

A woman stood from one of the armchairs beside the fireplace. She wore dark green trousers and flat pumps, a white blouse and floral cardigan. She looked to be in her sixties, with hair left to whiten and cut above the neck, but her skin seemed to glow, and her eyes were alive; she looked the healthiest there. Just the sight of her gave Rose hope: it was possible to survive grief, at least on the surface.

'Rose,' the woman said with a kind, closed smile. 'I'm Annette.'

'Hi, Annette.'

'Can I get you a drink?' Lucy asked. She signalled to the tray on the coffee table with an open palm: a pot of tea and cafetière of coffee; sugar cubes, milk and cream, a plate of biscuits left untouched.

'Black coffee would be lovely,' she said.

'Take a seat,' Lucy said and tapped a man on the shoulder where he sat in one of the armchairs. He stood nervously and signalled for Rose to sit.

'Thank you.'

Rose sat down in the chair and wiped her moist palms on her jeans. Everyone was looking at her, taking in her grief just as she had theirs. Lucy took her time to prepare the coffee, as if to put off the subject that awaited them. Silence rang behind her movements, the occasional clearing of someone's throat, shuffling in chairs.

'Thank you,' Rose said as she took the coffee cup. It shook against the saucer.

'There's no easy way to get into this,' Annette said as Lucy sat on the arm of the sofa. 'So I guess we'll jump right to it. All of us have had someone we love either go missing or die. We believe the same person is responsible.'

A woman from the sofa in the bay window snatched a tissue from the coffee table, dabbed the corners of her eyes. No matter how many years passed, the grief was always there, so close to the surface.

'And we believe the person responsible for the deaths and disappearances of our sons, our nephews and grandchildren, is the same man who is behind Finn's disappearance.'

'What makes you think that?' Rose asked.

Annette took out an envelope from her bag and handed it to her.

'Here.'

Rose took the envelope, opened the flap with shaking fingers. They watched her every movement. The air was alive with tension, itching at her skin and eyes.

She pulled out a collection of photos. A young man stared up at her.

'These are our loved ones,' Annette said, as Rose looked through them, eyeing each man.

They were a unique mixture of men: they varied in age and height; dark hair, blonde hair, red hair, eyes of emerald, blue, to the darkest brown. There would only be one factor that could possibly connect them all.

'Were they all attracted to men?'

'Yes.'

'I. . .' Rose looked at each of them and slipped the photos back in the envelope. 'I don't know what to say. I'm not sure what I can do to help.'

'You're looking into the disappearance of Finn Matthews, and we want to help in any way we can. If you find something, it could help us too.'

'We aren't expecting you to solve this,' a man said, the one whose seat she had claimed. 'But if there's a chance you might, any chance at all, we want to help.'

'Perhaps we should introduce ourselves,' Annette said. 'And those we lost.'

She stood up and took the envelope from Rose, and passed out the photos. Some shared a picture, others sat alone. Rose wondered how many families had broken from the grief.

'I'm Annette,' she said. 'And this is my grandson, Zach.' She held the photo so the young man's eyes were another pair searing into Rose. Fair hair, blue eyes, young, plump skin. He couldn't have been more than eighteen. 'The police decided he killed himself by throwing himself from the Rearwood bridge. I believe he was killed before he hit the water.'

'We're Edward and Meredith,' the man said from the sofa in the bay window, beside the woman who was back dabbing away tears. 'This is our son, Jamie. He has been missing for ten years.'

Jamie had dark brown hair, hazel eyes, a boyish body not yet filled out.

'Phillip,' Lucy said, the photo trembling in her grasp. The woman beside her patted Lucy's thigh. She was older, perhaps her mother, an aunt. 'Found dead in the woods, not far from the riverbank. The police said it was suicide.'

'It wasn't,' the woman beside her said.

A man cleared his throat from the other end of the sofa; a

younger woman who had his eyes sat on the arm. 'I'm Andrew. My son Johnny has been missing for fourteen years.'

Johnny had fair hair. He was young, but his eyes were old; she wondered what he had seen.

Rose looked at each of the four men, staring out at her from their loved ones' grasps. Zach, Jamie, Phillip, Johnny. With Finn and Adam, she was dealing with six potential victims now. Two dead, three missing, one driven mad and locked away. And she'd only signed up for one.

Lucy crossed the room and took a pile of folders from the top of the sideboard.

'These are the police reports,' she said, handing them to her. 'We made copies, so these are yours to keep.'

Rose took the files, felt the weight of them in her lap, the crushing responsibility.

'What we'd really like to know is,' Annette said, 'why are you doing this? Did you know Finn?'

'I lost my brother when I was young. He was harassed and abused for being. . . who he was. I couldn't help him, but I can help Finn. I found out about him when I found a journal. Finn's journal. He wrote of a stalker. The police wouldn't help, so I'm looking into it alone.'

'The police are useless,' Andrew said. He was dangerously thin. Days' worth of stubble coated his cheeks and neck. 'Couldn't give a toss about us.'

Rose thought to tell them that there was a lot more to the police than just ignorance, but held back. They needed all the hope they could get.

'So. . .' Annette said, demanding the attention of the room again. Everyone seemed to revolve around her word. 'Will you help us?'

Rose looked at each of them, witnessing their hope, their pain. She looked down at the files, the men in her lap. She scanned the room and saw their faith, a way she hadn't been looked at in a long time.

'Yes,' she said. 'Yes. I will help you.'

TWENTY-NINE

Rose stopped outside Finn's old apartment building in the same spot she imagined his stalker standing, watching for him at the windows, hour after hour.

The road itself was quaint for this part of town. The old street was lined with trees shedding gold and copper leaves, cars parked along either side of the pavement with permits stuck to the windscreens. The building was made up of bricks chipped from years of British winters, sash windows that looked old enough to let in a draught when the wind blew. Finn's apartment was on the first floor, comprised of two windows facing the street. From his writings in the journal, she felt she knew the place already; she could imagine the worn sofa he sat on as he bit his nails to the quick; the kitchen used less and less as fear ate away at his hunger; the bedroom where he tossed and turned in bed, his mind filled with nightmares, spawned by a man who stood exactly where she was.

Finn had made it so easy for her. He had described his walk to work; all she had to do was retrace his steps from his office. The police were wrong; he was clearly a man who wanted to be found.

When she had left Lucy's home that morning, she had waited until the turn in the road before bursting into tears. There were finally others who believed there was more to Finn's disappearance. There had been moments when she had doubted herself, wondered if she was going mad, but to look into their eyes and have their support gave her the confidence to continue. The purpose of the ad had been to enlist help, and now she had it.

On the corner of Lucy Nightingale's street, Rose had skimmed through the journal for the name of Finn's landlord. When she had searched for his contact details online, she discovered that Finn's old apartment was up for rent and available to view. The landlord had answered on the third ring, believed her when she enquired after the flat in the hope of viewing it, and agreed to meet her there at one.

She crossed the street and stood before the steps. This was where they had stopped, the night the stalker walked Finn home and forced a kiss on his lips. She looked up at the door and imagined Finn fighting his key into the lock, feeling the heat of the man's glare on his back. She took to the steps.

Buzzers lined a panel beside the door, with old names of tenants crossed out or stickers peeling away. Finn's was still there, fresher and bolder than the rest.

The pace of her heart quickened, beating in her ears. She licked her drying lips and pressed the buzzer for Finn's apartment.

'Hi, it's Rose Shaw, enquiring after the apartment,' she said when the landlord answered.

'I'll be right down.'

She took a step back, smoothing down her hair and clothes.

The door opened with a creak. A man stood in the doorway; his skin was too tanned, weathered like leather. She forced a smile.

'Nice to meet you,' he said. 'I'm Lee.'

His teeth looked as though they were rotting in his mouth, stained from nicotine. She shook his hand and almost flinched at the roughness of his palms. His finger had grown too big for his wedding ring.

'Come in,' he said.

The hall was almost exactly how she had pictured it. Pigeonholes on the left wall filled with post, off-white walls scuffed with dark scratches and chips in the paint. Her shoes stuck to the floor with each step. She scanned the pigeon holes for Finn's name and found it had been replaced with another, presumably the name of the tenant who had rented the apartment after him. Finn had lived and breathed in this space, stood in the same spot, yet his existence had been covered up as though he had never been there at all.

'The apartment is on the first floor,' he said, heading up the stairs. 'Great natural light.'

She took to the stairs behind him, followed close to his heels until they stopped before the door to the apartment. She imagined all of the nights Finn had spent behind the door that refused to lock when he needed it to most; the fear seemed to have bled into the wood of it, as though if she were to touch its surface, she would feel his pulse, his pain, beating beneath.

Lee took a ring of keys from his pocket and opened the door.

The flat was brighter than she had imagined, but as she stepped into the room, she smelt the fresh paint, felt the newly laid carpet beneath her feet. The landlord had tried to make the place like new, forgetting the past, forgetting Finn, but he was still there, claiming the air of the place.

'Great space,' he said. 'One bed, one bath, large open-plan living space as you can see. The windows, they let in such good light through the morning to afternoon, and—'

'I'm not here about the apartment.'

The smile dropped from his face.

'I'm here about Finn Matthews.'

He crossed his arms.

'You could have told me that from the beginning.'

'Would you have seen me if I had?'

He looked back to the open door, as if he was about to ask her to leave.

'Finn is missing. I'm trying to find him. I was hoping you knew of a forwarding address, so I can confirm he's all right.'

'Wouldn't give it to you even if I had,' he said. 'I respect people's privacy.'

Not enough to give them a working lock on their door, she thought.

'So you don't have a forwarding address?'

'No. He up and left overnight. Didn't even take half his stuff. I'm holding on to it for another month before I take it to the tip. Spoke to the police about it, they said I've hung on to it long enough.'

'You have his things? Why would he leave belongings behind?'

'How should I know? He was trouble from the beginning. I should just chuck the lot now. No sign he's coming back for it. And after the break-in, I should try and find him myself, charge him for the damage.'

'What break-in?' she asked.

'I've got some garages in town I keep for storage; stuff for decorating, old furniture I use to furnish empty homes I'm trying to flog. I kept his stuff in one of the garages and it was broken into. Someone hacked the lock clean off.'

'Was. . . was anything stolen?'

'I didn't have an inventory of his shit, love,' he said, huffing. 'Nothing that I could see.'

'When was this? The break-in?'

'Couple of weeks ago.'

She acquired the journal a couple of weeks ago.

'What night?'

'A Thursday, I think.'

270

The night she had bumped into the man was the night the garage was broken into. Was that why the man had been running – running from the break-in? She knew now that it couldn't have been Finn she bumped into. All he would have had to do was call the landlord and ask for his belongings back. It hadn't been him that night – it had been his tormentor.

'Finn Matthews was nothing but hassle. His buzzer would sound throughout the night: eleven p.m., one a.m., three. Shouting from his apartment in the middle of the night. The police always pulling up outside. He upset my other tenants, caused a leak and did things in the flat that I would've kicked him out for, had he not left on his own merit. I don't know where he is, but good riddance to him.'

Rose looked around the apartment one last time. Even with the fresh paint and the lack of furniture, she could feel him there, as though it was the sound of his heart beating in her ears rather than her own.

'He was in trouble and needed help,' she said. 'And you turned your back. Frankly, you and every person in this building should be ashamed of yourselves.'

'Out,' he said firmly, pointing towards the door.

She headed back down the stairs, feeling the heat of Lee's breath on the nape of her neck. He shot forwards for the door, opened it quickly to snatch back control, and slammed it behind her the second she was out on the steps.

The man had stolen the journal; he must have known what lay inside and tried to cover his tracks. But the only way he could have known about the journal was if someone had told him. . . if Finn had told him. Which meant the man knew where he was.

She walked down the steps and onto the street, a smile creeping across her face. She was getting closer.

Her phone vibrated in her pocket and broke her from her thoughts. She rummaged in her pocket, only remembering how tired she was when she felt the tug of her muscles, the start of a headache pulsing at her temples. Investigating the disappearance gave her the best distraction; she wasn't just helping Finn – he was helping her, too.

She glared down at the screen. A text from Christian.

Get home as soon as you can. The police are here. They're asking for you.

THIRTY

C

Rose turned onto the driveway and saw the police car stationed on the gravel. She had thought of possible reasons they had for coming to her home without warning. Maybe they had decided to look into Finn's case. Maybe they had been contacted with a lead after her advertisement in the newspaper. But in her gut she knew: they weren't there to help her, they were there to silence her. Shane had tried to help and had been beaten to a pulp. She wondered what they had in store for her.

Her phone vibrated again. Rob had been messaging her the whole way home, asking if she was okay, if he had moved too quickly, acknowledging that she appeared uncomfortable when she left. She couldn't see him again. Not if he was one of them.

She walked up the driveway to the door, rummaging through her bag for her keys, and stopped when the door opened.

Christian stood in the doorway.

'They're in the kitchen,' he said, his tone flat. But it wasn't his voice that showed her his fury; it was his eyes.

He turned and headed back down the hall.

Rose stepped inside and shut the door behind her. The air of the house felt different; she could almost taste the testosterone in the air.

She walked down the hall to the kitchen. Christian was standing in the corner with his arms crossed tightly across his chest, his brow furrowed. The officers stood at the breakfast bar.

They were the same officers from the gun range.

'Mrs Shaw?'

'Yes.'

'I'm Police Constable Leech, and this is my colleague, Constable Watts.'

She immediately saw flashes of the naked men on the ground, glistening with the urine from the men who stood in her kitchen.

'Fucking pussy,' Watts spat.

'We can sort him out too, then we almost have one each,' Leech said.

PC Leech was tall with broad shoulders, thick sideburns creeping from beneath his hat. His eyes were blue, cold.

PC Watts was smaller in height, but wider in girth, muscle bulging from beneath his uniform, his neck as thick as her thigh.

Both of them wore wedding rings. She couldn't fathom the idea of people loving them, promising their lives to them.

'You went to visit Adam Morant, didn't you?' Watts asked.

'Who's that?' Christian asked.

'Why do you want to know?' she asked.

They all stood eyeing each other, each waiting for one another to crumble and answer first.

'He's dead,' Leech said finally. 'Hung himself in his room the same night you went to visit him.'

Her legs almost buckled. She looked from officer to officer, waiting for them to burst into laughter, to tell her it was a joke, but all she saw were the crude smirks creeping across their faces, the mischievous glints in their eyes. Her head felt light.

'What did you say to him to make him do that?' Watts asked.

'What the hell is going on, Rose?' Christian asked. She met his eyes and flinched; the anger in them was searing. 'What are they talking about? Who's Adam Morant?'

He was standing straighter; his eyes were wider. The anger was rising like heat, and she immediately thought of him on the bridge, beating the asphalt with his fists as though it were her.

The downstairs toilet flushed. The door unlocked and Detective Inspector Montgomery emerged.

'Hello, Rose.'

Her eyes shot to Christian. It was a reunion none of them ever wanted.

'You need to think about the consequences of your actions, Mrs Shaw,' Leech said, putting on his hat. 'A man is dead. This isn't a game.'

'Rose,' Christian said sternly. 'I asked you what's going on.'

'Is that all you came here for?' she asked Leech. 'To make me feel bad?'

Christian scoffed and strode out of the room, passing Montgomery in the doorway.

'I'll go to him,' Montgomery said, and gave her a closed smile.

Each of them remaining waited to hear the lounge door click shut before speaking again.

'I won't stop looking into this,' she said, clenching her hands into fists. 'I know what you've done. You hurt Shane, those men in the park. No matter what you do to me, I won't stop.'

'You might want to reconsider,' Leech said, stepping closer until she could feel the heat of his breath. He stared into her eyes, but she refused to look away.

'Is that a threat?'

'No, love, that's a promise.'

They stared at each other until her whole body was twitching under his glare. He smirked again, showing uneven teeth. He was enjoying every second of it. Did Montgomery know what they were really doing here? Did he know that the officers had come to antagonise her, or did he truly think checking in on her was going to help?

'We suggest you stop this,' Watts said, behind him. 'For your sake. Your family's sake.'

She leaned in closer, until her nose almost touched Leech's.

'Over my dead body,' she whispered.

Leech breathed a laugh, hot on her cheeks. He adjusted his cap and headed through the doorway. Watts winked at her as he followed behind and whispered beneath his breath.

'See you soon.'

She stood stock-still until she was sure they were gone. When the door clicked shut, she heaved for air. Christian stormed back into the room.

'Tell me what's going on. Now.'

She slipped her bag from her shoulder and removed the journal. It fell on the countertop with a loud clap.

'What's that?'

'It's a journal. It belonged to a man called Finn Matthews. He's gone missing, and the police don't give a damn. I've been trying to—'

'The man from the paper,' he said.

'Yes. I placed the ad.'

He looked at her, bewildered.

'Why?'

'Because I can't stand by as the police bury the case of a missing man. He could be in danger. He could be dead.'

'But you don't know him.'

'Why does that matter?'

'Because it's madness, Rose. If the police don't think there's

276

enough to go on, what makes you think you can do anything?'

'It's not that they believe there isn't enough evidence. There's plenty. They just don't care. The whole establishment is homophobic. If Finn were a missing white woman, they would be all over it.'

'Christ, Rose. Listen to yourself.' He paced.

'You don't know what they've done.'

'Is this why you've been out at all hours? The bruise on your face?' A thought came to him, like the flick of a switch. 'That's why someone took your bag, left the message on your phone. What the hell have you got yourself into?'

'No one is looking for him, Christian. No one cares. But I do. I had the opportunity to help someone before, and I didn't. I won't let the opportunity pass again.'

'Jay,' he said and sighed. 'You're doing this because of Jay.'

'I'm doing this because it's the right thing to do.'

'So what, you think finding this man will bring your brother back? Make you feel less guilt for something that was never in your control? Shit, maybe even make you feel less guilt for killing Violet?'

Killing Violet, as if she had wrung the life from her neck. Tears pricked. Montgomery walked back into the kitchen the second Christian said the words. She thought of the day on the bridge, Montgomery holding her back as Christian took Lily away.

'You wouldn't understand,' she said hoarsely.

'You're right, I don't. What you're doing, it's insane.'

Christian stormed towards the front door. She followed behind him, her shoes clipping the backs of his heels. Montgomery stayed behind. Déjà vu had truly set in.

'Well, maybe I am,' she shouted after him. 'And with the life I live, would you blame me?'

She watched him get inside his car and swing around in the driveway, gravel spitting into the air. He sped out of the drive and down the road.

'I hope they weren't too hard on you,' Montgomery said behind her. 'But you need to understand that you're not just meddling with your own life here. A man has died.' He raised his hands. 'I'm not saying you had anything to do with it, but you need to consider that your actions have consequences.'

She stepped aside and held the door open.

'Good day, Detective Montgomery.'

He cleared his throat and gave her a nod.

'Good day.'

He just managed to pass the threshold before she slammed the door behind him.

FINN'S JOURNAL

18th February 2018 continued

    I arrived at the office dripping with sweat. I had practically marched the whole way, my eyes constantly darting to my watch.

    I was so racked with nerves I could almost taste them. I stepped out of the lift and into the office.

    A sudden silence fell upon the room.

    Everyone was looking at me. They didn't smile, they didn't drop their gazes when they recognised me, they just continued to stare.

    'Good morning,' I said.

    Everyone looked away.

    I walked on with my head down and let myself into my office, left the door ajar. I chucked my bag down beneath the desk and took off my blazer, only to spot the sweat patches soaked beneath my arms and shrug it back on.

    'Finn, can I speak with you a moment?'

    I looked up. Jonathan Cunningham, the editor of the Evening Herald, *was standing in the doorway, the girth of his waist almost meeting either side of the door frame. The strip lighting reflected off his bald scalp.*

    'Yes, of course.'

'I'll meet you in my office.'

When he left the doorway I saw everyone looking at me through the glass partition, shooting their attention back to their computer screens when I met their eyes.

I couldn't tell him why I was late. I was new to the role, I had expectations to meet. Telling him of my stalker would only make him worry about my commitment. So many bad things could come from this.

I left the comfort of my office and walked across the open-plan room, sweating further, my skin burning with the tension. I stepped inside his office and closed the door behind me.

Jonathan was a man of business. Although his appearance was unkempt, with sparing tufts of hair on his scalp and fingerprints on the lenses of his glasses, he was focused on keeping everyone in line. This was the first time I had strayed. I looked down at the food stain on his shirt before meeting his eye as he clasped his hands together on top of the desk.

'I'm so sorry I was late.' I picked the first lie that formed. 'I woke up feeling nauseous and faint, and didn't feel safe walking to work until it had passed.'

He went to reply. I spoke again before he could.

'I've never experienced anything like this before. Perhaps I've been over-eager this first month, working late and weekends.'

'I'm sorry to hear you were unwell,' he said. 'And it was unfortunate that you were late this morning, but that's not the reason I've called you in here.'

The looks everyone had given me in the office now felt more sinister. They hadn't stared at me because I was late, but for another reason entirely. I tried to swallow, but couldn't.

'Something has come to my attention.' He looked down at his hands. 'Something quite disturbing.'

He turned his computer monitor to face me, and every drop of blood left my face.

I looked at the social media page dedicated to my slander, eyed the photos that had edited me into explicit images with a man weighing over three hundred pounds, an array of animals in pigsties, barns, a cage with my head between the bars. Sick rose to my throat. I looked away.

'You've been very dedicated this first month, so I'm not worried about your commitment. However, we can't have anything like this affecting the company.'

'I. . . I obviously don't need to tell you that it wasn't me who created those. . . images. They aren't real.'

'We know that,' he said. 'Of course we know that.'

We. More people knew.

'And there are emails,' he said. 'Photos of this nature were sent to everyone in the office, our contacts at the printers, our shareholders.'

I couldn't process any of it. I stared at him, tears slipping down my cheeks, watching his lips move, but I couldn't hear him any more. It was too much.

'We think it's the right thing to do at this stage.'

I blinked furiously to focus.

'. . .For you to take a leave of absence while we consider the best way forward.'

'But you can't fire—'

But I knew they could. I hadn't passed my probation period. At this point, they could fire me for any reason they chose.

'I'm sorry, Finn.'

'I understand,' I croaked, but I didn't. My whole world had been ripped from me like the flesh from my back, and I couldn't do a thing about it.

I left his office in a blur and made my way to my own, eyes following me, pity scorching into my skin. I took my bag from beneath the desk and waited until I was in the lift before letting the sobs burst from me and echo all the way down.

By the time I returned home, I was trying to stop myself from hyperventilating. I got a taxi from door to door, too nervous to walk alone, which made me think of the police officer smirking at me, thinking I was a joke, less of a man for fearing another.

I let myself inside the building and trudged up the stairs. The two bottles of wine I'd bought from the off-licence as I waited for the cab clinked and chimed together with every step.

I reached the first floor and stopped.

My door was ajar.

The wine bottles smashed on the hard floor. Wine leaked from the bag and pooled around my feet. The shrill sound of smashing glass echoed up the stairwell.

The lock was faulty. It must have clicked open. The landlord must have checked the property while I was at work and forgotten to shut the door behind him. But all the excuses I tried to conjure faltered before I'd even finished the thought in my mind. I knew the truth. I knew it was him.

I pushed the door open all the way, listening to the squeal of its hinges, and stepped inside.

I tried to remember how the flat had looked that morning, whether it was me who'd left the mug on the dining table, who had plumped up the cushions on the sofa. I heard the sound of running water.

The tap was on in the kitchen, overflowing from the sink and pouring down the cupboards and onto the floor.

I rushed through the flat and snatched at the tap. The metal scorched my skin. I jumped back and slipped, slamming down onto the wet floor with a splash. My hand was red raw and shaking; hot water spat over the edge of the counter and onto my face.

I jumped up, my clothes soaked through, and snatched a spatula from the utensils pot to breach the water, a tea towel to grip the tap. I dislodged the blockage in the sink and watched the water slowly disappear. When the water was gone, I saw what had caused the blockage. A mass of pubic hair had been lodged in the drain.

I stumbled out of the kitchen, water soaking into the carpet at my feet, a stranger's pubic hair coating my fingers. He had been right there in my house. I felt tears slip down my cheeks and left them there. I heard more water and looked behind me at the kitchen sink, doubting whether I had stopped the leak at all. I listened out for the direction of the sound: it was coming from the bathroom.

I shot towards it and stopped in the doorway, flinching back at the stench.

The toilet had overflowed. Toilet paper and excrement floated in the film of water on the floor. Faeces had been smeared across the white tiles. Both taps were running.

I stepped backwards, shaking my head and dislodging fresh tears, and checked my bedroom.

The bed had been disturbed. Just that morning I had pressed the sheets flat with my hands, but now they were bunched together as though someone had been writhing amongst them. A pair of my boxers were on the bed. My top drawer was left ajar. I imagined him there, my underwear pressed to his nostrils with one hand, the other beneath the waist of his jeans.

I couldn't stay there a second longer. I snatched my phone from my pocket to call the police and bumped into someone in the hall.

'Is this your doing?' the man asked. It was the tenant from

the flat downstairs, Eddie; the odd man from the basement was standing behind him on the stairs, looking at me. I could never remember his name; he was one of those people who were instantly forgettable. 'Well?'

I couldn't speak, couldn't think. I looked down at my hands, the stranger's hair on them.

He stepped inside the flat.

'Wait!'

He glanced over the kitchen, stared up at the ceiling to check for water damage to confirm whether the leak had come from my apartment or the one above. He passed through to the bathroom and stumbled back at the smell.

'Jesus, what the hell?'

'I can explain,' I said, except I couldn't. I couldn't explain any of it.

'And what about this?' he asked, and pulled a folded piece of paper from his back pocket. He thrust it towards me. His brow was knitted together, his lips formed into a snarl.

I took it from him and unfolded the paper to see one of the edited photos of me. This one was of me in the pigsty, being defiled by the beasts. I instantly felt ill again.

'I've got kids, you sick fuck.'

'I didn't do it. I—'

I stepped backwards and felt something beneath my heel. The man from the basement had followed behind us. I was standing on the tip of his boot. He smelt of stale sweat and something sour.

'I need to call the police,' I stammered, and headed outside the flat. Sweat had broken out on my forehead. All I could smell and taste was the excrement staining the air. I covered my mouth and gagged.

'What's this mess?' the old woman said, coming down the flight of stairs. She stood before the broken wine bottles. 'Someone could seriously get hurt.'

'I'm sorry, I was—'

'What's the commotion?' she asked, her interest peaking. She peered through the open door over the tops of her glasses, moved to go inside.

'Can people stop walking inside my bloody flat without asking?' I snapped, loud enough for the men to hear.

'You're paying for the damage to my place,' Eddie said as he stepped out onto the landing.

'It wasn't me!'

'It came from your flat, you'll fix it.' He looked at the woman. 'You opened your post yet?'

'No, I do that after my dinner.'

'Don't open the brown envelope signed by hand – this guy's got a funny way of making friends with his neighbours.'

'I didn't do it!'

Eddie headed down the stairs. The man from the basement was still lurking inside my flat. He had wide eyes like a doe; the top of his shaved head looked too big for the slimness of his jaw and chin.

'Out!'

He scuttled out, tripping over the bag on the floor and kicking broken glass along the hall.

The woman was heading down the stairs. I heard her file through her post as I slammed the door shut behind me.

Furious tears burnt in my eyes. My chest felt tight, ready to explode. I took my phone from my pocket and called the officer on the contact card, just as the woman screamed in the lobby. I wondered what photo she had received, and a reel of them filled my mind. I ran to the sink and vomited, just as the officer picked up on the other end of the phone. I wiped my lips with the back of my hand and rambled into the receiver, bile on my breath. When I had finished I sat down on the sofa and buried my face in my hands, the sound of Officer Lycett breathing calmly down the phone.

'We spoke to him, Finn,' he said. 'He told us that you're harassing him, not the other way around.'

'What?'

'He has asked to press charges for harassment.'

'That's insane!'

'We need to sort this out once and for all. Would you meet him?'

My heart stopped.

'What?'

'Face to face, at the station. We can sit you both down in the same room and get to the bottom of this.'

I took a deep breath, tasted the foul stench of him in the air, the sick on my breath. How could I meet the man who had done this?

'Finn?'

The police would be there to intervene should anything happen. I would be protected. If I wanted this to end, I had to look him in the eye.

'Finn? What do you want to do?'

'Yes,' I said finally. 'I'll meet with him.'

THIRTY-ONE

C

Rose stood before her father's front door with the box of post beneath her arm. It had been a week since the ad was printed in the paper, and it had taken her as many days to face her father again. Every time she saw or thought of him, she remembered Jay floating in the water, remembered whose hate had put him there. But there was no escaping him now. The PO box she had opened for potential leads from the newspaper advertisement had been close to bursting with envelopes, a shoebox taped shut. The clerk had huffed and sighed as she bagged them all up before telling her to empty it sooner next time. But Rose had been too excited to care: she was walking out of the post office with dozens of potential leads.

She rang the bell and looked up and down the street. The day was cold but fresh. By the time she left it would be night-time with numerous shadows for strangers to lurk in. She had read Finn's journal so many times that she was starting to think like him, fear his fears.

Rob had stopped calling. She wanted him, but if he was close to Seb and his officers, there was a chance that he was just like them. It didn't matter if he was kind to her if he tortured others behind her back.

The door opened. Her father stood in the doorway, bloodshot

eyes peering out at her from beneath sagging lids. He looked worse than he had before. But when he recognised her, life seemed to seep back into his eyes.

'Rosie,' he said.

'Rose,' she corrected.

'Yes, sorry. Rose.' They stood awkwardly on either side of the threshold. 'Come in.'

He moved aside for her to enter. The hallway had been cleared of boxes, the carpet vacuumed. Only the dust on the skirting boards and the smears on the mirror gave any indication that she was staring at the same house she had fled from just weeks ago.

'You've tidied up,' she said, unable to hide the admiration in her tone. He shut the door behind her.

'Yes,' he replied.

Silence swelled between them.

'Tea? Coffee?'

'Coffee.'

She followed him to the kitchen.

The counters were almost clear; the only stains that remained were the ones that had baked into the material. The sink had been emptied and bleached, the floor freed of debris. But even though she could see the floor, she still looked around for any sign of mice, listened out for the tiny clip of their claws.

'Just a couple more rooms to do now,' he said over his shoulder as he boiled the kettle, arranged two mugs on the counter. 'Please . . .' he signalled the table in the centre of the room. She took a seat and admired the room.

'Well done,' she said. It sounded forced. Giving him even a sliver of kindness felt too much of a betrayal.

The kettle boiled, silencing them both. They had never been

good at talking to each other; the only thing they had ever had in common was the same blood running through their veins and dark memories of the past. If they hadn't been family, they would have made the perfect strangers.

'You're probably wondering why I'm here.'

'You don't need a reason to come and visit me, Rose,' he said as he stirred the coffee and placed it before her. 'You're welcome any time.'

He turned back to squeeze the teabag against the side of his mug with the teaspoon, like he always had.

'I need your help,' she said.

She listened to the spoon twirl in the mug and clink against the sides, and thought of her mother standing before the very same stove making her and Jay hot milk before bed. Her throat thickened. Everything she looked at provoked a memory.

Tony took the seat opposite her, mug of tea in hand.

'I found a journal written by a missing man. He wrote of being stalked, and how the police did nothing to help him. I've been looking into it, trying to find out what happened to him, but I discovered that this is much bigger than just one missing man. There are more. I posted an ad in the newspaper and numerous families have come forward. I want to find out the truth about what happened to them, but. . . I can't do it alone.'

They sat in silence for a while, the words sinking in.

'Well,' he said finally. 'I didn't expect that.'

'I think the police have swept the missing cases aside because the men were attracted to men. I spoke to an ex-police officer, and he told me about how the whole force is built on institutionalised homophobia, and spoke about the harassment he received himself. He tried to help me and got hurt.'

'Hurt?'

She nodded, and sipped her coffee.

'Are you sure this is something you want to get into?'

'Yes, I'm sure. I can't stand by while another innocent life is. . .'

They both looked away at the mention of him. Whatever happened, Jay would be between them, pushing them apart.

'Are you doing this because of him?' he asked.

You can't even say his name.

She took another sip of coffee. It burnt all the way down.

'It won't bring him back.'

'I know that.'

It wouldn't bring Violet back either, but doing something good, saving someone else, felt like a small step towards finding herself again.

He nodded solemnly and looked down at the box by her feet. 'What's all this?'

'Responses I received from the newspaper ad, and the police files on the other missing men. I met with their families. At first, I thought the only connection between Finn and the others was the awful treatment by the police, but the families seem to think they might be connected by the same man who stalked Finn.'

'A serial killer?'

'I don't know. Only two are confirmed dead.'

'What do you believe?'

She took another sip of coffee. She didn't know what to believe.

'I certainly think there's more to it.'

'Then we'd best get started.'

She couldn't help it: a thankful smile pulled at the corners of her lips. He smiled back with water in his eyes.

Her eyes had blurred over. So many words, never enough sleep. She read and read until they streamed and yawns tore at her lungs. She sat before the fireplace in the living room, her feet dead beneath her weight, and looked at the opened letters arranged in piles: possible leads, no leads, hate mail.

She hadn't expected that. Vile words etched onto paper, sick individuals hoping Finn had suffered in death, was burning in hell because of who he was. They had been directed towards her too: she was an enabler, a freak, a kid-killer. Every time she thought she had finally been forgiven, the town reminded her of her past. She hadn't mentioned her identity in the ad, which meant the town was starting to talk, her name spreading through the streets in whispers. She wondered what the police were saying about her.

Tony sat in the armchair, his eyes moving down the pages of the police reports. His head had bobbed as the monotony of reading tried to drag him under, until he made a fresh pot of coffee and filled each of their mugs. Before reading the police reports, he had read the journal from front to back and looked up at her stunned, his face a shade whiter.

Rose stood, groaning from her aching joints, and stared at their work spread out on the floor. Photos of the men from the files and the locations where their bodies were found or where they were last seen, a map of the town with red crosses marking each key location: home addresses, last known whereabouts. She stared at the photos of the victims, and each of them stared back at her. If she was going to make sense of it, she had to spew the crowded thoughts from her mind and speak them aloud.

'Andrew's son, Johnny, was the first to go missing in 2005,' she said aloud, staring at his photo. She heard the ruffle of paper behind her as her father sat up in the chair, followed her hand as she traced the road on the map. 'He was last seen walking down

Military Road, heading out of town. The police report said Johnny and his father had an argument before he left the house; the police believe he ran away. But he was only nineteen and had nowhere to go, no other family to stay with. Andrew didn't know of any friends his son had out of town. Neither his phone nor his bank card were used after he went missing. He simply vanished.

'In 2009, Jamie went missing. He used to walk across the fields to and from work. A dog walker saw him cross the stream in the woods and over the open field, but no one saw him leave. The police searched the woods and found nothing. They pinned him down as another runaway.'

Lucy's son Phillip stared up at her from the floor. He had his mother's smile, the same jaw and chin. She thought of the pain in Lucy's eyes, the garden groomed to within an inch of its life.

'Phillip was found dead in 2011, in the woods by the riverbank, with cut wrists.'

'How could he cut one wrist, and then the other?' Tony asked.

They both had to be thinking of Jay. He had only cut himself once; the damage he had done wouldn't have permitted another. She thought of the red water splashing against her jeans, the starkness of his bloodless skin. Her stomach twisted.

'Exactly,' she replied, and coughed to clear the croak in her voice. 'But the two victims before him just vanished, and suddenly we are meant to believe the killer changed tactics.'

She looked at their youngest victim, the youthful glow of his eyes, the freckles on the bridge of his nose, the puppy fat still clinging to his cheeks. A lump formed in her throat.

'Annette's grandson Zach had just turned eighteen when he was found in 2013. He had his whole life before him, but the police believe he took his own life. His body was found a mile from the bridge, naked on the bank with broken bones from the current. He didn't leave a note.'

Jay didn't leave a note, she thought. *He didn't need to. We knew he ended his life because each one of us failed him in one way or another.*

'Adam was admitted to the Lakes three years ago. He was found wandering in the same woods, almost like it's the killer's hunting ground. He didn't speak of the man who harassed him, but admitted enough for us to know that he was scared into submission, harassed until he broke.'

Adam, the man I killed.

Even saying his name aloud brought pain to her chest. She knew deep down that she wasn't responsible for Adam ending his life – if someone was going to commit suicide, they would find a way to do it – but having been the person to give him an out, to give him a reason to believe he was allowed to die, would stay with her for ever. She looked away from his photo, considered kicking it under the sofa so as not to feel his eyes on her.

'And then there's Finn.'

She ran her hand through her hair.

'What I don't understand is why the police didn't investigate Finn's claims more seriously. They say they had insufficient evidence, but his flat was crawling with it. The stalker left pubic hair and faeces and fingerprints all over the place, and yet the police didn't even test them for a third party.'

'They believed Finn was mad from the off,' Tony said.

'Or pursuing the idea that he was mad was easier for them to control, gave them the right to overlook so many clues.'

She stopped before their work on the floor, eyeing each of the victims' faces. 'I find it hard to believe they didn't do a single test,' Tony said. 'They must have done something.'

'Shane Hughes told me this had happened before, when Stephen Port murdered those men in London. The Metropolitan Police didn't test vital evidence, and if they had, they would have caught their killer. If I hadn't known that, I wouldn't have believed it either.'

Tony rose from the chair and stood next to her. They both looked down at Finn's photo.

'Let's assume for a moment that they're all dead. What I'm struggling to understand is, if the murders were orchestrated by the same man, why did he hide the first two bodies, but leave the next two to be found? And we don't even know what he did with Finn.'

'Maybe he was trying to throw them off the scent,' she replied. 'If he followed the same pattern each time, it would be clear the police were dealing with a serial killer. If they were different from time to time, it would be difficult to connect them.'

They both looked at the map, the red crosses identifying the victims' last whereabouts.

'But he made a mistake,' Tony said, taking the red pen and connecting the crosses. A jagged circle surrounded the centre of town. 'He didn't stray far enough. He worked in a six-mile radius.'

'And the years are almost evenly staggered. He left a few years between each of them, as if hoping the attention would die down so he could strike again.'

Their killer didn't seem to act on impulse, he planned each move meticulously, had done from the start.

Rose looked at the photos, trying to find a similarity.

'The victims didn't know each other. The only connection between them was their sexuality.'

'And something else,' Tony said.

He dropped one file on the floor, then another, and another.

'In each of the police files, one name sticks out.'

He looked down at his notes.

'Dr William Hunter. He was assigned to each of the patients. He used to work for the NHS, and although he operates from a private practice now, it appears he still works with police.'

The name rang a bell. She searched through her tired brain for a spark of connection, the waking of a memory.

'The same man Finn was assigned to.'

'What was his name again?' she asked.

'Dr Hunter.'

The memory came to her like a slap.

'I know him.'

'What?'

'He's. . . he's Christian's therapist.'

She rummaged around in her bag. She had almost forgotten that she had booked an appointment with Dr Hunter. So much had happened since then.

'What're you doing?'

'I'm calling his office.'

'Wait,' Tony said as she put her phone to her ear. 'Think it through before you jump into any—'

'Shh, it's ringing.'

'Rose, I really think we should talk about this first. If he's involved, we have no idea what he's—'

'Hi, my name is Rose Shaw. I have an appointment but I'm hoping to reschedule.'

It was the same receptionist as before. She had a kind voice, but she sounded tired, ready for the day to end.

'When were you thinking? Your appointment is booked in for the end of the week,' she asked.

'I was hoping to see him today, if possible.'

'I'll see if we've had any cancellations. One moment, please.'

Hold music rang down the line.

'What're you doing?' Tony asked.

The receptionist picked up the call again.

'You're in luck. We have an appointment free this evening at six.'

'Perfect. See you then.'

Rose hung up the phone and slung her bag on her shoulder.

'What are you doing?' Tony asked.

'I'm going to find out what Dr Hunter knows.'

PHILLIP

4th December 2011

Phillip woke with a jolt as something wet and heavy hit his face. He looked up and saw dark, leafless branches, knits of twigs splayed out like fingers. Moonlight sliced between them in dull beams. Snow slipped from a branch and fell next to him with a quiet thump.

His skin was so numb it burnt, and his face felt frozen in place, as if smiling would cause his skin to crack. His whole body was trembling.

In the distance, he heard the whisper of a river, but the rest of the woodland was silent. There was no breeze, no wildlife, just the sound of his breaths wheezing in and out of his lungs, the crunch of snow as he tried to move.

Something hard scratched against his back. He looked up again through a squint. He was resting against a tree.

He had no idea how he'd got there, or why he would be in woodland in the middle of the night, half-dressed during the height of winter. He should be scared, he thought, but he was too tired, too cold. A strange calmness had him in its grasp.

He looked down. The snow around him wasn't white, but red. His arms had been cut from the elbows to the wrists, exposing parts of him no person should ever see of themselves. His skin was blue, but the blood was warm as it trickled around his arms and dripped to the snow on the ground.

He should be crying, screaming, but he could only think in facts. *That's my arm. That's my blood. Those are my veins.*

Metal glinted in his hand. A razor blade. Did he do this? He couldn't remember dragging it down each arm, or even wanting to die, but there was so much he couldn't remember, as if the cold had frozen his memory solid and he wouldn't know what had happened until it thawed.

He licked his cracked lips, longed for snow to fall again so he could taste it and wet his tongue. The moon was high in the sky. Dawn was a long way off yet. Through the cold and the pain, he knew he would be dead by then.

He closed his eyes and rested the back of his head against the bark, causing a cold pain to run down his neck. An owl hooted, the sound echoing between the trees. At least he wasn't alone.

He opened his eyes with the memory, the reason why his head hurt. He remembered seeing the metal pipe swing through the air, remembered turning to run and falling to the ground as it landed against his skull with a crack. But that didn't explain why the razor was in his hand and the life was trickling out of him and onto the snow.

Fresh flakes began to fall. Even then, he thought how beautiful they were, the way they fell to the ground in silence. He closed his eyes as they landed on his face and rested into the tree.

He didn't want to remember any more.

THIRTY-TWO

R ose stepped out onto the quiet street and headed towards the
bus stop. The breeze stung her cheeks like a wakeful slap.

She had to find out how the doctor was connected to each of the
victims. He could have simply been doing his job, his name linked
to the victims because they needed the same support; or it could be
something more sinister. Finn never met the doctor, he had simply
mentioned him by name as the man the police planned to refer him
to, before he fell off the face of the earth. Had Finn had the chance
to meet him, would he have come face to face with his stalker?

A car engine grumbled to life behind her as it pulled out of a
parking spot along the road, continued to growl behind her back.
She turned and stopped in her tracks.

A police car was following her at a crawl. The window wound
down. Officer Leech's face appeared, with that familiar smirk
pulling at the corners of his lips, as Watts sat behind the wheel.

'Been to see Daddy, have we?'

She continued walking up the street, at a faster pace than
before. The police car crept along beside her.

'No talking today? Cat got your tongue?'

'Don't you have a job to do?' she asked. 'Maybe if you spent
your time looking into crimes rather than harassing people, I
wouldn't be doing this.'

'Who says we haven't been assigned to follow you everywhere you go?'

Detective Clark. He would want them watching her, making sure she didn't unearth evidence of their barbaric acts.

Leech watched her walk, scanning her up and down with disdain or desire, or a concoction of both. He wasn't getting off on *her*, but the power he had over her, his smile widening whenever he spotted her eyes shift towards the car, each time her pace quickened. She stumbled on a raised slab on the path and reddened as he laughed, a raucous howl deep from his gut, clapping his hand against the body of the car.

She turned onto the main road, walking so fast that she almost broke into a jog, and managed to drag the distance between them as the police car waited at the junction. But soon enough, it crawled up behind her, lights flashing. Other cars overtook. No one would stop to help her; if anything, passers-by were far more likely to think she was the troublemaker rather than them. Leech and Watts could do anything they wanted, and the cars would continue to pass.

'Shouldn't you be at home making dinner for your kid?' Leech asked. 'Lily, of course. Not the one you killed.'

'Don't say her name,' she spat.

'How do you forget something like that?' he asked. He was leaning out the window, both elbows hanging over the edge. 'How do you leave the house every day knowing that everyone knows exactly what you did?'

He wanted her to snap. She would love nothing more than to stride over to the car and slam the butt of her hand into his nose until it broke, grab him by the hair and thrust his face against the dashboard, but all she could do was continue to walk and listen to everything he said.

She could see the bus stop now, the glass of it reflecting the setting sun.

'You talk of injustice for Finn Matthews,' Leech said. 'But what about your daughter? All you got was community service and a hefty fine. Does that sound like justice to you?'

'I'm living my life sentence,' she choked, her chest so tight she could barely breathe. 'I'm punished every day.'

'Not enough, it seems,' he said. 'We're passionate about justice too, Mrs Shaw. We'll work day and night just like you. Isn't that right, Watts?'

Twenty steps and she would be at the bus stop, but what then? She would have to stand and wait, listen to the abuse. By the time the bus came, she would be a heap on the ground.

'But you can stop all this,' he said, his tone lighter. 'Stop what you're doing and all of this goes away.'

'You'd like that, wouldn't you? Well, don't hold your breath.'

She heard the familiar whine of the bus trundling up the street. She picked up her pace, waved her hand frantically at the driver as it neared.

'Last chance, Rose,' Leech said.

She reached the bus stop just as the bus pulled up and jumped on, her whole body shivering with adrenaline. She paid for her ticket and made her way to the back on soft legs, sat down in the last row before they buckled. As the bus pulled away, she peered out the rear window. The police car followed them the rest of the way.

She got off at an earlier stop and slipped down the first side street, risking glances over her shoulder to see if Leech and Watts were following her on foot. The police car pulled up at the mouth of the alley before shooting out of sight. They were going to try and catch her down one of the side streets.

She turned off the next street and ran, the shocks of her feet slamming against the asphalt reverberating up her spine.

Back street after back street she ran, glancing over her shoulder in case the fluorescent body of the police car turned round the bends in the roads, waited for the call of its sirens or the flash of its lights reflecting in the windows lining the streets. She stopped down an alley and pressed herself against the brick wall, panting for air and blinking away the lights bursting in her eyes. Her legs gave out. She held her face in her hands as everything spun. She would have struggled to run so fast and so far when she was rested, let alone without a wink of sleep.

When the fainting spell passed, she stumbled to her feet and rested against the wall. It was dark. She had run in various different directions to lose the officers, but now she was lost herself. She checked the time. Ten minutes until her appointment. She typed the address into the maps app on her phone; only four streets away.

She walked as quickly as she could. Sweat had dampened her hairline, stuck wet strands against her temples, her chest still heaving. The moment she spotted the psychiatrist's building on Moorcroft Road, she shot inside without a second's hesitation. If Detective Clark's officers were going to follow her everywhere she went, she would have to make it difficult for them.

She stood in the small hallway before the staircase and caught her breath.

Christian came here every week. Before, it had been another mystery attached to him, another part of his life she didn't know a thing about. But now that she was here, it didn't seem to fit.

She couldn't see him here, walking up the stairs, confessing his deepest, darkest thoughts.

She climbed a narrow staircase and followed the directions to the third floor.

The doctor would want to talk about her, but she had to find a way to move the conversation to the missing men. She only had one chance. If he was tied up in this, and she spoke of it face to face, he wouldn't want her to come back. His schedule would suddenly become fully booked, the receptionists would stop answering her calls. If she was going to unearth the truth, it had to be now.

She pushed open the door and stepped into the reception. Plastic chairs lined the walls with a large coffee table covered in old magazines. Music played quietly in the background like a whisper. She walked up to the reception desk.

'How can I help?' the receptionist asked.

Rose recognised her voice from speaking to her on the phone.

'I have an appointment with Dr Hunter.'

'Take a seat. He will be with you shortly.'

Rose took a seat in the waiting area and sank against the plastic; only then did the exhaustion hit her. It was like a wave: her eyelids immediately felt heavy, as though they were made of lead instead of flesh. Her muscles ached whenever she moved. Sweat had soaked into her clothes and stuck to her skin.

She had tried sleeping tablets for so many years, but they never seemed to work for her. Some were too weak, merely exhausting her as she remained awake, exacerbating her struggle to put one foot in front of the other. Others practically put her in a coma, and left her groggy when she woke so she could barely string a sentence together or think a coherent thought. But as she sat in the waiting room, she craved one of the small pills that would knock her out for days.

A door opened and a man appeared.

'Rose Shaw,' he said.

She recognised him immediately. It was the man she had seen in the waiting room at the police station after her meeting with the Chief Constable. The same man who'd had a meeting with Seb Clark that very same day.

She stood, her head swimming, and walked towards him, knocking her shin against the corner of the coffee table. A pile of magazines slipped to the floor. She bent down in a fluster, her cheeks reddening as he watched her, like she was a specimen to study, a mouse in a maze.

He was assigned to each victim; he knew every single one of them, and Seb Clark, the man trying to bury the case.

'I'll get it, don't worry,' the receptionist said from behind the desk.

'Thanks,' she said and stood, straightening her top, fixing her hair behind her ears.

'This way,' said Dr Hunter.

He opened the door and held it for her, watching each one of her movements with such intensity that she wondered if he would have her all figured out before she had even sat down and opened her mouth.

The office was dimly lit. Bookshelves lined the back wall, a large desk that felt too big for the room. She found that, with shorter men. They had to make up for their height in other ways: expensive watches and oversized furniture. She looked at his wrist: saw the designer logo on the face of his watch. She had him all figured out too. Two armchairs sat on the opposite side of the room by the window, the blinds drawn. A standard lamp hovered over the chairs, lighting up the side table between them, with only a small clock and a box of tissues on the surface. She wondered how much this was going to cost. A lot, by the looks of the office.

'Please,' he said, signalling the chairs.

She didn't know which one to take, which was his. She chose the one closest to the door and placed her bag by her feet. The seat was too soft, as though it was dragging her back, forcing her to relax, and there was a familiar scent in the air. When it hit her, her whole body steeled against the memory. The smell was citrus, just like the scent of the satsuma Violet had been eating before the crash. The memory flooded her mind like water. She heard the screams, the crunch of metal.

'I'm William Hunter. Nice to meet you.'

He held out his hand for her to take. She shook it with as much strength as she could muster, all the while looking for the cause of the smell. She spotted the orange peel in a waste bin beside his desk.

'Rose,' she said, and took her hand back. 'Although I'm sure you've heard about me from my husband.'

'I feel we need to jump right in the deep end,' he said, taking out a notebook with notes already scrawled on the pages. He slipped on a pair of glasses.

'You've bottled up a lot of grief over the years, and it's time we tackled it head on, before things get out of hand.'

'Out of hand?' she asked.

'It has come to my attention that you are looking into a missing person's case.'

'Shouldn't you hear what I have to say, rather than going off what my husband has told you?'

'Is what I've said untrue?'

'No, but I don't see how that's relevant to my grief.'

'On the contrary, I think there's a direct correlation.'

She immediately disliked the man. She had come across his kind before when going through the treatment process for her insomnia: consultants with egos too big for their small frames, speaking over her before she had the chance to respond to anything they said. Every time, she had left appointments enraged, and sensed quickly that this would be another meeting that would make her blood boil. But one good thing: he had mentioned the investigation first. She had a way in.

'You lost your brother,' he said.

'I'm not here to talk about him.'

'You're looking into the whereabouts of a man you don't know because he shares a likeness to your brother, are you not? Perhaps we should talk about him.'

'I'm looking into the case of a missing man because no one else gives a damn. A missing man you yourself were assigned to treat.'

He was silent for the first time, as though each of her words had lashed at his tongue, rendered him speechless.

The scent crept back to her again. Screams echoed in her ears. Her skin turned ice cold, as though she was there again, submerged in the water. She pinched her thigh to bring herself back.

'Investigating Finn's disappearance has unearthed others. There isn't just one victim, there're six. And what I find interesting is that you were assigned to treat every single one of them.'

'Is no one safe from your suspicions?' he asked.

'Not everyone is connected to the missing men, or has had their names mentioned in police files, or had meetings with Detective Seb Clark, who has been trying to bury these cases for years.'

He sighed into his lap.

'This is what I was afraid of,' he said. He took off his glasses and huffed a breath on each of the lenses, rubbed them clean with the end of his tie.

'It's good for people to distract themselves from grief with other activities, recommended even, but only when the activity isn't destructive. This. . .' He waved his hand through the air, as though her efforts were flippant, a child's game. 'This isn't good. You're hunting people down to punish them in some way. I believe this is because you're being punished by your own grief, a grief you cannot escape unless it is faced head on, in here, with me.'

She scoffed a laugh. 'That's quite a conclusion,' she said. 'You've only known me for five minutes.'

'On the contrary, I've known of you a lot longer than that.'

At first, she thought he knew of her because of Christian, but as he continued to belittle her, she wondered if his information came from the police, the officers who he knew well from past cases.

He spoke again, before she could. 'I'm concerned about your mental well-being. You've had to deal with a lot of grief in your life. Your brother. Your mother. Your daughter. Perhaps you see this man from the journal you speak of as the brother you lost. Maybe you're trying to help a stranger, who may very well not even need it, to make up for your past failings.' She went to speak, but he spoke over her again. He wasn't talking with her, but at her. She wanted to scream, demand to be heard. 'You suffer from insomnia, which inhibits mental processing and the ability to make good decisions, to see the truth for the truth, a lie for a lie. In fact, I'd say this game you're playing, this wild-goose chase that has you running all over town, is more of a break with reality.'

She stood up quickly.

'You don't even know me,' she scoffed. 'You're absurd.'

'Am I? Or have I seen this countless times, and hope to strike before it's too late? I would never usually jump to the core problem so quickly with a client, but I'm worried that if I don't do this now, there will be no stopping you. I want to help.'

She picked up her bag and hooked it over her shoulder.

'I see what you're doing. You're going to make me out to be insane, a fantasist, all with the help of the police. Well, it won't work. I won't give in. Goodbye, Dr Hunter.'

She headed for the door.

'If you won't look after yourself for you, then do it for your family. Your daughter is growing up fast. Your husband is suffering too. You all are. Perhaps you should focus on the problems closer to home, rather than running around after a man you don't even know.'

'Perhaps you should go fuck yourself.'

She left his office and strode for the stairwell, ignoring the receptionist as she called after her to pay, and raced down the stairs with her heart thumping hard in her chest, the smell of citrus stained into her airways and tainting every breath.

Either Dr Hunter was simply another arrogant prick, or he was trying to throw her off track. In this case, she suspected him of both.

THIRTY-THREE

As Rose sat in the cab outside the doctor's office, she wondered if he was right, if she really was mad after all.

The meter had been ticking over for the last two hours, racking up a bill she couldn't bring herself to look at.

'You've got the money for this, right?' the taxi driver asked.

'Yes,' she said, her eyes never leaving the door to the building.

'I'll need half of it now.'

She sighed and pulled her purse out of her bag. Thrusting the notes towards him she returned her eyes to the window.

She wasn't sure what time the doctor finished for the day, but she would be ready. She had left the building and walked up the street, only to draw out as much money as she could, call a cab, and turn back the way she'd come. If he was hiding something, she was going to find out what it was.

The driver drummed his fingers against the steering wheel, turned up the radio as though she wasn't there.

The door to the building opened. The receptionist stepped out first, keys in hand, followed by the doctor himself. She watched them make their goodbyes and lock up for the night before heading towards their cars parked up on the side of the road.

'Follow the Mercedes,' she said, as she watched the doctor get behind the wheel.

The cab driver hesitated.

'I'm not looking for trouble,' he said.

'Good, neither am I.' She took the rest of the notes from her purse. The total amount of money she had given him added up to £250. 'The Mercedes.'

He took the money and started the engine, following the doctor's car as it left the parking space and headed up the road.

Her heart began to race. She didn't know what she expected to uncover, but she wouldn't find all the answers in the journal or the police reports. If she had a hunch she had to follow it, no matter where it led.

'He your husband or something?'

'No,' she replied, sternly enough to keep him from asking any more questions.

The taxi followed the Mercedes down every street, hanging back a car or two behind, speeding up when the Mercedes got too far out of sight. For someone who wasn't looking for trouble, he seemed to have done this before.

They followed the doctor through the night, out of the town and into the country, down dark, unlit lanes winding through the fields.

It was thirty minutes before the doctor stopped. He pulled into a cul-de-sac made up of seven large homes, each with double garages and expensive cars outside. The Mercedes pulled into an empty driveway. The taxi driver pulled up two houses away.

'What do you want me to do?' he asked.

'Will you wait?'

'I'm not staying here if there's going to be trouble.'

She watched the doctor leave the car and head inside the house.

'Wait for me down the road. I'll call you.'

'All right.'

She took his number and looked up at the house again. The cul-de-sac looked familiar, but she couldn't place why. She sat in the back of the cab and considered asking the driver to take her home again. This was her stupidest idea yet. What was she going to do, peer through the window and watch the man eat his dinner?

'I can't be on this job all night,' he said.

It was the push she needed. She stepped out and crossed the road towards the house.

The taxi drove away and left her in the dark. She stood before the house, watching as lights were turned on from the inside as the doctor settled in. It was a large house, too large for one person. For someone who seemed to exude confidence, she wondered if it was all an act, whether he was lonely.

Another car pulled into the cul-de-sac. She jumped behind the nearest hedge in the doctor's front garden and peered between the leaves. The car pulled up right outside the house. The headlights split through the branches and shone in her eyes. She covered them with a protective hand until she was thrown into darkness again. Car doors slammed shut. Voices edged closer.

She peered through the branches and gasped.

Christian and Heather both whipped around at the sound.

She covered her mouth with her hand, held her breath.

'Come on,' Heather said and took his arm, but Christian hung back with his eyes on the hedge, as if he could see right through it. Her lungs burnt for air. She clamped her hand down and begged for him to move along.

'Christian,' Heather said, pulling at him softly until he followed.

They headed up the path and rang the bell, spoke too quietly for her to hear. When the front door opened the doctor greeted them like old friends. They stepped inside, shutting the door behind them.

Her heart was racing, her mind quicker still. Why would Christian and Heather visit the doctor together? Christian truly did have another life that she had no idea about. She remembered the pair of them sitting in her kitchen, falling silent when she entered, the guilt in Heather's eyes. Perhaps they were seeing the doctor to help them bring their affair to light without breaking Christian's deranged wife for good. The doctor seemed convinced she had broken from reality; she wondered which of them had planted that seed in his mind.

She got up and crossed the lawn, stopping before the lit window on the ground floor. The curtains were drawn but for a small crack between them. She moved left to right to take in the whole of the room.

The living room was similar to the doctor's study: an impressive array of books, large armchairs, furniture she knew would feel as expensive as it looked. The doctor was sitting in an armchair with his legs crossed and his hands in his lap. Christian and Heather sat together on the sofa, taking it in turns to speak.

'What're you doing?'

Rose whipped around to the sound of the voice.

Adeline.

Immediately Rose felt like a school mum again, turning up to football tournaments to be met by Adeline's judgemental glare. She had always been the ringleader. If she had been kinder to Rose, the rest of them would have been too.

Rose hadn't seen or spoken to her since the day of the crash. She was sure she had caught glimpses of her in town over the years: whipping down an aisle in the supermarket, driving past her in a blur. By the tautness of the skin of her cheekbones and the sockets of her eyes, she'd had work done. Her face was so smooth it reflected the light from the window. Her eyes had a slight slant to them now. She remembered why the cul-de-sac looked so familiar: Adeline lived here, directly next door to the doctor.

'I asked you what you're doing,' Adeline said.

'I. . . I'm sorry.'

She stumbled away with her head down, her heart caught in her throat.

'Come back here!'

Adeline grabbed her arm and spun her round.

'Rose, I asked what you were doing, peering into the window of someone else's home.'

Adeline dropped a black bin bag from her hand to the lawn.

'It doesn't concern you.'

Rose took a step back. Adeline took a step forward.

'Maybe I should call the police.'

'Do what you like,' Rose said, and yanked her arm away.

Then she stormed off and broke into a run, almost fell as she turned the corner and stopped down the lane, panting in the dark. She pulled out her phone and called the cab driver. Knowing Adeline, she would knock on the doctor's front door and tell him what had happened. If Rose was going to lie her way out of it, she had to get home before Christian.

THIRTY-FOUR

Rose stepped inside the house and called Lily's name. Her voice echoed through the empty rooms.

The house was freezing, enough for her to see her breath. The lights were on but there was nobody home. The air seemed to move like a breeze, slipping between the open doorways. She put her keys in the dish on the side table and caught her breath.

The cab driver had sped all the way home. Every time a pair of headlights had appeared behind them, she thought of Christian gripping the steering wheel and pressing his foot down on the accelerator. But she had been paranoid. Each time, the suspected car turned off the road and down another. But she knew he wouldn't be far behind. If Adeline had exposed her, Christian wouldn't hesitate to chase after her.

She would take a plate of leftovers from the fridge, scrape it in the bin and leave the plate in the sink so it looked as though she had been home all along. She made to rush down the hall for the kitchen and stopped before the doorway to the living room. The door was open, revealing uneven shadows that didn't fit her memory of the room. She flicked on the light.

The room was trashed.

The sofa cushions had been slashed, the white filling torn out and scattered across the room in clouds. Drawers hung open with their contents spewed all over the floor. Someone had flipped over the rug, presumably to look beneath. Nothing was untouched.

A burglary.

She turned from the room and raced up the stairs to her bedroom. The mattress had been cut open, the memory foam topper cut away in chunks. Feathers covered the carpet where the pillows had been searched. The wardrobe doors were ajar; clothes lay crumpled and shoeboxes were turned over in front of them. She rushed to her jewellery box, knocked to the floor beneath the dressing table. Each piece was accounted for, chains and jewels tangled together on the carpet.

No, this wasn't a burglary.

She shook her head. This seemed different from the attack on Shane's home. There were no words cut into the walls, no messages for her to take as a threat. But then the sight of her home ripped to shreds might be the message in itself. Or maybe the person who did this was looking for the journal. She felt her bag hanging over her shoulder and touched the notebook's cover through the fabric. It hadn't been an opportunistic burglar. If it wasn't the police, it must have been about Finn's journal. The intruder's frustration was etched into his handiwork: each slash and cut and emptied drawer messier than the last, as if he was getting his revenge with every thrust of the knife: she had taken something from him, so he had to take something from her.

Her stomach dropped instantly.

The study.

She rushed back downstairs, slipping as she turned the corner by the foot of the stairs and bolted along the hall.

Each kitchen drawer and cupboard was left open, the contents littering the floor in a sea of steel and smashed crockery. She stopped in her tracks.

The study door was open.

Her legs threatened to buckle. He had destroyed everything in the house, no room left unscathed. She knew what she was going to find. Tears bit at her eyes. Her heart jumped in her chest. She pushed the door open all the way and instantly fell to the floor.

The paintings.

Violet's face had been defiled with the knife again and again, holes in the material where her eyes should be, stabbed directly in the heart, her lips cut into a sinister smile.

She sobbed and tore her eyes away, staring down at the carpet through tears.

Jay too. She had almost forgotten how many paintings she had of him; they had been buried behind the layers of Violet. He had been dragged out of the past and into the middle of the room, stabbed in the face and chest again and again in such a violent attack that only she would ever know who the paintings had depicted before. All except one. It was her favourite painting of him, worked from a photo taken in a field of corn, the gold of it shimmering in his eyes, the sun lighting his hair in white-blond and copper strands. The painting rested against the pile of others, his eyes on the door, waiting for her. She met them through the tears; he stared back at her.

The bay window had been smashed, and the curtains were billowing and whipping up with the breeze. Glass littered the carpet, reflecting the glare of the moon above the river. The wind carried the sound of it until she could hear the water chopping in her ears.

She lay down on the carpet and sobbed, the fibres bristling against her cheeks. She clawed at it, thrust her fists against it until the skin was red raw with burns and she heard a loud click from one of her knuckles. A scream ripped from her chest and echoed through the house.

'What have you done?'

She sat up and whipped around. Christian stood behind her, keys in hand. The front door was left open, swaying with the through-breeze, and slammed shut until the whole house seemed to shake. He stepped around her and froze.

'Why?' he asked croakily. His face was an ashy-white. He stepped deeper into the room, glass crunching under the soles of his shoes, then sank to the carpet and cradled a painting of Violet to his chest, the wooden frame snapped and dangling from his grasp. '*Why?*'

'I didn't do this!' She stood as she spoke, stumbling on shaking legs.

'You've gone mad,' he whispered. Tears rolled down his face and zigzagged through the stubble along his jaw.

'I didn't do this, Christian! How could you even suggest—'

'Do you blame me?' He let the canvas go and stood as the anger rose. 'What you're doing, it's madness!'

'Someone broke in. . .' she stammered. She pointed to the window. 'Someone broke into our home and did this!'

'Because of *you*,' he spat. 'Because of everything you've done. Why were you at the doctor's house tonight, Rose?'

'I wasn't—'

'Don't lie to me!'

She gritted her teeth and looked away. He wouldn't understand.

'If I was at the doctor's house, how would I have had time to do this? You can hate me for one or the other, but not both.'

'I'm calling the police.'

'Don't,' she said quickly. 'They might be responsible for this.'

'Christ, *listen* to yourself!'

'You don't know what they've done,' she said. 'You have to believe me, Christian. If only you'd listen—'

'Don't you care what happens to Lily? What if she had been home?'

'But she wasn't. She's never home. Neither of you are. It's just me in the great big fucking house!'

Anger clotted in her throat. She could feel that her face was as flushed as his.

'Violet's dead,' he shouted. 'You hear me? Violet's dead, but Lily's still here!'

He stepped closer, the veins in his neck swelling, the pulse visibly beating at his temples. Even with his face contorted with anger, his lips pressed into a thin line, she wanted all of him, every breath, word and inch. If she touched him now, she wondered if he would take her right there on the floor beneath the rubble in a fit of rage, or swat her away, sickened by the thought. She wasn't sure if her heart could take either possibility.

'But she hates me – you both hate me. What can I do? What can I possibly do to make her love me?'

He looked away, disdain etched into his brow.

'No, please, Christian. Enlighten me. Tell me what to do that I haven't already tried.'

'I'm calling the police.' He strode out of the room and snatched the phone from its cradle.

'You can't.' She chased behind him and snatched his arm. 'You don't know what they've done!'

He yanked his arm from her grasp and headed down the hall, took the stairs two at a time. He had to be as far away from her as possible.

She returned to the door and looked back at the paintings, years of work and pain torn to pieces.

Either the killer did this searching for the journal, or the police wanted her to know that this was a fight they planned to win.

Whoever the culprit, they had wanted to scare her, know that they could invade every part of her life. But what should have scared her into silence only made her more eager for the truth. They had wanted to silence her, but instead they had ignited a fire that she wouldn't let die. They had made it personal.

C

The three police officers stood in the kitchen, each with their arms crossed and fluorescent coats reflecting the spotlights in the ceiling. Leech, Watts, Benson. Detective Clark's hounds sent to do his dirty work, to cover up crimes they themselves might have committed. But she didn't shout, she didn't scream, she remained silent. If they were responsible, they had to believe their tactics had worked. Only when they got off her back could she move freely again. She couldn't get justice for Finn and the others with the police following her everywhere she went. Christian had to believe she was sane, and the police had to believe she was finished. Only the killer needed to know that she was coming for him.

Photographs had been taken of the mess, statements conducted in separate rooms. If Christian thought she was mad, mad enough to trash her own home and smash the window to make it look like the work of a suspect in her investigation, he would tell the police exactly what they wanted to hear: she was mad, and everything she said and did was invalid. They would have it down on paper, and from her own husband, no less. It didn't matter what she found in the investigation; if she were considered mad, the whole force would laugh her out of the station.

She stood in the corner of the room near the study, occasionally looking inside and catching the sight of Violet's sinister glare, slashes where her eyes had been.

'You're aware that your behaviour may have triggered this,' Leech said. 'Digging up other people's pasts, getting beneath their skin.'

'She's aware,' Christian said from the other side of the room. He looked at her for the first time in hours. 'Aren't you, Rose?'

She had never noticed how he spoke to her like a child. Maybe he had only started to do so because he thought she was mad. Or maybe it was because she had started to think for herself.

'Yes,' she said croakily.

Watts spoke next. 'You need to think of your family's safety now, Rose.'

Stop what you're doing, and all of this goes away. She remembered Leech's words as he stalked alongside her in the police car as she headed to the bus stop, the intensity of his glare, the sly, sideways grin. He performed well. He stood in the kitchen and appeared forlorn, but when she met his eye, she saw the shimmer of enjoyment in it. She wanted it gone, wiped out for good.

'Yes,' she repeated.

'So you'll stop this?' Christian asked.

'Yes.'

She looked at each of the men who had worked so hard to silence her, thinking they had won.

'We'll be in touch,' Watts said, and headed for the hall. Christian followed behind him. Leech and Rose remained in the room, their eyes meeting.

'You'll end all this?' he asked.

'If I do, it'll all go away, right?'

'Right.'

'Yes,' she said. 'I'll stop.'

He looked at her for the longest time, searching her eyes for the truth. He exhaled in a laugh.

'Liar.'

He left the room for the hall and listened to them speak before the door shut. She stepped forward and looked down the hall. Christian had left too.

Her phone rang in her pocket. She took it in her hand and saw her father's name flashing on the screen. Just seeing it brought her comfort, something she never would have foreseen.

'Hi,' she said.

'Hi. Look, I found something. Something we didn't look at earlier.'

Fear shivered in his voice, crackled in the silence that followed.

'You need to see this,' he said.

'I'll be there as quickly as I can.'

She ended the call and tapped the cab driver's number again, hoping he was still on shift for the night.

By the tone of her father's voice, she knew she wouldn't like what she was going to see.

FINN'S JOURNAL

6th March 2018

I'd vomited three times that morning.

Every time I thought of seeing my tormentor, my stomach would twist into knots, send me lurching to the nearest toilet.

I looked up at the police station and stumbled to the nearest bush, retching into the dirt.

He had broken me. He hadn't physically hurt me, and yet he had instilled a fear so deep that I no longer remembered who I'd been before he appeared. I didn't recognise myself in the mirror. My hair was thinning, my skin a pasty white and thin on my bones. My thoughts and dreams were so dark, filled with a reel of blood and murder, because I cannot think of another way this will end. I dreamt of my death every night, still do as I write this at three in the morning, after a dream so vivid that the moment I woke up I felt the skin above my heart for the wound his knife had made.

I got up from the dirt and clapped my hands together to dust off the filth. Once I faced him, it would all be over. Everyone in the room would see what he had done to me. The truth of my trauma could not be covered with another man's lie.

I made my way inside the station, introduced myself at the reception in no more than a whisper. I barely had time to get comfortable in my seat in the waiting area before the officers emerged.

Lycett took one look at me and said, 'You'll be okay.'

I couldn't nod. I couldn't speak. I couldn't even meet his eye. I stared at his feet, longing for it to be over, to have my life back.

I couldn't remember standing from the seat or following them through the station. One minute I was looking at his shoes, wondering how he kept them so clean, focusing on anything but the event that awaited me. The next I was standing before a door, waiting to be led inside.

'You'll be okay,' he repeated.

Officer Byrne opened the door.

I froze to the spot. Every airway sealed shut. My lungs shrank in my chest. I stumbled back into the wall of the corridor.

'No.'

'You can do this, Finn,' Lycett said. 'We'll be with you the entire time.'

I couldn't breathe. Why couldn't I breathe? I snatched my neck, clawed at it with my nails until there were red marks streaked down my throat.

'Close your eyes,' Officer Lycett said. 'Take a deep breath, and hold it for five seconds.'

I tried. The breath spluttered out. I heaved for air, and exhaled with a sob. I was suffocating, drowning in my fear, and no one could do a thing to stop it. My head felt light. My vision seemed to blur. I was dying.

'Finn, listen to me. Breathe in through your nose, hold it for five seconds, and then breathe out through your mouth.'

I heard him doing it with me. I mimicked his breaths, inhaling the scent of his aftershave and the stale air of the station. Slowly, my heart calmed. Air returned to my lungs with each growing breath. I relaxed against the wall, reluctant to open my eyes.

'You've got this,' he said. 'Come on.'

Officer Lycett led me inside. I was too weak to fight him. Officer Byrne followed behind me. I wondered if he thought this was funny too.

It was a conference room with a long table and fourteen chairs. Large windows overlooked the roofs of the town, treetops moving with the breeze.

Sitting at the table was a man I didn't recognise. He wore a brown suit and a sour expression on his face, lines deeply etched into his forehead and the corners of his eyes. It would be my stalker's lawyer. I wondered when he would arrive. Officer Lycett ushered me into the nearest seat, my back to the door. He would enter the room behind my back. I felt my chest tighten again, my pulse quicken.

Officer Lycett sat next to me. Officer Byrne sat beside the man I didn't know.

'Thank you for both attending today,' Officer Lycett said.

'Shouldn't we wait?' I asked.

'For what?'

'For Michael.'

The officers looked at each other.

'This. . . this is Michael King.'

The man looked at me, his eyes searing with contempt. He was around the same age as my stalker, but they were completely different men. This one had longer hair, tanned skin and darker eyes.

The man who was harassing me had lied.

I bowed my head. Of course he had lied. Why would he give me his real name?

'This isn't him,' I said into my lap.

'Great,' the real Michael King said. 'So I can go?'

'This isn't the man who has been harassing you?' Officer Lycett asked. 'You're sure?'

'I'm sure,' I whispered.

Lycett nodded to his colleague. The real Michael King was escorted out of the room, muttering under his breath. When the door clicked shut, I let the tears fall. I hid my face in my hands.

'You said his name was Michael King.'

'Because that's what he told me. He must have given me a false name.'

Silence fell upon the room, and I buried my face in my hands again. At that moment, I knew this would never end. My stalker, whoever he was, would continue to hunt me undetected, closing in until he had the perfect time to strike. My phone vibrated in my pocket. After several attempts to unlock it with shaking hands, I opened the message.

Nice try.

THIRTY-FIVE

Rose stared inside the shoebox, flinched when the stench hit her. If her father hadn't been holding it, she would have dropped it to the floor.

'I found it in the box you brought the letters in. I thought the boiler was playing up, but it was the sound of the flies.'

No one could refute her case now, not even the police. The rat was almost as large as the box, its eyes closed and mouth open. The needle had penetrated straight through its chest and into its heart, blood dried onto the metal. Maggots crawled around inside the box and along the rat's matted fur. She turned away with a shaking hand over her lips.

'We should stop,' Tony said.

'We can't,' she said, turning back. She watched him put the lid back on the box and place it on the coffee table. Even with the lid closed, she could still smell death contaminating the air.

'This is a threat,' he said.

'Because we're getting close to the truth.'

He sat down on the sofa, his eyes never leaving the box.

'Are you willing to risk your life for this? Mine? Lily's?'

'I'll work alone,' she said.

'That's not what I'm suggesting.'

'I know what you're suggesting. You think that I should stop this, but I can't. If I don't find out the truth, we will have failed Finn just like the police have. We will be as bad as them.'

She bit her lip and paced. The anger rose again. It seemed she felt nothing but fury now, as if she was becoming a new woman, forever raging, the weak woman she had once been shed like old skin.

'Every time I ask for help I'm told to stop. You, Christian, the police. Hell, for all I know the police could have sent this.'

She sank onto the opposite sofa. Every time she got closer to the truth, someone stood in her way. She didn't want to do this alone; she had spent too many years with her own thoughts and memories. Tears stung her eyes. She crossed the room and knelt before him.

'Please. Please don't make me do this alone. I know I'm asking for a lot. I'm asking you to put yourself in danger, but. . . I can't do this on my own.'

He went to speak. She spoke over him.

'If not for me, then for Jay. We failed him, but we don't have to fail the other men. We can do something about it this time. . . together.'

She took his hand and stared up at him. He met her eye, watering at the sound of his son's name, and looked away.

'I'm not worried about my safety,' Tony said hoarsely. 'I'm worried about yours. Let me take over. I've lived my life. It doesn't matter if something happens to me. But you. . .'

'I got you into this. I can't stop now. I don't *want* to stop.'

He sighed and rubbed his eyes until they were a furious red. 'Then we'll do it together.'

She sighed with relief. 'Thank you.'

She let go of his hand and returned to the other sofa. Silence hung over them except for the quiet wriggle of the maggots against the walls of the box.

'How are things with Christian?' he asked.

'He thinks I'm insane.'

'And Lily?'

'I wouldn't know, she's never home. Sometimes I feel like they've both died, that I'm mourning both of my daughters.'

Silence fell upon them. Her eyes drifted to the shoebox. She breathed in the deathly stench.

'You can stay here tonight, if you like.'

She thought of her home torn apart. She had tried to tidy up the mess before leaving for her father's, but the memory would always be there. Someone had been inside their home. There was a different air about it now – it had been claimed by another. If she returned home, she wouldn't sleep a wink.

'Thank you.'

'When was the last time you slept? Properly?'

'I can't remember.'

'Come,' he said.

He heaved himself up from the sofa with a groan, and she followed him into the kitchen and sat at the table. He took milk from the fridge and a saucepan from the drawer. He was making her hot milk, just like her mother used to do for her and Jay. A notch formed in her throat.

'Do you still think of her?' she asked.

'Every day.'

She had spent so long resenting him for what he'd done, that she had failed to think of how her mother's death had affected him. He had been the one to stick it out. He was the one who stayed and watched her die.

'How was it, when she. . .?'

She couldn't bring herself to watch her mother reach the end of the line. She had witnessed her wither away for years, until it was like greeting a stranger every morning. Her eyes had lost any sign of the woman she had been before. She hardly ate, only drank tea and smoked cigarettes as she stared mindlessly at the television, clearly thinking of nothing but Jay. By the time Rose had packed her bags to leave, her mother wouldn't even get out of bed. The last time they saw each other, she had changed the sheets with her mother still in the bed, rolling her from one side and then the other, shimmying the sheet beneath her light frame. She had said goodbye through tears, but her mother showed no sign that she'd even heard.

'Her mind was dead already,' he said, as he set the stove to a simmer and stirred the milk. 'I don't even think she knew she had cancer; with her, words never really sank in. Her mind was filled with him and him alone. The woman we knew and loved was gone; it was just her body in that hospital bed. It wasn't *her*.'

The house looked exactly as it had when she was a child. The table was the very same surface where she had eaten her breakfast before school, where her mother and father would sit once she and Jay had gone to bed. When Rose turned eleven, she made a habit of sitting at the top of the stairs and listening to their conversations. It was at that age when their relationship had started to sour; a new friction sat between them, stifling them all. They argued over Jay.

'I want you to know,' he said, turning to face her, 'I regret every hateful word I said to him. I loathe myself for pushing him away because he was different.' He shook his head. 'Not abnormal, that's not what I mean. I know it's normal now, but back then, he was different to what I expected a boy to be, the idea I had been raised to believe. I pushed my own son away for nothing, and I regret it every day.'

The milk hissed. He turned back to the stove and turned down the gas.

She couldn't tell him he was forgiven. His epiphany was years too late. Jay would never know that he was loved or missed, that the man whose love he had craved had finally shed his prejudices. But she wouldn't make him feel worse.

'Your mother never forgave me,' he said. 'Even on her deathbed, she called for him, for you, but never for me.'

He poured the milk into two mugs, added sugar and blew the surface of each to cool them down.

'I never got the chance to tell him that I loved him, that I was sorry, and I can't let the opportunity pass with you.' He placed the mug before her and tucked a lock of hair behind her ear. She felt like a child again. 'I love you with all my heart.'

He stroked her cheek and left the room, climbed the stairs with his mug in hand.

Lily and she would be like this, if Rose didn't do something to bring them together. Lily would hate her just as Rose had hated her father for all those years. She couldn't let history repeat itself. Once this was over, she would do everything she could to earn Lily's love again.

If she could learn to love her father once more, perhaps Lily could learn to love her too.

THIRTY-SIX

Rose lurched awake.

She was twelve again, waking in her bedroom to the smell of fried bacon drifting up the stairs, the patter of rain against the window. A phone was ringing. It would be one of Mum's friends; she always seemed to be on the phone. If Rose ever had to use it to call a friend, the earpiece would be warm from her mother's ear.

But the ringing sounded different, and her body felt older, aching at every joint. Her eyes burnt with every blink. She wasn't a child, but a grown woman back in her old bedroom. She shook the past from her mind and sat up, snatching her mobile from the floor where her clothes lay inside out in a tangled mess. She cleared her throat before answering.

'Hello?'

'Rose?'

'Detective Montgomery.'

There was something in his tone that made the hairs on her arms raise, her skin come out in goosebumps.

'What. . . what is it?'

'I'm afraid something's happened,' he said.

They could have found Finn's body.

Her house could have been broken into again.

Something could have happened to Lily.

Oh God, Lily.

There were dozens of scenarios, all of them bad. She longed to shut off her brain and focus only on what he had to say, but all she could think of was Lily, hurt because of her actions. Another daughter she had harmed.

'What's happened?'

'There are. . .' He cleared his throat. She could hear the rush of traffic on the other end of the phone, the odd gale cracking into the receiver. 'Posters have been left around the town. Posters with slanderous comments. . . about you.'

Slanderous material shared with the town, just as the stalker had done with Finn. 'We've got a team assigned to take them down,' he added.

'Don't,' she said. 'I need to see them.'

She jumped out of bed and stumbled around for her clothes, half blind in the dull light illuminating the curtains.

'Where should I meet you?' she asked. 'Where have the posters been displayed?'

'They're everywhere, Rose.'

She imagined them stapled to doors, taped to shop windows, drifting down the street and collecting in the gutter. Her head spun.

'Just. . . just tell me where to meet you.'

She heard the shuffle of paper and wondered if he was looking at a map. He breathed heavily down the line. She stopped in the centre of the room and closed her eyes to calm the thoughts hurtling around inside her head.

'Osborne Street at ten. That should be the last street to be touched.'

'All right.'

She ended the call and listened to the empty ring of the room.

The man who was responsible for Finn's misery was closing in, like the clamping of a vice.

What had happened to Finn was happening to her. The man who destroyed his life was trying to destroy hers too. He wasn't just after the journal – he was after her.

She dressed quickly, fumbling for her clothes in the shadows, and rushed towards the bathroom to use the toilet and brush her teeth. Montgomery had made it sound as though the police were taking the posters down at that very moment. She had to get to Osborne Street before all traces had been removed and see them for herself. She opened the bathroom door and froze.

The past was waiting for her. The bathwater was thick and red. She stared at her brother's body, the shadows framing his ribs, every eyelash on his closed lids. Her jeans weren't blue any more, but soaked through. She clenched her eyes shut and shook her head roughly. When she opened them again, the bath was dry and white. Jay was gone. She used the toilet and brushed her teeth, splashed cold water against her face, all the while keeping her eyes on the floor, closing them when red water slithered between the tiles and etched towards her feet, and rushed out of the bathroom before the past could drag her back again.

'Dad!' she called as she headed down the stairs, moving about the house like it was hers again. She entered the kitchen and found him standing at the counter preparing breakfast for them both. He turned with a smile, which fell the second he saw the fear in her eyes and the shake to her frame.

'What's happened?' he asked.

'I need a ride.'

Montgomery was right. The posters were everywhere.

Her own eyes stared back at her a hundred times, stuck to the glass of shop windows, every lamp post and wall; drifting down the road in the wind and stuck to the ground, soaked through with the rain. The large black words ran down the walls where the rain had got them.

KID-KILLER.

Montgomery stood beside her silently. People muttered about them as they passed. Rose snatched a poster from a passing woman.

'Hey!'

The anger slipped from the woman's face the second she recognised Rose from the flyer. She carried on along the street with her head down.

Rose looked at the flyer, damp and shaking in her grasp.

'When did this happen?' she asked croakily.

'The first call came in after six. We're searching CCTV back at the station and should have footage of who did this by noon.'

'Doesn't this seem familiar to you?' she asked.

He turned away from her and lit a cigarette in a cupped palm, breathed out the smoke in a sigh.

'This happened to Finn,' she said.

She thought of the social media pages that had been created overnight, and wondered which had been completed first: the posters or the online slander. There was one page called *#JusticeforViolet*, another simply called *The Kid-Killer of Rearwood*. Photos of Violet had been posted on the social media accounts, photos of Rose, pictures she had forgotten existed. Post after post defiling her, demanding that she serve time in prison for her crime, random users suggesting the return of capital punishment and that she hang for what she'd done. How had someone got hold of these photos? Had they found their way online somehow? Or had they been hunted out? Lily hadn't posted about this yet, but Rose knew she would. She regularly refreshed Lily's social media pages.

'It could be a coincidence,' he said. 'Bringing up the past can get people riled.'

'Are you sure your colleagues didn't do this?'

'Of course they didn't.'

'Please,' she said with a snort. 'Please don't act like you don't know what goes on.'

She eyed the posters on the walls until her whole body shook with rage. She lunged forwards and snatched at them, one by one, wet paper digging beneath her fingernails and a path of it left behind her, soaking into the puddles.

'Do you take me seriously now?' she shouted, storming back to him. 'Surely now you and your colleagues can't write me off as a crazy woman making up lies.'

'I've never believed that,' he said. 'It's the lack of—'

'Bullshit! You want this buried just like the rest of them. You might not have hung these posters or followed me down the street in a patrol car, but your silence, your inability to act, makes you complicit. You're just as bad as them.'

'What do you want us to do, Rose? Arrest everyone in Rearwood?'

'I want you to take this seriously, look into the case and get justice for the victims. Finn might be dead, for all we know.'

'You can't possibly know that.'

'And don't pretend you aren't aware of the others. Johnny. Jamie. Phillip. Zach. Adam. They're dead or missing, and undoubtedly connected to this. Open your eyes!'

He crushed the ember of his cigarette beneath the tip of his shoe.

'We'll analyse the CCTV and be in touch.'

Then he turned down the street and blended in with the crowd, the last lungful of cigarette smoke billowing over his shoulders.

She waited a beat for her heart to calm, but tears fell instead. Stumbling back against the wall she breathed in the crisp, cold air as tears chilled on her cheeks. It wasn't the hateful comments about her, or the people who wished her dead, but the invasion into her past. Violet's photo had been taken by someone and re-posted by dozens of others, using her sweet, angelic face to push a cause that wasn't theirs to claim.

She dashed the tears away with her sleeve and followed down the street. People on the path looked her up and down, muttered behind her back. Whoever had done this wanted the town to turn on her, for her to take the heat while the killer slipped beneath the radar. And to all intents and purposes, it seemed to be working.

She turned onto the high street with her head down, just as her phone rang in her pocket. She checked the screen and saw Christian's name. He must have seen the posters or the social media pages. She put the phone back in her pocket, ignoring the dozens of texts that Rob had sent her, asking if she was okay, if he could do anything to help. He'd obviously seen the posters too. If he hadn't known about her past before, he did now: she was a kid-killer. She turned off her phone and thrust it back in her pocket.

She didn't want to talk to either of them; all she wanted was for her world to stop spinning out of control, just for a second, so she could catch her breath.

Her father was waiting for her further down the street, his BMW dented in the side, old bird shit baked onto the bonnet. She was about to cross the street when she spotted a familiar face and stopped.

Not one familiar face, but two.

Lily was sitting inside the café at a table by the window.

With Heather.

Lily appeared to be on the verge of tears. Rose watched Heather take her hand from the other side of the table and give it a comforting squeeze.

Rose crossed the street in a haze, not caring if cars came in either direction, or if people on the street recognised her from the posters and took a tentative step back. She couldn't escape the sight of her daughter seeking comfort from the woman who had betrayed her again and again. Tears collected in her eyes. She pressed her hand against the glass.

When Heather glanced up, her eyes widened and her jaw fell.

She immediately let go of Lily, who followed her gaze to the window. Lily scowled and looked away.

She's ashamed of me.

Rose turned quickly and headed up the street. She couldn't let them see her break down. Tears fell in endless streams; her throat ached. She had to get home, had to get away from them, the posters, the whole town closing in.

'Rose!' Heather said, coming up behind her.

Rose spun around, giving Heather a look that stopped her in her tracks.

'Her too? First my husband, and now my daughter? You had to take her too?' Heather stared at her with her lips parted, words caught in her throat.

339

Rose turned and rushed up the street, finally letting the sobs free.

She had lost everyone and everything. The past was closing in, dug up by a man who would do anything to keep his secret buried. She had nothing left.

Nothing but the truth.

FINN'S JOURNAL

4th April 2018

I woke up, unsure if it was night or day. The bed sheets hadn't been changed for weeks. I could smell my nervous sweat on them from where I'd jolted out of my dreams, the sheets twisted around my limbs. It was dark; I had slept through the day again.

Outside, winter had turned to spring, but I rarely saw it except for the occasional glance between the slats to check whether he was standing on the other side of the street.

I kept the blinds closed. If I opened them, I immediately felt his eyes on me, watching my every move; even if he wasn't there, his presence was. I would move around in the dark, my eyes accustomed to the dim light of day behind the blinds and the deep, black shadows of the night. The fridge was empty, the cupboards bare but for the last few tins of beans and soup. Each time I prepared to leave the house to go shopping, I stood by the door with my wallet in my pocket and the key in my hand and broke down. It always ended with me returning them to the sideboard before crawling back into bed, fully clothed and weeping at my weakness. Leaving the house meant facing him. I would rather have starved.

I looked through the darkness to where I had left my phone on the bedside table.

I turned on my phone twice a day: once in the morning, and again in the evening, to check if my boss had given me a call or sent an email, with a small sliver of hope that he would take me back. He never did. Instead, I had messages filled with hate pouring into my inbox. My voicemail was full with messages I didn't have the strength to listen to. The police hadn't been in touch either. I left all the texts and other communications from him unread, turned off my phone again, and closed my eyes.

I remember everything about this night. The building was quiet, except for the occasional gurgle of the pipes within the walls. I couldn't hear the usual mutter of the television downstairs, or the heavy footsteps from the flat above. Even the street was quiet: no breeze, no sirens, no vixens wailing into the night.

The bedroom door creaked.

My eyes flew open.

He was standing in the doorway, a silhouette against the darkness.

I screamed so loud, so suddenly, that pain burst in my throat, as though it had erupted with the force, split from the back of my tongue to the depths of my stomach, stealing away my voice. I pressed myself against the headboard and pulled my knees up to my chest. He stepped forward, so I backed away, falling from the bed to the floor with a jarring thump, and pressed myself in the corner of the room, making myself small. Hot, salty tears shot down my face and wet my lips. My lungs shrank. I couldn't breathe.

He stepped further into the room with his hands up. I could just see the whiteness of his palms.

'No! No, no, no, please! Just leave me alone!'

I clamped my eyes shut, waiting for the moist press of his hands on my body. I wondered what he would touch first: the parts he desired, or my neck to silence me.

I tried to scream again but couldn't, steeled my teeth shut until pain shot down to the roots.

Further away in the apartment, the front door clicked shut.

I opened my eyes.

He was gone.

I paced the apartment from one end to the other, entering every room with a nervous glance to make sure he was definitely gone.

I hadn't left the flat, so he'd come inside. I couldn't even lock myself away.

I had stayed in the corner of the room for what felt like an hour, struggling to find my breath, to stop the tears. Someone had banged on the front door. I thought they were worried about me, following the scream. But it was the man from upstairs, telling me to keep the noise down in a trail of expletives and threats.

Eventually I found the strength to stand, sliding up the wall, and stumbled over to the bed for my phone. I turned it on, ignoring all the messages he had sent.

I blinked away the tears and called the police, barely able to speak clearly, stumbling over every word, my breathing inconsistent.

All I could do was pace as I waited for them to arrive – I can't remember how much time had passed. And all I could think about was him inside the flat, staring at me through the darkness, asking myself how he'd got inside after the landlord had finally got around to changing the locks.

When the door buzzed from downstairs, I froze. It could be the police, or it could be him. He had let himself in before, but maybe he was trying a different approach, wanting me in the doorway so he could silence me faster, shield my mouth mid-scream.

It buzzed again. If I didn't answer, the police would leave. But if it was him, I would be powerless again. I could already hear Byrne's tone, asking why I didn't defend myself, speaking through the smirk that made me blush whenever I thought of it.

When it buzzed a third time, and I heard the movement of feet from upstairs, pounding against the ceiling, I made for the door and rushed down the stairs to the front door of the building.

It was dawn. The sky was waking in colour and reflecting in the glass of the cars lining the street. Officers I hadn't met before stood on the step, with a man in a suit behind them, a detective perhaps. I stayed behind the door and stared past the officers, scanning the opposite side of the street, to where he usually stood. He wasn't there.

The male officer made to speak, but I pressed a finger against my lips. I beckoned them inside with my hand. They glanced at one another with an expression I was too slow to catch, and the man in plain clothes watched me intently from behind his spectacles, reflecting the officers' high-vis jackets.

I made my way up the stairs and flinched when the shout came.

'Arrest this fucker!' my neighbour shouted from the top of the stairs, in nothing but a vest and boxers. Hair on his chest crept around the limits of the vest.

'He's making our lives hell. Shouting all night. Slamming doors. Causing leaks in the building. He smeared his own shit on the walls, did you know that? He's fucking loony!'

'Sir, we'll need you to calm down,' the female officer said from behind me. She walked past me on the stairs and moved him aside. I couldn't go any further.

'Come on,' the man in the suit said.

I met his eyes, confused by the look in them, as though he had seen all this before.

I climbed the rest of the stairs on shaking legs and fumbled with my keys at the door of the flat, the male officer breathing heavily behind me.

I opened the door and let them in, and it was only having left the apartment that I could smell the decay of it when I returned. Stale sweat stained the air, the musk of damp from the constant state of darkness clinging to every fabric and surface. The damage from the leak had been put right, and I had scrubbed the faeces from the walls, but I could still smell it in the small space, the lingering scent of him.

'He was here,' I said quickly, turning to look at them.

The female officer finally entered, shutting the door behind her. The man in the suit had crossed the room while my back was turned, and opened the blinds, the morning light slicing through the dust in the air. I squinted against the glare.

'He was here,' I repeated. 'I woke up and. . . and. . .' I was stammering, couldn't think clearly. I shook my head. 'He-he-he was at the foot of my bed.'

'Why don't we all sit down,' said the man in the suit. He perched on the edge of the sofa, as though he didn't want to spoil his clothes on the fabric. The female officer sat beside him, the male officer remained on his feet. I sat down in the chair opposite them and jittered my leg, unable to stop myself from moving. The female officer looked at me intently.

'Finn, you remember us, don't you?' she said.

'What?'

I had seen so many different police personnel that each of

345

them became the same, a blur of high-vis jackets and strange, shared glances. Perhaps I had met them.

They glanced at the man in the suit, who nodded.

'Finn, my name is Dr Thew. I'm the on-call psychologist for cases such as these.'

Cases such as these, *I remember thinking, unable to understand why a psychologist would be needed for a call-out about an intrusion.*

'We're concerned,' the man said. He kept on speaking but I tuned in and out, unable to believe the words coming from his mouth. Paranoid. Psychosis. Wasting police time. A place you could go to get help. *It was only when he stopped speaking and I felt the heat of their glares on me, waiting for me to respond, that his words sank in.*

'You. . . you think I'm lying?'

'Finn. . .' This was the female officer.

'Get out.'

'Mr Matthews, we've had complaints from your neighbours. We—'

'Get out!'

They all stared for a moment, meeting each others' eyes, and then back to me. I rose on numb legs and strode to the door, opened it for them.

'I thought. . . I thought you were on my side,' I said as they stood and made their way over.

'We are on your side, Finn,' the shrink said. 'All we want to do is help you.'

They left in single file. I stayed there, listening to the descent of their footsteps, the front door opening and shutting. I closed my own door and returned to bed.

They thought I was crazy, that I was making it all up.

Through it all, I had thought I had their help, and was keeping myself going until they got him and stopped him for good. But it was then that it hit me. I didn't have their help at all. I was on my own, always had been, except for him.

It was just us now, me and him locked in some vile game, a game he was set to win.

THIRTY-SEVEN

Rose stepped inside the house and shut the door behind her with an unintentional bang that made her wince. She slumped against it and closed her eyes, quivering from the cold. The rain had plastered her clothes and hair to her skin, and her thoughts seemed diluted, as though it had seeped in through her skin and filled her skull. Each move she made felt disjointed and delayed. Her head hadn't stopped spinning since seeing her face plastered all over town. Exhaustion and stress had finally caught up with her, and it was as though she was losing herself, unable to think or act straight.

When she opened her eyes again, her gaze spun, failing to focus on any one thing, before falling on the suitcases resting against the wall. She was used to seeing Christian's suitcase at the foot of stairs, but not Lily's. She blinked furiously to check she was really seeing them, and that it wasn't just a memory that had bled into the present, knocked from another part of her brain. She reached forward and touched the tag on Lily's suitcase. They were definitely there.

Christian stood in the doorway of the living room. She couldn't be sure if he had just appeared, or had been standing there the whole time. The house had been cleaned up as though nothing had happened.

'Rose, a moment please,' he said, and stepped back out of sight.

Her thoughts and emotions couldn't connect, like crossed wires in her brain. She walked towards the doorway, focusing on each step, and stopped in her tracks.

Christian. Lily. Heather. Dr Hunter. Adeline. They all stared at her, all but Lily, who sat with her arms crossed and her eyes on the floor. An empty chair was placed before them, like a seat before a jury.

'Sit down, please, Rose,' said Dr Hunter.

She had lost all will to fight. She walked into the centre of the room and sat heavily in the chair. Rainwater dripped from her clothes and soaked into the carpet. A high-pitched squeal rang in her right ear. From where she sat, she could see their cars parked in the driveway on the other side of the window. She had walked right past them.

'Rose,' the doctor said. 'We're here today because we're worried about you.'

Adeline scoffed. 'And for our own safety.'

Heather shot her a look. 'Adeline.'

Rose's eyes flitted from one to the other, each of them diverting their eyes, except for the doctor.

'We would all like you to hear what we have to say about this. . . situation. Heather, why don't you go first?'

She nodded quickly and sat forward in her chair, choosing her words for a moment. Rose watched her eyes move left and right, before finally settling on hers.

'Rose, we're all worried about you. This thing you're doing, this. . . *investigation,* it's destroying you. I've known you for a long time and I've never seen you like this. You've lost weight. You're still not sleeping. You're acting oddly. It seems like you've lost a part of yourself, worse than before, before Vi—'

'Are you sleeping with my husband?'

The anger had risen the moment she'd seen Heather in the room. She had the audacity to enter her home and pity her, when she was helping to tear them all apart.

Heather's face fell slack. Christian sat straighter in his chair.

'Of course not, I would never—'

'You were alone together, right here. In my house. You went to the doctor's house together.'

'To talk about how best to help you,' Heather said. 'We're all very worried. I promise you, Rose, I am not sleeping with your husband.'

'Well, at least she admits she was at your house, doctor,' put in Adeline. 'Not that it would matter if she denied it   I saw her with my own two eyes.'

'Why are you here?' Rose spat.

Adeline had the nerve to laugh.

'The doctor invited me, probably in the hope that seeing you break down will stop me pressing charges for you stalking our street.'

Christian sat forward. 'Adeline. . .'

'One at a time please,' said the doctor.

'Then I'll take my turn.' Adeline fixed her eyes on Rose. 'Unlike everyone else, I don't care what you do with your life, but I do care that you're stalking around in the dark, right outside my home where my children sleep.'

'Adeline. . .' Heather warned.

'What? It's the truth, and if it happens again, I'll call the police.'

'Enough,' Christian said.

'Why don't you speak, Christian?' suggested the doctor.

Christian sighed into his lap, wrung his hands together.

'You said you would stop this,' he said. 'You promised you

would stop and yet here you are, staggering in like you're drunk, soaked through from the rain. You look. . .'

He looked away, as if the sight of her was too much.

'I trusted you when you said you would stop this, and you broke that trust. The police have asked you to stop. Dr Hunter has asked you to stop. I have asked you to stop. But you won't listen. You're obsessed with finding a man you've never met, a man you're willing to throw your life away for. I'm worried that one day I'll come home to find you've been arrested, or harm will have come to Lily because of your actions. I can't risk that, Rose. So, I will ask you one more time: please stop this.'

The room fell silent but for the sound of her heart beating in her ears.

'Thank you for your honesty, Christian,' said the doctor. 'Lily, why don't you speak now?'

Lily seemed to have shrunk in her chair, as though she wished she was anywhere but here, sitting before her mother.

'Do you really want to know why I hate you?' Lily asked.

Rose flinched. Tears fell but she didn't notice them, just the searing hate in Lily's eyes.

'You grieve for the daughter you lost, my sister – the sister you killed. But you only have one person to grieve for. I didn't just lose my sister that day, I lost my mother too.'

She spoke with such force that spit flew from her mouth with her words. Lily didn't sound like a child any more, but a grown woman.

'It's not just because of what you did. . .' She looked away and the venom dissolved. She sank back in her chair, bit her lip to stop herself from crying, the child in her creeping back. 'It's because of what you said.'

'What did I say?' Rose asked in barely a whisper.

'You said you'd saved the wrong one. You wished you'd saved Violet instead of me.'

The air slammed from her lungs and she breathed out in a sob. She hadn't thought the words – she had said them aloud. . . and Lily had heard her.

'No. . .'

Rose could feel the heat of the others watching them, but she couldn't tear her eyes away from Lily's.

'I lay there in the mud, barely alive, and heard my own mum wish I was *dead*!'

'No. . .' Rose could barely speak through the sobs. Her whole body shook with them. Her throat was on fire.

'I couldn't grieve for Violet because I resented her. I hated that you loved her more. You stole my chance to miss her, and you stole my chance to love you, and I will never, *ever* forgive you for that.'

'Lily, I'm. . . I'm so. . . sorry.'

Rose covered her face with her hands, sounds escaping her like a wounded animal: whines, screeches. The room began to spin again.

'You must stop this, Rose,' the doctor said. 'You've followed people to their homes, watched through windows. You've put your family and yourself in danger, and accused your husband and your friend of having an affair.'

She couldn't look at him. She couldn't speak, couldn't think of anything other than Lily. The tears wouldn't stop coming. The pain was like a gunshot wound to her chest, ripped open, ribs broken, the cavity bare for all to see, watching as her heart broke.

'Paranoia is a side effect of sleep deprivation. I know it's difficult for you to see this for what it is, but paranoia can feel incredibly real; it can even make you act in destructive ways to prove your own point. It could explain the trashing of your home, your burnt bag, the sinister messages, as if from someone else. Without sleep, the brain works in ways that are difficult to understand. You're not entirely at fault here.'

She was too distraught to defend herself, to correct his lies. It was as though they had each shared a knife to cut at her tongue, passing it between them until Lily made the last cut and ripped the flesh from her mouth. But as the doctor spoke, her anger rose, the heat of it dissolving her tears and stifling her sobs. She lowered her hands. Lily had left the room. Rose shot a look at the window to see her getting into the passenger seat of Christian's car and slamming the door behind her.

'There is a place you can go, to get the rest and help you need.'

'You want to lock me away.'

'No, Rose. We want to help.'

Christian was deathly pale. Heather was biting on her lip to stop herself from crying. Adeline had been stunned into silence. The doctor sat before her with a smug expression, his hands cupped neatly in his lap.

'You think I'm mad? That I'm making all this up?'

She snatched her bag from her shoulder and took the journal in her hand. She opened it at a random page and read a line.

'*My thoughts and dreams were filled with a reel of blood and murder, because I cannot think of another way this will end.*'

'Rose. . .'

'You think I made that up? That this is my handwriting?' She showed them the page, pointed at it with a shaking finger. 'Speak to Shane Hughes if you don't believe me. Speak to Anna, a detective at the police station. I'm not lying. I'm not mad. This man went missing and *no one cares*! Why don't any of you care? Don't you have hearts? Don't you have any decency at all?'

'You need help, Rose.' Christian's voice was hoarse.

'No, Christian, Finn does.'

He shook his head in disbelief, wiped a tear from his cheek.

'We're leaving, and we're not coming back.'

The day had finally come. She had waited years for this, almost hoped for it to end the torment, but it still didn't feel real.

Christian stood, wiping his palms on his trousers.

'Goodbye, Rose.'

He left the room until it was just the four of them listening to the wheels of the suitcases dragging against the floor in the hall and the click of the door as it shut behind him.

'It's time we all left, I think,' the doctor said.

Adeline was the first to go, without a single glance at Rose. The doctor followed. Heather hung back, tears rolling down her cheeks.

'Rose, I. . .'

'Heather,' the doctor said behind Rose's back. 'We have tried our best. There is nothing more we can do.'

Heather nodded, wiping her eyes as she left the room.

Rose sat in the chair and listened to the final slam of the door.

No, she thought suddenly. *I can't lose her.*

Still unsteady on her feet as though her skull was full of water, she rushed to the door. She opened it and squinted against the sun. When her eyes settled, she saw Rob making his way up the driveway.

No. Not now.

She looked at Christian, staring from Rob to her behind the steering wheel. Heather watched in wonder before getting inside her own car.

'Rose. . .' Rob said as he approached the steps. 'What's happened?'

'Not now, Rob, please.'

She broke, tears swimming down her cheeks.

'What's going on?' He shot a look at Christian's car as it pulled away. 'Has he done something?'

'No,' she said, her tone sharp. 'Now please, just go. I can't do this right now.' She watched the hurt take over his face.

'All right,' he nodded, jaw clenched, and turned to leave.

'How do you know where I live?'

He turned back. 'I. . . you signed up to the newsletter, remember?'

He was friends with Seb, Leech, Watts. He knew where she lived. She had let him into her life without really knowing him. She had trusted people because she couldn't bear to be alone; she might have let one of her tormentors straight into her life.

'I'm sorry, I thought we. . .' He looked at her, shook his head. 'I'm sorry.'

The last of the cars turned out of the driveway. It was just the two of them. Rob turned towards the road and didn't look back.

Rose watched him leave, and continued to stare out long after he'd gone. The moment she turned around and closed the door behind her, she would be alone again, the ring of silence waiting for her, ready to turn her mad.

Too late, she thought. *I already am.*

She walked inside and closed the door behind her.

THIRTY-EIGHT

Two days had passed since the intervention, but Rose's tears were still as fresh, the pain searing like a new wound. Her scent was sour; saliva had dried to a paste on her tongue.

It all made sense now. No wonder Lily hated her. She had heard her own mother wish her dead. Every time she thought of Lily confessing the secret she had kept for years, her heart broke again and again, fresh tears swelling in her eyes, sobbing herself into a light slumber, only to wake and remember it all over again. Her only sense of time was the sun in the sky and the smell of her scent spoiling with each hour.

How could she possibly fix this? It was a wrong she could never put right. She couldn't go back and unsay the words, couldn't raise Violet from the dead. She had accepted losing Christian, had quietly resigned herself to the idea a long time ago, but she couldn't let go of Lily.

Before saying those fatal words, she had never admitted to herself that she had a favourite. It wasn't that she had loved Violet more, but she had been *allowed* to love her more. Violet wanted her affection, whereas Lily had always been a daddy's girl, a free spirit she couldn't pin down, with a wilfulness that made it so much harder for Rose to exist on so little sleep. Violet was subdued, whereas Lily knew how to push her buttons. Did that mean she had a favourite? It didn't matter now. Her own words had tarnished her relationship with her daughter for ever.

She moved in the chair for the first time in what seemed like days and flinched from the burning pain in her bladder. She took her phone from her pocket and called the only person who could possibly understand.

He picked up after three rings.

'Rose,' her father said. 'I've been trying to get hold of you for days. Are you all right?'

'I've lost her.' Rose's voice was hoarse from so long without speaking.

'Who? Who have you lost? What's going on?'

'Lily. I'll never get her back. They've left for good. I. . .'

She couldn't bear to repeat the words. The moment she spoke them, they wouldn't just be inside her head; they would solidify, become something she could never take back.

'The day of the accident, after Lily and I got out of the water, I. . .' She bit her tongue, blinked away the tears. 'I thought something disgusting, something evil, and I found out that I didn't think it at all. But I said it aloud.'

'What did you say?'

Another sob burst from her. Tony waited patiently on the other end of the line.

'I wished. . . I wished I had saved Violet instead.'

'Oh, Rose. . .'

What had she expected him to say? What could anyone possibly say to ease the guilt?

'She will never forgive me, but. . . I can't lose her. I can't accept that I've lost her too.'

She cried for a while, comforted by listening to him on the other end of the line. After two full days of being alone with her thoughts, it felt good to be near someone, even if it was just the sound of them.

'How did you do it?' she asked.

He had to have felt the same pain she was feeling now: the responsibility of killing one child and losing another. For years, Rose had feared she would turn into her mother, overcome by grief, but in the end she had become her father.

'I don't know,' he said. 'But somehow I did. I can't tell you how, only that it's possible. All you can do is hope that one day they will forgive you.'

'You waited over two decades,' she said.

'You may have to as well,' he said softly.

'But what if I can't wait that long? What if I can't live without her?'

'I'm sorry, my darling. That isn't up to you.'

She thought of Lily as a baby, holding her in her arms, stroking the soft skin on her plump cheeks, eyeing the moist bow of her lips, the long auburn lashes that were blonde at the tips. Her love for her, and the pain of losing her, rivalled no other. People say burning alive is the worst way to die, but they're wrong. Killing one's child and then losing another is the longest, most agonising death a person could be dealt.

'Do you want to come and stay here? So you're not alone?'

'No,' she said. 'Not yet. I just need. . .' She looked out at the bridge, further memories filling her head, then closed her eyes and sank back into the seat. 'Time. I just need time.'

'Okay.'

She ended the call. Silence rang back into the room.

She got up from the seat and almost doubled over. The pain in her bladder screamed. Her legs burnt as blood rushed back into each limb. She hobbled to the bathroom to relieve herself and then took a bottle of wine from the kitchen cupboard. She would sleep upstairs in her own bed, the bed she used to share with her husband. Could she still call him that? *Husband*. The law still recognised them as a married couple, but it felt wrong. They were more like strangers.

She headed for the stairs, listening to the satisfying slosh of the liquid in the bottle, and walked along the dark landing. She screamed as she was thrust into the wall.

A heavy body pressed into her back, slamming her face against the plaster. Stale breaths blasted the back of her head and whipped her hair against her cheek. Her arm was twisted behind her with a sudden thrust. She screamed, the pain causing her to drop the bottle to the carpet and her legs to buckle beneath her until she was a heap on the ground. She untangled herself in a manic hurry and looked up. The silhouette of a man towered over her in the dark.

The journal was in his hand.

She had left it in her bag on the island unit in the kitchen. He must have been in the house while she slept and was forced to run upstairs when she woke.

She reached out to snatch it from his grasp. He turned to leave. 'No!'

She latched her arms around both of his ankles and braced herself. The floor shuddered with the impact. She clambered over him for the journal, tugging at the cover. He twisted beneath her in one violent thrust and knocked her against the wall with a bang. All the air left her chest.

She put her hands out to steady herself and felt the cool glass of the bottle beneath her fingertips. She swung it by the neck with all her might. Glass exploded with an ear-ringing shatter, ricocheted off him and onto her. He cried out and thrust her into the wall again, her head cracking against it. She fell limp and slumped to the carpet, with small bits of glass pressing against her cheek.

The man staggered to his feet and down the hall, swaying as if he had drunk from the bottle. Her eyes flickered shut to the creak of the stairs. The front door opened and closed.

The journal was gone.

ZACH

C

3rd December 2013

Run.

The woodland floor had sliced up the soles of his feet, but he could barely feel the pain through his fear. The night air had scorched his lungs and throat until each breath tasted of blood. The thud of footsteps not far behind him masked the sound of his own.

Just keep running.

His legs shook. Tears continually streamed down his cheeks, slanting with the wind. If he stopped he'd be dead, but he couldn't run for ever. The wilderness seemed never-ending, and however fast he ran, the man behind him only seemed to get faster. Zach could hear the man's trouser legs brushing against each other with his strides, his quick breaths, the power of his footsteps as they snapped twigs and turned dead leaves into dust. Each time he bellowed his name, fear exploded in Zach's chest and spread through him like a current.

And then he saw it: a small dot of light flickering between the trees.

He sobbed without stopping. More lights flickering silently, like fireflies in the dark.

He raced towards them, dodging the trees in his path, vaulting over a fallen trunk, until he passed through two trunks and was out in the open, falling. He stumbled down the verge, running too fast to stop so suddenly, and fell to the muddy bank. The Rearwood river bustled before him; moonlight shimmered on the chopping surface, forming quick flickers of light before the ripples in the water changed. Those were the lights he had seen, not headlights passing on a motorway or a row of houses. He was still alone with him in the dark.

The bridge was just in sight. Zach scrambled to his feet and made to run in the same direction. He could flag down a car, stand in the middle of the road and force a driver to stop.

A hand snatched his hair.

A yelp ripped from his mouth.

He pulled forwards and into a sprint. Fresh pain pricked his scalp where hair had once been. The river roared beside him.

'Zach!'

Fear bled through him. The mud was soft and sucked at his soles. The man was so close that Zach could smell the sweat on him, feel the swipe of his hand through the air as he tried to grab him.

The bridge was close. He watched a car moving along it, its headlights illuminating the metal structure from one end to the other until it was gone.

He set his eyes on the slope of the bank leading up to the bridge. It would only take him another minute to reach the road and flag down a car. He would be safe. He would live.

Zach landed on the bank with a deafening thud. His head slammed against it and his senses spun. Hands were on him, pinning him down at the nape of his neck and the small of his back. He tried to breathe and inhaled dirt.

'You did this,' he spat at Zach's back. 'This is your doing!'

Another car drove along the bridge, so close that he could hear the distant sound of music playing on the radio, and yet the driver had no idea what was happening below. He screamed for help, but the word was cut short. His face was forced into the ground until he felt the gritty earth between his teeth.

'Quiet!' he hissed.

Zach lay still on the bank, listening to the car pass them on the bridge. Mud stuck to the tears on his cheeks. He wondered how long it would take for the man to kill him if he screamed. He listened to his escape pass him by until the sound died and they were alone again.

He was going to die.

Strong hands snatched him up to his feet and led him forwards. He tried to blink away the dirt, cough it up from his lungs. He saw the water just before he was thrust face first beneath the surface.

The water was so cold it felt like needles stabbing his skin and eyes. It numbed his teeth down to the roots, forced its way into his lungs when they mechanically drew for breath. He thrashed beneath the man's hold. His feet kicked against the bank until dirt flew into the air in clumps as he thrashed his arms through the water, desperately trying to find the surface for leverage.

Play dead.

It took every ounce of concentration for his body to fall still beneath the man's grasp. His heart was racing, his chest was filled with water, but he stayed still for second after second, waiting.

His grip weakened, and after a few seconds, he turned Zach over in the water until he was floating on his back.

Sounds exploded in his ears as they breached the surface. The night air cooled the water on his face. He heard the bustle of the river, the sway of the trees in the breeze, the man's sobs above him. He took small, controlled breaths through his nostrils, begging his lungs not to take over and force him to gasp for air.

The man took hold of his arms and held him to his chest, sobbing into his neck.

He must feel my heart. I'm trembling. He must know I'm alive.

But the sobbing continued, hot and wet.

Zach opened his eyes, stinging from the breeze, and sank his teeth into the man's neck, turning his sobs into screams. Blood pooled on his tongue, spewed out when the man's fist flew into his gut and unhinged his jaw.

He clambered on top of Zach and pinned him down. All Zach could do was watch helplessly as the man covered his mouth with one hand and pinched his nostrils closed with the other. They stared into each other's eyes, tears falling, bodies squirming for control.

'You did this,' he whispered. 'You did this.'

Zach closed his eyes.

THIRTY-NINE

Rose lay in bed looking up at the same ceiling she had stared at sleeplessly for years, only this time she lay in the bed alone. It was as if the attack in her home had woken her from a slumber, one in which she was stuck in a revolving nightmare and unable to escape. She had been overcome by grief, thinking of Lily and nothing more, but having the intruder's presence in her house made her remember why it all began: Finn.

Christian and Lily had left. The man who had harmed Finn had entered her home and taken the journal with him. Her life had been decimated, but she couldn't let it end like this. She had come so far, sacrificed so much. All of her losses couldn't be for nothing.

The police wouldn't help; the force had worked against her from the beginning, except for Montgomery who seemed to be working to keep the peace, whether for her or himself. The only people who had helped her along the way was a man who had fled the town for his own safety and a detective who had refused to help further. She thought of Shane trying to start over again, Anna working in the same building as the corrupt officers, and fought the urge to bury herself beneath the duvet and forget. She sat on the edge of the bed and rested her face in her hands.

There was only one person she could potentially win over, one person who didn't see her as a madwoman: Montgomery. But he was tied up amongst the mess, part of the same force who had tried to silence her.

Rose showered for the first time in days, washing away the sweat and tears, and scraped her hair in a messy, wet bun. She stepped out onto the landing.

The house was cold, silent, as though having just her inside wasn't enough to warm it and make it a home. This was her future: just her and the incessant silence ringing in her ears, the sound she was sure would turn her mad. Glass still covered the carpet, and dark splashes of wine stained the walls.

When she told Montgomery of the attack in her home, he would have to act. All she had to do was get to him without being followed.

She thought about how she was going to do it. It would be too risky to go to the police station when Dr Hunter had branded her as insane, the same man who seemed to be in Seb Clark's pocket. Montgomery had told her he lived on the farm on the edge of town; she could go there and wait for him to return. She took her phone from her pocket and called a local taxi firm as she headed downstairs, wandering into the living room with her phone to her ear. The operator spoke just as she reached the window.

'Lion Town Cars.'

She continued to stare out the window, her eyes locked on the police car parked on the opposite side of the street. Watts and Leech were inside. They were waiting for her.

'Is anyone there?'

There was only one other option.

'Hello?'

She ended the call and strode through the house to the back door.

This time, she would make sure she wasn't followed.

By the time Rose arrived at Montgomery's farm, the sun had almost set. Her mouth and throat were so dry that her tongue kept sticking against the roof of her mouth. She had passed puddles on her journey and had to stop herself from falling to her hands and knees and lapping up the murky water. Her bladder was burning, longing to be released, but each time she had tried to relieve herself, bobbed down in the treeline of the fields, it wouldn't come. Her whole body was tight like a fist, too tense to unfurl. Ever since leaving the house, she had been on high alert, flinching at the slightest sound.

She had kept to the backstreets, walking fast with her head down until she reached the fields where she could finally breathe with ease. But she felt as though she was on borrowed time, forever looking over her shoulder, listening out for the call of sirens, the sound of thudding footsteps coming up behind her. Leech and Watts would come looking the moment they knew she had left the house. It wasn't a matter of if, but when.

She had thought to call a cab from a backstreet so many times, but each time she stopped, she felt too exposed, and pictured the police car coming round the corner the second she dared to lower her guard. Each time, she kept on walking. She had tried to trust people before this, and her world had fallen apart. The only person she could rely on now was herself.

It was the only house for miles, lost amongst acres of sprawling fields. The windows reflected the sky, mimicking fire.

Everything hurt. Just when she thought she couldn't take another step, she forced one foot in front of the other.

She walked up the path to the front door, panting and coated in sweat. Her knock on the door was barely audible. She clenched her fist as tight as she could and put the last of her strength into it, banging on the wood until it shuddered in its frame.

Nothing.

She pressed her forehead against the door, her hot breaths bouncing back at her. All those miles, and Montgomery wasn't home. She had expected he would have returned from work by now, but as the sun set behind her, doubt crept in like a chill.

No. I won't let all of this be for nothing.

She straightened her spine and banged on the door again. Birds burst from the trees and took to the sky. She leaned down and opened the letterbox, squinted to see through the semi-darkness.

'Detective Montgomery? It's Rose Shaw.'

Years of mud were trodden into the carpet. The wallpaper dated back to the seventies, psychedelic patterns faded with age, strips of it peeling in yellowing curls. With so much land to care for, the house must be their last concern.

The farm. Perhaps his wife was working out the back.

She followed the house around and spotted a decaying barn a few hundred feet from the house. The metal skeleton of a tractor was stationed outside the barn's tall doors, brown with rust.

She turned to the house again and peered through the glass in the back door. The room was dark with dusk, but she could just see the glint of the steel kitchen tap beneath one of the windows, shining in the last of the sun.

If she could have salivated at the thought of water, she would have, but her mouth had been leeched dry. If she could just get inside and have a glass of water, the wait wouldn't be so unbearable. She spotted an outside tap and practically ran to it. The tap had rusted and refused to budge.

Small pots filled with overgrown weeds lined the back of

the house. She thought of her own garden and how she used to keep a spare key beneath one of the pots in case of emergencies. She checked under each one, disturbed insects running in all directions. No key. She plunged her hand in the pot nearest the door in case it had been hidden out of sight. The nettles stung at her hands and dirt dug beneath her fingernails. She stopped the moment she felt cold metal and yanked it free, mud littering her trousers, and rubbed the key until it shone.

This is insane, she told herself as she stood. *You can't do this. It's wrong.*

She eyed the tap through the glass again and licked her cracked lips. The key was stiff in the lock but it turned. She wove around the breakfast table for the sink, ignoring the slop encrusted in the bowl, the limescale coated around the base of the tap and framing its spout. She turned it on and lapped up water until it ran down her cheek and wet locks of her hair.

When she was done, she rested against the counter to catch her breath, water dripping from her chin. It was only then that she took in the room.

The place wasn't just neglected – it was abused. Her palms stuck to the edge of the counter from years of stains. The slate-tiled floor was encrusted with flakes of dirt and grime. Unopened post littered the round breakfast table with a bowl of blackened, rotting fruit in its centre, surrounded by a cloud of flies. Wherever she looked, the dirtier the place seemed. Ashtrays filled to the brim were dotted on every surface, the smell lingering in the air.

The sun had almost set. She moved across the room and flicked on the light. Dust on every surface; spiderwebs had been spun in each corner. The flies buzzed in a frenzy, zinging this way and that.

She should leave, wait outside the front of the house until he returned, but night was falling, and the temperature with it. She would be a shivering mess by the time he came home. If he came home at all. And if his wife returned home first. . .

She stood in the kitchen against the filthy counter with her eyes on the door leading further into the house. She wondered where the toilet would be in a house as old as this, debating if she could hold it for another hour or so. She couldn't. She would use the toilet and then wait for him outside.

The door opened with a long, drawn-out creak. The hallway was dark and smelt of damp and soot from a coal fire. She walked down the hall and opened the first door. The living-room. Shadows of furniture stood out in the darkness; she spotted the coal fire, lurking in the shadows of the brick chimneybreast. She passed the front door and looked up the stairs.

She would be quick. They would never know she had been inside.

'Hello?' she called.

Her voice rang up the staircase, echoed back at her.

She climbed the stairs, flinching with each creak of the boards, and stood on the small, dark landing. She opened the first door and peered inside, her hand feeling the wall for the light switch. The bulb dangling from the centre of the ceiling flickered to life, revealing flashes of the room.

She moved into it, her eyes never leaving the photos plastered to the walls. She stopped beneath the bulb.

The victims stared back at her.

He *was* working on the case.

She looked at each one of them in turn, meeting their eyes, saying their names inside her head, remembering each of their families, the pain in their eyes. There was a gap in the line-up, as though someone was missing. She imagined Montgomery waiting to hang a photo of the killer in that spot, directly in the centre of the victims, of all the chaos he had caused.

Someone on the force was just as passionate about justice as she was. Montgomery must have known what was going on inside the station and had been working on the case in secret. She closed her eyes and sighed with relief, a smile creeping across her cheeks. She wasn't alone. Montgomery had been her last chance before the other police closed in. Now he could protect her, and convince others that there was something to her claims.

When she opened her eyes again, her gaze fell on a photo that had fallen to the floor. Her eyes drifted to the gap in the line-up and back to the photo lying below it. She picked it up and inspected it.

It was a photo of them all.

Parts of the victims had been torn out and stuck together, the rips around each chosen feature like scars on the face. Adam's hair. Finn's eyes. Jamie's smile. Zach's nose. Phillip's jaw and cheekbones, Johnny's neck.

She inspected the back of the photo and stuck it on the wall, pressing hard on the Blu Tack. She stepped back, looking at it, waiting to see what Montgomery saw.

'No. . .'

She stumbled back, shaking her head in disbelief. Her heart hammered against her ribs. Tears immediately formed and fell, dashing down her cheeks.

The victims made up one person.

The victims, when pieced together, looked like Jay.

A door creaked open downstairs. She shot a look at the open doorway.

The kitchen light was on.

The key was still in the back door.

'Hello?'

FINN'S JOURNAL

19th April 2018

I have told you my story. Only he and I will know how it ends.

My hair started to fall out by the handful a few days ago. My nails are torn and bitten to the quick, the skin around them gnawed and scabbed. I have some sort of stress rash all over my body. I don't know who the man in the mirror is, nor do I want to know him, but it's who my stalker has made me become.

To the landlord's joy, I've ended the lease on my flat, with the plan of leaving Rearwood at the end of the week. I don't know where I'll go, only that I need to get away from here. But deep down I realise that anything I do is fruitless. He's coming for me. I can feel it, like an aching in my bones. I can't stop myself from moving: tapping my foot, grinding my teeth, drumming my fingers against my knee. I never thought I would surrender, but I find that I'm waiting for him, accepting my death. I have nothing else to give. The fight inside me died a long time ago.

But just because I'm giving in doesn't mean I don't want to be found. Don't let him do this again. I promise you: waiting for death as it lurks around every corner, locking myself away until the end like a convict on death row, is the worst death imaginable.

The buzzer's just sounded. My time is up.

If you're reading this, please believe me. I'm not mad. This is all too real, and if it can happen to me, it can happen to you. I'm not special or unique, I'm normal – I'm just like you. As long as he is still out there, no one is safe.

I should write something poignant for my last words, shouldn't I? But then they would only be words on paper. Only he will know what I say before my death. I wonder what I will say.

FORTY

Rose stood frozen to the spot, her eyes never leaving the open door.

'Who's there?' he asked. He was walking up the hall, heading towards the stairs.

Hot urine soaked through her jeans.

It couldn't be him. She had got it wrong. She met Jay's eyes as the other victims stared out at her, their smiles frozen onto their faces for eternity.

Her first thought was to kill him. If Jay had been on his wall, it meant Montgomery had something to do with his death. But her brother had taken his own life – she had found him herself, saw his body floating in the bloody water with her own eyes.

But she never did find out why.

The stairs creaked.

He was coming up.

He had her cornered. She had to get out of there. She rushed to the window and raised it, stiff in its frame. The night air ripped into the room, raising the hairs on her arms and cooling the wet patch in the crotch of her jeans. The banister whined beneath his weight. He was almost at the top of the stairs.

She placed one leg over the ledge and then the other. When she looked down her mind spun. It was a long way to fall.

The sun had set and the grass was dark with dusk, hiding any uneven ground, any dips in the earth. Her heart was beating so hard and fast that she could taste it. Nervous sweat dripped into her eye.

'Rose?'

She whipped around.

Montgomery was in the doorway. He looked from her to the wall and then back again. His eyes changed in an instant. She saw the real him in his eyes, the man with a secret, a sickness.

And she was the only living person to know what he had done.

He took a step towards her.

She leapt from the ledge without a second thought.

The force of the fall slammed through her, rattled every bone, jarred her brain against the sides of her skull. It felt as though all the vertebrae in her spine had locked together with the impact. Her mind took a second to reboot, but when it did, pain screamed up her calf from her ankle.

She looked up at the window. Montgomery was staring down at her, his pale face lit by the moon, before he dashed out of sight.

She scrambled to her feet and fell with a scream as the pain seared from her ankle to her hip. Biting her lip, she forced herself to stand again.

She couldn't head for the road, he would catch her in a second. Despite his limp, he would be faster than her now. If she wanted to get away without being seen, she had to hide until she had a chance to flee.

She tried to walk. The pain in her ankle made her fall to her knees, her second scream echoing across the vast land. Hot tears landed on the grass. Her foot felt useless now, a limp, fleshy weight to carry behind her as she fled. She had a strange instinct to get rid of it, like a fox with its leg caught in a trap, chewing down to the bone until it was free.

She spotted the barn through the shadows just as it began to rain, and crawled on her hands and knees, moving as fast as she could. Mud packed beneath her fingernails and the cold wind lashed her hair into her eyes. She bit down on her lip to silence her groans as pain echoed through her body, pulsed at the joint. She could barely see her hands through the tears.

'Rose!'

His deep voice echoed across the open space, carried with the wind and rain from the east. She reached the towering doors of the barn and squinted against the raindrops. She took hold of the handle and stood, shaking with the strain, before stumbling inside.

The air inside the barn smelt of rotten wood and dung, but it was so dark that she couldn't see an inch from her face. She ripped off her coat and discarded it in the shadows. It was only slowing her down. She swiped her hands through the air and knocked something cold. Metal clanged together again and again. She lowered her hands and felt a thick wooden stick resting against the wall, so she picked it up and felt it with her hands. It was heavy at the bottom, as though a weight was attached to the end. Splintered wood. Chipped metal.

An axe.

She used it like a walking stick, the metal head pressed into the barn floor, and edged forward with her spare hand searching the darkness. Mud and hay shifted beneath her feet, bunching around them, slowing her down. She stopped when she felt a ladder, rungs so soft with age that they were almost damp. Dropping the axe, she pulled herself up with her arms and her one good foot, the other dangling behind her and sending shooting pains up to her kneecap. A harsh gale curled around the barn, causing the wooden panels to shiver and creak. Rain thrashed against the roof, dripped through the cracks. She reached the top and felt hay. A hayloft.

The door handle sounded through the darkness, twisted by a heavy hand. She dragged herself upwards with her elbows and crawled into the rotting hay, holding her breath as hay dust coated the inside of her mouth, stung her eyes. She arranged herself so she was facing the door and could watch his every move.

The door creaked open. Lightning slashed through the barn, projecting his shadow across the dirty ground in a succession of flashes. She saw the glint of metal tools hanging from a suspended rack: metal hooks, saws, blades of different widths and lengths. It wasn't a barn, it was a bloody abattoir. Something scurried amongst the hay with her, a mouse or a rat.

'Rose,' he said. His voice echoed in the vast barn, mimicking the shake of his voice. It sounded as though he was crying.

'I'm sorry, I. . .'

She watched him limp towards the wall and flick a switch. Strip lighting stuttered awake, suspended from wires attached to one of the beams. She shrank back into the hay and saw flashes of the space: the tools, workbenches, rotten hay parted where she had shuffled to the ladder. Old pigeons' nests lay abandoned amongst the beams, the wood coated in their white faeces.

'Something's wrong with me, I know it. And. . . now you know it too.'

He looked up at the hayloft, searching for her. Her heart leapt as his eyes scanned past her.

'Your brother, he was. . .' Montgomery was sobbing. He covered his face with his hands. 'I loved him. I loved him so much.'

She eyed the tools on the rack and wondered which one she would use to kill him. Her brother, her sweet baby brother. Furious tears burnt in her eyes and mixed with the hay dust on her cheeks. She should have known what was going on. She should have helped him.

'I can't describe it. I wanted all of him. Whatever he gave me, I wanted more, as if even devouring him whole wouldn't be enough. I loved him too much. We were young; seventeen and twenty-one. We didn't know any better, it was all so new.'

Her fingernails dug into the rotting boards beneath her. She wanted to claw his eyes out of his skull, tear his tongue from his mouth with her bare hands.

'He loved me too, Rose. He did.' He walked out of sight and stood at the foot of the ladder, talking up to her. She had nowhere to run. Panic rose again, shoving down the fury.

'He talked to me. He cried over your father, how he could never earn his love or respect, how terrified he was to tell him about us, about himself.'

She watched the top of the ladder move against the loft with his weight. The rungs creaked beneath him. She shuffled backwards, further into the hay.

'He talked about you. He loved you, but he couldn't talk to you, you were never home. He came to me because he had no one else.' He reached the top of the ladder and met her eyes. 'He loved me, until our love got so strong that it terrified us both. I scared myself.'

'Leave me alone. . .' she said, shuffling back, her arms and legs tangling in knots of hay. The boards moved beneath her, soft as mud.

'I couldn't lose him. . . but I couldn't replace him either.' He rose, towering over her. 'Whenever I saw men who looked just like him, my heart broke. But I was able to see parts of him in others: the same smile, the same eyes, the same laugh. I had to keep his memory alive, to keep the monster inside me satiated. I know what I am.'

'Montgomery, please. . .'

The loft wobbled beneath their weight. She heard a creak from one of the floorboards.

'I'm sick, Rose. I can't stop myself.'

The structure whined like a sinking ship. She froze and looked down, felt it straining beneath her weight. She could hear the wood snapping away in splinters, cracking to the centre.

'And now you know. . .'

The boards crumbled beneath her, until her stomach rose to her throat with the fall and she plummeted to the ground. Sheets of hay fell with her as she landed with a bang.

'And I can't have that.'

Everything went dark.

JAY

☾

Jay stopped at the front door of his home and wiped his eyes until the skin beneath them felt grazed, raw when the breeze touched them. Monty had dropped him at the end of the street like he always did, so no one knew where Jay went or with whom, but for once he wished he had been dropped off right outside the house so they would ask questions. That way, he could tell them everything.

Something stopped him from getting his keys out of his pocket. He knew what it was, but he didn't feel strong enough to think it through, let alone step inside and say the words: *Help me.*

In order to tell them what was going on, how Monty was taking over, controlling everything he did, he would first have to tell them his secret, the secret they already knew but which none of them dared to address. It was like a fifth person living in the house with them, sitting at the table during dinner, standing between them whenever they spoke, its shadow cast over him, keeping him in the dark.

He had tried to tell them so many times: he loved a man who frightened him, who refused to let him go anywhere without him, scolding him for doing or saying the wrong thing when they were reunited. When he met Monty, Jay had felt free for the first time ever, but now his life was even more confined than it had been before. He couldn't think, couldn't breathe, without worrying whether Monty would disapprove and what would happen to him if he did, and when he returned home, he stepped into a different kind of prison, but stifling all the same. From the second he woke up to the last beat of consciousness before he drifted off to sleep, there was a weight on his chest, crushing his lungs, his heart.

Life whispered behind the door. He heard the thud of Rose's feet racing up the stairs, shouting to Mum over her shoulder. Mum would be in the kitchen cooking dinner, and Dad would be sitting in front of the telly with his feet up and the top button of his jeans undone. He liked listening to this, the unforced normality. The moment he stepped inside, everything changed. The air stifled with a buzzing tension. His very existence caused a silence that made him want to claw at his own skin.

He took the keys from his pocket and unlocked the door. The smell of dinner hit him instantly. Music was playing upstairs; Rose would be getting ready to go out again. He walked along the hall and stepped into the dining room, the living room in view through an arch, the kitchen through another.

'Hiya, lovey,' his mum said from the stove.

'Hi.'

His father turned immediately and his whole body seemed to harden. He nodded in Jay's direction before glancing back at the TV.

He stepped into the kitchen and stared at his mother's back as she stirred something in the pan. He could do it, he just had to find the words.

Help me.

'Hungry?' she said and turned to look at him.

Jay nodded. The words were clogged in his throat.

'Have you had a good day?'

He scares me, Mum. I don't know what to do.

'Yeah,' he forced.

'Good. Stew and mash for tea.' She leaned over and kissed him on the forehead before turning her back again to face the stove.

The moment had passed. He turned back into the dining room with tears pricking his eyes and glanced briefly in his father's direction. He was laughing at something on the TV. He had to feel Jay standing there, but he wouldn't look his way.

Jay stepped back into the hall and climbed the stairs, stopping before Rose's door, and knocked too timidly to be heard over the beat. He knocked again with more weight.

'Yeah?' he heard her shout.

He opened the door and saw her slip into her dressing gown, catching a glimpse of her breasts in the mirror. He blushed as she turned, tying the gown shut, and smiled.

'Hey, bud.' She turned back to her wardrobe and moved clothes along the rail. 'Hay fever playing up again? Your face is all red.'

He nodded quickly.

All he had to do was say it: *Help me.* Two words, and this would all be over. She would help him, he knew that – she loved him, perhaps more than anyone else in the house. But the thought of her hating him for who he was, for the secret that kept him prisoner, was too painful to bear.

'You all right?' she asked.

'I. . .'

I'm scared. Please help me. Please don't hate me.

She looked at him intently. Her eyes were genuine, but there was an impatient shift in her body. She wanted to get ready in peace; he was invading her time.

'I'm going to have a bath,' he said.

'Don't be too long, I need to shower before I go out.'

He nodded, swallowed the words down, and closed the door behind him.

Jay stood on the landing and listened to the house: the music from Rose's room, the clatter of a pot from the kitchen, the laughter from a televised audience drifting up the stairs. He wondered what it was like to live without fear.

Stepping inside the bathroom, he turned on the taps. The sound of the water masked everything else in the house but the faint beat of Rose's music. He stripped off his clothes and sat on the toilet seat, silent tears streaming down his face. He had never felt more alone.

He turned off the taps and lowered himself into the bath, enjoying the sting of the water that reminded him he was alive. He let himself slip beneath the surface to wash away the tears and listened to the thrum of his heart against the base of the tub, the pop of bubbles as they rose. He screamed as loud as he could beneath the water, his pain erupting in bubbles, then sat up again, wiped his eyes.

His gaze settled on Rose's disposable razor on the side of the bath.

FORTY-ONE

Rose resurfaced to heavy thuds, the ground shuddering beneath her. She opened her eyes and looked directly into the lights dangling from the roof of the barn, so bright that her eyes stung and watered. She tried to sit up. Her vision spun violently and she fell back to the ground.

'I had to do it. . .' he said. 'I had to.'

She tried to find his voice, but her senses refused to settle, overwhelmed by all the other elements: the rotten musk of the barn, the scratch of hay, thuds against the ground. The pain in her ankle was nothing compared to that in her head. It felt as though her skull had cracked down the middle.

Thud. Thud. Thud. The ground continued to vibrate with the blows.

'They knew too much. If I'd let them go, they would have talked. . . Everyone would know what I am.'

Tears filled his eyes.

'I hate who I am, Rose. I hate it.'

'Jay. . .' It was all she could say.

'I didn't mean to scare him,' he said through the tears. 'I never thought that he would. . . It was all my fault. I hate myself for it every day.'

She opened her eyes and searched for him. Montgomery was

hunched over, his shirt removed. Sweat had seeped through his undershirt and his shoulder blades moved beneath it with each thrust. He was digging. The spade glinted in the light as it rose, crunched back into the earth floor.

'I *told* you. . .' he said, turning to look at her over his shoulder. 'I told you not to pursue this, but you wouldn't listen. Why didn't you listen? Everything I did to stop you, and you still kept going. I burnt your bag. I set a trap for a bloody rat and sent it your way. I broke into your house and destroyed your paintings, posted about you all over town, snatched the damn journal out of your hands and you still wouldn't stop. I don't want to kill you, I *have* to. Why couldn't you just leave it alone?'

The man in the alley, her bag and phone burnt to a crisp, the break-ins, the attacks, the rat, the posters strewn all over town. It had all been him.

'Of all the people I could have bumped into that night, it had to be you. I'd finally got the journal back, after almost two years of trying to find it. I'd worked so hard, and you swooped in and took it from me. I'd formed a relationship with the landlord when Finn was still living in the apartment while pretending to enquire about the neighbours' complaints, but it was so I could swipe a key for the new lock. It was me the landlord called about the legal aspect of disposing of Finn's belongings, and he told me exactly where they were. All of that took *years,* and in seconds, you snatched it away.'

Swipe a key, she thought. She remembered the day he had come to her home with Leech and Watts. The key to the side door off the kitchen would have been left in the lock, ready for the taking. She hadn't used the door in years, just the French windows leading to the porch. That's how he got into her house.

'Your wife. . .' she said, and realised the truth the moment she spoke the words. Montgomery had never had a wife.

'I had to look like I had a normal life,' he said. 'I couldn't let anyone know what I am.' He released a bellowing scream, threw the spade against the wall. 'I'm a *monster*!'

She lay there helpless as he sobbed into his hands, watched his back racked with the sobs. It was over now. Whatever he had in store, she wouldn't win. He wiped his eyes and turned towards her. They were red raw. His face was streaked with mud, glistening with sweat and tears.

He limped towards her, reminding her of the night the hooded man had tried to snatch her bag and how he had limped away. It hadn't been from injuries she had caused; the limp had been there all along. He took her ankles and dragged her. She screamed with the pain and snatched at the ground, but it crumbled under her fingers.

'I keep some of them here. . .' he said. Sweat dripped from his brow and onto her T-shirt. 'I wanted to keep them safe, before I had to cover my tracks.'

She didn't understand. He was talking in a crazed reel of words that only he could decipher. All she could think about was the pain.

'I hid them at first, but I couldn't keep them all here. The number kept growing, so I had to stage the rest. I couldn't have their disappearances lead back to me, look similar to the last.'

He stepped down into a pit, dragged her with him. The hard landing silenced her mid-scream, falling against wood and rubble. Dirt walls towered either side of her. He climbed out of the pit and looked down at her; a drop of sweat fell from his chin.

'He. . . Johnny, he was the first I. . .' He picked up a large piece of wood. 'Look after him.'

She clawed at either side of her, felt hard wooden panels.

'Finn. . . Tell me what you did with Finn.'

'He's here.'

She stared at him, at the madness in his eyes, the incoherent spiel falling from his lips.

'I'm sorry. . .'

He stepped down and placed the wood over her, smothering her in darkness. She gasped for breath as she finally understood, the realisation firing inside her brain like a gunshot.

He was burying her alive.

She screamed to the sound of nails banging into the wood, to the dirt hitting the lid of the coffin, and sobbed in the dark as the sound got further and further away. She felt the rubble beneath her, her sight useless in the dark. She latched on to something and inspected it with her fingers and the grasp of her palm.

Bones.

Look after him.

She was lying on Johnny's bones.

She screamed until her ears rang, the sound bouncing off the wooden walls of the coffin. She couldn't hear the crunch of the spade any more.

She would die beneath the earth, and no one would ever know.

Just like Finn.

FINN

☽

19th April 2018

Finn stood before the door, knowing his tormentor was waiting for him on the other side.

He thought he would be terrified, but his heart was calm, his skin was bone dry.

Before all this began, he would never have understood why someone would put their life in another man's hands for him to do what he wished with it, but now all that separated him from death was a wooden door, and he was almost grateful. This was finally going to end.

He reached for the latch. Cold air seeped into the hall. The street lights were out, and the road was completely silent but for the occasional swish of leaves as the breeze picked up and fell again. His tormentor stood in the shadows, a sympathetic smile crawling across his cheeks.

'This way,' he whispered softly.

Finn nodded and followed him down the steps towards a parked car. His head was light and his legs felt disconnected from his hips, moving without thought, driven by instinct. The man opened the door for him and leaned over to buckle him into the seat. His breath smelt of cigarette smoke and mint, his clothes of fresh sweat. Finn could feel the heat of his body, the shake of his fingers as he fumbled with the buckle. The night air drifted around him; it had a metallic smell to it, as if the wind was carrying the scent of rain that had yet to reach them. When they caught each other's eyes, the man blushed and went to leave the car.

'Will you tell me your real name?' he heard himself ask. He sounded broken, distant.

'Montgomery,' he said through a smile, and shut the door behind him.

Finn glanced out the window and up to his flat. He would never see it again. There were so many things he would never do or see: smell the sea or feel the chill of snow, close his eyes against the sun and see blazing orange behind his eyelids. He would never rekindle the relationship with his parents, who had failed to accept him for who he was, something that, in the back of his mind, he'd always hoped would happen, the sort of hope he knew would never materialise but imagined all the same. He would never fall in love. He was thirty years old and had never been loved. The realisation was sadder than the fate that awaited him and the injustice he had been served. He would never look into another man's eyes and know that he was that person's entire world. He was going to die without ever truly living. Tears scratched at his eyes. He blinked them away.

Montgomery settled behind the wheel and started the engine, Finn's fate sealed with the click of the locks.

'Are you okay?' he asked. 'Ready to go?'

Finn stared out the window at his flat. He thought the move was going to be the start of a new beginning; now all he wanted was for the misery to end.

'Yes,' he whispered. 'I'm ready.'

They drove for miles in silence. The town thinned until they were surrounded by nothing but dark, open fields, with the occasional vehicle passing them on the other side of the road, headlights filling their car before they were thrown into darkness again. But Finn barely noticed – he stared out of the windscreen but didn't really see. He could only think of the past, the life he had lived and the events he had overcome. For all those years, he told himself that the pain would be worth it in the end, that one day he would have a life that made the past seem as though it had belonged to someone else.

'I did this all for you,' Montgomery said suddenly.

Finn jolted back into the present. Montgomery was wringing the steering wheel; he looked anxiously into the rear-view mirror before returning his eyes to the road.

It was as if he had been asleep this whole time and now he was finally awake. Nervous energy surged through him, pulsed inside his skull until a splitting headache formed behind his eyes. In an instant, he realised he wasn't ready to die.

'I needed to make you see. . .'

He looked around the inside of the car for a weapon, a way out. His eyes fell on the door handle, and glanced up at the scenery passing the glass in a blur. He could unbuckle his seat belt, open the door, and jump. But all Montgomery had to do was slam on the brakes, turn around and speed after him. He couldn't outrun a car.

'When we first met,' Montgomery said, 'I couldn't get you out of my head, I. . .'

Finn looked for a cigarette lighter in the dashboard to press it against Montgomery's face, blind him in both eyes with scorching halos, but he couldn't spot one in the dark.

Montgomery shifted the car down into second gear. Finn flinched as his hand neared his thigh. The car slowed.

'You were driving me mad. I just needed to see you. Be with you. Jay, I. . .'

Finn wasn't even sure Montgomery realised he had called him by the wrong name. The car turned off the lane and onto a gravel drive, rolling to a stop outside a pebble-dashed cottage. His whole body was shaking now, and however hard he tried, he couldn't fill his lungs. He took quick, small breaths through his nose.

Montgomery switched off the engine and turned in his seat.

'What I did to your apartment. . . I had to make my colleagues think that you were mad.'

Colleagues.

Finn immediately felt sick. His mind spun.

'You're. . . with the police.'

Montgomery nodded.

Suddenly it hit him: he would never get help. The police would always be on Montgomery's side. Finn already looked mad. If he escaped, got out of this alive, and went to the police station and told them it was one of their colleagues who had been harassing him, they would have him sent away to a facility for the deranged. That day in the police station, when he met the wrong Michael King – the text had come through the moment he left the room. Montgomery must have been so close, watching it all unfold.

I will never escape you, he thought, as he eyed his face in the dark, the way the shadows collected on the right of his face as the moon shone through the windscreen. He had seemed so normal in the café that day. He wondered how he did it: hid the madness from sight until he was ready for it to be seen.

'I love you,' Montgomery said.

Finn watched his eyes. Montgomery truly believed he loved him, a man he barely knew. How could he not see the terror in his eyes? The repulsion?

A thought came to him suddenly. It was his only way out.

'Prove it to me,' Finn said.

Montgomery laughed nervously.

'Prove it to you?'

'Kiss me,' Finn said. He smiled as he fought back bile. It would only be for a second.

Montgomery eyed him cautiously, before smiling back and edging closer, bringing the scent of sweat and smoke with him. His breath was sharp with nerves.

Every part of Finn recoiled: his heart raced, his limbs shook, sweat ran down his body.

Montgomery moved closer, until their noses were almost touching, and pressed his lips against his. Finn watched and waited for his eyes to close. As Montgomery's tongue broke between his lips, Finn snatched the man's groin and twisted.

Montgomery shot back in his seat. He yelled behind clenched teeth as bubbles of saliva broke on his lips. Finn let go and quickly rammed his elbow into Montgomery's face. He heard the cartilage in his nose break with the blow.

Montgomery yelled and caught hot blood in his palms as Finn fumbled to unclip his belt. He opened the door wide, squirming out of Montgomery's grasp as he slapped a bloody hand on his arm.

Bolting out of the car, Finn stumbled, grazing his arms, slamming his face against the grass. Shock had turned the muscles in his legs to useless wet strips. He scrambled to his feet and staggered across the field eyeing the thick shadows of woodland in the distance. Once he got to the woods, he would lose him. He would run all night until he was safe. He knew Montgomery's name and where he lived. They had to believe him now.

The engine revved to life behind his back. He looked over his shoulder to see the car spit gravel as it headed in his direction. He turned back and kept running, the trees getting so close he could smell their sap in the air, hear the wild rush of their leaves moving in the wind. He didn't move left or right, but ran in a straight line so as not to cut his speed. The engine got louder behind him, edging so close he could feel the heat of the headlights on his legs and back. He would reach the woodland and lose him. A car couldn't fit between the trees.

His legs flew out from under him and his back slammed against the bonnet. The windscreen cracked beneath him. He landed on the ground with a final blow, breathing in the dirt.

He instantly smelt his own blood. His whole body felt broken. The car had stopped, its brake lights turning everything red: his skin, his clouds of breath, the grass beneath him. As his eyes closed, he heard the opening and closing of the car door, the pad of footsteps, and Montgomery's sobs by his side.

Finn woke to the sound of a man crying. He felt weightless somehow, as though he was floating through the air. The chill cooled something wet on his skin as pain seared through him. He couldn't feel his legs.

He looked up and saw Montgomery carrying him through the night. A cold tear fell onto Finn's face.

As his head lolled to the side he caught sight of a derelict barn, his vision jolting with Montgomery's steps.

'It's always the same,' Montgomery whispered above him.

He kicked open the barn door and carried him into the darkness.

'I can't feel my legs,' Finn whispered. His own voice sounded distant and strange, as if the blow had made him drunk.

'I'm sorry,' Montgomery said, flicking on the light with his elbow.

Strip lights flickered to life. Birds flapped in their nests perched high up on the beams. Finn watched a feather drift down from the rafters.

'Why can't I feel my legs?'

'You were going to get away. I didn't mean to. I never planned...'

Montgomery settled him on a pile of hay. Finn looked down at his legs. His scream ripped through the air and sent the birds fleeing from their nests and through a hole in the roof.

His legs were mangled, twisted this way and that; a bone had broken through the fabric of his jeans.

'WHY?'

He was really going to die. He clawed at the mud and hay, desperate to escape, but pain shot up his arms, and his legs were deadweight, pinning him down.

Montgomery came towards him.

'Don't touch me!' Finn bellowed. 'Don't fucking touch me!'

But Montgomery knelt and cupped Finn's face in his hands. Tears slithered down his cheeks as he frantically scanned for a speck of love or forgiveness. Finn spat in his eye.

'I'd rather die than let you touch me!'

Finn watched his saliva slither down Montgomery's face, watched as fury seeped into his eyes like ink and his grip hardened. He pushed Finn onto his back and rose.

Finn sobbed into the hay, his screams echoing above the rafters, as Montgomery paced the barn with his head in his hands, muttering frantically beneath his breath. He burst suddenly with a roaring scream and pushed the contents of the workbench to the floor. Tools flew through the air, disappearing into the hay. He stormed out of the barn and locked the door behind him.

All Finn could do was cry. The pain was rising now, stabbing in his legs, all the way to the bone, pulsing where it had broken through the skin. If he survived this, he might never walk again.

He looked around the barn, blinking away the tears. He had no way of knowing how long he would be left alone.

This was his only chance.

He heaved air into his lungs and clawed at the dirt, pulling until his legs moved behind him. He dragged himself across the barn floor on his elbows and searched amongst the hay for the scattered tools, tears falling. He found a wrench, but it wouldn't be enough. Birds that had stayed behind flapped above him, cooing quietly. He spotted the shimmer of metal from amongst the hay and crawled for it. He snatched it up and shook away the strands: a screwdriver.

He placed the screwdriver between his teeth and dragged himself back to where Montgomery had left him. Sweat ran into his eyes. Tears lined his jaw and shivered with his movements. He could taste the metal against his tongue. By the time he had arranged himself as he had been before and hidden the tool amongst the hay, he was panting against the ground.

The door burst open.

Montgomery stood in the doorway, rage radiating off him, his face ugly and contorted with it.

A shotgun quivered in his grasp.

He strode across the barn and held the end of the gun to Finn's face.

Finn stared up the dark barrels. He could smell the metal, the twang of rust.

'You. . . you don't. . .' He tried to speak through the sobs, to beg for his life, but just the sight of the gun stalled the words in his throat. 'You don't have to do this.'

With his eyes on Montgomery, he closed his hand around the screwdriver hidden in the hay.

'You know I do.'

They stared at each other for a long time, the gun shaking between them.

'You have no idea how much I hate this. . .' Montgomery said. 'How I wish that I wasn't like this. When I look at you I see him, and who you are doesn't matter any more. I know that's wrong, that I'm mad. I know I am and I hate it. But I can't unsee him. I can never let him go.'

Finn launched upwards and stabbed the screwdriver through Montgomery's shoe, watching it pierce the leather before he yanked it out again. Montgomery screamed and fell, his free hand rushing to his foot. Finn dragged himself up and launched the screwdriver into Montgomery's thigh next, stopping at the bone. Saliva burst from his mouth as he fell onto his back, but he didn't scream again. The pain had rendered him speechless.

Finn clambered up the man's body, straddled his hips, and raised the screwdriver above his head, his broken legs beneath him.

The gun flew up and pressed against his cheek. Montgomery stared at him from the other side of the gun.

'Open your mouth,' he said.

A tear slid down Finn's cheek. The end was there, right in front of him. He had tried and failed.

But I didn't go down without a fight.

Finn opened his mouth, closing his eyes as the barrels passed his lips. He listened to the cocking of the gun. His teeth clinked against the metal. Tears slid to his jaw.

'I just wanted to love you,' Montgomery said. 'Why wouldn't you let me?'

Finn sobbed silently, and waited for the blast of the gun that would rip his life away. He waited. And waited.

'Look at me,' Montgomery whispered.

Finn opened his eyes and met his gaze.

Montgomery pulled the trigger.

FORTY-TWO

C

R ose woke to the dark and the cold.

Rubble dug into her back. When she tried to adjust her position, a searing pain shot from the back of her skull and down her spine.

Except that it wasn't rubble, but bones.

Her breaths were amplified in the confines of the coffin. Dirt crumbled through the planks and dusted over her chest as she clawed at the wood.

'No! No, no, no, no, no!'

She scratched at the roof until her fingernails cracked. Dirt continued to fall on her face and neck; it stuck to her tongue, nestled between her eyelashes. The small space began to close in around her until the darkness thickened and her lungs shrivelled. She thrashed in panic, knocking her head and limbs against the confines of the coffin. Sharp corners of Johnny's bones jabbed into the groove of her ribs and cut the backs of her hips and thighs. The fear swelled, crushing every organ within her ribcage. Her head became light.

No.

She couldn't fall unconscious again. There would only be so much air inside the coffin – the more she panicked, the more she used – and it wouldn't last for ever. She covered her face with her hands and willed her heart rate to slow, breathing in through her nose and out through her mouth. Every time her heart began to calm, she would hear the tinny echo of her breaths or smell the richness of the dirt slipping between the boards, and her panic would take hold again.

A tear slipped down her temple. Violet would have felt the same fear beneath the water, confined in a metal coffin of her own. She sobbed in the dark. She had left Violet to die just like this, but she had been so much younger, so helpless. The only comfort she had was that her daughter's death had lasted minutes, not hours like this death that awaited herself.

Don't think of her, she thought. *Breathe.*

Slowly, her heart calmed. She uncovered her face and blinked against the darkness. She needed to see what she was up against. She felt the boards with her hands, squinting when dirt fell, and snatching her hands back when splinters lodged into the pads of her fingers.

Her phone.

She fumbled for it at her pocket and squinted against the bright display.

No signal.

She hadn't expected it to work, but reading *No Service* in the corner of the screen still made her heart sink. She shone the light around her. Dirt slipped beneath the slats and coated her jeans. Small insects slowly made their way inside, scurrying away from the light and into the shadows. Each time it shone on the bones, she tried to focus on something else, but when she saw the skull, she couldn't look away from where the eyes should have been and only sockets remained.

Finn was down here too, buried in another coffin somewhere close. The man she had dedicated her days to finding hadn't needed her help; he had been here the whole time, lying in the silence of the earth. A part of her had hoped he was living in hiding and that the victims who were never found had made it out alive, but the truth was beneath her, each vertebra of Johnny's spine digging into hers. She thought of his parents, the deathly thin Andrew whose grief had eaten away at him. She had found the answers, but couldn't give them to him. If she didn't escape, he would never know.

Had Finn died before he was buried, or had Montgomery put him out of his misery first? Finn had fought for so long, but Montgomery's perseverance had won in the end. But this hadn't been for nothing. She might not have saved Finn, but she could still work to put his killer away.

Montgomery couldn't be left to kill again.

She pushed against the boards with her palms to see if they would give, but all she felt was the earth pushing back at her. The panic rose. She would never get out. This was impossible. But the only alternative was to give up and wait to rot. She imagined the incessant buzz of flies, the wriggle of maggots, worms working their way between the boards. If she wanted to get out, she needed tools. She looked around the coffin.

No, she thought. *I can't.*

She eyed the bones. They were all she had that remotely resembled tools. Without them, she wouldn't have a way out at all. She'd had no idea that one of the men who she had dedicated her life to saving would in fact save her.

She placed her phone on her chest so the light beamed up towards the roof of the coffin, and felt the bones beneath.

Don't think of them as bones. You can't lose your mind, not down here.

But even while she told herself this, she felt her hands shaking as they hovered across them, flinching as she felt their sharp edges.

The grooves between the planks of wood were fine. She would need a bone thin enough to fit between them but strong enough to break them. She gripped one and brought it up towards her chest, inspecting it with a crooked neck in the tight space. A thigh bone.

Her breaths shortened. Her heart quickened. The coffin began to shrink again.

'No,' she said aloud. 'No!'

She clamped her eyes shut, breathed deeply. She couldn't lose sight of this now.

She opened her eyes and inspected the bone again. She was surprised by how light it was, how smooth it felt against her palm, but it was far too thick to fit within the grooves. She put it down as gently as she could and searched again with sweat forming in beads on her brow, even though it was cold beneath the earth and she could see her breath. She found something long and thin and brought it up to her chest to inspect it: a collarbone. She placed the end against one of the grooves. The way the end sharpened into a point worked in her favour: it just fit, with enough tension to apply pressure. She wedged the bone between it as much as she could and held it with two hands, cranking it like a crowbar. The boards moved and whined. She spat out dirt and cranked again. The bone snapped in the middle.

'Shit!'

She covered her face with shaking hands and tried to hold back the tears. This would never work. She was going to die down here, waiting for the air to thin until there was none left.

Christian and Lily had gone, and wouldn't know or care if she didn't return home. The police would assume she had stopped looking for answers. Only her father would go looking for her, but he had no idea where to start. She would never be found. Just like Finn.

Like Johnny.

Like Jamie.

She wondered if they had tried to get out just as she was, clawing at the wood with bloodied fingertips, how long it had taken before they gave up.

No, there has to be another way.

She moved to the side and searched down the left of her, pulling back with a wince as splinters poking out of the wall of the coffin scratched her right shoulder. She picked them out, one by one, and stopped.

The sides of the coffin were rough. She could find a strong bone and whittle down the end. She searched frantically for the thigh bone again, her hands shuffling the last remaining parts of Johnny against the sides of the coffin and her own body. She snatched it up and chose the smallest end, where the bone would have met the kneecap, and began to work it against the side of the coffin, clenching her teeth against the sound. It would take hours, but she had no other choice. It was her only way out.

Her phone died suddenly and plunged her into darkness.

FORTY-THREE

C

As the hours wore on, the air thinned. Each breath wheezed in and out of her lungs. Her muscles shook in a continuous spasm from dragging the bone against the side of the coffin. The space was hot from her rigorous work, her breath and sweat. It was impossible to tell how much time had passed in the dark. All she knew for sure was that the air was running out, and if she didn't have a drink of water soon, dehydration would kill her first.

She had been ready to give up so many times, but the thought of lying back and waiting for death forced her into action again, raking the bone against the wood, albeit slower than before. And Lily – she couldn't die without telling her how much she loved her, how much she wished she could take back the words she had spoken on the bank.

She brought the bone to her chest and felt the end with her fingertips. It was blunt in places, sharp in others, but had slimmed significantly. She raised it to the roof of the coffin and felt for one of the grooves with her fingertips. It was so dark she couldn't even see her hands. She tried the bone between the grooves.

It fitted.

She sighed and dropped it to her chest. A slim tear slipped down her cheek in silent celebration. It was done.

Except this was only the beginning.

She thought of how much work she had left to do: she still had to break through the wood, claw up through the mud and somehow survive with one held breath. That's if she even got that far.

Her body was broken. The muscles in her arms felt taut and useless, her head was light from lack of oxygen. She had used up all of her energy whittling down the bone, and now she had to muster more to break through the lid of the coffin.

She closed her eyes and almost let sleep take her. Except it wasn't sleep at all – she was dying. She had been dying for hours, a slow, drawn-out death as she got less and less oxygen. Her body wasn't just tired. It was shutting down. The air was so sparse she could hear breaths crackling in and out of her lungs. If she was going to survive, she had to get out now.

She fitted the bone between the planks and cranked like she had before, coughing as dirt rained down on her. She bit her lip and carried on until she heard a crack.

She stopped immediately and felt the length of the bone, waiting to find a break in the middle. Nothing. It wasn't the bone that had cracked. It was the board.

It was working.

She worked quicker than she had before, pushing the last of her strength into it, until the cracking got louder; the earth fell in constant, heavy loads, and the pressure of it filling the coffin was stronger than her. She pressed her hands against the boards to think.

She hadn't planned this far ahead. Surviving entirely depended on how deep he had buried her. Had he gone for the standard six foot? She couldn't remember falling that far into the coffin. It had to be shallower. The earth would still be heavy, but she would have more of a chance of escape. If it was deeper than she thought, she would have been dead the moment the earth breached the boards, stealing the last of the air, crushing her beneath its weight. She had to cover her mouth and nose somehow to allow herself to breathe. She tried to bring her knees up to her chest to keep the boards from bowing inwards, but there wasn't enough room. To cover her mouth and nose, she needed to take off her T-shirt and cover her head with it. The only way to do that was to let go. Either she would have just enough time to act, or it would cave in with the pressure and immediately bury her alive.

There's only one way to find out.

Slowly, she lowered her hands from the boards. They whined beneath the pressure, cracking deeper and deeper to the centre. She had just seconds to get the job done. She pulled at her T-shirt, struggling in the confined space, bashing her elbows into the sides of the coffin, scratching the backs of her hands against the rough roof. She pulled at the fabric until it tore at the seams. Just as she moved the T-shirt up to her head, she felt the earth fall in heavy clumps on her chest and stomach, ricocheting off the fabric against her face. She worked furiously, tying the sleeves around her neck. It was unbearably hot inside. Her breath moistened her cheeks and lips. She raised her hands in the darkness again and found the bone. She pulled and pushed, pulled and pushed, until the earth poured around the breaking boards, and one plank came free, crashing down against her. She had to manoeuvre herself so she could escape the coffin before the earth filled the inside and flattened her beneath, but there was no space; the bowing roof had stolen the little space she'd had.

Just keep going.

She took the bone again and worked at the wood, listening to the splintering, the shifting of earth, her hot, frightened breaths. The dirt falling inside was heavier now, accompanied by sharp rocks that slammed down on her hip bones. A second board broke free and earth poured in, pinning down her legs. She put both hands out, grappling at the sides of the lid of the coffin to pull herself up. The earth forced her back down. She tried again, shifting her legs to the side and pushing upwards with them, making her way through the moving earth. The further she rose, the more space she left in the coffin for the earth to fill, giving her further leeway as it shifted and filled the space beneath her. Earth flattened the shirt against her face until she could taste it through the fabric and it was almost impossible to draw breath. The pressure was strong, pushing down on her head and shoulders, but all she had to do was push up.

She screamed against the pressure in her head as she forced one foot onto the lid of the coffin and then the other. Her hands breached the surface, the cold air above the earth nipping at her fingers. The pressure flattened the fabric against her mouth and nose until she couldn't breathe at all. She clawed the flat earth above, digging her nails into it. The dirt around her thinned as she got further to the surface, allowing her to move her head and neck. When her head broke the surface, she gasped for air, sucking in the T-shirt until she gagged. She dragged herself up and clawed blindly against the dirt until her shoulders were free, then dug her elbows into the barn floor and army-crawled forwards, freeing her back, her hips, kicking the last of the strength from her legs until she was lying on the barn floor soiled with mud, yanking desperately at the T-shirt over her head. She tore it away and lay on her back, staring up at the roof of the barn, heaving for air.

She was free.

FORTY-FOUR

Lightning flashed through the gaps in the wooden walls. The thunder was seconds behind, blaring down to her eardrums as it clapped overhead.

Rose closed her eyes against the downpour entering through a hole in the roof and opened her mouth to catch the drops. Mud coated her from head to toe where the earth had poured into the coffin before she had managed to fix the T-shirt over her head. The wind whistled around the barn in endless screams. The air was thick with the smell of the rain and earth. She had managed to free herself from the coffin, but the question that followed taunted her from the back of her mind.

What now?

She couldn't walk home, not in this state. Her ankle was throbbing. She was miles from town, from any neighbouring houses. To get to them, she would have to trek through acres of woodland. Her phone was dead, so she couldn't call the police. The only way she could do that was if she got inside the farmhouse and used the phone without being seen.

She sat up and forced herself to stand, stumbling as she got to her feet and landed against a workbench, her hair moving with her frantic breaths. Her ankle. She looked down and lifted the hem of the jean leg. The ankle had swollen to twice its usual size.

She closed her eyes, waited for her legs to stop shaking. When she opened them again, she saw it.

The shotgun resting in the corner of the barn.

She slipped into her T-shirt again and took the gun in both hands, resting her weight on her one good leg. Rob had taught her the basics, but to say she could use this because she had used another was like saying she could fly a plane because she had driven a BMW. She thought back to how he unlocked the nose, loaded the cartridges, clicked it back into place. There were two triggers, one for each barrel. Rob had used one in front of her, pulled both at the same time and blown a gaping hole in the target. She inspected the gun and unclipped the barrels on the third try. There were two cartridges inside. She put the weapon on top of the workbench and frantically searched the drawers for spare cartridges.

The first drawer was filled with nuts, bolts, rusted tools, industrial tape. She opened the second and froze.

Mobile phones of different brands, sizes, ages. She knew immediately whom they belonged to. Montgomery had confiscated their phones, but not hers. Perhaps he had forgotten her phone because she took him by surprise. Or maybe she was the only one he buried alive. She checked each phone but the batteries had been removed and the sim cards were missing.

She closed the drawer and opened the third.

Amongst the mess were some shotgun cartridges, two full, the others empty. She pocketed the full ones inside her mud-caked jeans, picked up the shotgun again, and faced the entrance to the barn.

The door opened and shut in violent shivers as the whole barn creaked with the storm. She tested her ankle by taking a step. Pain shot up her leg to her hip and tears filled her eyes in a second, but she didn't buckle.

I can do it, she thought, and limped towards the door with the gun pressing into the ground like a crutch. She stood on her strong leg for support and eased open the door with the barrel of the gun. A flash of lightning lit up the sky.

The house looked smaller against the darkness. Had it not been for the lightning or the lit window on the ground floor, she might not have seen the house at all.

If the light was on, there was a chance he was still awake.

When she had entered the house earlier that day, she had seen a house phone on a small table in the entrance hall, coated in a thick layer of dust. Or she could have been imagining things, seeing what she wanted to see. But she had to know for sure. She could slip inside and call the police and return to the barn or hide on the outskirts of the woodland until they arrived. They would see the mobiles in the open drawer and the grave he had dug for her. They would dig further and bring up the bodies of the first two victims and find Finn; then they would know she had been telling the truth all along.

She stared up at the house again, her eyes honing in on the lit window.

Every fibre in her body told her not to go back to the house, but her ankle was barely able to take her weight, and the only way to get away was on foot. The farm was at least ten miles from the town centre, and even further from home, and she hadn't seen a single neighbouring house on her trek to the farm. It would take twice as long to get back in her condition, perhaps longer, and if Montgomery checked the barn and saw she was gone, it would take half the time for him to catch up. If she followed the road, he could stop her just by jumping in the car. If she headed through the woods, he would know the only direction in which to go. All of her energy had been spent escaping the coffin, and now she could barely stand. The only way she would survive the night was if she went back inside Montgomery's house and used the phone.

She raised the shotgun and limped out into the rain, never once lowering the gun.

Slowly, she made her way up towards the house, squinting as her hair thrashed against her face with the wind, biting her lip against the pain in her ankle, which worsened with every step. Rain ran from the tip of the gun, the end of her nose, stalked down her face in muddy brown streaks. She spotted a puddle and fell to her knees, cupping the muddy rainwater in her hand and gulping it down. He had turned her into an animal, a wild, feral thing. She wiped her lips with the back of her hand, raised the gun again, and headed towards the house.

Her eyes scanned each of the windows, looking for his silhouette in the dark, but they always returned to the kitchen window, which shed a beam of light across the lawn. She got close enough to see the grime coated on the windows, the flies buzzing around the room. She stopped and peered inside.

Montgomery was sitting at the table with his back to her. She limped round the side of the house and stood at a distance to look through the second window.

He was asleep. His head was down, his chin on his chest. A half-empty bottle of Scotch was on the table, with no sign of a glass. A handgun was resting beside it. She wondered if he had planned to end his life, or whether he was getting ready in case she returned.

There was no way she could enter the house with him so close. One wrong move and she might wake him. Yes, she had the gun, but she didn't want to use it. Hell, she wasn't even sure if she could.

Her heart raced in odd, frantic beats. Her palms moistened around the gun. She looked over her shoulder at the miles of woodland in the distance, the rain pouring down. She would have pneumonia by sunrise, or collapse with exhaustion, or be unable to travel any further when the pain in her ankle grew too great. There were so many ways she might die.

It's the only way.

She walked around to the window facing the barn again and moved towards the back door, peering through the glass panel and down the hallway to where she could see the phone in its dock.

It would only take a minute.

But if she slipped up, even for a second, she was dead.

She stood outside the house shivering in the rain, trying to talk herself into it while also trying to think of any other way to get out of this alive.

Reaching out for the handle, both her hand and the metal dripping with rain, she pressed it downwards as quietly as possible.

The door opened.

The wind pushed against it, whistling through the gap. She slipped inside, taking almost a minute to return the handle to its upright position so it didn't screech in her grasp. Raindrops fell from her and patted on the floor, sounding like a ream of gunshots in the silence.

She turned and eyed the back of him in the chair, watched his shoulders move with sleeping breaths.

Her heart was in her throat. Her breaths whistled in and out of her nose. Her whole body shook violently. She almost couldn't feel the pain in her ankle any more, only the pounding of her heart, the rush of adrenaline surging through her. A clock ticked from another room. The wind howled on the far side of the glass.

She took a step forward. Her shoe squeaked.

She froze on the spot and held her breath, waiting for him to move in his sleep, jolt awake with the slightest sound.

Nothing.

In the corner of her eye, she saw someone's reflection in the window. She flinched at the sight and stared at the monster across the room, until it dawned on her: the reflection was hers. She was covered in mud from head to toe. All she could see were beady white eyes staring back at her, flashes of skin where the rain had caused it to run.

She considered untying her shoes to pad across the floor on bare feet, but couldn't shift her weight onto her bad ankle to remove them.

Cautiously she took a step, and then another. Her shoes squeaked from the rain, drops of it pattered on the tiled floor.

As she reached the doorway to the hall, a phone rang behind her. She pressed herself against the wall, covering her mouth with one hand and holding the gun to her chest in the other.

Montgomery jolted awake, banging his knees against the table. 'Montgomery,' he said gruffly into the phone.

She clamped her eyes shut, bit her lip.

'Her dad's not talking? Then make him. Threaten him with any charge you can think of.'

Dad.

'Keep him awake all night. If he doesn't tell us where she is by morning, let him go. We can follow him; hopefully he'll lead us right to her. . . and Seb –' he paused – 'don't call me again. Only get in touch if he talks.'

He ended the call and dropped the phone to the table. She listened to him sigh heavily and clear his throat. Scotch moved up and down the bottle as he gulped from the neck.

She had to move.

The living-room door was shut, and she had no idea if it made a sound when it opened. If she went for the front door, he would hear the storm. She could creep upstairs, find a place to hide until she was able to call the police.

She moved along the wall and held out her hand for the banister.

A floorboard creaked.

A shot blasted. She fell with a scream and landed on her back, then scrambled frantically for the shotgun and pulled the left trigger. The gun jolted in her grasp and blew away a chunk of the kitchen door frame.

Incessant ringing pierced her ears. A mist of plaster and wood drifted to the floor. The noise settled until all she could hear was the shrill ring of the shot in her ears.

'Rose?' he said.

She strengthened her grip on the gun and trained her finger on the right trigger. If he turned the corner, she would shoot again.

'Is that you, Rose?'

'Don't. . . don't come any closer.'

'Okay, okay,' he said.

She watched the door, waiting for him to appear.

'Put down your gun,' she said.

'Only if you put down yours.'

'No way.'

'Then we're in a bit of a pickle, aren't we?'

She heard movement, the shuffle of shoes.

'I said don't come any closer!'

He fell silent again. She lay there on her back, looking down the barrel of the gun as it quivered in her grasp. Her breaths rattled with her. She couldn't move.

'How confident are you with that thing?' he asked. 'I've known how to shoot a gun since I was seven years old. I've fired every model you can think of. I know them well enough to know when they will perform and when they won't. Like that shotgun you're holding. You took that shot with the left barrel, didn't you? I know that because the right barrel sticks.'

He could be lying, trying to psyche her out. Would he know which barrel she'd shot, just by the sound? She looked down at the gun for a brief second and he shot round the corner, gun raised. A bullet blasted splinters of wood an inch from her face. She instinctively pulled the second trigger, blowing a chunk of plaster from the ceiling until it rained down on them both. She squinted through the dust and saw him covering his head from the debris, and launched her good foot into his groin, which sent him to his knees. She scrambled to her own and reached for the phone. It was an old one, with a ring cord connecting the phone to the base. Her hand had just clasped the cord when she was yanked back by her hair. She slammed to the ground with a scream, bringing the phone with her, and scrambled beneath his grasp as he wrestled his way on top of her and pinned her down.

It all happened so fast. In an instant, the gun was out of her hand and clasped in his, the barrel pressing into her neck. She watched his face turn red and a vein swell in his forehead as he put all of his weight into it, crushing her windpipe. She could feel it splitting, the skin bruising. She clawed at his hands on the gun, dug her nails into the backs of them until she broke the skin, but he wouldn't stop. The pressure of the barrels reached all the way to the bones of her spine, forcing tears down her temples. She reached for his face, scratching at his eyes where he leaned into the gun, but he clenched them shut. She thrashed and clawed, the cord still in her grasp and the phone knocking against her arm. She had just seconds of consciousness left; her lungs were ready to rupture. She snatched the phone cord in both hands and wrapped it around his neck. His eyes widened as she pulled down, tightening the noose. His hands rose to his neck.

She gasped for air as the gun tilted, but still, she couldn't breathe. He had broken her. She pulled tighter on the cord. He grabbed at her hands. She pulled tighter. He was panicking. His eyes looked bigger, as though they were bulging from the sockets. She let go and snatched the gun, swung it as hard as she could as he drew a desperate breath. The butt met his temple with a violent crack. All of the colour left his face. His jaw fell slack as he slumped against the wall. She dropped the shotgun and scurried away, pressing her back against the opposite wall and trying to draw breath, but couldn't. Her hand met with something cool on the floor beside her.

Montgomery's handgun.

She snatched it up. The safety would be off. A bullet would have shifted into the cylinder automatically, ready to be shot. She trained her sight line on the centre of his face.

His eyes looked lost inside his skull, drifting but never settling. He was trying to speak but only formed mumbles. But the second his eyes trained in on hers, she saw the realisation seep in. She had won. He took his phone from his pocket and slammed it against the wall again and again until the screen cracked. She looked down at the house phone and saw how it had broken in the struggle. He was destroying her last chance to call for help. She tried to protest but pain exploded in her throat. He banged it into the wall one last time before letting it fall to the ground.

His strength was returning. Soon he would have enough clarity to fight her again.

If she wanted to live, she had to pull the trigger.

But she couldn't. She wasn't the killer, he was.

And then he said the one word that would seal his fate.

'Jay. . .'

The gun stopped shaking.

'All I ever wanted was Jay.'

She pulled the trigger.

FORTY-FIVE

☾

Rose sat with the gun in her lap and the sound of the shot ringing in her ears. She'd watched Montgomery's brains spray up the wall, his body slide down to the floor, all with his eyes open, the shock seared into them.

She had to leave, but her whole body felt broken. She had jumped from a window, been buried beneath the earth and dug her way out, and killed a man before he could kill her, and now she had no way to call the police for help. She eyed his mobile and reached for it as quietly as she could, as though Montgomery would jolt back to life and grab her. But the phone was as dead as he was. She chucked it aside and looked at the landline. The buttons on the phone had been forced into the plastic base, and the cord had split until wires were exposed within.

She struggled to her feet and stumbled into the door frame. When she tried to draw a deep breath, she coughed it up and into her palm. She opened her eyes and saw the blood speckled on her hand.

Through the windows, the sun was rising in the distance, its rays bleeding into the clouds.

She looked up and scanned the room until her eyes fell on the ring of keys on the table where Montgomery had sat with his bottle and his gun.

Car keys.

Immediately she heard the girls' screams, the twisting metal as the car crashed through the barrier of the bridge.

She hadn't driven since the day of the accident. She stood in the kitchen and eyed them for so long that the sun rose higher in the sky and started to leak through the windows in warm golden beams.

Before she could stop herself, she snatched them from the table and stumbled out of the house.

The morning air was ice cold and sliced at her throat when she breathed, like salt in a wound. She limped around the house to the driveway and stopped before the car.

She couldn't do it. But she didn't have a choice. There was no way of contacting the outside world from the farm. Either she drove, or she walked, both too difficult to fathom. She unlocked the car, slipped inside, and shut the door behind her.

Her hands shook as they hovered over the steering wheel.

She stayed there, sobbing behind the wheel, as the memories seeped into her, the way the river water had filled the car to the brim. She heard their screams, felt Lily's nails dragging along her skin, tasted the water on her lips and tongue. Violet's eyes, looking up from the tooth in her palm, just before the windscreen caved in and the current ripped them apart. She clenched her eyes shut and shook her head until the memories broke away.

Taking a deep breath, she turned the key in the ignition until the engine grumbled to life. She found the pedals with her muddied feet and pulled the chair closer to the steering wheel. When she pressed down on the clutch with her bad foot, fresh tears formed and fell from her eyes. Her hands wrapped around the wheel, gripped so tightly that the leather squeaked beneath them.

She moved the stick to first gear and lowered the handbrake, allowing the car to roll forwards before she found the courage to press down lightly on the accelerator, and drove to the gate before turning off down the lane.

It had been so long since she'd sat behind the wheel that she fumbled with the gears, the biting point of the clutch and the accelerator, braked so sharply on the bends that the car jolted, all while trying to block out the memory of water filling the car, leaving Violet behind.

She drove for miles, too frightened to go above second gear, until she remembered: the old phone box by the bridge. It had to still be there. She put her foot down, biting her lip against the agony of her ankle, and changed up the gears, taking the corners too wide, staying in too high a gear so the car felt on the verge of tipping. She drove on autopilot, attempting to block out the memory of the gun firing in her hands, the sight of Montgomery's brains splashing up the wall, Violet's ghostly face on the bank.

When the bridge came into view, she slammed on the brakes.

The car sat in the middle of the road, the engine grumbling. She stared from behind the wheel, up at its steel skeleton sparkling with dew, the fog drifting with the river and slicing through its structure.

She couldn't do this.

The bridge was the only way in and out of Rearwood; she hadn't left in all these years specifically to avoid this very trip.

The phone box was on the other side.

She looked down at her ankle. The skin was so bruised it was almost black, and had swollen beyond all recognition. She couldn't walk another step.

The past screamed in her ears. She revved the engine to block out the sounds, the screams. She had overcome so much. This was the last hurdle. The moment she did this she would be free; the night would finally end.

423

Panic rose up to her mangled throat. She pressed down on the accelerator and crawled forwards. The fog helped, dimming her view of the river beneath, but she could still hear the chopping water, the loud rush of it as it bustled beneath. She couldn't breathe, couldn't think. Sweat ran down her ribs, stuck her T-shirt to her back. She didn't know she was crying until she tasted the salt of the tears on her lips.

Her body went ice cold, as though she was back in the water, holding on to Lily's wrist, feeling it break beneath her grasp. The past was creeping in, taking over.

Oh, fuck this, she thought, and pressed down on the accelerator. The car jerked forwards. She moved up to second gear, then third.

The screams. The blood. The punch of the airbag against her nose.

She saw the phone box and slammed on the brakes.

She heard the whine of the bridge breaking open, felt her stomach lurch with the memory of the fall.

She opened the car door and stumbled, scraping her palms and knees on the tarmac. The same surface Christian had beaten with his fists, the same road that had been littered with glass.

She got to her feet.

A flash of Violet drawing hearts on the glass.

She limped towards the phone box, her mind swirling.

Lily was beside her, clawing at her, screaming for her.

She stumbled to the ground. The past bled into the present, turned the tarmac into mud on the riverbank, projected Violet's body beneath her.

She screamed up the agony, speckles of blood spraying the ground. She screamed for Violet, for Lily, for Christian. For herself.

Then she crawled towards the phone booth as the car edged to the side of the bridge, its door still open and beeping at the dashboard, and stopped to the sound of a shattered headlight. She reached the shelter of the phone box and tugged at the door, stiff with rust, and fought her way inside. Rotten leaves had stuck to the floor; cigarette ends had browned with age. Graffiti had been written all over the glass. She snatched the phone and dialled 999, and waited with baited breath, the sound amplified in the closed space when she breathed out and then held her breath again.

An operator answered and diverted her to the local police. She waited, her head going light, her whole body shaking, and sank to the bottom of the booth. When the operator answered, she burst into tears.

'Can you hear me? I asked, what is your emergency?'

She tried to speak, but her throat felt utterly broken, and the tears wouldn't stop.

'It's okay,' the kind voice said. 'You're okay. Tell me what's happened, where you are.'

She couldn't speak a word. She sobbed into the receiver, croaking sounds instead of words.

'All right, hang in there, officers are on the way – we'll trace the number. I'll stay on the line, all right?'

Rose nodded, knowing the woman couldn't see her, and sobbed, letting the phone hang from the metal cord. She closed her eyes and rocked.

It's over, she thought. *It's finally over.*

EPILOGUE

Rose lay in bed and scanned the room that she had once seen as a prison, admiring the changes she'd made. The Artex swirls had been sanded away and covered with a new coat of plaster, the floral wallpaper had been stripped and replaced with eggshell-blue paint, a new bed put in a different position in the room, facing the windows with blinds that rose on a timer and shed light into the room. Each morning, she woke to the view of the river.

Facing it first thing meant she could grieve, cry if she needed to, and then get on with her day. She would never forget, but she had to exist. If cheating death had taught her anything, it was that she couldn't hide in the past, not any more.

She sat up in bed and swung her legs over the edge.

Her ankle wasn't bad this morning. Sometimes she woke without pain, other times she woke in tears. The physiotherapy was working, but no one could promise her a pain-free future. It hadn't been the injury that caused complications, but everything she did after the fall, worsening its condition until over time, her damaged muscles healed in scars; her ankle bone had broken away in chips.

She did the stretching exercises the physio had taught her and left the room. Lily's door stood ajar, just like it had been all those years before, the morning her whole world imploded. Rose crept down the hallway and pushed the door lightly on its hinges.

427

They had decorated her room together, made it something that was just hers. Lily was barely visible huddled beneath the duvet, only the mess of red hair creeping onto the pillow. Rose smirked and closed the door.

Some things never change.

She made her way downstairs, holding the banister with an intense grip to ease the pressure on her ankle, and headed into the kitchen to fix some tea. The house wasn't a prison any more. She would never be able to remove the history from its walls, but she had found a way to make room for it. This was still the room where Violet ate her last meal, but her memory didn't poison the air the way it used to; it simply lingered.

Rose took her mug of tea and stepped out onto the porch.

Tony was already up, perched on his stool before the easel, paintbrush in hand. Out of all of them, he had changed the most. He seemed younger, with his back held straighter, his eyes brighter. From where he sat at the easel, she could just see the corner of his contented smile.

'Morning,' she said.

He turned, smile widening.

'Morning, Rosie. How did you sleep?'

'Six hours.'

'In human terms that's twelve,' he said with a chuckle. 'You must feel amazing.'

'I do,' she said, and meant it.

She sat in her rocking chair and swayed lightly, cradling the mug in her hands. They fell into a comfortable silence. Tony painted, the breeze blowing wisps of his hair. Rose sat listening to the river and watching the sun shimmer on its surface.

'What time is Christian coming to pick Lily up?' he asked.

'Midday, I think.' She thought of the week ahead, seven

days of just her and her father. Her chest ached.

'I should be used to it by now.'

'Missing her for the week?' he asked.

She nodded and took a sip.

'Gives me a chance to beat you at Scrabble. She's too good, puts us both to shame. How did therapy go on Friday?'

'Better. She hugged me. I felt like I'd won the lottery ten times over.'

'That's good. And what about you? How's it going for you?'

'Good.'

'You still take the sleeping pills?'

'Not every night.'

'That's good.'

'Thanks, doc,' she said, and smirked, raising the mug to her lips.

He laughed. 'Sorry. Seeing Rob today?'

Whenever she heard Rob's name, she immediately felt guilty for suspecting him, even for a minute. There had been so many people to suspect, people like Dr Hunter who had seemed so corrupt, and Rob who was so new in her life. But not all of her suspicions had had foundation; Dr Hunter was right, in a way – paranoia had worked its way in.

When Rob learned of what the police had done to the victims, and to her during her investigation, he was adamant that he had had no idea, and swiftly denounced them. If any officers came to the range, he turned them away, and he spent many months trying to prove that he was good enough for her. It took more strength to let him in than it had to push him away, but now that she had him and the intimacy she had craved for so long, she felt close to becoming whole again.

'I think so.'

He chuckled and turned back to the painting. Her eyes drifted to the bridge. A year ago to the day, she had driven across it after lodging a bullet in a man's brain and uncovering a truth that caused a ripple through the town. Three hundred and sixty-five days, and she could still feel the dirt closing in around her as she escaped the coffin, hear the grind of the gears as she sped across the bridge for the phone box.

'It's a year today,' she said.

'I know,' Tony said, and turned on his stool. 'How're you feeling?'

'Angry.'

'They'll charge them, Rose. They have to.'

'The justice system protects their own. Seb Clark, Leech, Watts, they'll all walk free – just watch.'

'You did everything you could.'

'And still, it wasn't enough. I just. . . I want them to pay, truly, truly pay. I want them to know what it feels like to have your whole world ripped away from you, to understand the true pain of injustice. The police will drag the investigation out for years, and that's before they even get to court.'

'But they're looking into it, Rose. They ignored so much evidence, put so many lives in danger. That Anna, the detective, she'll give evidence. So will Shane. There are lots of people to back this up. They can't weasel out of it this time. One of their own was responsible for the murders, for Christ's sake.'

'Watch them, Dad.'

Tony sighed into his lap, looked out at the view again.

'Well, whatever happens, know that you did more than anyone to end this. You risked your own life for those men, and gave their families the closure they needed. You did this. Not the police, not the town, *you*.'

She looked out at the river, at the trees swaying on the bank at the other side. 'Do you want to know the worst part?' she said. 'Montgomery blackmailed his victims into staying quiet. He used their secrets, their sexuality, against them. If society didn't keep people from being themselves, they could have come forward – they would still be alive. We're all responsible for that.'

'I know,' he said.

We would still have Jay, she thought.

Rose sat and listened to the bustle of the river, the sway of the trees, thinking of those left behind. She longed for Shane to be happy, to finally put his demons to rest. The families of the victims who finally had answers, and the new reality of acceptance to grapple with. It was easier to go through life angry and hunting for justice, but when it was served, the real struggle began. Like her, they would have to accept what had happened if they stood any chance of moving on.

The papers had been reporting the case every day, updates plastered on the front cover, mentioning the victims by name, printing their photos again and again, milking her connection to Jay for everything they could, and bringing up Violet's death when the slightest opportunity arose. But the other victims, the ones left alive, were forgotten. Montgomery hadn't just taken the lives of Jay, Finn, Johnny, Jamie, Phillip, Zach and Adam, but of their families, of Shane, of the men in the park. Even if the case was ruled in their favour and Seb Clark and his colleagues were sent down, injustice would continue to thrive. She had accepted a lot of things in the last year, but she wasn't ready to accept that.

Her phone vibrated in her pocket.

Just a text to say I love you.

She read Rob's message and smiled. Happiness had breached her life again, even when she had tried to keep it at bay and continue to punish herself for what she had done. Allowing herself to move on was the hardest part. She hadn't suffered for long enough. How dare she, when Violet was dead in the ground? But she had watched her own mother kill herself slowly, punishing herself day after day, until she finally closed her eyes and didn't wake up again. She left a daughter behind who loved her, needed her. Rose couldn't do the same to Lily. And although progress was slight, and Lily's anger seemed indestructible, Rose could almost feel Lily learning to love her again. She would work as hard as she could to earn every bit of love her daughter was able to give.

She eyed the bridge, lit up with the sun, the water bustling beneath, the stroke of her father's brush as he detailed the leaves on the trees, and thought of her.

Good morning, Violet.

The wind swept in, the breeze like a warm, tender touch to her cheek.

I love you too.

ACKNOWLEDGEMENTS

As always, many thanks to my agent, Sarah Hornsley of the Bent Agency, for your unwavering support and dedication, and to my editors, Sara O'Keeffe and Poppy Mostyn-Owen at Atlantic, for believing in this story so ardently.

Many thanks to Mary Chamberlain for your sharp eye and attention to detail while copy-editing this novel – you're fantastic.

To my friends and family, who haven't seen much of me while I've been writing this book (or the one before that, and most likely the one after). I promise I'm working to achieve that work–life balance people speak of. Special thanks to my main support system: Sandra Jarrad, Carl Jarrad and Pamela Jordan – this career wouldn't be possible without you. Thank you also to my number one fans Josie Sinead Kendall and Vicki Kettle.

A thousand thanks to the team at Waterstones Colchester, who backed *Before Her Eyes* with the sort of passion that authors can only dream of: Helen Wood, Karl Hollinshead, Mark Vickery, Joe Oliver Eason, Liv Quinn, Jon Clark, Chloe Denton and Clive Parsons. Your support has been so genuinely moving. I will never forget it.

A huge thank you to everyone who has read and loved my books and helped to spread the word: every copy sold, every social media message, photo, review and word-of-mouth comment means the world. Special thanks to the Book Club on Facebook and to all the wonderful bloggers I'm lucky to know, as well as to Charlotte at *what.i.read* who has always been so supportive.

Another heartfelt thank you to the team at my local Costa Coffee for knowing my coffee order off by heart, allowing me to overstay my welcome to write, and for not asking me to pay towards the rent, despite me being there so often.

ABOUT THE AUTHOR

Jack Jordan wrote his first novel at seventeen and self-published two e-book bestsellers, *Anything for Her* and *My Girl*, by the age of twenty-four. Jack's much-anticipated third novel *Before Her Eyes* published in Summer 2018. He lives in East Anglia.

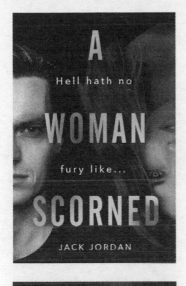

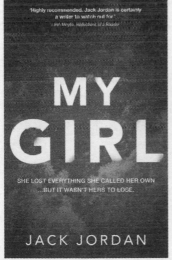